*Jonah and Co*

NOVELS BY DORNFORD YATES

*The "Berry" Books*

THE BROTHER OF DAPHNE

THE COURTS OF IDLENESS

BERRY AND CO

JONAH AND CO

ADELE AND CO

AND BERRY CAME TOO

THE HOUSE THAT BERRY BUILT

THE BERRY SCENE

AS BERRY AND I WERE SAYING

B-BERRY AND I LOOK BACK

# DORNFORD YATES

---

# *Jonah and Co*

---

## WARD LOCK LIMITED
## LONDON

Designed by Humphrey Stone
Text set in Intertype Baskerville
Printed by The Compton Press Ltd.
Bound by Leighton-Straker Ltd.

## To Elm Tree Road

My Lady,

It is hard, sitting here, to believe that, if I would call for a cab, I could be in St. James's Street in less than ten minutes of time. Nevertheless, it is true. I have proved it so many times. Soon I shall prove it for the last time.

Better men than I will sit in this study and pace the lawn in the garden with the high walls. The lilies and laburnums and all the gay fellowship of flowers will find a new water-man. The thrushes and blackbirds and wood-pigeons will find a new victualler. The private forecourt, so richly hung with creeper, will give back my footfalls no more. Other eyes will dwell gratefully upon the sweet pretty house and look proudly out of its leaded window-panes.

The old order changeth, my lady. And so I am going, before I am driven out.

Nine years ago there was a farm upon the opposite side of the road—a little old English farm. Going out of my door of a morning, I used to meet ducks and geese that were taking the air. And horses came home at even, and cows lowed. Now the farm is gone, and a garage has taken its room. And other changes have come, and others still are coming.

So, you see, my lady, it is high time I was gone.

This quiet study has seen the making of my books. This—the last it will see—I make bold to offer to you for many reasons, but mainly because, for one thing, this house belongs to you and, for another, no hostess was ever so charming to the stranger within her gates.

I have the honour to be,

Your ladyship's humble servant,

DORNFORD YATES.

Number Six.

# Contents

# BERTRAM PLEYDELL
### (of White Ladies, in the County of Hampshire)

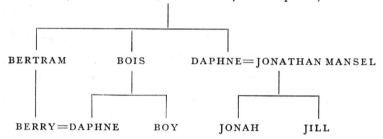

## CHAPTER I

# How Berry Stepped into the Breach, and Jonah Came First and was First Served

"Shall I massage it?" said Berry. The suggestion was loudly condemned.

"Right," replied my brother-in-law. "That reduces us to faith-healing. On the command 'One', make your mind a blank—that shouldn't be difficult—realise that the agony you aren't suffering is imaginary, and close both legs. One! On the command 'Two'——"

"You can go," I said wearily. "You can go. I'll write to you when I want you. Don't bother to leave your address."

"But how vulgar," said Berry. "How very vulgar." He paused to glance at his watch. "Dear me! Half-past ten, and I haven't had my beer yet." He stepped to the door. "Should the pain become excruciating, turn upon the stomach and repeat Kipling's 'If'. Should——"

My sister and Jill fairly bundled him out of the doorway.

Sitting by my side upon the bed, Adèle laid her cheek against mine.

"Is it any better, old chap?"

"The pain's practically stopped," said I, "thank Heaven. Putting it up's done that. But I'm in for a stiff leg, dear. I know that. Not that that matters really, but it means I can't drive."

It was unfortunate that, before I had been upon French soil for half an hour, I should be kicked by a testy cab-horse of whose existence—much less proximity—thanks to the poor lighting of Boulogne, I had been totally unaware. I had been kicked upon the same knee in 1916. On that occasion I had gone with a stiff leg for a fortnight. It seemed unpleasantly probable that history would wholly repeat itself.

"I can travel," I continued. "I shall be able to walk with a stick, but I shan't be able to drive. And, as Jonah can't drive more than one car at a time, Berry'll have to take the other."

At my words Daphne started, and Jill gave a little cry.

"B-but, Boy, he's only had three lessons."

"I know, but he'll get through somehow. I'll sit by his side. It'll shorten my life, of course, but what else can we do? Even if

Fitch was here, there's no room for a chauffeur. And you'd find towing tedious after the first five hundred miles."

With a white forefinger to her lips, my sister regarded me.

"I know he's a disgrace," she said slowly, "but he's—he's the only husband I've got, Boy, and—he has his points," she concluded softly with the tenderest smile.

I stretched out a hand and drew her towards me.

"Isn't he my only brother, darling? Isn't he—Berry? I'll see he comes to no harm."

"You really think it's safe?"

"Perfectly. For one thing, I shall be able to reach the hand-brake rather more easily than he will. . . ."

My sister kissed me.

"I like the sound of that," she said cheerfully.

It was the fifth day of November, and all six of us were for the Pyrenees.

A month ago Adèle and I, new-wed, had visited Pau. We had found the place good, conceived the idea of spending the winter there, and wired for instructions. Within three days we had received four letters.

The first was from Jill.

ADELE DARLING,

How sweet of you both to think of it! We're all simply thrilled. Try and get one with a palm-tree and some wistaria. We miss you awfully. Tell Boy Nobby is splendid and sends his love. Oh, and he smells his coat every day. Isn't it pathetic? My hair won't go like yours, but I'm going to try again. All our love to you and your HUSBAND,

JILL.

Then came Jonah's.

DEAR BOY,

What about tobacco? You might examine the chances of smuggling. I'm sending you a hundred cigarettes conspicuously labelled BENGER'S FOOD, to see what happens. I suppose the roads are pretty bad. What about fishing?

Yours,

JONAH.

(I subsequently received a curt communication to the effect that there was a package, addressed to me and purporting to contain "*Farine*," lying at the local custom-house. Adèle was horrified. I endeavoured to reassure her, tore up the notice, and cursed my cousin savagely. When three days had passed, and I was still at liberty, Adèle plucked up heart, but, for the rest of our visit, upon sight of a *gendarme* she was apt to become distrait and lose the thread of her discourse.)

A letter from Daphne had arrived the next day.

DEAREST ADELE,
   We're all delighted with the idea.
   I don't think six months would be too long. I agree that a villa would be much the best, and we're perfectly content to leave the selection to you. You know what room we must have. I suppose two bathrooms would be too much to expect. About servants: we can bring some, but I think we ought to have a French cook to do the marketing, and perhaps one other to keep her company and help in the kitchen and house. Will you see what you can do? Plate and linen, of course, we can bring. By the way, Madge Willoughby tells me that last year in France they had some difficulty about coal; so tell Boy to see if he can order some now. All this, of course, if you can get a villa.
                                        Your loving sister,
                                                DAPHNE.
Berry's came last.

DEAR BROTHER,
   So we shall ourselves winter this year at Pau? *Eh bien!* There are, perhaps, worse places. At least, the sun will shine. *Ma foi*, to think that upon you depend all the arrangements. *Tant pis!* My suite must face itself south and adjoin the bathroom. Otherwise I cannot answer for my health, or, for the matter of that, yours either.
   Kindly omit from your next letter any reference to the mountains. "Impressions of the Pyrenees" by a fool who has been married for less than three weeks not only are valueless, but make my gorge rise—*une élévation très dangereuse*.
   Which brings me to your wife. How is the shrew? Tell her I have some socks for her to darn on her return.

It was thoughtful of you to emphasise the fact that the season of green figs, to a surfeit of which I sincerely hope you will succumb, will be over before I reach Pau. I am inclined to think that the five hundred cigars George sent you will be over even earlier. Besides, I shall at once console and distend myself with *foie gras*.

We must have a French cook, of course—a very priestess of Gluttony—skilful to lure the timid appetite from the fastness of satiety. *Enfin* ...

I ask myself why I shall have made the trouble to write to you. You have, of course, an opportunity unique of making a mess with a copper bottom of my life for six months. *Mais, mon Dieu, que vous serez puni!*

*Je t'embrasse, vieil haricot, sur les deux joues.*

BERRY.

P.S.—This here letter is a talisman, and should be worn upon the exterior of the abdominal wall during a drought.

Considering the nature of our holiday, Adèle and I did not do so badly. Before we left Pau, I had signed the lease of an attractive villa, standing well in its own grounds and commanding a prospect of the mountains as fine as could be. Adèle had engaged a Frenchwoman and her daughter, both of whom were well spoken of, and had been in the service of English and American families before the War. A supply of fuel had been reserved and various minor arrangements had been concluded. Ere we were back at White Ladies, October was old.

It had been Jonah's belated suggestion that our migration should be accomplished by car. It was Jonah's enterprise that reduced the upheaval of our plans, consequent upon the instant adoption of his idea, to order and convenience. By the third of November everything had been arranged. The heavier stuff had been embarked for Bordeaux; the servants were ready to accompany the rest of the luggage by way of Paris; the Rolls had been sold. In the latter's place we had purchased two smaller cars—both new, both of the same make, both coupés, both painted blue. Indeed, but for their numbers, which were consecutive, we could not have told them apart. Each seated three inside—comfortably, while a respectable quantity of baggage could be easily bestowed in each of the capacious boots.

Certainly my cousin's staff work had been superb.

In the circumstances it seemed hardly fair that upon this, the first night of our venture, he should be faced with the labour of shepherding both cars, single-handed, first clear of the Customs, and then, one by one, through the cold, dark streets which led from the quay to the garage of the hotel.

As if she had read my thought—

"Poor Jonah!" said Adèle suddenly. "I wonder——"

A knock upon the door interrupted her.

This, being opened, admitted Nobby, two porters, our luggage, two waiters, a large dish of sandwiches, some beer, coffee and its accessories, Jonah, and finally Berry.

"You must be tired," said the latter. "Let's sit down, shall I?" He sank into a chair. "And how's the comic *patella*? I well remember, when I was in Plumbago, a somewhat similar accident. A large cherry-coloured *gibus*, on its wrong side——"

"At the present moment," said I, wrestling with the Sealyham's advances, "we're more concerned with your future than with your past. It's the Bank of England to a ha'p'orth of figs that to-morrow morning I shall have a stiff leg. Very good." I paused. "Those three lessons you've had," I added carelessly, "will come in useful."

Jonah, who was filling a tumbler, started violently and spilled some beer. Then he leaned against the wall and began to laugh helplessly.

Coldly Berry regarded him.

"I fail," he said stiffly, "to see the point of your mirth. I gather that it is proposed to enjoy my services for the propulsion of one of the automobiles—that, while you will be responsible for the 'shoving' of Ping, these delicate hands will flick Pong across France. Very good. Let the Press be informed; call forth the ballad-mongers. What would have been a somewhat sordid drive will become a winged flight, sublime and deathless."

"I trust so," said Jonah. "Six hundred miles with a fool at the wheel is a tall order, but, if your companions survive the first two days, they ought to pull through. Try not to do more than five pounds' worth of damage to the gallon, won't you?"

"Sour grapes," said Berry. "The professional reviles the distinguished amateur."

"Seriously," said I, "it's no laughing matter."

"I agree," said Daphne. "You'll have to just crawl along all the way. After all, we've got six months to get there in. Promise me you won't try and pass anything."

"I promise," replied her husband. "Should another vehicle approach, I'll stop the engine and go and hide in a wood till it's gone."

"Fool," said his wife. "I meant 'overtake anything' of course. You know I did. Promise you won't try and rush past things just to get in front of them."

I took up the cudgels.

"We've got to get along, darling, and he can't give a promise like that. You wouldn't want to do fifty miles behind a traction-engine, would you? Remember, I shall be by his side. He may be holding the wheel, but I shall be driving the car. Make him promise to obey me implicitly, if you like."

"That's right," said Jill. "You will, won't you, Berry?"

The latter looked at Adèle.

"Do you also subscribe to my humiliation?" he said.

Adèle smiled and nodded.

"Unquestionably," she said. "By the time you get to Pau, you'll be an expert. And then you can teach me."

"The pill-glider," said my brother-in-law. "Well, well. So far as in me lies, I'll do as I'm told. But I insist upon plain English. I'm not going to be suddenly yelled at to 'double-clutch', or 'feel the brake', or 'close the throttle', or something. It makes me want to burst into tears. That fellow who was teaching me asked me, without any warning and in the middle of some sheep, what I should do if one of my 'big ends were to run out'. I said I should consult a specialist, but the question upset me. Indirectly, it also upset the shepherd. . . . Which reminds me, I never knew a human being could jump so far. The moment he felt the radiator . . ."

"You never told us this," said Daphne reproachfully. "If I'd known you'd knocked somebody down——"

"I never knocked him down," said Berry. "I tell you he jumped. . . . We stopped, of course, and explained. He was a little nettled at first, but we parted on the best of terms."

"It's all very well," said my sister, "but I'd no idea——"

"Every dog must have his bite," said I, laughing. "He won't do it again. And now, since I'm tethered, will somebody give me some beer?"

Then and there supper was consumed.

A vigorous discussion of the turn events had taken, and the advancement and scrutiny of a variety of high speculations regarding the probable style of our progress to Pau, prevailed until past twelve o'clock, but at length the others were evicted, and

Adèle, Nobby, and I were able to prepare for the night.

Out of the luxurious silence of a hot bath Adèle's voice came floating into the bedroom.

"Boy!"

"Yes, lady?"

"I wish I was going with you to-morrow instead of Daphne."

"So do I," I said heartily.

Adèle sighed. Then—

"It can't be helped," she said. "I think, on the whole, she would have worried more than I shall."

"Not a doubt of it," said I cheerfully. "As she said, Berry's the only husband she's got."

Adèle choked. Presently——

"The real reason," she said, "is because she mistrusts her husband even more than I trust mine."

When I had worked this out—

"Aha," I said pleasedly.

"But then, of course," said Adèle, "she's been married much longer."

\*      \*      \*      \*      \*

With Rouen as our objective, we left Boulogne the next morning at ten o'clock. To speak more accurately, we left the hotel at ten o'clock and Boulogne itself some forty minutes later. The negotiation of an up-gradient leading out of the town was responsible for the delay.

My sister and I shall remember that hill so long as we live. So, I imagine, will Berry. We were half-way up when he stopped the engine for the first time. We were still half-way up when he stopped it for the eighth time. Indeed, it was at this juncture that I suggested that he should rest from his labours and smoke a cigarette.

My brother-in-law shook his head.

"Shall I slide down backwards and begin again?" he inquired.

"No thanks," said I. "I have a foolish preference for facing death."

"D'you think we could push it up?" said Daphne.

"Frankly," said I, "I don't. You see, she weighs over a ton without the luggage."

Berry cleared his throat.

"I am not," he said, "going through the farce of asking what I do wrong, because I know the answer. It's not the right one, but you seem incapable of giving any other."

"I am," said I.

"Well, don't say it," said Berry, "because, if you do, I shall scream. No man born of woman could let in that clutch more slowly, and yet you say it's too fast. The truth is, there's something wrong with the car."

"There soon will be," I retorted. "The starter will fail. Then every time you stop the engine you'll have to get out and crank. That'll make you think."

"Make me think?" yelled Berry. "D'you think I haven't been thinking? D'you think I'm not thinking now?" Haven't I almost burst my brains with thinking?" Daphne began to laugh helplessly. "That's right," added her husband savagely. "See the humorous side. I may go mad any minute, but don't let that stop you." And, with that, he set his foot upon the self-starter.

When he had stopped the engine another three times, he applied the hand-brake with unnecessary violence, sank back in his seat, and folded his hands.

My sister and I clung to one another in an agony of stifled mirth.

Berry closed his eyes.

"My work," he said quietly, "is over. I now see that it is ordained that we shall not leave this spot. There's probably an angel in the way with a drawn sword, and the car sees it, although we can't. Any way, I'm not going to fight against Fate. And now don't speak to me. I'm going to dwell on bullock-carts and goat-chaises and other horse-drawn vehicles. I shan't last many minutes, and I should like to die in peace."

With a swift rush, Ping drew up alongside. From its interior Adèle, Jill, Nobby and Jonah peered at us excitedly.

"Hullo!" said the latter. "What's up?"

"Go away," said Berry. "Drive on to your doom. An apparition has appeared to us, warning us not to proceed. It was quite definite about it. Good-bye."

"Jonah, old chap," said I, "I'm afraid you're for it. Unless you take us up, we shall be here till nightfall."

With a groan my cousin opened his door and descended into the road. . . .

One minute later we were at the top of the hill.

"And now," said Daphne, with the *Michelin Guide* open upon her knees, "now for Montreuil."

When five minutes had passed and my brother-in-law was

breathing through his nose less audibly, I lighted a cigarette and ventured to look about me.

It was certainly a fine highway that we were using. Broad, direct, smooth beyond all expectations, it lay like a clean-cut sash upon the countryside, rippling away into the distance as though it were indeed that long, long lane that hath no turning. Presently a curve would come to save the face of the proverb, but the bends were few in number, and, as a general rule, did little more than switch the road a point or two to east or west, as the mood took them. There was little traffic, and the surface was dry.

Something had been said about the two cars keeping together, but I was not surprised when Jonah passed us like a whirlwind before we were half-way to Samer. He explained afterwards that he had stuck it as long as he could, but that to hold a car down to twenty on a road like a private racing-track was worse than "pulling."

Fired by Jonah's example, Berry laid hold of the wheel, and we took the next hill at twenty-five.

It was a brilliant day, but the cold was intense, and I think we were all glad that Pong was a closeable car. That Winter's reign had begun was most apparent. There was a bleak look upon the country's face : birch-rods that had been poplars made us gaunt avenues : here and there the cold jewellery of frost was sparkling. I fell to wondering how far south we must go to find it warmer.

Presently we came to Montreuil.

As we entered the little town—

"This," said I, "was the headquarters of the British Expedition-ary Force. From behind these walls——"

"Don't talk," said Daphne, "or I shall make a mistake. Round to the left here. Wait a minute. No, that's right. And straight on. What a blessing this *Michelin Guide* is ! Not too fast, Berry. Straight on. This ought to be Grande rue." She peered out of the window. "Yes, that's right. Now, in a minute you turn to the left. . . ."

After all, I reflected, we had to get to Rouen, and it was past mid-day.

We had sworn not to lunch before we had passed Abbeville, so, since we had breakfasted betimes, I furtively encouraged my brother-in-law to "put her along".

His response was to overtake and pass a lorry upon the wrong side, drive an unsuspecting bicyclist into a ditch and swerve, like a drunken sea-gull, to avoid a dead fowl. As we were going over forty it was all over before we knew where we were, but the impression of impending death was vivid and lasting, and nearly a minute had elapsed before I could trust my voice.

"Are we still alive?" breathed Daphne. "I'm afraid to open my eyes."

"I think we must be," said I. "At least, I'm still thirsty, if that's anything to go by."

"I consider," said Berry, "that the way in which I extricated us from that *impasse* was little short of masterly. That cyclist ought to remember me in his prayers."

"I don't want to discourage you," I said grimly, "but I shouldn't bank on it."

The plan of Abbeville, printed in the Guide, was as simple to read as were my sister's directions to follow. At a critical moment, however, Berry felt unable to turn to the right.

"The trouble is," he explained, as we plunged into a maze of back streets, "I've only got two hands and feet. To have got round that corner, I should have had to take out the clutch, go into third, release the brake, put out a hand, accelerate, sound the clarion and put the wheel over simultaneously. Now, with seven limbs I could have done it. With eight, I could also have scratched myself—an operation, I may say, which can be no longer postponed." He drew up before a *charcuterie* and mopped his face. "What a beautiful bunch of sausages!" he added. "Shall we get some? Or d'you think they'd be dead before we get to Rouen?"

In contemptuous silence Daphne lowered her window, accosted the first passer-by, and asked the way. An admission that it was possible to reach the Neufchatel road without actually retracing our steps was at length extracted, and, after a prolonged study of the plan, my sister gave the word to proceed. Save that we twice mounted the pavement, grazed a waggon, and literally brushed an urchin out of the way, our emergence from Abbeville was accomplished without further incident.

With the knowledge that, barring accidents, we ought to reach Rouen by half-past five, we ventured to devour a wayside lunch some ten minutes later.

It was after Neufchatel that the surface of the great grey road argued neglect in no uncertain terms. For mile after mile, fat bulls of Basan, in the shape of gigantic pot-holes, gaped threateningly upon us. Berry, who was driving much better, did all that he could, but only a trick-cyclist could have picked his way between them. The car hiccoughed along piteously. . . .

With the approach of darkness, driving became a burden, being driven a weariness of the flesh, and we were all thankful when we slid down a paved hill into the Cathedral City and, presently, past the great church and on to the very bank of the River Seine.

The others had been awaiting us for nearly two hours.

\* \* \* \* \*

"With this sun," said Adèle, "they ought to be glorious."

Impiously I reflected that Berry was almost certainly enjoying his breakfast in bed.

"I expect they will," I said abstractedly.

Adèle slid an arm through mine.

"It's very sweet of you to come with me, Boy."

I stood still and looked at her.

"You're a wonderful child," I said. "When you speak like that, I want to kick myself and burst into song simultaneously. I suppose that's Love."

"I expect so," said Adèle mischievously.

Five minutes later we were standing beneath the shadow of Chartres Cathedral.

We had come, my wife and I, to see the windows. The day before had been dull, and what light there was had been failing when we had visited the shrine. To-day, however, was all glorious.

If we had risen early, we had our reward.

The place had become a gallery with jewels for pictures. Out of the sombre depths the aged webs of magic glowed with the matchless flush of precious stones. From every side colours we had not dreamed of enriched our eyes. To make the great west rose, the world herself might have been spoiled of her gems. Looking upon this mystery, no man can wonder that the art is lost. Clearly it went the way of Babel. For of such is the Kingdom of Heaven. Windows the sun was lighting were at once more real and more magnificent. Crimsons and blues, purples and greens, yellows and violets, blazed with that ancient majesty which only lives to-day in the peal of a great organ, the call of a silver trumpet, or the proud roll of drums. Out of the gorgeous pageant mote-ridden rays issued like messengers, to badge the cold grey stone with tender images and set a smile upon the face of stateliness. "Such old, old panes," says someone. "Six hundred years and more. How wonderful!" Pardon me, but I have seen them, and it is not wonderful at all. Beneath their spell, centuries shrink to afternoons. The windows of Chartres are above Time. They are the peepholes of Immortality.

We returned to the hotel in time to contribute to a heated argument upon the subject of tipping.

"It's perfectly simple," said Berry. "You think of what you would hate to have given before the War, double it, add forty per cent. for the increased cost of living, halve it because of the Exchange, ask them whether they'd like it in notes or gold, and pay them in postage-stamps."

"I want to know," said Daphne, "what to give the chamber-maid."

"Eight francs fifty. That's the equivalent of half-a-crown before the War."

"Nonsense," said his wife. "Five francs is heaps, and you know it."

"I think it's too much," said Berry. "Give her one instead, and tell her you've hidden the rest in the bathroom and that, when she touches the towel-rail, she's warm."

"As a matter of fact," said Jill uneasily, "it's all over. I've done it."

There was a dreadful silence. Then—

"Tell us the worst," said I, "and get it over."

"I'm—I'm afraid I gave her rather a lot, but she had a nice face."

"She had a nice step," said Berry. "I noticed that about five this morning."

"How much?" said I relentlessly.

Jill looked round guiltily.

"I gave her fifty," she said.

There was a shriek of laughter.

"Did she faint?" said Berry. "Or try to eat grass, or anything?"

Gravely Jill shook her head.

"She talked a great deal—very fast. I couldn't follow her. And then she turned away and began to cry. I was so glad I'd done it."

"So are we all," said Daphne.

She was supported heartily.

Jonah looked at his watch.

"I suggest," he said, "that we start at eleven, then we shall fetch up in time to see the cathedral."

"How far is Tours?" said Daphne.

"Eighty-six miles."

"Let's keep together to-day," said Jill. "It's much more fun."

Her brother shook his head.

"I don't want," he said, "to be arrested for loitering."

"Don't you worry," said Berry. "We wouldn't be seen with you."

Jonah sighed.

"Where there's a will there's a way," he murmured.

"More," said Berry. "We regard you rather less than the dust beneath our detachable wheels. You pollute the road with your hoghood. I suppose it's no use asking you to keep behind us."

"None whatever," replied our cousin. "Why should we?"

"Well," said Berry, "supposing a tyre discovers that I'm driving and bursts with pride, who's going to change the wheel?"

Jonah stifled a yawn.

"You can't have it both ways," he said. "If we're to warn people not to shoot at you, we must be in front."

Berry regarded his finger-nails.

"Perhaps you're right," he said. "Think of me when you get your third puncture, won't you? And remember that my heart goes out to you in your tyre trouble and that you will have all my love. Then you won't sweat so much."

Half an hour later Pong stormed out of the garage and into the place des Epars.

Adèle's wish had been granted, and she was travelling with Berry and me instead of with Jonah.

For this new order of battle Nobby was solely responsible. Upon the first day's journey the terrier had whined all the way to Rouen because he had wanted to be with me. As one of his audience, Jonah had been offensively outspoken regarding this predilection. Upon the following day the dog's desire had been gratified, whereupon he had whined all the way to Chartres because he was apart from Adèle. Commenting upon this unsuspected devotion, Berry had been quite as outspoken as Jonah, and much more offensive. Naturally, to withstand such importunity was out of the question, and, since it was impossible for me to leave Berry, the line of least resistance was followed, and Daphne and Adèle changed places.

Our way out of Chartres was short and simple, and, with the exception of temporarily obstructing two trams by the artless expedient of remaining motionless upon the permanent way, Pong emerged from the city without a stain upon his character.

The Vendôme road looked promising and proved excellent. Very soon we were flying. For all that, Jonah overtook us as we were nearing Bonneval. . . .

It was some thirty minutes later, as we were leaving Châteaudun, that a sour-faced *gendarme* with a blue nose motioned to us to stop. Standing upon the near pavement, the fellow was at once conversing with a postman and looking malevolently in our direction. I think we all scented mischief.

"What can he want?" growled Berry, as he brought the car to a standstill.

"He's probably being officious," said I, getting our papers ready. "We're strangers, and he's in a bad humour. Consequently, he's going to scrutinise our *triptyque*, passports, passes and certificates, to see if he can accuse us of anything. Happily they're all in order, so he'll be disappointed. When he's thoroughly satisfied that he can bring no charge against us, he'll order us to proceed."

"He's taking his time about it," observed my brother-in-law.

I looked up from the documents.

My gentleman was still talking to the postman, while his pig's eyes were still surveying the car. From his companion's demeanour, he seemed to be whetting his wit at our expense.

"This is intolerable," said I. "Ask him what he wants, lady."

Adèle leaned forward and put her head out of the window.

"I think you wished us to stop, *Monsieur*?"

The *gendarme* waved his hand.

"Wait," he said insolently.

The postman sniggered shamefacedly.

Adèle sank back in her seat, her cheeks flaming.

In a voice trembling with passion I conjured Berry to proceed.

The moment the car moved, the official sprang forward, gesticulating furiously.

As we passed him, I put out my head.

"Now it's our turn," I said warmly, "to make the postman laugh."

From the hoarse yells which followed us, it was clear that we had left the fellow beside himself with rage. Looking back through the little window, I could see him dancing. Suddenly he stopped, peered after us, and then swung about and ran ridiculously up the street.

"Blast him, he's going to telephone!" said I. "Where's the map?"

Together Adèle and I pored over the sections.

"If," said Berry, "you're going to direct me to turn off, for Heaven's sake be quick about it. At the present moment I'm just blinding along into the blue and, for all I know, an oversized hornets' nest. Of course they mayn't sting when there's an 'r' in the month, but then they mightn't know that. Or am I thinking of oysters?"

"They'll stop us at Vendôme," said I. "Not before. Right oh! We must turn to the right at Cloyes and make for St. Calais. We can get round to Tours that way. It'll take us about twenty miles out of our way, but——"

"Yes, and when we don't show up at Vendôme, they'll wire to Calais. Seriously, as Shakespeare says, I'm all of a doo-dah."

That we should be stopped at St. Calais was not likely, and I said as much. What did worry me, because it was far more probable, was that when they drew blank at Vendôme, the authorities would telephone to Tours. Any apprehension, however, regarding our reception at that city was soon mercifully, unmercifully, and somewhat paradoxically overshadowed by a more instant anxiety lest we should never arrive there at all. From the moment we left the main road, the obstacles in the shape of uncharted roads and villages, pavements, cattle, goats, a horse fair, and finally a series of appalling gradients, opposed our passage. All things considered, my brother-in-law drove admirably. But it was a bad business, and, while my wife and Berry were very staunch, I think we all regretted that I had been so high with Blue Nose.

Night had fallen ere we slunk into Tours.

Fully expecting to find that the others had well-nigh given us up, we were astounded to learn at the hotel that Ping had not yet arrived. Indeed, we had finished dinner, and were debating seriously whether we should take a hired car and go to seek them, when there was a flurry of steps in the corridor, Nobby rushed to the door, and the next moment Daphne and Jill burst into the room.

"My darling," said Berry, advancing, "where on earth have you been?"

My sister put her arms about his neck and looked into his eyes.

"Kiss me 'Good-bye'," she said. "Jonah's just coming."

Her husband stared at her. Then—

"Is it as bad as all that?" he said. "Dear, dear. And how did he get the booze?"

Somebody cleared his throat.

I swung round, to see Jonah regarding us.

"You three beauties," he said. "Four with Nobby."

"But what do you mean?" said Adèle. "What have we done?"

"Done?" cried Jonah. "Done? Where d'you think we've been?"

"It can't have been goats that stopped you," said Berry, "because I had all the goats. There was a great rally of goats at St. Calais this afternoon. It was a wonderful smell—I mean sight."

"Guess again," said Jonah grimly.

"You haven't been waiting for us on the road?" said I.

"You're getting warmer," was the reply.

Adèle gave a sudden cry.

"O-o-oh, Jonah," she gasped, "you've been at Vendôme!"

I started violently, and Berry, who was about to speak, choked.

"That's right," said Jonah shortly. "Nice little place—what I saw of it. . . . Lovely view from the police-station." He leaned against the mantelpiece and lighted a cigarette. "It may amuse you to know," he added, "that the expiation of your crime took us six and a half hours and cost five hundred francs."

In response to our thirsty enquiries, the tale came bubbling.

My surmise that the blue-nosed *gendarme* would telephone to Vendôme had been well-founded. He had forwarded an exact description of Pong, together with the letters and the first three figures of the four appearing upon the number-plate. Six minutes later Ping had sailed innocently into Vendôme—and up to her doom. . . .

The Vendôme police could hardly believe their eyes. Here was the offending car, corresponding in every particular to the one described to them, admittedly fresh from Châteaudun, yet having covered the thirty-nine kilometres in eleven minutes. It was amazing . . . almost incredible . . . almost. . . . Of outlaws, however, all things were credible—even a speed of one hundred and thirty-six miles an hour. For it was without doubt that outlaw which had flouted Authority at Châteaudun. Oh, indubitably. And, having thus flouted Authority, what was more natural than that it should endeavour to outstrip the consequences of its deed? But, *mon Dieu*, what wickedness!

In vain had Jonah protested and Daphne declared their innocence. The telephone was again requisitioned, and the blue-nosed *gendarme* summoned and cross-examined. As luck would have it, he could not speak to the passengers, beyond affirming that they included one man and one woman. . . . When he gratuitously added that the reason why he could not swear to the whole of the number was because of the terrible pace at which the car was moving, the game was up. . . .

Finding that the accusation of travelling at a horrifying speed was assuming a serious look, my sister and cousins at length decided that they had no alternative but to give us away. They had, of course, realised that Pong was implicated from the beginning. Consequently, with the flourish of one who has hit upon the solution of a problem, they divulged our existence. They were politely, but wholly disbelieved. In reply, they had politely but confidently, invited the police to wait and see. . . .

For over four hours they had anxiously awaited the arrival of Pong. When at last the humiliating truth began to dawn upon them, and it became evident that we had ruled Vendôme out of our itinerary, the shock of realising, not only that they were to be denied an opportunity of refuting the charges preferred, but that they were destined to leave the town branded as three of the biggest and most unsuccessful liars ever encountered, had well-nigh reduced Daphne and Jill to tears. And when, upon the sickly resumption of negotiations, it appeared highly probable that they would not be permitted to proceed, Jill had wept openly. . . .

France is nothing if not emotional.

Visibly affected by her distress, the police had immediately become less hostile. Observing this, Daphne had discreetly followed her cousin's example. Before the sledge-hammer blows of their lamentation two *gendarmes* began to sniff and a third broke down. The girls redoubled their sobs. They were practically there.

"You never saw anything like it," concluded Jonah. "Within three minutes four of the police were crying, and the head bottle-washer was beating his breast and imploring me in broken accents to explain away my guilt. I threw five hundred francs on his desk and covered my eyes. With tears rolling down his cheeks, he pushed the notes under a blotting-pad and wrote laboriously upon a buff sheet. Then a woman was produced. Between explosions of distress she made us some tea. In common decency we couldn't push off for a while. Besides, I wasn't quite sure that it was all over. However, everybody seemed too overcome to say anything, so, after a bit, we chanced it and made a move for the car. To my relief, they actually helped us in, and two of them fought as to who should start us up." He looked round coldly. "And now, perhaps, you'll be good enough to tell us what we've been punished for."

I told what there was to tell.

As I came to the end, Berry nodded at Jonah.

"Yes," he said unctuously, "and let this be a lesson to you, brother."

Speechless with indignation, our cousin regarded him.

At length—

"What d'you mean?" he demanded.

Berry raised his eyebrows.

"I hardly think," he said, "the penalty for—er—loitering would have been so vindictive."

<br>

CHAPTER II

# How Three Wagers were Made, and Adèle Killed Two Birds with One Stone

We had slept, risen and breakfasted: we had visited Tours Cathedral: finally, we had mustered in the lounge of the hotel. It was when we had there been insulting one another for nearly an hour, that Jonah looked at his watch.

"We have now," he said, "wasted exactly forty-nine minutes in kicking against the pricks. Short of a European war, you can't alter the geography of France, and the laws of Mathematics take a lot of upsetting. It's no good wishing that Bordeaux was Biarritz, or that Pau was half the distance it is from Angoulême. If you don't want to go right through, you must stay at Bordeaux. It's the only possible place. If you don't want to stay at Bordeaux, you must go right through. I don't care which we do, but I do want to see something of Poitiers, and, if we don't get a move on, we shan't have time."

All the way from Boulogne France had made an excellent host. So far she had never failed to offer us a good night's lodging, with History as a bedfellow, at the end of a respectable run. Indeed, from the point of view of they that go down to the South in cars, her famous capitals could hardly have been more conveniently disposed. This very evening, by lodging us at Angoulême, she was to repeat such hospitality for the last time. Upon the morrow we should be faced with a choice of making a dash for the villa which was awaiting our arrival at Pau, or breaking the journey asunder—but by no means in half—by sleeping at Bordeaux.

"I must confess," said Daphne, "that, for some reason or other, Bordeaux doesn't attract me. Incidentally, I'm getting rather tired of unpacking and packing up."

"So far," said her husband, "as the bestowal and disinterment of my effects are concerned, I can confirm that statement. Indeed, if we had another week on the road, you'd both be exhausted. You left my sponge and bedroom-slippers at Boulogne, my dressing-gown at Rouen, and my pyjamas at Chartres. I wish you'd tell me what you've left here. I'm simply dying to know."

"No," said Daphne. "You must wait till Angoulême. I wouldn't spoil it for anything."

"Jade," said her husband. "And now, stand back, please, everybody. I want to do a little stock-taking." With that, from every pocket he produced French notes of all denominations, in all stages of decay, and heaped them upon the table. "Now, this one," he added, gingerly extracting a filthy and dilapidated rag, "is a particularly interesting specimen. Apparently, upon close inspection, merely a valuable security, worth, to be exact, a shade under twopence-halfpenny, it is in reality a talisman. Whosoever touches it, cannot fail to contract at least two contagious diseases within the week. In view of the temperature of my coffee this morning, I'm saving it for the head-waiter."

"When," said I, "do you expect to go down?"

"The pure in heart," said Berry, "are proof against its malignity. Don't you come too near. And look at this sere and yellow leaf. Now, that represents one franc. When I think that, upon offering that to a bar-tender, I shall not only not be assaulted, but shall actually receive a large bottle of beer and be lent a two-and-sixpenny glass from which to imbibe the same, I feel the deepest reverence for the French Government. No other authority in the world could possibly put up such a bluff and get away with it."

"They are awful," said Jill, peering.

"They're perfectly beastly," said Berry, "and wholly ridiculous. However, since they're also legal tender, I suppose I may as well try and sort them out. What I really need is some rubber gloves and a box-respirator. Hullo! Just catch that one, will you? He's seen that dog over there. . . . You know, I'm not at all sure that they get enough air in my pocket. I suppose we couldn't get a hutch for the more advanced ones. I mean, I don't want to be cruel."

Again Jonah looked at his watch.

"We have now," he said, "wasted fifty-five minutes in——"

"Excuse me," said Berry, "but isn't this touching? Here's affectionate Albert." With the words, he laid a two-franc note tenderly upon my sleeve. "Now, I bet you don't get him off without tearing him."

Disgustedly I managed to detach Albert, who instantly adhered to my fingers.

There was a shriek of laughter.

"Stick to him," said Berry. "I've lost the bet."

The injunction was unnecessary.

After Albert had clung once to Adèle's—happily, gloved— fingers and twice to each of my hands, I trod upon him. Some of Albert was still upon my boot that evening at Angoulême.

"For the last time," said Jonah, "I appeal to you all to let that dog-eared mountebank rake over his muckheap, and attend to me."

My brother-in-law addressed Adèle.

"It is," he said, "a discreditable but incontrovertible fact that saints have always been reviled. I suppose it's jealousy." He turned to his wife. "By the way, did you pack my *aureola*? I left it hanging on the towel-rail."

"If," said Daphne, "you're referring to your body-belt, it's with your bed-socks."

"And why not between your flannel vests?" said her husband. "The grey ones we found at Margate, I mean. With the imitation bone buttons. Ah, here we are. Now, if half a franc's no earthly, what'll who give me for two-thirds of fifty centimes?"

Jonah sank into a chair and closed his eyes.

"Look here," said I desperately. "Once for all, are we going to stay at Bordeaux, or are we going right through?"

"I think we'd all rather go right through," said Jill.

"I know I would," said her brother. "And if Boy's leg was all right, I shouldn't hesitate. I'll answer for Ping. But, frankly, with Berry driving, I doubt if Pong'll fetch up. I mean, two hundred and twenty-two miles takes some biting off."

There was a pregnant silence. Then—

"He'll never do it," said Daphne.

Her husband, who was still busy with his paper, looked up defiantly. Then he took a thousand-franc note and laid it apart from its fellows upon the table.

"I will wager that shekel," he said deliberately, "that, with a start of one hour to-morrow, Pong reaches Pau before Ping."

There was a gasp of astonishment.

"Done," said Jonah. "What's more, I'll bet you another you don't get in before ten."

Berry raised his eyes to heaven.

"An insult," he said. "Never mind. Your dross shall wipe it out. I take you."

"And I," said I, not to be outdone, "will put another on Pong for the double."

I felt that my honour was involved. After all, if I had not trained the mount, I was training the jockey.

"Right," said Jonah. "Will you both pay me now, or wait till you're out of hospital?"

"I think," said I, "we'll have a run for our money."

The bets were made, and there was an end of it. But when we were again in the car, and my brother-in-law was threading his way out of Tours, I began to repent my rashness.

Considering that, when he took the wheel at Boulogne, Berry had had only three lessons in the management of a car, he had done most creditably. My brother-in-law was no fool. Moreover, on leaving Rouen, he and I had joined forces. Sitting beside him in the coupé, I had driven the car with his hands—after a little practice—with astonishing results. In two days we had, we prided ourselves, raised such collaboration from the ranks of the Mechanical to the society of the Fine Arts. My part was comparatively easy. Sinking his initiative he had more nearly converted himself into an intelligent piece of mechanism than I would have believed possible. It would, of course, be vain to suggest that Pong would not have gone faster if I had been able to drive with my own hands, or Berry had had my experience. Still, we had come very well, and with a start of a whole hour and a little luck . . . Another point in our favour was that Adèle, who with Nobby completed our crew, had a pronounced gift for map-reading. She had an eye to country. She seemed to be able to scent the line we ought to take. The frequent treachery of signposts she laughed to scorn. Upon the morrow her confident assistance would be invaluable. . . .

What, when I made my bet, I had entirely forgotten, was that we were not always upon the open road. There was the rub. From Angoulême to Pau towns would have to be penetrated—among them Bordeaux itself—and in the towns our system had broken down. In a crowded street, though I could still administer, Berry could not execute. When I endeavoured to allow for his inexperience of traffic, I found it impossible accurately to gauge his capabilities. After a failure or two, it had been agreed that he should negotiate such streets as we encountered without my interference. . . . Of my haste to support Pong's honour, I had forgotten the towns.

With years of practice behind us, Jonah and I could thrust through traffic, happy enough with an odd inch to spare. Naturally enough, Berry had no such confidence. An inch was no use to him. He must have a good ell, and more also, before he would enter a gap. In the trough of a narrow street he laboured heavily. . . . There was no doubt about it. The towns through which we should have to pass on Wednesday would settle our chances. My money was as good as gone.

It seemed equally probable that Berry would save his stake. Barring accidents of the grosser sort, if we started betimes, we were bound to reach Pau before ten. Such a protasis robbed the bet of its savour. With a thousand francs at stake, it would be foolish not to take reasonable care. And the taking of reasonable care would all but eliminate the element of uncertainty. . . . There was no getting away from it. Of the two wagers, only the first was worth winning. To reach Pau before Jonah would be a veritable triumph.

Moodily I communicated my reflections to Adèle.

"I thought it was rather rash at the time," she replied. "But I think there's a sporting chance."

"That's right," said Berry. "Put your money on uncle. With enough encouragement I can do anything."

"Permit me to encourage you to blow your horn," said I. "That child in front of you is too young to die." My brother-in-law obeyed. "All the same, I'm afraid we're for it. It isn't so much a question of pace, pure and simple, for Jonah's a careful driver. But his street work is beautiful."

Berry sighed.

"I suppose he'd pass between those two waggons," he said sarcastically.

"He would," said I.

"I don't think you quite see where I mean," said Berry, pointing. "I mean along that temporary passage, which would admit a small perambulator."

As he spoke, Ping brushed past us, slipped between the two wains, and disappeared.

Berry stared after it in silence. At length—

"I withdraw," he said. "I'm not a conjurer. If everybody stood well back I used to be able to produce an egg, broken or unbroken according to the temperature of my hands, from a handkerchief about six feet square. People were very nice about it, very nice. But an inability to introduce a quart into a pint pot has always been among my failings. Don't say I've got to turn to the left here, because I can't bear it."

"No," said Adèle, smiling. "Straight on."

"What—past the steam roller? How very touching! Excuse me, messieurs, but would you mind suspending your somewhat boisterous *travail*? My little car is frightened. . . . No answer. I suppose I must pass it. Or shall we turn back? You know, I didn't really half see the cathedral!"

"Go on," I said mercilessly. "Jam your foot on the accelerator and shut your eyes. Oh, and you might hold Nobby a minute, will you? I want to light a cigarette."

Adèle began to shake with laughter.

"With pleasure," said Berry acidly. "And then I'll help you on with your coat. I may say that, if you touch me with that mammal, I shall press and pull everything I can see and burst into tears. I'm all strung up, I am."

There was not much room, and the roller was ponderously closing in, but with a protruding tongue our luckless chauffeur crept slowly past the monster in safety, and a moment later we were scudding up the Poitiers road.

Now that we were clear of the town, we set to work diligently. Adèle pored over the map and the *Michelin Guide*; Berry turned himself into a mechanical doll; and I maintained a steady issue of orders until my throat was sore.

The weather was fair and the going was good. Her new-born stiffness beginning to wear off, Pong went better than ever. Berry excelled himself.

With every kilometre we covered my spirits rose, and when we overtook Jonah on the ouskirts of Châtellerault, I could have flung up my cap.

The latter was clearly immensely surprised to see us, and when we stopped, as was our custom, at a *charcuterie* to buy our lunch, and Ping had followed our example, leaned out of his window and asked me pointedly whether my leg was yet stiff.

Concealing a smile, I regretted that it was.

Jonah fingered his chin.

"Of course," he said warily, "it's a condition precedent that you don't drive to-morrow."

"Of course," I agreed.

The confession of uneasiness, however, did my heart good. It was plain that my imperturbable cousin was getting nervous.

As we moved off again—

"We must lunch soon," said Berry. "My mouth's watering so fast, I can't keep up with it."

I patted Adèle's arm.

"Now you know the way to his heart," I said. "Straight through the stomach, and——"

"But how gross!" said Berry. "And how untrue! Naturally ascetic, but for the insistence of my physicians, I should long ago have let my hair grow and subsisted entirely on locusts and motionless lemonade, but a harsh Fate ruled otherwise. Excuse me, but I think that that there basket or ark in which the comfort is enshrined is rather near the conduit through which flows that sparkling liquid which, when vapoured, supplies our motive power. And *foie gras* is notoriously susceptible to the baneful influence of neighbouring perfumes. Thank you. If those bits of heaven were to taste of petrol, it would shorten my life. And now, where was I?"

I turned to Adèle.

"He's off," said I. "The prospect of gluttony always loosens his tongue. There's really only one way to stop him. What about lunching at the top of this hill? Or can you bear it till we've passed Poitiers?"

A mischievous look came into Adèle's brown eyes.

"It's not half-past twelve yet," she said slowly. My brother-in-law groaned. "Still . . . I don't know. . . . After all, we did have breakfast rather early, didn't we?"

Berry smacked his lips.

"A sensible woman," he said, "is above boobies."

As he spoke, Ping swept by stormily.

There was a moment's silence. Then—

"Hurray," cried Adèle excitedly; "we've got a rise!"

It was patently true. Jonah was wishful to reassure himself upon a point which an hour ago he had taken for granted. The reflection that at the moment we had not been trying to outdistance him increased our delight. All the same, his ability to outdrive us was unquestionable. But whether he could give us the start he had agreed to was another matter.

We ate a festive lunch. . . .

An hour with Poitiers is like a sip of old wine.

The absence of the stir and bustle which fret her sister capitals is notable. So reverend and thoughtful is the old grey-muzzled town that it is hard to recognise the bristling war-dog that bestrode the toughest centuries, snarled in the face of Fate, and pulled down Time. The old soldier has got him a cassock and become a gentle-faced dominie. The sleepy music of bells calling, the pensive air of study, the odour of simple piety, the sober confidence of great possessions, are most impressive. Poitiers has beaten her swords into crosiers and her spears into tuning-forks. Never was there an old age so ripe, so mellow, so becoming. With this for evidence, you may look History in the eyes and swear that you have seen Poitiers in the prime of her full life. The dead will turn in their graves to hear you; children unborn will say you knew no better. And Poitiers will take the threefold compliment with a grave smile. She has heard it so often.

Celt, Roman, Visigoth, Moor, Englishman—all these have held Poitiers in turn. Proud of their tenure, lest History should forget, three at least of them have set up their boasts in stone. The place was, I imagine, a favourite. Kings used her, certainly. Dread Harry Plantagenet gave her a proud cathedral. Among her orchards Cœur de Lion worshipped Jehane, jousted, sang of a summer evening, and spent his happiest days. Beneath her shadow the Black Prince lighted such a candle of Chivalry as has never yet been put out. Not without honour of her own countrymen, for thirteen years the High Court of Parliament preferred her to Paris. Within her walls the sainted Joan argued her inspiration.

I have dived at random into her wallet, yet see what I have brought forth. If memories are precious, Poitiers is uncommon rich.

As if to console us for our departure, the road to Sister Angoulême was superb. Broad, straight, smooth as any floor, the great highway stretched like a strip of marquetry inlaid upon the countryside. Its invitation was irresistible. . . .

We reached the windy town in time for a late tea.

As soon as this was over, Berry and I escaped and carried Pong off to a garage, there to be oiled and greased against the morrow's race. Somewhat to our amusement, before we had been there ten minutes, our cousin arrived with Ping and the same object. Had the incident occurred at Poitiers, I should have been encouraged as well. It was another sign that Jonah did not despise his opponents, and his opinion was worth having. As it was, the compliment left me unmoved. . . .

The truth was, Berry had that afternoon contracted two habits. Again and again on the way from Poitiers he had shown a marked tendency to choke his engine, and five times he had failed to mesh the gears when changing speed. Twice we had had to stop altogether and start again. He had, of course, reproached himself violently, and I had made light of the matter. But, for all the comfort I offered him, I was seriously alarmed. In a word, his sudden lapse suggested that my brother-in-law was entering that most unpleasant stage which must be traversed by all who will become chauffeurs and are taught, so to speak, to run before they can walk.

It was after we had dined, and when my wife and I were seated —myself, by virtue of my injury, upon a couch, and she upon a cushion beside me—before the comfort of a glowing log-fire, that Adèle laid down the *Guide* and leaned her head against my knee.

"I'm glad I married you," she said.

I looked at Nobby.

"So are we both," said I.

"I wonder," said Adèle, "whether you are really, or whether you're just being nice."

"Personally, I'm just being nice. Nobby is really. Of course, he may be making the best of a bad job. As a worldly good of mine, I just endowed you with him, and that was that."

"You were both very happy before—before I came."

"We thought we were."

"O-o-oh," said Adèle twisting her head around, to see my face. "You were. You know you were."

The gleeful accusation of the soft brown eyes was irresistible. To gain time, I swallowed. Then—

"So were you," I said desperately.

"I know I was," was the disconcerting reply.

"Well, then, why shouldn't we——"

"But you said you weren't."

I called the Sealyham.

"Nobby," said I, "I'm being bullied. The woman we love is turning my words against me."

For a moment the dog looked at us. Then he sat up and begged.

"And what," said Adèle, caressing him, "does that mean?"

"He's pleading my cause—obviously."

"I'm not so sure," said Adèle. "I wish he could talk."

"You're a wicked, suspicious girl. Here are two miserable males,

all pale and trembling for love of you—you've only got to smile
to make them rich—and you set your small pink heel upon their
devotion. I admit it's a soft heel—one of the very softest——"

"——I ever remember," flashed Adèle. "How very interesting!
'Heels I have Held', by Wild Oats. Were the others pink, too?"

Solemnly I regarded her.

"A little more," said I, "and I shan't teach her to drive."

Adèle tossed her head.

"Berry's going to do that," she said. "Directly we get to Pau."

I laughed savagely.

"I'm talking of automobiles," I said, "not golf balls."

"I know," said my wife. "And Berry's going to——"

"Well, he's not!" I shouted. "For one thing, he can't, and, for
another, it's my right, and I won't give it up. I've been looking
forward to it ever since I knew you. I've dreamed about it.
You're miles cleverer than I am, you're wise, you're quick-witted,
you can play, you can sing like a nightingale, you can take me on
at tennis, you can ride—driving a car's about the only thing I can
teach you, and——"

Adèle laid a smooth hand upon my mouth.

"Nobby and I," she said, "are very proud of you. They're not
in the same street with their master, they know, but they're
awfully proud to be his wife and dog."

To such preposterous generosity there was but one answer.

As I made it—

"May I teach you to drive, lady?"

A far-away look came into the soft brown eyes.

"If you don't," said Adèle, "nobody shall."

\*     \*     \*     \*     \*

The day of the race dawned, clear and jubilant. By eight
o'clock the sun was high in a blue heaven, new-swept by a steady
breeze. Limping into the courtyard before breakfast, I rejoiced
to notice that the air was appreciably warmer than any I had
breathed for a month.

We had hoped to leave Angoulême at nine o'clock. Actually it
was a quarter to ten before the luggage was finally strapped into
place and my brother-in-law climbed into the car. With a sigh
for a bad beginning, I reflected that if we could not cover the two
hundred and twenty odd miles in twelve and a quarter hours, we
ought to be shot.

Jonah stood by, watch in hand.

"Are you ready?" he said.

I nodded.

"Right," said my cousin. "I'm not sure we've picked the best route, but it's too late now. No divergence allowed."

"I agree."

"And you don't drive."

"It's out of the question."

"Right. Like to double the bets?"

"No," said Adèle. "they wouldn't. I won't allow it. But I'll bet with you. I can't afford much, but I'll bet you a hundred francs we're there before you."

"I'll give you tens," said my cousin. "And I start in one hour from *Now*!"

When I say that, upon the word being given, Pong, whose manners had been hitherto above reproach, utterly refused to start or be started, it will be seen that Fate was against us. . . .

It took us exactly two minutes to locate the trouble—which was in the magneto—and just over two hours to put it right.

As we slid out of Angoulême, an impatient clock announced that it was mid-day.

At least the delay had done something. So far as the second wager was concerned, it had altered the whole complexion of the case. We were no longer betting upon anything approaching a certainty. Indeed, unless we could break the back of the distance before daylight failed, our chances of reaching Pau before ten were worth little. If the road to Bordeaux were as fine as that from Poitiers, and Berry could find his form, we should probably run to time. We could not afford, however, to give a minute away.

As luck would have it, the state of the road was, on the whole, rather worse than any we had used since we left Boulogne. Presumably untouched for over six years, the wear and tear to which, as one of the arteries springing from a great port, it had been subjected, had turned a sleek highway into a shadow of itself. There was no flesh; the skin was broken; the very bones were staring.

For the first half hour we told one another that we had struck a bad patch. For the second we expressed nervous hopes that the going would grow no worse. After that, Berry and I lost interest and suffered in silence. Indeed, but for Adèle, I think we should have thrown up the sponge and spent the night at Bordeaux.

My lady, however, kept us both going.

She had studied our route until she knew it by heart, and was just burning to pilot us through Bordeaux and thence across Gascony.

"They're sure to make mistakes after Bordeaux. You know what the sign-posts are like. And the road's really tricky. But I spent two hours looking it up yesterday evening. I took you through Barbezieux all right, didn't I?"

"Like a book, darling."

"Well, I can do that every time. And I daresay they'll have tyre trouble. Besides, the road's no worse for us than it is for them, and after Bordeaux it'll probably be splendid. Of course we'll be there before ten—we can't help it. I want to be there before Jonah. I've got a hundred——"

"My dear," I expostulated, "I don't want to——"

"We've got a jolly good chance, any way. While you were getting her right, I got the lunch, and we can eat that without stopping. You can feed Berry. We'll gain half an hour like that."

Before such optimism I had not the face to point out that, if our opponents had any sense at all, they had lunched before leaving Angoulême.

"Here's a nice patch," added Adèle. "Put her along, you two."

Spurred by her enthusiasm, we bent again to the oars.

Contrary to my expectation, my brother-in-law, if unusually silent, was driving well. But the road was against him. He had not sufficient experience to be able to keep his foot steady upon the accelerator when a high speed and a rude surface conspired to dislodge it—a shortcoming which caused us all three much discomfort and lost a lot of mileage. Then, again, I dared not let him drive too close to the side of the road. Right at the edge the surface was well preserved, and I knew that Jonah's off wheels would make good use of it. Such finesse, however, was out of Berry's reach. We pelted along upon what remained of the crown painfully.

Seventy-three miles separate Bordeaux from Angoulême, and at the end of two hours fifty-four of them lay behind us. All things considered, this was extremely good, and when Adèle suggested that we should eat our lunch, I agreed quite cheerfully.

The suggestion, however, that I should feed Berry proved impracticable.

After four endeavours to introduce one end of a *petit pain* into his mouth—

"Would it be asking too much," said my brother-in-law, "if

I suggested that you should suspend this assault? I don't know what part of your face you eat with, but I usually use my mouth. I admit it's a bit of a rosebud, but that's no excuse for all these 'outers'. Yes, I know it's a scream, but I was once told never to put *foie gras* upon the nose or cheeks. They say it draws the skin. Oh, and don't let's have any comic nonsense about the beer," he added shortly. "Pour it straight into my breast-pocket and have done with it. Then I can suck my handkerchief."

As he spoke, Nobby leaned forward and took the dishevelled sandwich out of my unready fingers.

"That's right," added Berry, with the laugh of a maniac. "Cast my portion to the dogs." He dabbed his face with a handkerchief. "Never mind. When his hour comes, you'll have to hold him out of the window. I'm not going to stop every time he wants to be sick."

Eventually it was decided that, since we should have to stop for petrol, Berry must seize that opportunity to devour some food.

"Besides," I concluded, "a rest of a quarter of an hour will do you good."

As the words left my mouth, I noticed for the first time that my brother-in-law was tiring.

For the moment I thought I was mistaken, for upon our previous runs he had never turned a hair. Now, however, he seemed to be driving with an effort. As if to confirm my suspicions, at the very next hill he missed his change.

"I think," I said quickly, "you ought to have your lunch right away. It's no good getting done in for want of food."

Berry shot me a pathetic glance.

"It isn't that, old chap. It's—— Hang it all, it's my shoulder! That cursed muscular rheumatism cropped up again yesterday. . . ."

The murder was out.

After a little he admitted that, ever since we had left Poitiers, any quick movement of his left arm had caused him intense pain.

Of course both Adèle and I besought him to stop there and then and let the race go to blazes. Of this he would not hear, declaring that, so long as Jonah was behind, Victory was not out of sight, and that nothing short of paralysis would induce him to jilt the jade. After a little argument, we let him have his way . . .

The road continued to offer an abominable passage, and when we stopped at a garage in Bordeaux, it was five minutes to three of a beautiful afternoon.

The third *bidon* was discharging its contents into Pong's tank, and Berry was sitting wearily upon the running-board, with his mouth full and a glass of beer in his hand, when, with an apologetic cough, Ping emerged from behind an approaching tram and slid past us over the cobbles with a smooth rush. The off-side window was open, and, as the car went by, Jonah waved to us.

There was no doubt about it, my cousin was out to win. It was also transparently clear that Adèle and I, at any rate, had lost our money. We could not compete with an average of thirty-six miles an hour.

"Boy!"

"Yes, darling?"

"Is that the last *bidon*?"

"Yes. But Berry won't have finished for a least ten minutes. Besides——"

"Couldn't I drive for a bit, just till he's finished his lunch?"

I stared at my wife. Then—

"I don't see why you shouldn't, dear, except that the streets of Bordeaux are rather rough on a beginner."

"I'll be very careful," pleaded Adèle, "and—and, after all, we shall be moving. And it can't affect the bets. Nothing was said about Berry having to drive."

I smiled ruefully.

"As far as the bets are concerned, we might as well stay here the night. We've got a hundred and fifty miles in front of us, and seven hours—five of them after dark—to do them in. Berry's shoulder has put the lid on. We shan't get in before midnight."

"You never know," said Adèle.

Berry suspended the process of mastication to put his oar in.

"Let her drive," he said huskily. "One thing's certain. She can't do any worse than I have."

"You never know," said Adèle.

A minute later she was in the driver's seat, and I had folded the rug and placed it behind her back.

As Berry took his seat—

"That's right," I said. "Now let in the clutch gently. . . . Well done. Change. . . . Good girl! Now, I shouldn't try to pass this lorry until——"

"I think you would," said Adèle, changing into third, and darting in front of the monster.

"Good Heavens!" I cried. Then: "Look out for that tram,

lady. You'd better . . ."

As the tram was left standing, I caught my brother-in-law by the arm.

"*She can drive!*" I said stupidly.

"Nonsense," said Berry, "I'm willing her."

"*You fool!*" I shouted, shaking him. "*I tell you she can drive!*" We flashed between two waggons. "*Look at that! She's a first-class driver, and she's going to save your stake!*"

"What's really worrying me," said Adèle, "is how we're to pass Jonah without him seeing us."

There was an electric silence. Then—

"*For-rard!*" yelled Berry. "*For-r-a-r-d!* Out of the way, fat face, or we'll take the coat off your back." A portly Frenchman leaped into safety with a scream. "That's the style. For-rard! Fill the fife, dear heart, fill the blinkin' fife; there's a cyclist on the horizon. For-rard!"

To sound the horn would have been a work of supererogation. Maddened by our vociferous exuberance, Nobby lifted up his voice and barked like a demoniac. The ungodly hullaballoo with which he shook the dust of Bordeaux from off our tyres will be remembered fearfully by all who witnessed our exit from that city.

When I had indulged my excitement, I left the terrier and Berry to finish the latter's lunch and turned to my wife.

Sitting there, with her little hands about the wheel, she made a bewitching picture. She had thrown her fur coat open, and the breeze from the open window was playing greedily with the embroidery about her throat. Her soft hair, too, was now at the wind's mercy, and but for a little suède hat, which would have suited Rosalind, the dark strand that lay flickering upon her cheek would have been one of many. Chin in air, eyebrows raised, lids lowered, the faintest of smiles hovering about her small red mouth, my lady leaned back with an indescribable air of easy efficiency which was most attractive. Only the parted lips at all betrayed her eagerness. . . .

I felt very proud suddenly.

The road was vile, but Pong flew over it without a tremor. Looking upon his driver, I found it difficult to appreciate that a small silk-stockinged foot I could not see was setting and maintaining his beautiful steady pace.

As I stared at her, marvelling, the smile deepened, and a little gloved hand left the wheel and stole into mine.

I pulled the glove back and kissed the white wrist. . . .

"And I was going to teach you," I said humbly.

"So was I," wailed Berry. "I'd arranged everything. I was going to be so patient."

"I was looking forward to it so much," I said witsfully.

"Oh, and don't you think I was?" cried Adèle. "It was so dear of you, lad. I was going to pretend——"

"It was much more dearer of me," said Berry. "But then, I'm like that. Of course," he added, "you ought to have driven from Boulogne. Don't tell me why you held your peace, because I know. And I think it was just sweet of you, darling, and, but for your husband's presence, I should kiss you by force."

The car fled on.

There was little traffic, but thrice we came upon cows and once upon a large flock of sheep. We could only pray that Jonah had endured the same trials.

As we slid through Langon, thirty miles distant from Bordeaux, I looked at my watch. Two minutes to four. Adèle noticed the movement and asked the time. When I told her, she frowned.

"Not good enough," she said simply.

The light was beginning to fail now, and I asked if she would have the lamps lit.

She shook her head.

"Not yet, Boy."

At last the road was presenting a better surface. As we flashed up a long incline, a glance at the speedometer showed me that we were doing fifty. As I looked again, the needle swung slowly to fifty-five. . . .

I began to peer into the distance for Jonah's dust.

With a low snarl we swooped into La Réole, whipped unhesitatingly to right and left, coughed at cross-streets, and then swept out of the town ere Berry had found its name in the *Michelin Guide*.

Again I asked my wife if she would have the headlights.

"Not yet, Boy."

"Shall I raise the wind screen?"

"Please."

Together Berry and I observed her wish, while with her own right hand she closed the window. The rush of the cool air was more than refreshing, and I turned up her coat collar and fastened the heavy fur about her throat.

The car tore on.

Lights began to appear—one by one, stabbing the dusk with their beams, steady, conspicuous. One only, far in the distance, seemed ill-defined—a faint smudge against the twilight. Then it went out altogether.

"Jonah," said Adèle quietly.

She was right.

Within a minute we could see the smear again—more clearly. It was Ping's tail-lamp.

I began to tremble with excitement. Beside me I could hear Berry breathing fast through his nose.

Half a dozen times we lost the light, only to pick it up again a moment later. Each time it was brighter than before. We were gaining rapidly. . . .

We could not have been more than a furlong behind, when the sudden appearance of a cluster of bright pinpricks immediately ahead showed that we were approaching Marmande.

Instantly Ping's tail-light began to grow bigger. Jonah was slowing up for the town. In a moment we should be in a position to pass. . . .

In silence Berry and I clasped one another. Somewhere between us Nobby began to pant.

As we entered Marmande, there were not thirty paces between the two cars. And my unsuspecting cousin was going dead slow. A twitch of the wheel, and we should leave him standing. . . .

Then, without any warning, Adèle slowed up and fell in behind Ping.

I could have screamed to her to go by.

Deliberately she was throwing away the chance of a lifetime.

Desperately I laid my hand on her arm.

"Adèle!" I cried hoarsely. "My darling, aren't you——"

By way of answer, she gave a little crow of rejoicing and turned sharp round to the right.

Jonah had passed straight on.

As Pong leaped forward, the scales fell from my eyes.

Adèle was for the side-streets. If she could only rejoin the main road at a point ahead of Jonah, the latter would never know that we had passed him. If . . .

I began to hope very much that my wife knew the plan of Marmande rather better than I.

Through the dusk I could see that the street we were using ran on to a bridge. It was there, I supposed, that we should turn to

42

the left. . . .

To my horror, Adèle thrust on to the bridge at an increased pace.

"A-aren't you going to turn?" I stammered. "I mean, we'll never——"

"I said the road was tricky," said Adèle, 'but I hardly dared to hope they'd make such a bad mistake." We sailed off the bridge and on to a beautiful road. "Ah, this is more like it. I don't know where Jonah's going, *but this is the way to Pau.* . . . And now I think it'll be safe to have the lights on. You might look behind first to see if they're coming. You see, if they'd seen us go by, the game would have been up. As it is . . ."

\*     \*     \*     \*     \*

At half-past seven that evening we drove into Pau.

Arrived at our villa, we put the car away and hurried indoors.

It was almost eight o'clock when Ping discharged his passengers upon the front steps.

In silence and from the landing we watched them enter the hall.

When they were all inside, I released Nobby.

CHAPTER III

# *How a Golden Calf was Set Up, and Nobby Showed Himself a True Prophet*

Five fat weeks had rolled by since Adèle had eased Jonah of sixty pounds, and the Antoinette ring we had given her to commemorate the feat was now for the first time in danger of suffering an eclipse. In a word a new star had arisen.

"I dreamed about it," said Daphne. "I knew I should."

I knitted my brows.

"I wish," said I, "I could share your enthusiasm."

"Ah, but you haven't seen it."

"I know, but I don't even want to, If you'd come back raving about a piece of furniture or a jewel or a picture, I should have been interested. But a shawl . . . A shawl leaves me cold."

"I agree," said Jonah. "I've learned to appear attentive to the description of a frock. I keep a special indulgent smile for the incoherence inspired by a hat. But when you pipe to me the praises of a shawl—well, I'm unable to dance."

"Wait till you see it," said Adèle. "Besides, there were some lovely rugs."

"That's better," said I. "I like a good rug."

"Well, these were glorious," said Jill. "They had the most lovely sheen. But, of course, the shawl . . ."

"If anyone," said Jonah, "says that ugly word again, I shall scream."

It was half-past nine of a very beautiful morning, and we were breakfasting.

The last two days had been wet. In the night, however, the clouds had disappeared, leaving the great sky flawless, an atmosphere so rare as tempted shy Distance to approach and the mountains in all the powdered glory of their maiden snow.

Seventy miles of magic—that is what Pau stares at. For the Pyrenees, viewed from this royal box, are purely magical. They do not rise so high—eleven thousand feet, as mountains go, is nothing wonderful. There is no might nor majesty about them— distant some thirty odd miles. They are just an exquisite wall, well and truly laid, and carved with that careless cunning of the great Artificer into the likeness of some screen in Heaven.

Where, then, is the magic? Listen. These mountains are never the same. To-day they are very nigh; to-morrow they will stand farther than you have ever seen them. On Monday they will lie a mere ridge above the foot-hills; on Tuesday they will be towering, so that you must lift up your eyes to find the summits. But yesterday you marvelled at this stablishment; this morning they will be floating above the world. One week the clear-cut beauty of their lines and curves gladdens your heart; the next, a mocking mystery of soft blurred battlements will tease your vision. Such shifting sorcery is never stale. Light, shade, and atmosphere play such fantastic tricks with Pau's fair heritage that the grey town, curled comfortably in the sunshine upon her plateau's edge, looks not on one, but upon many prospects. The pageant of the Pyrenees is never done.

As for the wedding garment which they had put on in the night—it made us all late for breakfast.

The door opened to admit Berry.

The look of resignation upon his face and the silence in which he took his seat were highly eloquent.

There was no need to ask what was the matter. We knew. Big with the knowledge, we waited upon the edge of laughter.

As he received his coffee—

"I'm not going on like this," he said shortly. "It's insanitary."

Adèle's lips twitched, and Jill put a hand to her mouth.

"I can't think how it is," said Daphne. "Mine was all right."

"Of course it was," retorted her husband. "So was Adèle's. So was Jill's. By the time you three nymphs are through, there's no hot water left."

"That," said I, "is where the geyser comes in. The agent was at some pains to point out that it was an auxiliary."

"Was he, indeed?" said Berry. "Well, if he'd been at some pains to point out that it leaked, stank, became white-hot, and was generally about the finest labour-wasting device ever invented, he'd've been nearer the mark. If he'd added that it wasn't a geyser at all, but a cross between a magic lantern and a money-box——"

"Knack," said Jonah. "That's all it needs. You haven't got the hang of it yet."

The savagery with which my brother-in-law attacked a roll was almost frightening.

"W-why money-box?" said Jill tremulously.

"Because," said Berry, "it has to be bribed to devil you. Until you've put ten centimes in the metre, you don't get any gas. It's a pretty idea."

Adèle began to shake with laughter.

"You must have done something wrong," said I.

Berry shrugged his shoulders.

"Provided," he said, "that you are fairly active and physically fit, you can't go wrong. But it's a strain on one's sanity. . . . No, I don't think I'll have any omelet. They're so impatient."

I decided to apply the spur.

"But the agent showed us exactly——"

"Look here," said Berry, "you enter that bathroom, clothed—after a fashion—and in your right mind. Then you leave it for some matches. On your return you turn on the gas. After wasting four matches, you laugh pleasantly, put on your dressing-gown again, and go about the house asking everyone for a ten-centime piece. . . . This you place in the slot. Then you go out again and try to remember where you put the matches. By the time you're back, the whole room is full of gas, so you open the window wide and clean your teeth to fill up the time. Long before it's safe you strike another match. The thing lights with an explosion that shortens your life. . . . In about two minutes it emits a roaring sound and begins to shake all over. By now all the taps are red-hot, and, by the time you've burnt yourself to hell, you're wondering whether, if you start at once, you'll have time to leave the house before the thing bursts. Finally, you knock the gas off with the cork mat. . . .

"After a decent interval you start again. This time you turn on the water first. Stone cold, of course. When you've used enough gas to roast an ox, you hope like anything and reduce the flow." He paused to pass a hand wearily across his eyes. "Have you ever seen Vesuvius in eruption?" he added. "I admit no rocks were discharged—at least, I didn't see any. There may be some in the bath. I didn't wait to look. . . . Blinded by the steam, deafened by the noise, you make a rush for the door. This seems to have been moved. You feel all over the walls, like a madman. In the frenzy of despair—it's astonishing how one clings to life—you hurl yourself at the bath and turn on both taps. . . . As if by magic the steam disappears, the roaring subsides, and two broad streams of pure cold water issue, like crystal founts, into the bath. Now you know why I'm so jolly this morning."

With tears running down her cheeks—

"You must have a bath in the dressing-room," wailed Daphne. "The others do."

"I won't," said Berry. "It faces North."

"Then you must have it at night."

"Not to-night," I interposed. "Nobby's bagged it."

With the laugh of a maniac, my brother-in-law requested that the facts should be laid before the Sealyham, and the latter desired to waive his rights.

"Of course," he concluded, "if you want me to become verminous, just say so."

There was a shriek of laughter.

"And now be quick," said Daphne, "or we shall be late for the meet. And I particularly want to see Sally."

Sarah Featherstone was the possessor of the coveted shawl.

We had met her by chance upon the boulevard two days before. No one of us had had any idea that she was not in Ireland, whither she had retired upon her marriage, and where her passion for hunting kept her most of the year, and when we learned that she had already spent six months in the Pyrenees, and would be at Pau all the winter, we could hardly believe our ears. Her little son, it appeared, had been ailing, and the air of the Pyrenees was to make him well. So their summer had been passed in the mountains, and, with three good hunters from Ireland, the winter was to be supported under the shadow of the healing hills.

"It hurts me to think of Ireland, but I'm getting to love this place. I want the rain on my face sometimes, and the earth doesn't smell so sweet; but the sun's a godsend—I've never seen it before —and the air makes me want to shout. Oh, I've got a lot to be thankful for. Peter's put on a stone and a half to date, George'll be out for Christmas, and, now that you've come to stay. . . ."

We were all glad of Sarah—till yesterday.

Now, however, she had set up golden calf, which our woman-kind were worshipping out of all reason and convenience.

At the mention of the false prophet's name, Jonah and I pushed back our chairs.

"Don't leave me," said Berry, "I know what's coming. I had it last night until I fell asleep. Then that harpy"—he nodded at Daphne—"dared to rouse me out of a most refreshing slumber to ask me whether I thought 'the Chinese did both sides at once or one after the other'. With my mind running on baths, I said they probably began on their feet and washed upwards. By the time the misunderstanding had been cleared up, I was thoroughly awake and remained in a hideous and agonising condition of sleepless lassitude for the space of one hour. The tea came sharp at half-past seven, and the shawl rolled up twenty seconds later. I tell you I'm sick of the blasted comforter."

A squall of indignation succeeded this blasphemy.

When order had been restored—

"Any way," said Jill, "Sally says the sailor who sold it her'll be back with some more things next month, and she's going to send him here. He only comes twice a year, and——"

"Isn't it curious," said Jonah, "how a sailor never dies at sea?"

"Most strange," said Berry. "The best way will be to ask him to stay here. Then he can have a bath in the morning, and we can bury him behind the garage."

*   *   *   *   *

With that confident accuracy which waits upon a player only when it is uncourted, Jill cracked her ball across the six yards of turf and into the hole.

"Look at that," said Adèle.

Jonah raised his eyes to heaven.

"And the game," he said, "means nothing to her. It never has. Years ago she and I got into the final at Hunstanton. She put me dead on the green at the thirteenth, and I holed out. When I turned round to say we were three up, she wasn't there. Eventually I found her looking for her iron. She'd laid it down, to start on a daisy chain."

"I only put it down for a second," protested Jill, "and you must admit the daisies were simply huge."

"What happened?" said Adèle, bubbling.

"The daisy chain won us the match. She was much more interested in the former, and actually continued its fabrication between her shots."

We passed to the next tee.

As I was addressing the ball——

"Don't top it," said Jill.

"Have I been topping them to-day?"

"No, Boy. Only do be careful. I believe there's a lark's nest down there, and it'd be a shame——"

"There you are," said Jonah.

"Now," said I, "I'm dead certain to top it."

"Well, then, drive more to the right," said Jill. "After all, it's only a game."

"I'll take your word for it," said I.

Of course, I topped the ball, but at the next hole my grey-eyed cousin discovered that our caddie had a puppy in his pocket, so we won easily.

As we made for the club-house——

"Only ten days to Christmas," said Adèle. "Can you believe me?"

"With an effort," said I. "It's almost too hot to be true."

Indeed, it might have been a June morning.

The valley was sleepy beneath the mid-day sun; the slopes of the sheltering foot-hills looked warm and comfortable; naked but unashamed, the woods were smiling; southward, a long flash spoke of the sunlit peaks and the dead march of snow; and there, a league away, grey Pau was basking contentedly, her decent crinoline of villas billowing about her sides, lazily looking down on such a fuss and pother as might have bubbled out of the pot of Revolution, but was, in fact, the hospitable rite daily observed on the arrival of the Paris train.

"I simply must get some presents," continued my wife. "We'll start to-morrow."

I groaned.

"You can't get anything here," I protested. "And people don't expect presents when you're in the South of France."

"That's just when they do," said Adèle. "All your friends consider that it's a chance in a lifetime, and if you don't take it, they never forgive you."

"Well, I haven't got any friends," said I. "So that's that. And you used to tell me you had very few."

"Ah," said Adèle, "that was before we were engaged. That was to excite your sympathy."

I appealed to my cousins for support.

"Nothing doing," said Jonah. "If you didn't want this sort of thing, what did you marry for? For longer than I can remember you've seen your brother-in-law led off like an ox to the shambles —he's there now—financially crippled, and then compelled to tie up and address innumerable parcels, for the simple reason that, when they're at the shops Daphne's faculty of allotment invariably refuses to function."

Jill slid an arm through her brother's, patted his hand affectionately, and looked at Adèle.

"If Boy breaks down," she said sweetly, "I'll lend you my ox. He's simply splendid at parcels."

"You've got to find something to do up first," said I. "This isn't Paris."

A colour was lent to my foreboding within the hour.

As we sat down to luncheon—

"Yes," said Berry, "my vixen and I have spent a delightful morning. We've been through fourteen shops and bought two amethyst necklets and a pot of marmalade. I subsequently dropped the latter in the place Royale, so we're actually twelve down."

"Whereabouts in the place Royale?" I inquired.

"Just outside the Club. Everybody I knew was either going in or coming out, so it went very well indeed."

There was a gust of laughter.

"N-not on the pavement?" whimpered Jill.

"On the pavement," said Daphne. "It was dreadful. I never was so ashamed. Of course I begged him to pick it up before it ran out. D'you think he'd do it? Not he. Said it was written, and it was no good fighting against Fate, and that he'd rather wash his hands of it than after it, and that sort of stuff. Then Nobby began to lick it up. . . . But for Fitch, I think we should have been arrested. Mercifully, we'd told him to wait for us by the bandstand, and he saw the whole thing."

"It's all very fine," said her husband. "It was I who furnished and suggested the use of the current issue of *Le Temps*, and, without that, Fitch couldn't have moved. As it was, one sheet made a shroud, another a pall, and Nobby's beard and paws were appropriately wiped upon the ever-burning scandal of 'Reparations'."

"I gather," said Jonah, "that the dissolution of the preserve turned an indifferent success into a howling failure. Of course, I haven't seen the necklets but . . ."

"I can't pretend it's easy," said Daphne. "It isn't that there aren't any shops——"

"No," said Berry emphatically, "it isn't that."

"—but somehow . . . Still, if we go on long enough, we shall find something."

"That's it," said her husband. "We're going to put our backs into it this afternoon. After we've done another twelve shops without buying anything, we're going to have police protection. Not that we need it, you know, but it'll improve my morale."

"If only Sally was here," said Jill, "she could have told us where to go."

"If only her sailor would turn up," said Adèle, "we might be able to get all our presents from him."

"That's an idea," said Jonah. "What was the merchant's name?"

Amid a buzz of excitement, Daphne sent for the letter which had announced Sarah Featherstone's departure from Pau. When it arrived, she read the material portion aloud.

". . . George can't get away, so Peter and I are going home for Christmas. We'll be back the first week in January. I've told the Marats that if Planchet (the sailor who sold me the shawl, etc.) turns up before I get back, he's to be sent on to you. If he's got anything extra-special that you're not keen on, you might get it for me. . . ."

"Well, I never thought I should live to say it," said Berry, "but, after what I've gone through this morning, if Planchet were to totter in this afternoon, laden with at once cheap and pretentious goods, I should fall upon his bull neck."

"Who," said I, "are the Marats?"

"They're the married couple who run the flat. I believe they're wonderful. Sally says she never knew what service was before."

"I do hope," said Jill, twittering, "they don't make any mistake."

"I've no fear of that," said Adèle. "I can't answer for the man, because we didn't see him, but Madame Marat's no fool."

"Incidentally," said I, "it's one thing giving Planchet our address, but it's quite another persuading him to fetch up. He may have other sheep to shear."

"We can only pray that he hasn't," said Daphne. "It's too much to expect him to have another shawl, but I should like the first pick of what he has."

Berry regarded his wife.

"If," he said, "you will swear to select from his wares all the blinkin' presents with which you propose to signalise this Yuletide, I'll—I'll tie them all up without a word."

"Same here," said I. "Our gifts will cost us more, but we shall live the longer."

"Ditto," said Jonah.

The girls agreed cheerfully, and, before luncheon was over, it had been decided to give Planchet three days in which to make his appearance, and that, if he had not arrived by that time, then and then only should we resort to the shops.

Less than an hour had elapsed, and we were just about to make ready to take the air by the simple expedient of proceeding at a high speed in the direction of Biarritz, when Falcon entered the room.

"There's an individual, madam, 'as come to the door——"

"Planchet? Is it Planchet?"

"I'm afraid I can 'ardly say, madam, but 'e 'as this address upon a piece of note-paper, madam, and——"

"All right, Falcon, I'll come."

The butler's valiant endeavours to cope with the heritage of Babel were better known to us than he imagined. More than once his efforts to extract from strangers that information which was his due, and at the same time, like a juggler of many parts, to keep the balls of Dignity and Courtesy rolling, had been overheard, and had afforded us gratification so pronounced as to necessitate the employment of cushions and other improvised gags if our faithful servant's feelings were to come to no harm.

"I'll go," said Jill and Adèle simultaneously.

We all went, and we were all just in time to see our visitor precede the Sealyham in the direction of the lodge.

Aghast at such ill-timed pleasantry, we erupted pellmell into the drive, all frantic by word or deed to distract the terrier from his purpose. Shrieks, curses, and a copy of *La Fontaine's Fables* were hurled simultaneously and in vain at our favourite, and it was Berry, to whom the fear of further acquaintance with the emporiums of Pau must have lent wings, who actually overtook and discomfited the pursuer some three yards from the road.

It was with feelings of inexpressible relief that we presently beheld the three returning—Berry alternately rebuking the Sealyham, who was under his arm, and apologising to his guest, the latter wide-eyed, something out of breath, and anything but easy, and Nobby apparently torn between an aggressively affectionate regard for his captor and a still furiously expressed suspicion of the stranger within our gates.

As the trio drew nigh—

"It is Monsieur Planchet," called Berry. "He's brought some things for us to see. His man's behind with a barrow."

With beating hearts we trooped back into the house. . . .

As I returned from thrusting Nobby into a bedroom, Monsieur Planchet's hireling staggered into the hall, a gigantic basket-trunk poised precariously upon his hunched shoulders.

The inspection was held in the drawing-room.

It was rather late in the day to assume that nonchalant air which has, from time immemorial, adorned the armouries of all accomplished hucksters.

Our instant recognition of the salesman, our energetic solicitude for his safety, and our obvious anxiety to dissociate ourselves from the policy of direct action adopted by the terrier, had not only betrayed, but emphasised, the fact that the sailor's arrival was very much to our taste. Clearly, if we did not wish to pay through the nose for what we purchased, our only course was to feign disappointment when the wares were produced.

For what it was worth I circulated a covert recommendation of this wile, which was acknowledged with sundry nods and inaudible assurances—the latter, so far as Jill was concerned, too readily given to inspire me with confidence.

Sure enough, when the lid of the trunk was lifted, and Planchet plucked forth a truly exquisite rug and flung it dexterously across a chair, my grey-eyed cousin let out a gasp which an infant in arms could not have misinterpreted.

There was only one thing to be done, and Daphne did it.

With a heroic disregard for her reputation, she shook her head.

"Too bright," she said shortly. "Don't you think so?" she added, turning to Berry.

The latter swallowed before replying.

"It's positively gaudy," he said gloomily.

Planchet shrugged his shoulders and began to unfasten a bale. . . .

By the time seven more Persian rugs—all old and all more than ordinarily pleasing in design and colouring—were sprawling about the chamber, any organised depreciation was out of the question. Where all were so beautiful, it required a larger output of moral courage than any one of us could essay to decry the whole pack. By way of doing his or her bit, everybody decided to praise one or two to the implied condemnation of the remainder. In the absence of collusion, it was inevitable that those rugs which somebody had thus branded as goats should invariably include somebody else's sheep. The result was that every single rug had its following. A glance at their owner, who was standing aside, making no offer to commend his carpets, but fingering his chin and watching us narrowly with quick-moving eyes, showed that he was solely engaged in considering how much he dared ask.

I moved across to him.

"You only come here twice a year?" I inquired.

"That is so, *Monsieur.*"

"And how do you get these things? By barter?"

"Yes, *Monsieur.*"

After a little encouragement, he explained that before each voyage he laid in a stock of knives, gramophones, mirrors, trinkets, and the like, these to exchange with the natives in the bazaars of the smaller Eastern ports at which his ship touched. From Bordeaux he used to set out, and to Bordeaux he as regularly returned. An aunt dwelling at Pau was responsible for his selection of the town as a market for his goods. I should not have taken him for a sailor, and said as much. With a shy smile, he confessed that he was a steward, adding that he was a landsman at heart, and that, but for the opportunities of trading which his occupation presented he should go to sea no more.

Suddenly—

"What else have you got?" said Daphne.

Six panels of Chinese embroidery—all powder-blue and gold, "laborious Orient ivories", a gorgeous hanging that had been the coat of a proud mandarin, three Chinese mats, aged and flawless, a set of silken doilies—each one displaying a miniature landscape limned with a subtlety that baffled every eye—one by one these treasures were laid before us.

Even Jonah went down before the ivories.

Ere the trunk was empty, we had, one and all, dropped our

masks and were revelling openly.

"Now, isn't that beautiful?" "Sally's got a ball like that, but it isn't so big." "It's just as well she's in Ireland, or we shouldn't have had those mats." "You know, that rug on the chair's a devilish fine one." "They all are." "Yes, but that—my dear fellow, it's the sort of rug they put in the window and refuse to sell, because it's such an advertisement." "I'll tell you what, if we had those panels made into curtains, they'd look simply priceless in the drawing-room." "Give me the ivories."

It was Adèle who pulled the check-string.

"What's the price of this rug?" she said quietly.

There was an expectant and guilty hush.

With a careless flourish we had called the tune—clamoured for it. . . . If the piper's fee was exorbitant, we had only ourselves to thank.

Planchet hesitated. Then—

"Five hundred francs, *Madame*."

Ten pounds.

You could have heard a pin drop.

The rug was worth sixty. In Regent Street or Fifth Avenue we should have been asked a hundred. If this was typical of Planchet's prices, no wonder Sally had plunged. . . .

I took out a pencil and picked up a pad of notepaper.

"And the other rugs?" I inquired.

"The same price, *Monsieur*."

The rugs went down.

Slowly, and without a shadow of argument, the prices of the other valuables were asked, received, and entered.

With a shaking hand I counted up the figures—eight thousand six hundred francs.

I passed the paper Berry.

"Will you pay him?" I said. "I haven't got enough at the bank here, and you can't expect him to take a foreign cheque."

"Right oh!"

"He may not want to part with them all at one house," said Daphne. "You'd better ask him."

Adèle smiled very charmingly.

"We like your pretty things very much," she said. "May we have what you've shown us?"

Planchet inclined his head.

"As *Madame* pleases."

I crossed to where he was standing and went through my list, identifying each article as I came to it, and making him confirm the price. When we had finished, I insisted upon him checking my figures. He did so with some show of reluctance. The total, seemingly, was good enough.

When the reckoning was over, I hesitated.

Then—

"You know," I said slowly, "we'd have to pay much more than this in the shops."

It seemed only fair.

Planchet spread out his hands.

"*Monsieur* is very kind : but for me, I should not obtain more from the merchants. I know them. They are robbers. I prefer infinitely to deal with you."

"All right. You don't mind a cheque?"

"A cheque, *Monsieur*?"

"Yes, on the bank here. We haven't so much money in the house."

The little man hesitated. Nervously the big brown eyes turned from me to fall upon his possessions. . . .

"That's all right," said Berry. "The bank's still open. Fitch can run up in the car and get the money. He's probably had a dud cheque some time or other. Anyway, considering he knows nothing of us, and Sally's out of reach, I don't blame him."

Such a way out of the difficulty was unanimously approved, and when I communicated our intention to Planchet, the latter seemed greatly relieved. It was not, he explained volubly, that he did not trust us, but when a poor sailor produced such a cheque to a bank . . .

As Berry left to give the chauffeur his instructions—

"Last time you came," said Daphne, "you brought a beautiful shawl. Mrs. Featherstone bought it."

Planchet frowned thoughtfully. Then his face lighted with recollection.

"Perfectly, *Madame*. I remember it. It was very fine. I have another like it at home."

My sister caught her breath.

"For sale?"

"If *Madame* pleases." Adèle and Jill clasped one another. "I will bring it to-morrow."

With an obvious effort Daphne controlled her excitement.

"I—we should like to have a look at it," she said.

Planchet inclined his head.

"To-morrow morning, *Madame*."

Without more ado he packed up his traps, announced that, as he was returning on the morrow, there was now no occasion for him to wait for his money, and, thanking us profusely for our patronage and assuring us that he was ever at our service, summoned his employee and withdrew humbly enough.

It was fully a quarter of an hour before the first wave of our pent-up enthusiasm had spent itself. After a positive debauch of self-congratulation, amicable bickering with regard to the precise order of precedence in which an antiquary would place our acquisitions, and breathless speculation concerning their true worth, we sank into sitting postures about the room and smiled affectionately upon one another.

"And now," said Berry, "what about tying them up?"

"What for?" said Jill.

"Well, you can't send them through the post as they are."

"You don't imagine," said Daphne, in the horrified tone of one who repeats a blasphemy, "you don't imagine that we're going to give these things away?"

Berry looked round wildly.

"D'you mean to say you're going to keep them?" he cried.

"Of course we are," said his wife.

"What, all of them?"

My sister nodded.

"Every single one," she said.

With an unearthly shriek, Berry lay back in his chair and drummed with his heels upon the floor.

"I can't bear it!" he roared. "I can't bear it! I won't. It's insufferable. I've parted with the savings of a lifetime for a whole roomful of luxuries, not one of which, in the ordinary way, we should have dreamed of purchasing, not one of which we require, to not one of which, had you seen it in a shop, you would have given a second thought, all of which are probably spurious——"

"Shame!" cried Jill.

"——only to be told that I've still got to prosecute the mutually revolting acquaintance with infuriated shopkeepers forced upon me this morning. It's cruelty to animals, and I shall write to the Y.M.C.A. Besides, it's more blessed——"

"I can't help it," said Daphne. "The man had absolutely nothing that would have done for anybody. If——"

"One second," said her husband, "I haven't parsed that sentence yet. And what d'you mean by 'done for'? Because——"

"If," Daphne continued doggedly, "we sent one of those rugs to someone for Christmas, they'd think we'd gone mad."

Berry sighed.

"I'm not sure we haven't," he said. "Any way—" he nodded at Jonah and myself—"I'll trouble each of you gents for a cheque for sixty pounds. As it is, I shall have to give up paying my tailor again, and what with Lent coming on . . ." Wearily he rose to his feet. "And now I'm going to have a good healthy cry. Globules the size of pigeons eggs will well from my orbs."

"I know," said Jill. "These things can be our Christmas presents to one another."

Berry laughed hysterically.

"What a charming idea!" he said brokenly. "And how generous! I shall always treasure it. Every time I look at my pass-book . . ."

Overcome with emotion he stepped out of the room.

A muffled bark reminded me that Nobby was still imprisoned, and I rose to follow my brother-in-law.

As I was closing the door, I heard my wife's voice.

"You know, I'm simply pining to see that shawl."

\*     \*     \*     \*     \*

At ten o'clock the next morning the most beautiful piece of embroidery I have ever seen passed into our possession in return for the ridiculously inadequate sum of two thousand francs.

Obviously very old, the pale yellow silk of which the shawl was made was literally strewn with blossoms, each tender one of them a work of art. All the matchless cunning, all the unspeakable patience, all the inscrutable spirit of China blinked and smiled at you out of those wonderful flowers. There never was such a show. Daring walked delicately, Daintiness was become bold. Those that wrought the marvel—for so magnificent an artifice was never the work of one man—were painters born—painters whose paints were threads of silk, whose brushes, needles. Year after year they had toiled upon these twenty-five square feet of faded silk, and always perfectly. The thing was a miracle—the blazing achievement of a reachless ideal.

Upon both lovely sides the work was identical: the knotted fringe—itself bewildering evidence of faultless labour—was three feet deep, and while the whole shawl could have been passed through a bracelet, it scaled the remarkable weight of nearly six pounds.

Daphne, Adèle, and Jill with one voice declared that it was finer than Sally's. As for Berry, Jonah, and myself, we humbly withdrew such adverse criticism as we had levelled at the latter, and derived an almost childish glee for the possession of its fellow.

It was, indeed, our joy over this latest acquisition that stiffened into resolution an uneasy feeling that we ought to give Sally a slice of our luck.

After considerable discussion we decided to make her a present of the three Chinese mats. She had bought three of Planchet upon his last visit, and those we had just purchased would bring her set up to six. Lest we should repent our impulse, we did them up there and then and sent them off by Fitch the same afternoon.

\* \* \* \* \*

Christmas was over and gone.

In the three days immediately preceding the festival, such popularity with the tradesmen of the town as we had forfeited was more than redeemed at the expense, so far as I was concerned, of an overdraft at the bank. Absurdly handsome presents were purchased right and left. Adèle's acquaintance was extremely wide. Observing that it was also in every instance domiciled in the United States, with the density of a male I ventured to point out that upon the day which my wife's presents were intended to enrich, all of them would indubitably be lying in the custody of the French postal authorities. Thereupon it was gently explained to me that, so long as a parcel had been obviously posted before Christmas, its contents were always considered to have arrived "in time"—a conceit which I had hitherto imagined to be the property of book-makers alone. In short, from first to last, my wife was inexorable. But for the spectacle of Berry and Jonah being relentlessly driven along the same track, life would have lost its savour. Indeed, as far as we three were concerned, most of the working hours of Christmas Eve were spent at the post office.

The registration of a postal packet in France is no laughing matter. When a coloured form has to be obtained, completed, and deliberately scrutinised before a parcel can be accepted, when there is only one pen, where there are twenty-seven people in front of you—each with two or more packages to be registered—when there is only one registration clerk, when mental arithmetic is not that clerk's *forte*, when it is the local custom invariably to question the accuracy first of the postage demanded and then of the change received, when the atmosphere of the post office is germane to poison-gas, and when you are bearing twelve parcels and leading a Sealyham, the act of registration and its preliminaries are conducive to heart-failure.

The miniature of herself, however, with which my wife presented me on Christmas Day atoned for everything. . . .

And now—Christmas was over and gone.

The New Year, too, had come in with a truly French explosion of merriment and good-will.

It was, in fact, the fourth day of January, and, with the exception of my cousins, who were upon the links, we were proceeding gingerly down the rue du Lycée, *en route* for Lourdes, when my sister gave a cry and called upon me to stop.

As I did so, I saw Mrs. Featherstone stepping towards us across the open space which fronts the market.

Berry climbed out of the dickey, and Adèle and Daphne got out of the car.

As I followed them—

"Sally, my dear," said Daphne, "I never knew you were back."

"I wasn't till this morning," panted Sally. "I only arrived at eight. For the last three hours I've been——"

"Before you tell us anything," said Daphne, "we want to thank you. Since you've been away, Planchet's been. He's sold us the most lovely things I've ever seen. We're so grateful to you, we don't know what to do."

"Well, for goodness' sake," rejoined Sally, "insure them to-day. I've just been cleaned out of everything I've got."

"Cleaned out?" cried Daphne. "D'you mean to say you've been robbed?"

"That's right," said Sally. "Peter and I got back this morning to find the Marats gone and the place stripped. Of course, the furniture belonging to the flat's there, but the only decent things were what I'd added, and those have vanished."

"Not all the things you got from Planchet?"

"Rather," said Sally. "Shawl and everything. Jolly, isn't it?"

"What an awful shame!" cried Adèle. "But who's taken them? Not the Marats?"

"Must be," said Mrs. Featherstone. She nodded over her shoulder. "I've just been to the police about it, but you know how hopeless they are."

"If I can do anything," said Berry, "you know I'd only be too happy. . . ."

"Thanks awfully," was the reply, "but to tell you the truth, I

don't see what there is to be done. As far as I can make out, they
left before Christmas, so they've got a pretty good start."

"I'm terribly sorry," said I. "Of course I never saw the goods,
but, if they were anything like the things we bought, it's a cruel
shame."

Mrs. Featherstone laughed.

"I do feel sore," she admitted. "The maddening part of it is, I
meant to take the shawl home to show George, and then, in the
rush at the last, I left it out." She turned to my sister. "And you
know I trusted that couple implicitly."

"I know you did."

"The queer thing is, they seem to have suffered one solitary
pang of remorse. Did I show you those Chinese mats I was so
crazy about? Well, after they'd gone, I suppose, their hearts smote
them, because they did the three up and sent them back."

For a moment we looked at one another.

Then—

"I'm sorry to disappoint you, Sally," said Daphne gently, "but
you mustn't give the brutes that credit. We sent you the mats as a
Christmas present." Sally knitted her brows. "They're not yours.
We bought them from Planchet. Directly I saw them, I thought
how beautifully they'd match yours, and we wanted you to have
a set."

Sally stared at her.

"But I could have sworn——"

"I know," said Daphne. "It was because they were such a
wonderful match that we——"

"What else did he sell you?"

A sudden thought came to me, and I turned to catch Berry by
the arm. . . . As men in a film, he and I looked at one another
with open mouths. . . .

Sublimely unconscious, Daphne and Adèle were reciting the
list of our treasures.

Mrs. Featherstone heard them out solemnly. Then—

"And what," she said, "does Planchet look like?"

It became Daphne's turn to stare.

I moistened my lips.

"Slight, dark, clean-shaven, large brown eyes, nervous manner,
scar on the left temple—*or am I describing Marat?*"

Sally spread out her hands.

"To the life," she said simply.

There was a dreadful silence.

At length—

" 'Sold,' " I said slowly. " 'By order of the trustees. Owner going abroad.' Marat was with you when you bought them, of course? But what a smart bit of work!"

Sally covered her face and began to shake with laughter. Daphne and Adèle stared at her as if bewitched.

At his third attempt to speak—

"Well, that's topping," said Berry. "And now will you come back and get your things now, or shall we bring them over to-morrow? We've taken every care of them." He sighed. "When I think," he added, "that, but for my good offices, Nobby would have sent that treacherous drawlatch away, not only empty, but with the modern equivalent of a flea in his ear, I could writhe. When I reflect that it was I who supported the swine's pre-dilection for hard cash, I could scream. But when I remember that ever since our purchase of the shawl, my wife has never once stopped enumerating and/or indicating the many superiorities which distinguish it from yours, I want to break something." He looked round savagely. "Where's a grocer's?" he demanded. "I want some marmalade."


CHAPTER IV

## *How Berry Made an Engagement, Jill a Picture, and Adèle a Slip of Some Importance*

A natural result of our traffic with Planchet was that we became temporarily suspicious and careful to a fault. The horse had been stolen. For the next three weeks we locked not only the stable door, but every single door to which a key could be fitted—and suffered accordingly. In a word, our convenience writhed. To complete our discomfort, if ever one of us jibbed, the others were sure to lay the lash about his shoulders. The beginning of the end arrived one fine February day.

An early breakfast had made us ready for lunch. As we were taking our seats—

"Are the cars locked?" said Daphne.

Adèle held up a key.

"Pong is," she said.

My sister turned to Jonah.

"And Ping?"

My cousin shook his head.

"No," he said shortly. "I omitted the precaution. If this was Paris, instead of Pau, if the cars were standing in an undesirable thoroughfare, instead of in the courtyard of the English Club, if——"

"It's all very well," said Daphne, "but you know what happened to the Rolls."

Berry frowned.

"Any reference," he said, "to that distressing incident is bad for my heart." He turned to Jonah. "As for you, you've lodged your protest, which will receive the deepest consideration. I shall dwell upon it during the soup. And now push off and lock the vehicle. I know Love laughs at locksmiths, but the average motor-thief's sense of humour is less susceptible."

When his sister threw her entreaties into the scale, my cousin took the line of least resistance and rose to his feet.

"For converting a qualified blessing into an unqualified curse," he said bitterly, "you three alarmists take the complete cracknel. Since the locks were fitted, I've done nothing but turn the key from morning till night. Before the beastly things were thought of, the idea of larceny never entered your heads."

The indignation with which his words were received would have been more pronounced if we had had the room to ourselves. As it was, Jonah made his way to the door amid an enraged murmur of expostulation, whose temper was aggravated by suppression almost to bursting-point.

There was much to be said for both points of view.

It was a fact that since the theft of the Rolls we had never felt easy about leaving a car unattended. Yet, though we had often discussed the matter, nothing had been done. Now, however, that we were in a strange country, where the tracing of a stolen car would, for a variety of reasons, be an extremely difficult undertaking, and staying withal only a handful of miles from the Spanish frontier, we all felt that action of some sort must be taken without delay.

An attempt to enlist the services of the Sealyham as a custodian had failed ignominiously. In the first place, unless fastened, he had flatly declined to stay with either of the cars. The expedient of closing one of these altogether and leaving Nobby within had proved quite as unsatisfactory and more humiliating. Had we been able to eradicate from the dog's mind the conviction that he

was being wrongfully imprisoned, the result might have been
different. As it was, after barking furiously for five minutes, he had
recourse to reprisal and, hardly waiting to remove the paper in
which it was wrapped, devoured half a kilogramme of ripe Brie
with a revengeful voracity to which the condition of the interior
of the car bore hideous witness. Finally, when the urchin who was
in our confidence, and had engaged for the sum of five francs
to endeavour to enter the car, opened its door, the captive leaped
out joyously and, after capering with delight at his delivery, wiped
his mouth enthusiastically upon a tyre and started on a recon-
naissance of the neighbourhood in the hope of encountering his
gaolers. As for the car, our employee might have driven it into the
blue. . . .

In the end, it was decided that a lock attached to the steering-
column would offer the best security. Accordingly, a device was
sent for, fitted to each of the cars, and proved. So far as we could
see, there was no fault in it. Once the key was withdrawn, the car
concerned was useless. It could be driven, certainly, but it could
not be steered. Indeed, short of getting it upon a trolley or taking
"the steering" down, its asportation could not be compassed.

New brooms sweep clean.

Delighted with the realisation that theft could now be erased
from the list of terrors of motoring, the girls insisted upon the
observance of the new rite upon every possible occasion. As drivers
of long standing, Jonah and I found this eagerness hard to indulge.
Use holds, and, try as we would, it was absurdly difficult to remember to do as we had never done before, whenever we evacua-
ted a car. Often enough, as now, it was a work of supererogation.

Berry turned to me.

"I observe," he said, "that for once you have not advanced
your opinion. Is this because you realize that it's valueless? Or
won't your mouth work?"

"Jonah was right," said I. "Insurance has its advantages, but
you don't register every letter you post. The truth is, what little
sense of proportion you have is failing. Of course you're not as
young as you were, and then, again, you eat too much."

"In other words," said my brother-in-law, "you attribute
caution to the advance of old age and gluttony. I see. To which of
your physical infirmities do you ascribe a superabundance of
treachery and bile?"

"That," said I, "is due to external influence. The sewer-gas
of your temperament——"

"I refuse," said Berry "to sit still and hear my soul compared to a drain at the very outset of what promises to be a toothsome repast. It might affect my appetite."

I raised my eyebrows.

"Needless anxiety again," I sighed. "I don't know what's the matter with you to-day."

"By the way," said Daphne, "I quite forgot. Did you cash your cheque?"

"I did," said her husband.

"What did they give you?" said Jill.

"Fifty-three francs to the pound."

"Fifty-*three*?" cried Daphne and Adèle in horror-stricken tones.

"Fifty-three francs dead. If I'd cashed it yesterday, as, but for your entreaties, I should have done, I should have got fifty-six."

"But when you found it was down, why didn't you wait?"

"In the first place," retorted my brother-in-law, "it isn't down; it's up. In the second place, I was down—to four francs twenty-five. In the third place, to-morrow it may be up to fifty."

"It's much more likely to go back to fifty-five."

"My dear girl," said Berry, "with the question of likelihood the movements of the comic Exchange have nothing to do. It's a law unto itself. Compared with the Money Market of to-day, Monte Carlo's a Sunday-school. I admit we'd have more of a show if we didn't get the paper a day late. . . . Still, that makes it more sporting."

"I don't see any sport in losing six hundred francs," said his wife. "It's throwing away money." Here my cousin reappeared. "Jonah, why did you let him do it?"

"Do what?" said Jonah.

"Cash such a cheque when the franc's dropped."

"It hasn't," said Jonah. "It's risen."

"How," piped Jill, "can it have risen when it's gone down?"

"It hasn't gone down," said I.

"But fifty-three's less than fifty-six."

"Let me explain," said Berry, taking an olive from a dish. "You see that salt-cellar?"

"Yes," said Jill, staring.

"Well, that represents a dollar. The olive is a franc, and this here roll is a pound." He cleared his throat. "When the imports exceed the exports, the roll rises"—up went his hand—"as good bread should. But when the exports exceed the imports, or the

President backs a winner, or something, then the olive begins to soar. In a word, the higher the fewer."

Jill passed a hand across her sweet pretty brow.

"But what's the salt-cellar got to do with it?"

"Nothing whatever," said Berry. "That was to distract your attention."

Jill choked with indignation.

"I'll never ask you anything again," she said severely. "After all, if you can't help yourself, it isn't likely you can help me. And, any way, I wouldn't have been so silly as to go and cash a cheque when the franc had gone down."

"Up," I said relentlessly.

"But how can it——"

"Look here," said I. "Imagine that all the francs in the world have turned into herrings."

"What a joy shopping would be!" said Berry.

"Yes," said Jill faithfully.

"Well, on Monday you go and buy a pound's worth of herrings. Fish is plentiful, so you get fifty-six."

"Yes."

"During the night herrings rise."

"Get quite high," said Berry. "You have to get out of bed and put your purse on the landing."

Adèle began to shake with laughter.

"Yes," said Jill earnestly.

"So that the next morning," I continued desperately, "when you come to buy another pound's worth of herrings, you only get fifty-three."

"That's right," said Berry. "And while you're trying to decide whether to have one or two pounds, they turn into bananas. Then you *are* done."

Jonah took up the cudgels.

"It's perfectly simple," he said. "Think of a thermometer."

Jill took a deep breath.

Then—

"Yes," she said.

"Well, on Monday you find it's fifty-six. On Tuesday you look at it again, and find it's fifty-three. That means it's gone down, doesn't it?"

"Yes," said his sister hopefully.

"Well, with the franc it's just the opposite. It means it's gone up."

"Yes."

"That's all," said Jonah brutally.

Jill looked from him to Daphne and from Daphne to Adèle—dazedly. The former put a hand to her head.

"My dear," she said, "I can't help you. Before they started explaining, I had a rough idea of how the thing worked. Now I'm confused for ever. If they are to be believed, in future we've got to say 'up' when we feel inclined to say 'down'. But don't ask me why."

She stopped to speak with a member who was leaving the room and had come to pay his respects. After a word or two—

"Visitors' weather," he said. "Perfect, isn't it? But, I say, what a fall in the franc! Three points in day. . . . Never mind. It'll go up again."

He made his adieus and passed on.

It was no good saying anything.

A prophet is not without honour, save in his own country.

\*　　\*　　\*　　\*　　\*

It was three days later that we were bowling along the road to Biarritz.

The morning was full and good to look upon. Sun, sky, and air offered the best they had. To match their gifts, a green and silver earth strained at the leash of Winter with an eager heart. The valleys smiled, high places lifted up their heads, the hasty Gave de Pau swirled on its shining way, a laughing sash of snow-broth, and all the countryside glowed with the cheerful aspect of a well-treated slave.

Wide, straight, and level, the well-built road thrust through the beaming landscape with a directness that took Distance by the throat. The surface improving as we left Pau behind, I drew on the seven-league boots—surreptitiously. Very soon we were flying. . . . With a steady purr of contentment, Pong, tuned to a hair, swallowed the flashing miles so easily that pace was robbed of its sting.

A dot on the soft bullock-walk that edged the road grew with fantastic swiftness into an ox-waggon, loomed for an instant life-size, and was gone. A speck ahead leapt into the shape of a high-wheeled gig, jogged for a moment to meet us, and vanished into space. A doll's-house by the wayside swelled into a villa . . . a chateau . . . a memory of tall thin windows ranged in a white wall. The future swooped into the present, only to be flicked into the past. The seven-league boots were getting into their stride.

Then came a level-crossing with the barriers drawn. . . .

For a minute the lady responsible for the obstructions seemed uncertain whether to withdraw them or no. After a long look up the line, however, she decided against us and shook her head with a benevolent smile.

"*Le train arrive,*" she explained.

With a sigh, I stopped the engine and lighted a cigarette. . . .

"What exactly," said Daphne, "did Evelyn say?"

"That," said Berry, "as I have already endeavoured to point out, will always remain a matter for conjecture. We addressed one another for more than twenty minutes, but our possession of the line was disputed effectively during the whole of that period."

"Well, what did you hear her say?"

"I heard her say 'Yes' twice, and 'Delighted', and 'One o'clock'. I'm almost certain that towards the end of our communion she said, 'Oh, hell!' Having regard to the prevailing conditions, she may be forgiven."

Daphne sighed.

"Well, I suppose she expects us," she said. "After all, that's the main thing. You made her understand it was to-day, didn't you?"

"That," was the reply, "remains to be seen. If I didn't, it's not my fault. It's no good pretending that 'Wednesday's' a good word to shout, but I made the most of it. I also said 'Woden's Day' with great clarity, and '*Mardi*'."

"*Mardi?*" shrieked his wife.

"Oh, much louder than that."

"B-but that's *Tuesday!*"

Berry started guiltily.

"I—I mean '*Mercredi*'," he said hurriedly.

I began to shake with merriment.

Suspiciously my sister regarded her husband.

"Which did you say?" she demanded.

" '*Mercredi*'."

"I don't believe a word of it," cried Daphne. "You said '*Mardi*'. You know you did."

Here a seemingly interminable freight-train started to lumber across our path. . . .

As the rumble began to die—

"I think," said I, "he must have got 'Wednesday' through. Otherwise Evelyn would have rung up last night."

Berry drew a case from his pocket and offered me a cigar. Then he turned to my sister and protruded his tongue. . . .

We had known Evelyn Fairie for years. It was natural that we should wish to know Evelyn Swetecote. That wedlock could have diminished her charm was not to be thought of. But we were forgivably curious to see her in the married state and to make the acquaintance of the man whom she had chosen out of so many suitors. Little knowing that we were at Pau, Evelyn had written to us from Biarritz. In due season her letter had arrived, coming by way of Hampshire. An answer in the shape of a general invitation to lunch had brought not so much a refusal as a definite counter-proposal that we should suggest a day and come to Biarritz. In reply, the services of the telephone had been requisitioned, and, if my brother-in-law was to be believed, Mrs. Swetecote had been advised to expect us on Wednesday.

In any event, expected or unexpected, here were we, all six, upon the road—my wife and cousins in one car, and Daphne, Berry, and I within the other.

As we swung into the paved streets of Orthez—

"And when," said Berry, "when am I to drive?"

"From Peyrehorade," I replied.

"Oh. I suppose that's where the stones begin, or the road stops, or something."

I shook my head.

"Not that I know of. And you can drive all the way back. But—well, there's a hill or two coming, and—and I'd like just to take her so far," I concluded lamely.

But for my sister's presence, I would have told him the truth. This was that I had bet Jonah that I could get from Orthez to Peyrehorade in twenty minutes. The distance was exactly thirty kilometres, and the road was perfect. There were no corners, and the bends were few, there were hills, certainly; but these were straight-forward enough and could be taken, so to speak, in our stride. Moreover, there were no cross-roads, and only two turnings worth thinking about. To some cars the feat would have been nothing. Whether it was within the reach of Ping and Pong remained to be seen. . . .

As we left Orthez, I looked at my watch.

Ten minutes to eleven.

I laid hold of the wheel. . . .

To this hour I cannot tell why Daphne did not exercise the prerogative of a passenger and protest against the pace. But neither at the time or thereafter did she so much as mention it. Berry confessed later that he had been frightened to death.

Three kilometres out, there was a bend, and the needle of the speedometer, which, after rising steadily, had come to rest against the stop, retreated momentarily to record fifty-five. . . . We sang past a wayside farm, dropped into a valley, soared up the opposite side, flashed in and out of an apparently deserted village, shot up a long incline, and slowed up for a curve. . . . Then some poultry demanded consideration. As we left them behind, the agitation of two led horses necessitated a still further reduction of speed. We lost such time as I had made, and more also. Still, we were going downhill, and, as if impatient of the check, the car sprang forward. . . . We rose from the bottom with the smooth rush of a non-stop elevator. As we breasted the rise, I saw another and steeper dale before us. The road was becoming a switchback. . . .

At the top of the opposite hill was a big grey cabriolet coming towards us. At the foot was a panting lorry going our way. An approaching Ford was about to pass it. The cabriolet and Pong fell down their respective slopes. . . .

The Ford was abreast of the lorry, and the cabriolet was prepared to pass the two when we arrived. It was a question of giving way—at least, it ought to have been. It was, however, too late. Happily, there was more room than time at our disposal—a very little more. There was no time at all. . . .

For one never-to-be-forgotten instant there were four vehicles in a row. I doubt if an ordinary matchbox could have passed between our near-side runningboard and that of the cabriolet. I could certainly have touched the lorry, had I put out my hand. . . .

Then we swept on and up and over the crest.

Thereafter all was plain sailing.

As we ran into Peyrehorade, I glanced at my watch.

I had lost my bet by about a quarter of a minute. But for the led horses, we should have run to time. . . .

Upon one matter we were all agreed, and that was that the driver of the grey cabriolet was going much too fast.

So soon as we had passed through the town, Berry and I changed places. Almost immediately the road deteriorated. Its fine straightforward nature was maintained : the surface, however, was in tatters. . . .

After ten kilometres of misery, my brother-in-law slowed up and stopped. Then he turned to me.

"Have you ever driven upon this road (sic) before?"

I shook my head.

"Well, you can start now," was the reply. "I'm fed up, I am. I'd rather drive on the beach." With that he opened his door. "Oh, and give me back that cigar."

"Courage," I said, detaining him. "It can't last."

"Pardon me," said Berry, "but it can last for blistering leagues. I know these roads. Besides, my right knee's getting tremulous."

"It's quite good practice," I ventured.

"What for?" was the bitter reply. "My future estate? Possibly. I have no doubt that there it will be my blithesome duty continually to back a charabanc with a fierce clutch up an interminable equivalent of the Eiffel Tower. At present——"

"And you were driving so beautifully," said his wife.

"What—not with *finesse*?" said her husband.

"Rather," said I. "Ginger, too."

"What d'you mean—'ginger'?"—suspiciously.

"Determination," said I hurriedly.

"Not the b-b-bull-dog b-b-breed?"

"The same," said I. "All underhung. 'Shove-me-and-I'll-shove-your-face' sort of air. It was most noticeable."

Berry slammed the door and felt for the self-starter. . . .

As we bucketed down the next slope—

"I only wish," he said, "that we could encounter the deceitful monger responsible for including this road among *les grands itinéraires*. I can stand pot-holes, but the remains of a railway platform which might have been brought from one of what we know as 'the stricken areas', laid, like linoleum, upon a foot of brickdust, tend to make you gird at Life. Incidentally, is this fast enough for you? Or are your livers still sluggish?"

"I think," said I, nodding at a huge pantechnicon, "that we might pass the furniture."

I know no horn whose note is at once so compelling and offensive as that of the usher with which Pong was equipped. I know no din at once so obliterative and brain-shaking as that induced by the passage of a French pantechnicon, towed at a high speed over an abominable road. That the driver of the tractor failed to hear our demand was not remarkable. That he should have elected to sway uncertainly along the very crown of the road was most exasperating. . . .

Three times did Berry essay to push by; three times at the critical moment did the tractor lurch drunkenly across our bows; and three times did Pong fall back discomfited. The dust, the reek, the vibration, the pandemonium, were combining to create an atmosphere worthy of a place in the Litany. One's senses were cuffed and buffeted almost to a standstill. I remember vaguely that Daphne was clinging to my arm, wailing that "it was no good". I know I was shouting. Berry was howling abusive incoherence in execrable French. . . .

We were approaching the top of a hill.

Suddenly the tractor swung away to its right. With a yell of triumph, my unwitting brother-in-law thrust at the gap. . . . Pong leapt forward.

Mercifully there was a lane on the left, and I seized the wheel and wrenched it round, at the same time opening the throttle as wide as I dared. I fancy we took the corner on two wheels. As we did so, a pale blue racer streaked by our tail-lamp with the roar of an avalanche.

When Daphne announced that, if she reached Biarritz alive, she should drive home with Jonah, I was hardly surprised.

It was perhaps an hour later that, after passing greyheaded Bayonne, we came to her smart little sister and the villa we sought.

The great lodge-gates were open, but Ping was without in the road, while Jonah was leaning languidly against the wall. As we slowed up, he took his pipe from his mouth.

"I shouldn't drive in," he said. "They're out. Won't be back before six, the servants say."

\*     \*     \*     \*     \*

Black as was the evidence against him, my brother-in-law stoutly refused to be held responsible for the affair. All the way to the Hôtel du Palais he declared violently that the engagement had been well and truly made, and that if Evelyn and her husband chose to forget all about it, that was no fault of his. Finally, when Jonah suggested that after luncheon we should return to the villa and inquire whether we had indeed been expected the day before, he assented with disconcerting alacrity. As we passed into the restaurant—

"And I'll do the interrogating," he concluded. "I don't want any of your leading questions. 'I quite expect we were expected yesterday, weren't we?' All sweet and slimy, with a five-franc note in the middle distance."

"How dare you?" said Daphne. "Besides, I'd be only too relieved to find it was their mistake."

"Blow your relief," replied her husband. "What about my

bleeding heart?"

"I'm not much of a physician," said I, "but there's some cold stuffed venison on the sideboard. I don't know whether that, judiciously administered . . ."

Berry shook his head.

"I doubt it," he said mournfully. "I doubt it very much. . . . Still"—he looked round hungrily—"we can always try."

We were at the villa again within the hour.

Almost immediately we elicited the information that Major and Mrs. Swetecote had spent the previous day at San Sebastian.

Turning a withering and glassy eye in our direction, my brother-in-law explained the position and desired permission to enter and write a note. This was granted forthwith.

My sister and I followed him into a pleasant salon meekly enough. When he had written his letter, he read it to us with the air of a cardinal.

DEAR EVELYN,

### "LEST WE FORGET"

Yes, I know, But you should be more careful. Old friends like us, too. Disgraceful, I call it. To have been unprepared to receive us would have been bad enough, but to be actually absent from home. . . . Well, as Wordsworth says, that's bent it.

When I tell you that, in the belief that she was to enjoy a free lunch, my beloved yoke-fellow, who is just now very hot upon economy, forewent her breakfast and arrived upon your threshold faint and ravening, you will conceive the emotion with which she hailed the realization that that same hunger which she had encouraged could only be appeased at an expensive hotel.

But that is nothing.

To bless your married life, I have hustled a valuable internal combustion engine over one of the vilest roads in Europe, twice risked a life, the loss of which would, as you know, lower half the flags in Bethnal Green, and postponed many urgent and far more deserving calls upon my electric personality. I was, for instance, to have had my hair cut.

Worse.

Upon hearing of your absence, the unnatural infidel above referred to charged this to my account. As is my humble wont, I bent my head to the storm, strong in the fearless confidence that France is France, and that, late as we were, the ever-open bar would not be closed.

"Tell me more of yourself," I hear you say.

That may not be, che-ild.

For one thing, that venison has made me sleepy. Secondly, I am off to find a suitable and sheltered grove, within sound of the Atlantic, where I may spend an hour in meditation. Thirdly, I live for others.

Jonah wants to know if your husband can play golf. He does, of course. But can he?

Your dear old friend,

BERRY.

P.S.—D'you happen to know who owns a large grey cabriolet with a "G.B." plate? I imagine it lives at Biarritz. Anyway, they ought to be prosecuted. Driving about the country like a drunken hornet. Mercifully we were crawling. Otherwise . . . I tell you, it made my b-b-blood b-b-boil. Not at the time, of course.

\*　　\*　　\*　　\*　　\*

The pine woods were wholly delightful.

The lisp of the wind among the branches, the faint thunder of the Atlantic, the soft sweet atmosphere showed us a side of Biarritz which we should have been sorry to miss. By rights, if music and perfume have any power, we should have fallen asleep. The air, however, prevented us. Here was an inspiriting lullaby—a sleeping-draught laced with cordial. We plucked the fruit from off the Tree of Drowsiness, ate it, and felt refreshed. Repose went by the board. We left the cars upon the road and went strolling. . . .

"D'you think you could get me that spray?" said Jill suddenly.

In my cousin's eyes flora have only to be inaccessible to become desirable. Remembering this, I did as Berry and Jonah were doing —stared straight ahead and hoped very hard that she was not speaking to me.

"Boy!"

"Yes, dear?"

"D'you think you could . . . ?"

By the time I had torn my trousers, strained my right shoulder, sworn three times, and ruined the appearance of my favourite brogues, the others were out of sight.

"Thanks awfully, Boy. You are good to me. And that'll look lovely in the drawing-room. The worst of it is, this stuff wilts almost at once."

"Seems almost a shame to have picked it," I said grimly, "doesn't it?"

"It does really," Jill agreed. "Never mind," she added cheerfully, slipping an arm through mine. "It was my fault."

Subduing a desire to lie down on my back and scream, I relighted my pipe, and we strolled forward.

A country walk with Jill is never dull.

To do the thing comfortably, you should be followed by a file of pioneers in marching order, a limbered waggon, and a portable pond. Before we had covered another two hundred yards, I had collected three more sprays, two ferns, and a square foot of moss— the latter, much to the irritation of its inhabitants, many of whom refused to evacuate their homes and therefore accompanied us. I drew the line at frogs, on the score of cruelty to animals, but when we met one about the size of a postage stamp, it was a very near thing. Finally, against my advice, my cousin stormed a bank, caught her foot in an invisible wire, and fell flat upon her face.

"There now!" I cried testily, dropping our spoils and scrambling to her assistence.

"I'm not a bit hurt," she cried, getting upon her feet. "Not a scrap. And—and don't be angry with me, Boy. Jonah's been cross all day. He says my skirt is too short. And it isn't, is it?"

"Not when you don't fall down," said I. "At least—well, it is rather, isn't it?"

Jill put her feet together and drew the cloth close about her silk stockings. It fell, perhaps, one inch below her knees. For a moment she regarded the result. Then she looked up at me and put her head on one side. . . .

I have grown up with Jill. I have seen her in habits, in balldresses, in dressing-gowns. I have seen her hair up, and I have seen it tumbled about her shoulders. I have seen her grave, and I have seen her gay. I have seen her on horseback, and I have seen her asleep. But never in all my life shall I forget the picture which at this moment she made.

One thick golden tress, shaken loose by her fall, lay curling down past the bloom of her cheek on to her shoulder. The lights in it blazed. From beneath the brim of her small tight-fitting hat her great grave eyes held mine expectantly. The stars in them seemed upon the edge of dancing. Her heightened colour, the poise of her shapely head, the parted lips lent to that exquisite face the air of an elf. All the sweet grace of a child was welling out of her maidenhood. Her apple-green frock fitted the form of a shepherdess. Her pretty grey legs and tiny feet were those of a fairy. Its very artlesseness trebled the attraction of her pose. Making his sudden way between the boughs, the sun flung a warm bar of light athwart her white throat and the fallen curl. Nature was honouring her darling. It was the accolade.

I could have sworn that behind me somebody breathed "Madonna!" but although I swung round and peered into the bushes, I could see no one.

"When you've quite done," said Jill. Clearly she had noticed nothing.

I returned to my cousin.

"Yes," I said, "it's too short. Just a shade. As for you, you're much too sweet altogether. Something'll have to be done about it. You'll be stolen by fairies, or translated, or inveigled into an engagement, or something."

Jill let her dress go and flung her arms round my neck.

"You and Berry and Jonah," she said, "are far too sweet to me. And—— Oh, I can see myself in your eye, Boy. I can really." For a moment she stared at the reflection. "I don't think I look very nice," she added gravely. "However . . ." She kissed me abstractedly and started to fix the tress errant. "If Jonah asks you, don't say it's too short. It's not good for him. I'll have it lengthened all right."

For the second time I began to relight my pipe. . . .

After examining the scene of her downfall, the witch caught at a slip of a bough and swung herself athletically to the top of the bank. Thence she turned a glowing face in my direction.

"No, I shan't, after all," she announced. "It's much too convenient."

Twenty minutes later we reached the point from which we had set out.

Adèle was awaiting us with Ping.

As soon as we saw her—

"Good Heavens!" cried Jill. "I quite forgot you were married. You ought to have been with Adèle." She ran to the car. "Adèle darling, what do you think of me?"

"I am blind," said Adèle, "with jealousy. Anyone would be. And now jump in. Berry has taken the others to look at La Barre, and we're to follow them."

Such of the landscape as I was bearing was thereupon bestowed in the boot, I followed my cousin into the car, and a few minutes later we were at the mouth of the Adour. Here we left Ping beside Pong, and proceeded to join three figures on the horizon, apparently absorbed in the temper of a fretful sea.

As we tramped heavily over the shingle—

"You're not cross with me, Adèle?"

"Why should I be, darling?"

"Well, you see," panted Jill, "I've known him so long, and he's still so exactly the same, that I can't always remember——"

"That he's not your property?" said my wife. "But he is, and always will be."

Jill looked at her gravely.

"But he's yours," she said.

Adèle laughed lightly.

"Subjects marry, of course," she said, smiling, "but they've only one queen."

Which, I think, was uncommon handsome.

Any way, I kissed her slight fingers. . . .

As we reached our companions—

"I could stay here for ever," said Berry. "Easily. But I'm not going to. The wind annoys me, and the sea's not what it was before the War."

"How can you?" said Daphne. She stretched out a pointing arm. "Just look at that one—that great big fellow. It must be the ninth wave."

"Nothing to the York Ham—I mean the Welsh Harp—on a dirty night," replied her husband. "Why, I remember once . . ."

In the confusion of a precipitate retreat before the menace of the roller, the reminiscence was lost.

It was certainly a magnificent spectacle.

There was a heavy sea running, and the everlasting battle between the river and the Atlantic was being fought with long swift spasms of unearthly fury. Continually recurring, shock, mellay and rally overlapped, attack and repulse were inextricably mingled, the very lulls between the paroxysms were big with wrath. There was a point, too, where the river's bank became coastline, a blunt corner of land, which seemed to exasperate the sea out of all reason. A stiff breeze abetting them, the gigantic waves crashed upon it with a concussion that shook the air. All the royal rage of Ocean seemed to be concentrated on this little prominence. The latter's indifference appeared to aggravate its assailant. Majesty was in a tantrum.

With the exception of Berry, we could have watched the display till, as they say, the cows come home. My brother-in-law, however, felt differently. The wind was offending him.

After a violent denunciation of this element—

"Besides," he added, "we ought to be getting back. It's nearly half-past three, and if we're to avoid the playground of the Tanks and return to Bidache, we shall be longer upon the road."

"Well, you go on," said Daphne. "Ask Adèle nicely, first, if she'll take my place, and then if she minds starting now."

"Fair lady," he said,

"The vay ith long, the vind ith cold,
It maketh me feel infernal old."

"I'm sorry," said Adèle hurriedly, "but I've left my purse at home. Try my husband."

Berry put on his hat, cocked it, and turned to me.

"D'you want a thick ear?" he demanded. "Or will you go quietly?"

"A little more," I retorted, "and you ride in the dickey."

Ten minutes later Pong was sailing into the outskirts of Bayonne.

To emerge from the town upon the Briscous road proved unexpectedly hard. The map insisted that we should essay a dark entry, by the side of which a forbidding notice-board dared us to come on. . . . Adèle and I pored over the print, while out of our bickering Berry plucked such instructions as his fancy suggested, and, alternately advancing and retiring, cruised to and fro about a gaunt church. After a while we began to ask people, listen carefully to their advice, thank them effusively, and then demonstrate to one another that they were certainly ignorant and probably hostile.

At length—

"How many times," inquired Berry, "did they walk round Jericho before the walls went?"

"Thirteen, I think," said Adèle. "Why?"

"Oh nothing," was the reply. "Only, if you aren't quick, we shall have this church down. Besides, I'm getting giddy."

"Then show some initiative," I retorted.

"Right," said Berry, darting up a side-street.

Calling upon him to stop, Adèle and I fought for the map. . . .
A sudden lurch to the left flung us into the corner, whence, before

we had recovered our equilibrium, a violent swerve to the right
returned us pell-mell. At last, in response to our menaces, Berry
slowed up before a sign-post.

Its legend was plain.

BRISCOUS 10

We stared at it in silence. Then we stared at one another.
Finally we stared at Berry. The latter spread out his hands and
shrugged his shoulders.

"Instinct," he said. "Just instinct. It's very wonderful.
Hereditary, of course. One of my uncles was a water-waste pre-
venter. With the aid of a cricket-bat and a false nose, he could
find a swamp upon an empty stomach. They tried him once, for
fun, at a garden-party. Nobody could understand the host's uneasiness until, amid a scene of great excitement, my uncle found
the cesspool under the refreshment marquee."

Eventually we persuaded him to proceed.

For a while the going was poor, but after we had passed
Briscous all cause for complaint vanished. Not only was the surface
of the road as good as new, but the way itself was winsome. The
main road to Peyrehorade could not compare with it. At every
twist and turn—and there were many—some fresh attraction
confronted us. The countryside, shy of the great highways, crept
very close. We slipped up lanes, ran side by side with brooks,
brushed by snug cottages. Dingles made bold to share with us
their shelter, hill-tops their sweet prospects, hamlets their quiet
content.

An amazing sundown set our cup brimming.

That this might run over, Bidache itself gave us a château—
ruined, desolate, and superb. There is a stateliness of which Death
holds the patent: and then, again, Time can be kind to the dead.
What Death had given, Time had magnified. Years had added to
the grey walls a peace, a dignity, a charm, such as they never
knew while they were kept. The grave beauty of the place was
haunting. We passed on reluctantly. . . .

A quarter of an hour later we ran into Peyrehorade.

Here Adèle relieved my brother-in-law and, encouraged by the
promise of a late tea, made the most of the daylight.

Eighty minutes later we slid into Pau.

As we swept up the drive of our villa—

"Well," said Berry, "I must confess it's been a successful day.
If we'd lunched with Evelyn, we should have missed that venison,

and if the main road hadn't been vile, we should have missed
Bidache. Indeed, provided no anti-climax is furnished by the
temperature of the bath-water, I think we may congratulate
ourselves."

Adèle and I agreed enthusiastically.

Falcon met us in the hall with a note and a telephone message.
The first was from Mrs. Swetecote.

DEAREST DAPHNE,

How awful of you! Never mind. I know how terribly easy
it is to forget. And now you must come over to us instead.
Falcon insisted that you would wish us to have lunch, so we
did—a jolly good one, too. And Jack smoked one of Berry's
cigars, and, of course, we both lost our hearts to Nobby. In
fact, we made ourselves thoroughly at home.

Your loving
EVELYN.

P.S.—Try and find out who's staying at Pau with a blue
all-weather coupé. They went by us to-day like a flash of
lightning. Fortunately we were going dead slow, so it was all
right. But they ought to be stopped.

The second was from Jonah.
As rendered by Falcon, it ran :—

"Captain Mansel's compliments, sir, and, as Mrs. Adèle
Pleydell was the last to drive Ping, 'e thinks *she must 'ave 'is key.*
. . . And as Love's the honly thing as laughs at locksmiths, sir,
will you kindly return this forthwith. . . . I asked Captain Mansel
where 'e'd like you to meet 'im, sir, but 'e said *you'd* know."

From Pau to La Barre is seventy miles—as near as "damn it."

\*     \*     \*     \*     \*

I covered the distance alone. All the way a memory kept
whispering above the rush of the tyres. . . . "Madonna!" . . .
"Madonna!" . . .

CHAPTER V

# *How Love Came to Jill, Herbert to the Rescue, and a Young Man by his Right*

A week of fine days had slipped by. Most of these we had spent upon the open road. For fifty miles about Pau we had proved the countryside and found it lovely. This day we had determined to fare farther afield. Perhaps because of this decision, Trouble had peered out of the bushes before we had gone twenty miles.

Had we, however, been advised to expect a puncture and requested to select the venue, we could not have chosen a more delightful spot.

Immediately upon our right there was a garden, trim and pleasing as the farmhouse it served. Stretched in the gateway lay a large white hound, regarding us sleepily. Beyond, on the greensward, a peacock preened himself in the hot sunshine. On the left, a wayside bank made a parapet, and a score of lime-trees a sweet balustrade. A glance between these natural balusters turned our strip of metalling into a gallery. The car, indeed, was standing upon the edge of a brae. Whether this fell sheer or sloped steeply could not be seen, for the first thing which the down-looking eye encountered was a vast plain, rich, sunbathed, rolling, three hundred feet below. North, south, and east, as far as the sight could follow, was stretching Lilliput. Meadows and poplars and the flash of streams, steadings and villages, coppices, flocks and curling roads glinted or glowed in miniature. Close on our right two toy towers stood boldly up to grace a townlet. Due east a long, straight baby avenue led to a midget city. Northward a tiny train stole like a snail into the haze of distance. Far to the south the mountain, blurred, snowy, ethereal, rose like a beckoning dream to point the fairy tale.

It was only when we had gloated upon the prospect for several minutes, identified the townlet as Ibus and the city as Tarbes, and, taking out powerful binoculars, subjected the panorama to a curious scrutiny, which might have shattered the illusion, but only turned Lilliput into Utopia, that we pulled ourselves together and started to consider our plight.

This was not serious. A tyre was flat, certainly, but we had two spare wheels.

I drew a sou from my pocket and spun it into the air.

"I maintain," said Berry, "that the obverse will bite the dust."

The coin tinkled to a settlement, and we both stooped to read our respective fates. . . .

A moment later, with a self-satisfied grin, I climbed back into the car, whilst Berry removed his coat with awful deliberation.

Jill was in possession of the paper, so I lighted a cigarette and turned up Tarbes in the guide-book. . . .

"Just listen to this," said my cousin suddenly.

" 'Of the four properties, the villa Irikli is the most notable. A well-known traveller once styled it "the fairest jewel in Como's diadem". Occupying one of the choicest situations on the famous lake, surrounded by extensive gardens, the varied beauty of which beggars description, the palace—for it is nothing less—has probably excited more envy than any dwelling in Europe. . . .'

"Then it speaks about the house. . . . Wait a minute. . . . Here we are.

" 'The heavily-shaded lawns, stretching to the very edge of the lake, the magnificent cedars, the sunlit terraces, the cascades, the chestnut groves, the orange and lemon trellises, the exquisite prospects, go to the making of a veritable paradise.'

"Doesn't that sound maddening?"

"It does, indeed," I agreed. "Whose is it?"

"I don't know," said Jill absently, staring into the distance. "But I can just see it all. Fancy living there, and going out before breakfast over the lawns to bathe. . . ."

Idly I took the paper out of her hand.

From this it appeared that the property had belonged to the Duke of Padua. Reading further, I found that the latter's whole estate had, upon his death nine months ago, become the subject of an action at law. The deceased's legitimacy, it seemed, had been called in question. To-day the Appeal Court of Italy was to declare the true heir. . . .

As I laid down the sheet—

"Somebody," I said, "will drink champagne to-night."

"Oranges and lemons," murmured Jill. "Cascades . . ."

A vicious grunt from below and behind suggested that my brother-in-law was standing no nonsense.

I settled myself in my corner of the car, tilted my hat over my nose, and closed my eyes. . . .

The sound of voices aroused me.

". . . your silly eyes. Didn't you hear me say 'Non'? *NONG,* man, *NONG!* You'll strip the blinkin' thread. . . . Look here. . . ."

"*A-a-ah! Oui, oui, Monsieur. Je comprends, je comprends.*"

"You don't listen," said Berry severely. "That's what's the matter with you. Valuable car like this, too." Jill buried her face in my sleeve and began to shake with laughter. "*Alors, en avant, mon brave. Mettez y votre derrière.* Oh, very hot, very hot."

"*C'est bien ça, Monsieur?*"

"Every time," said Berry. "Now the next. . . . *D'abord avec les doigts.* . . . That's enough, fathead. What's the brace done?"

"*Mais, Monsieur——*"

"*Si vous disputez,*" said Berry gravely, "*vous ne l'aurez pas seulement où le poulet a reçu la hache, mais je n'aurai pas de choix mais de vous demander de retourner à vos b-b-b-bœufs.*"

"*Pardon, Monsieur.*"

"Granted, Herbert, granted," was the airy reply. "But you must take off that worried look. *Ca me rappelle la maison des singes.* . . . *Oh, terrible, terrible. Et le parfum.* . . . My dear Herbert, *il frappe l'orchestre.* . . . And now, suppose we resume our improvement of the working day."

Except for the laboured breathing of Herbert, the remaining bolts were affixed in silence.

"*Bien,*" said Berry. "*Maintenant le* jack. I trust, Herbert, that you have a supple spine. *Voici. Tournez, mon ami, tournez.* . . . *Non, non, NONG!* You bull-nosed idiot! *A gauche!*"

"*A-a-ah! Oui, oui, Monsieur! A gauche, à gauche.*"

"All right," said Berry. "I said it first. It's my brain-wave. . . . That's right. Now pull back—*tirez. Bon.* Now shove it *ici, dans la bottine.* . . . And must you kneel upon the wing, Herbert? *Must* you? A-a-ah! Get off, you clumsy satyr!"

A yell of protest from Herbert suggested that Berry's protest had been reinforced *vi et armis.*

"*Non, non, Monsieur! Laissez-moi tranquil. Je ne fais que ce que vous commandez.* . . ."

"Dog," said my brother-in-law, "you lie! Never mind. Pick up that wheel instead. *Prenez la roue, Herbert.* . . . *C'est bien. Alors, attachez-la ici.* Yes, I know it's heavy, but *ne montrez pas la langue. Respirez par le nez,* man. And don't stagger like that. It makes me feel tired. . . . So. Now, isn't that nice? Herbert, my son, *voici la fin de votre travail.*"

"*C'est tout, Monsieur?*"

"*Cest tout, mon ami.* Should you wish to remember me in your prayers, *je suis le Comte Blowfly, du Rat Mort,* Clactonon-Sea. Telegraphic address, Muckheap. And there's ten francs towards your next shave."

"*Oh, Monsieur, c'est trop gentil. J'ai été heureux*——"

"*Pas un mot*, Herbert. Believe me, it's cheap at the price. What's more, *je suis enchanté d'avoir fait votre connaissance.*"

"*A votre service, Monsieur.*"

"Itch Deen," said Berry. "Itch Deen. And if ever one of your bullocks bursts and you have to put in a new one, I only trust I shall be out of earshot. *Au revoir, mon ami. Ne faites-pas attention au monsieur avec le nez rouge dans l'auto. Il est grisé.*"

The reverent look with which Herbert favoured me, as he returned to his oxen, I shall never forget. Clearly, to be in the arms of Dionysus by eleven o'clock in the morning was arguing at once an affluence and a discretion which were almost sacred.

"Ah," said Berry, making his appearance, "you're awake, are you? I've just finished. Herbert's been watching me. Have you got the beer-opener there? It's —it's tiring work."

"What is?" said I grimly. "Instructing?"

"That's it," said my brother-in-law. "I explained as I went along. Herbert was most interested. A little dense, you know, but such a nice fellow. He thinks the world of you. Now, I think the beer-opener's in the left-hand——"

"In you get," said I, starting the engine. "Philanthropy and beer don't go together."

With his foot upon the step, Berry regarded me.

"I should like Herbert's ruling on that," he said. "Besides, I've got a thirst which is above rubies."

"Think what it'll be like by lunch-time," said Jill. "Besides," she added, searching for her bag, "I've got some acid drops somewhere."

With an unearthly shriek Berry clawed at his temples. . . . For a moment he rocked to and fro agonisedly. Then he climbed heavily into the car.

As he sank back against the cushions—

"Murderess," he said. "And it was the best I've had since Egypt."

\*　　\*　　\*　　\*　　\*

Two hours later we ran into Montrejeau, crept by its exquisite market—roofed and pillared and carrying its four hundred years as they were forty—dropped down a wicked hill, and swept over an infant Garonne on to the Luchon road.

Before we had covered five kilometres we sighted our goal.

"A city that is set on a hill cannot be hid."

Out of the blowing meadows rose up an eminence. But for the snow-clad heights beyond, you would have called it a mountain. Its slopes were timbered, and if there was a road there, this could not be seen. High up above the trees was a city wall, standing out boldly, as ramparts should. Within the wall, still higher, were houses, white, ancient, stern-faced. And there, clear above them all, perched upon the very point of the hill, towered a cathedral. The size of it turned the city into a close. Its site, its bulwarks, however, turned the church into a castle. Here was an abbot filling the post of constable. The longer you gazed, the stronger the paradox became. Pictures of peace and war became inextricably confused. Men-at-arms mumbled their offices; steel caps concealed tonsures: embrasures framed precious panes: trumpets sounded the Angelus: mail chinked beneath vestments: sallies became processions: sentinels cried *"Pax vobiscum"*. . . . Plainly most venerable, the tiny city and the tremendous church made up a living relic, of whose possession Memory can be very proud. Saint-Bertrand-de-Comminges ranks with the Leaning Tower of Pisa. There is nothing like it in all the world.

Presently we passed through the meadows, climbed up the tree-clad slopes, and came to a little terrace under the city-wall. Full in the sunlight, sheltered from the wind, the pleasaunce made an ideal refectory. The view of the mountains, moreover, which it afforded was superb. I stole by the city gate and berthed Pong close to the low parapet. . . .

Ten minutes later Ping drew up behind us.

"Isn't this just lovely?" cried Adèle, applying the hand-brake.

"It's unique," said I, advancing. "How did the car go?"

"Like a train," said Jonah, helping Daphne to alight. "I may add that I've enjoyed being driven."

"Oh, Jonah, how nice of you!" cried Adèle.

It was, indeed, a compliment worth having.

"I told you so," I said unctuously.

"And now," said Berry, "if you've quite done scratching one another's backs——"

"Vulgar brute!" said Daphne.

"I beg your pardon?"

My sister repeated the appellative.

Instantly her husband assumed an attitude of listening ecstasy.

"Hark!" he exclaimed dramatically. "I he-ear my lo-ove calling." A rapturous smile swept into his face. "It must be clo-osing time." He changed his tone to one of indicative solicitude. "More to the left, sweet chuck. No. That's the water-trough. I've got the pram here."

A master of pantomime, Berry can create an atmosphere with a look and a word. "On the halls", he would probably be a complete failure. On the terrace beneath the walls of St. Bertrand he was simply side-splitting. Daphne and Jonah included, we collapsed tearfully. . . .

As we did so there was a roar of laughter behind us.

One and all, we turned blindly about, to see a slim figure in a grey tweed suit dash for the gateway. As we looked, a grey hat flew off. The next moment its owner was within the walls.

I ran to the gateway and stared up a little paved street. It was quite empty. After a moment I returned to pick up the hat. Looking at this, I saw that it came from Bond Street.

What was more remarkable was that twenty paces away was standing a grey two-seater. It was quite evident that, for car and passenger to approach without our knowledge, we must have been extremely preoccupied, and the new-comer's engine uncannily silent.

After some discussion of the incident, we placed the hat in the two-seater and proceeded to lunch. . . .

The meal was over, and Jonah and I were washing the glasses, when—

"Now, no guide-books, please," said my brother-in-law. "I've read it all up. Where we are now was the *ulularium*."

"Whatever's that?" said Jill.

"The howling-green," said Berry. "The monks used to come and howl here before breakfast."

"What did they howl for?" said Adèle.

"It was a form," was the reply, "of mortification, instituted by Aitchless the 'Alf-baked and encouraged by his successor, who presented an empty but still fragrant beer-barrel to be howled for upon Michaelmas Eve." After the manner of a guide, the speaker preceded us to the gateway. "And now we come to the gate. Originally one-half its present width, it was widened by the orders of Gilbert the Gluttonous. The work, in which he took the deepest interest, was carried out under his close supervision. Indeed, it was not until the demolition of the structure had been commenced that he was able to be released from a position which was embarrassing not only his digestion, but his peace of mind, inasmuch as it was denying ingress to a cardinal who had much influence at the Vatican and was wearing tight boots."

The steep, narrow street was walled by great houses of the fifteenth and sixteenth centuries, while at the top a little archway buttressed a mansion of obvious importance.

"We now enter," said Berry, with the time-honoured flourish of the hired conductor, "the famous Bishops' Row. At one time or another, in every one of these dwellings prelates of all sizes and shapes have snored, swallowed, and generally fortified the flesh. Upon that door were posted the bulletins announcing the progress towards recovery of Rudolph the Rash, who in the fifteenth year of his office decided to take a bath. His eventual restoration to health was celebrated with great rejoicing. From that window Sandwich, surnamed the Slop-pail, was wont to dispense charity in the shape of such sack as he found himself reluctantly unable to consume. Such self-denial surprised even his most devoted adherents, until it was discovered that the bishop had no idea that he was pouring libations into the street, but, with some hazy intention of conserving the remains of his liquor, invariably mistook the window for the door of a cupboard. The house on the left is of peculiar interest. Behind those walls——"

"I wouldn't interrupt you for worlds," said Daphne, "and I'm sure the cathedral won't be half so interesting, but, perhaps, if we saw that first...."

"That's right," said her husband. "Twist the sage's tail. Now I've lost my place. I shall have to begin all over again." He paused to pass his hand across his eyes. Then he flung out an arm. "We now enter the famous Bishops' Row. At one time or another, in every one of these dwellings prelates of all...."

We fairly fled up the street.

We had visited the shrine : we had wondered at the silver eloquence of architects : we had examined one by one sixty-six of the most exquisite stalls that ever graced a choir : we had stared at thrones, pulpit, organ-case and a great frieze—all of them carved with a cunning which money could never buy, and to-day great love and piety are too poor to purchase—we had walked in the cloisters : we had been shown the relics : and whilst the others were picking over some picture postcards, I was looking at an old fountain in the cathedral square.

"I say," said a pleasant voice.

Upon the other side of the basin with a slim figure in a grey tweed suit—a nice-looking boy of about twenty summers. His thick, dark hair was uncovered, and there was a grave look in the big brown eyes.

"Hullo," said I. "You're the runaway."

"That's right," he said quickly. "I only want to apologise. I'm afraid I was awfully rude to laugh like that, but I couldn't help it. I wasn't listening."

He turned away hurriedly.

"Here, I say!" I cried, stepping after him. With his chin on his shoulder the boy hesitated, like some wild thing. "Don't go," I added. "It's quite all right. If my brother-in-law likes to make a fool of himself, why shouldn't you laugh?"

"I know, but——"

"My dear fellow," said I, "the more the merrier. Besides, we use the same hatter. So let's be friends. You're all alone, aren't you?"

"Er—yes. I'm really staying at Pau, and, as I'd got noth-ing——"

"I knew I'd seen your car before. Didn't you go to Lourdes on Tuesday?"

The boy started.

"Yes, sir. I—I think I did."

He was really extraordinarily nervous.

"That's right," I continued. "We were on the way back from Cauterets. By the way, I see you've got one of the new models. How does she go?"

We walked down to the gate, talking easily enough. . . .

By the time the others arrived, the two-seater's bonnet was open, and I had promised to teach him to change speed without taking out the clutch.

"Isn't that sweet?" said Jill's voice.

My companion started upright.

"You like it?" he said, flushing.

"I think it's wonderful," said my cousin.

So it was.

I have seen many mascots. But, seated upon the cap of the radiator, a little silver reproduction of the Ares Ludovisi knocked memories of nymphs, hounds, and urchins into a cocked hat.

"I'd like you to have it," said the boy suddenly. "Which is your car?"

"Oh, but I can't take it," cried Jill breathlessly. "It's awfully generous of you, but I couldn't think of——"

"Well, let's just see how it looks. You were in the first car, weren't you?"

It was about a thousand to one against the two caps being interchangeable, but the miracle came off. Once Ares was in his new seat, nothing would induce his owner to disestablish him.

"Keep him to-day, at least," he insisted. "Please do. I think it —it'll bring me luck."

"You're awfully kind," said Jill. "Why did you run away?"

Daphne took my arm and called Berry. Together we strolled up the terrace. Jonah was showing Adèle the points of the two-seater.

"Who," said my sister, "is this attractive youth?"

"I've not the faintest idea," said I. "But he's staying at Pau."

"Well, Jill's got off," was the reply. "They're like a couple of children."

"Ah!" said Berry unexpectedly.

"What on earth's the matter?" said Daphne.

"Listen," rejoined her husband. "I've laid an egg—metaphorically. We're all terrified of Jill getting pinched—again metaphorically—aren't we? Very good. Let's encourage this friendship. Let it swell into an attachment. They're far too young to think about marriage. Of course, we shan't see so much of her, but, as the sainted Martin said, half a cloak's better than no bags."

"Dear lad," said Daphne, slipping her arm through his, "you're not laying at all. You're getting broody." With that, she turned to me. "And what do you think about it?"

"He's a gentleman," said I. "And he's a child. Children, I suppose, attract children. Let him be asked to tea, and they can play in the nursery."

"Thank you," said my sister. "Now I'll break it to you. Subject to the usual formalities, Jill will marry that boy within the year."

"B-but it's absurd," bubbled Berry. "It's out of the question. They'd be like the Babes in the Wood. What that he-child's doing on his own, I can't imagine. I should think he's a ward in Chancery who's given his guardians the slip. And the two together'd make a combination about as well fitted to cope with Life as a mute with a megaphone."

"On the contrary," said Daphne, "they'll get on splendidly. They'll turn the world into a playground. Wherever they go, everybody'll drop their tools and go down on their knees and play with them." She laughed delightedly. "I tell you, it'll be like a fairy tale."

"Of course," I said, "I see what it is. You're at your old games."

"I'm not," was the fierce retort. "D'you think I want to lose Jill? But she'll have to go some day. It's inevitable. And the only thing she could ever really love is a playmate. The finest lover in the world would never find the trick of Jill's heart. Only a child can do that. She might marry him easily—the lover, I mean. And she'd be happy, of course. But she'd miss the biggest thing in life. Well, eligible playmates are pretty scarce. I've been watching for one for years. Mind you, I don't say this boy's going to do. There may be a score of reasons that put his suit out of court. But, on the face of it, he's nearer the mark than anything I've seen."

Thoughtfully we turned back the way we had come. . . .

After a long silence—

"Any way," said Berry gloomily, "the first thing to do's to find out who he is. Perhaps Jill's done it."

"That," said my sister, "is the very last thing she'd think of."

We returned to where Ping and Pong were standing, to find that Jonah and Adèle had disappeared, while Jill was being taught to drive the two-seater. The environs of Saint-Bertrand-de-Comminges do not make a good school, but master and pupil cared not for that. Indeed, they were so engrossed in their exercise that our approach was unobserved.

The two were at the top of their bent.

Flushed with excitement, laughing, chattering like old friends, lady and squire were having the time of their lives. They were, certainly, wonderfully matched. If Jill was a picture, so was the boy. His gravity was gone. The fine, frank face was fairly alight with happiness, the brown eyes dancing, the strong white teeth flashing merriment. From being good-looking, he had become most handsome. If he was to find the trick of Jill's heart, she had laid a pink finger upon the catch of his charm.

For a moment we stood marvelling. . . .

Then Jill saw us with the tail of her eye.

"I say," she cried, twittering, "he's going to teach me to drive. He's coming to lunch to-morrow, and then we're going along the Morlaas road, because that'll be quiet."

As Adèle and Jonah emerged from the gateway—

"You can't have the Morlaas road to-morrow," said Berry, "because I've got it. I'm going to practise reversing through goats. It's all arranged. Five million of the best new-laid goats are to be in line of troop columns two kilometres south of the 'L' of a 'ill by three o'clock."

Jill addressed her companion.

"We'll go another way," she said. "I don't suppose he's really going there, but, if he did. . . . Well, when he says he's going backwards on purpose, we always get out of the car."

The naïveté with which this unconsciously scathing criticism was phrased and uttered trebled its poignancy.

Berry collapsed amid a roar of laughter.

Then Jonah pulled out his watch, and we began to arrange ourselves. That Jill might return with her brother and have her mascot too, we had to swap cars; for, as the only two mechanics, Jonah and I never travelled together. I was sorry about it, for Pong was the apple of my eye. Seldom, if ever, had we been parted before. Jonah, I fancy, felt the same about Ping.

Our new friend was going straight back. We, however, were proposing to return by Bagnères-de-Bigorre, and suggested that he should accompany us. He shook his head gravely.

"No. I—I have to get back," he said heavily. "I must." Then he bowed to Daphne and to us all. "You've been very kind to me. Good-bye."

As he turned—

"Till to-morrow," I cried heartily. "You know where we live?"

"Oh, yes. You're Captain Pleydell."

"That's right. Oh, and—er—by the way, I don't think we know your name."

For a moment the boy hesitated. Then he turned scarlet.

"N-neither do I," he said.

\*     \*     \*     \*     \*

It was four o'clock by the time we reached Lannemezan, so, after a little discussion, my wife and Berry and I determined to cut Bagnères-de-Bigorre out of our itinerary and return to Pau by the way by which we had come. Whether the others, who were ahead of us, had come to the same decision, we could not tell.

Berry was driving like a professional. The fact, however, that between Lannemezan and Tarbes the pleasant road was littered with more dog-carts and bullock-waggons than one would have expected any three departments of France to be able to furnish, tended to cramp his style. The uses, moreover, to which the occupants of these vehicles subjected the way argued a belief not so much in progress as in *esprit de corps*. As often as not the carts moved three abreast, their human complements comparing excited notes, gossiping and making merry with as much disregard of their whereabouts as if they were gathered in a familiar tavern. As for the waggons, these were frequently unattended, their custodians trudging disinterestedly in rear, absorbed in good-natured argument and leaving their bullocks to place their own interpretation upon the rule of the road. Such confidence was seldom misplaced : still, for the driver of an approaching car to share it, demanded, I suppose, an experience of oxen which we did not possess.

After a few miles my brother-in-law's patience began to show signs of wear and tear, and by the time we had reached Tournay it was positively threadbare. For this Adèle and I paid almost as heavily as he. But for the horn by his side, many an infuriated chauffeur would have lost his reason. It is a kind of safety-valve. Berry's employment of this convenient accessory was characterised by a savagery which, if deplorable, is not uncommon. The frequency, however, with which passage simply had to be asked was truly terrible. Disapproval at once so bitterly and constantly expressed was most distressing. Our heads began to ache violently. . . .

To crown our annoyance, we picked up a cast shoe—with the inevitable result. When, fortified by the knowledge that it was my turn to change the wheel, Berry ventured to point out that such an acquisition was extremely fortunate, the power of speech deserted me.

Dusk was falling as we ran into Tarbes. . . .

"D'you think," said Adèle, "that we could find a chemist? My head feels as if it was going to burst."

We sought diligently without success. After a little we stopped and asked a postman. An apothecary of sorts, it appeared, was plying his trade two side-streets away. Adèle and I descended to go and visit him.

I was rather sceptical about the virtue of the drug which was eventually produced to us, but, after a little discussion, we purchased the tablets and asked for some water with which to swallow them.

I must confess that when we returned to find no sign of the car, I was extremely annoyed. It was rapidly growing dark and it had become cold. Adèle was tired and had had no tea. The market was up, with the result that the streets were swarming. I cursed my brother-in-law with pardonable acerbity.

"It's all right, old chap," said Adèle, taking my arm. "He's probably just around somewhere. Let's go and look for him."

He was not around anywhere.

We struggled to the right, we fought our way to the left, we pushed and were pushed back to the *pharmacie*, and we returned laboriously to our starting-point. All the time we were devilled by the lingering idea that Berry was searching for us, and that we were just avoiding him at every turn. After another two minutes, I took my protesting wife back to the chemist's shop, requested his hospitality on her behalf, and, after seeing her received by a glowing Frenchwoman into an inner room, turned up my collar and advanced blasphemously into the street.

Almost immediately Berry stumbled into my arms.

"*The car!*" he gasped. "*A plant! Quick! Or they'll do us down!*"

I stared at him stupidly.

His coat was torn and he was streaming with sweat. Also his hat was missing, and there was a cut on his cheek.

"You're hurt," I cried.

"Right as rain," he panted. "Tell you 's we go." He started to pelt up the street. I ran by his side. " 'Bout two minutes after you'd gone—fellow ran up t' the car in hell of a state—firs' couln' make out what matter was—talked too fast—then gathered, you'd sent him—Adèle had been taken ill—lie, of course—see now—never occurred to me at time—told him to get on step and guide me—burst off up street—lef' ri' lef' stunt—'fore knew where I was, cul de sac—pulled up—nex' second, both doors open and toughest cove 've ever seen told me t' hop it—in bad American—round to t' left here—course I tumbled at once—dirty work—tried t' hit him—nothing doing—tried to lock car—couldn't—hauled out anyhow—no good yelling—ran find you—one ray hope—out of petrol—I never stopped engine—petered out on its own—can on step, I know—but they'll have to locate trouble—and then decant —left again here . . . no . . . wait." He looked from side to side anxiously. Then he swung round and glanced back. "Gad, I think we're wrong." He started back frantically. "No, that's right. I 'member that café." We swung round again. Arrived once more at the corner, again he hesitated, twitching his lips nervously and sobbing for want of breath. "These blasted streets," he jerked out. "I tried to memorise 'em, but—— *There they are, Boy! There they are!*"

It was true.

Turning away from us into a street on our left, about forty paces away, was our own blue coupé. . . .

But for the fact that a cart was presenting a momentary obstruction, our quarry would have been gone. As it was, I flung myself on to the running-board as she was gathering speed. . . .

Without a word, I thrust my arm in at the window and switched off the engine. As she slowed up I leapt for the bonnet, whipped it open and felt for the high-tension wire. At that moment the engine re-started. . . . For a second whoever was driving fumbled with the gears. . . . As the wheels meshed with a chunk, my fingers found what they sought. The next instant the car lunged forward—and the wire broke.

I fell on my back, certainly, and my hand was bleeding, but I could afford to smile. The gun was spiked.

As I rose to my feet, the car came gently to rest twenty-five paces away.

"All right?" panted Berry by my side.

"Every time," said I. "And now for it." I turned to a gaping youth. *"Allez cherche la police,"* I flung at him. *"Vite!"*

As we came up to the car—

"And may I ask," drawled a voice, "the meaning of this holdup? I guess you'll get tired of answering before you're through, but, as the owner of this vehicle, I'm just curious."

"Cut it out," said I shortly. "And just come out of that car. Both of you."

So far as the speaker's companion was concerned, my injunction was supererogatory. Even as I spoke, with a scream of agony the latter emerged from the car. Holding him fast by the wrist, Berry had almost broken his arm across the jamb of the door.

"And why?" said the voice imperturbably.

"Because the game's up." I opened the door. "Besides, to tell you the truth, we're rather particular about our cushions. Till now, no one with more than three previous convictions has ever sat on them."

With narrowed eyes, a very square-faced gentleman regarded me grimly.

"If you hadn't damaged my car," he said slowly. "I'd get out and refashion your physiognomy. But I guess I'll wait for the police." And, with that, he drew a cigar from his pocket, bit off the end, spat, and then lighted the brand with great deliberation.

I began to think rapidly.

Violence was out of the question. The fellow was far heavier than I, and obviously as hard as nails. Moreover, I felt instinctively that the Queensberry Rules did not mean much to him. As for cunning—well, we were not in the same class. Here was an audacity such as I had not dreamed of. Having lost one throw, the fellow was doubling his stake. Hook having broken in his hand, he had dropped it and picked up Crook. *His game was to bluff the French police.* That was why he was staying in the car —to give the impression of ownership. If he could maintain this impression, make it easy for the police to wash their hands of a dispute between foreigners, so find favour in their eyes, just turn the scale sufficiently to be allowed to proceed "pending the fullest inquiries"—it might go hard with us. . . .

I fancy he read my thoughts, for he took the cigar from his mouth and laughed softly.

"Up against it, aren't you?' he said.

At last a *gendarme* arrived, and five minutes later we were all on the way to the police-station.

This was not to my gentleman's taste, but he was too shrewd a knave to press his point. Honesty was his best policy. He did demand hotly that I should be taken in charge, but I had the better of him in French, and after a moment he let that iron go. He fought very hard for the services of a mechanic, but I was determined that the engine should remain out of action, and, calling for volunteers upon the crowd of onlookers, soon satisfied the *gendarme* that to push the car to the station was easy enough.

Holding fast to the accomplice, who, for reasons best known to himself, was adopting an injured air in sulky silence, Berry walked by my side.

"What's his game?" he muttered. "In the face of our papers, he's done."

"He'll swear they're his, for a monkey. They're in the car. Probably read them through, while you were looking for me. And all the details are on the Travelling Pass. But he's got to get over the photograph."

"Well, it's up to you," said Berry. "I used to think I could bluff, but this—this is beyond me."

When we arrived at the police-station the chief of the police was summoned, and we told our respective tales.

Our enemy spoke first—shortly, but much to the point.

He was returning, he said, to Pau, where he was staying with friends. Finding that he had run out of petrol, while he was passing through Tarbes, he had turned into a side-street to refill without obstructing a main thoroughfare. As he was starting again, an assault had been made—an unprovoked assault—

seriously damaging the car. Thereupon he had sent for the police. Now, foiled in their enterprise, the thieves, he understood, were actually daring to say that he had assaulted them. One of them —he nodded at Berry—had certainly been roughly handled, but, *Mon Dieu*, what did they expect? (Here he took out his watch and frowned at the dial.) And now would the police get to work? His friends at Pau would be wondering what had become of him.

I admit that you could have pushed me over.

Upon the question of ownership the rogue said not a word. The whole onus of raising that issue he had thrust on to me. I was to broach the barrel of improbability, and by so doing to taint my whole case. . . .

The police were manifestly impressed.

There was no doubt at all that we were up against it.

The asperity with which the official asked me what we had to say sent my heart into my boots.

I started to tell my story.

The moment I said that the car belonged to us, police and robber stared at me as if bewitched. Then the latter exploded.

It was certainly very well done.

Such fulminations of outraged dignity, such out-pourings of righteous indignation, never were witnessed. It took the united sympathy and assurance of the whole personnel of the station, to smooth the ruffian down. After a while, however, he condescended to see the humorous side. The police laughed with him. . . .

Throughout my recital I had to endure the like.

As for the chief of police, he was plainly extremely bored. He listened, patiently because it was his duty to let me speak. His cold, indifferent air, the way in which his eyes went straying about the room, were simply maddening.

Desperately endeavouring to keep my temper, I ploughed my way on.

At last—

"Listen," I said dramatically. "You do not believe me. I do not blame you. My friend has told a good tale. At present it is my word against his. Supposing I bring some evidence?"

"What evidence can you bring?"

"The papers belonging to the car." I pointed to the usurper. "On his own showing I cannot have seen them. Yet I will tell you their contents. I pray you, send for them. They're in the left——"

"Wrong, sonny," said my antagonist, tapping his coat. "I

always carry 'em here." And, with that, he drew out our wallet and flung it upon the desk.

With our Pass in his hands, the chief of the police blinked at me.

"The chassis number?" he said.

"P 1709."

Up went his eyebrows.

"And on the number-plates?"

"XD 2322."

The official folded the Pass and shook his head.

"Wrong," he said shortly.

As I stared at him, frowning—

"Yes, sonny," said the jeering voice. "An' don't go putting it up that you're J. Mansel, 'cause the picture's against you."

With the words the truth came to me.

It was Ping—Jonah's car—that was standing without in the street. *And I had given Pong's numbers....*

With a grin of triumph the impostor rose to his feet.

"So that's that," he drawled. "Well, I guess I'll be moving. As for these climbers——"

"Pardon me, sir," said Berry, in pretty fair French, "but you will do nothing of the sort." He turned to the chief of the police and inclined his head. "I am a nobleman, and—I should like a chair."

For a moment the other stared at him, then he sent for a seat. Had I stood in his shoes, I should have done the same. My brother-in-law's air was irresistible.

Berry sat down carefully.

"I shall not," he said, "keep you long. This is not my car. It belongs to my cousin, Captain Jonathan Mansel. Look at the Pass, please, and check me. Captain Mansel was born at Guildford, Surrey, is it not so? Good. Now I have given the birthplace." He shot out an accusing hand. *"Ask that gentleman the date."*

For the second time the tough exploded, but with a difference. This time the wrath was genuine, the passion real. There was something beastly about it. Beside this paroxysm the other outburst had been almost refined.

The official who had been about to speak looked at the fellow curiously, and when, a moment later, the latter stretched out his hand for the Pass, he held up a prohibitive palm.

As the storm died down—

"Good," said Berry. "The gentleman doesn't want to. The

date is December the fifteenth, 1891." He sighed profoundly. Then: "You have a *gendarme* here," he said musingly, "called Jean Laffargue."

The chief of the police stared.

"Yes, *Monsieur*. He is there, by the door."

Berry nodded.

"He has a twin brother, hasn't he?"

"Perfectly, *Monsieur*. He is called 'François'."

"Very likely," said Berry. "Very likely. I call him *Herbert*!"

"*Monsieur le Comte*," said Herbert, stepping into the room.

"Ah, Herbert," said Berry airily, "we meet again." He nodded at the official. "Just tell this gentleman about this morning, will you? He would, I think, be interested."

To say that Herbert came up to the scratch is to do scant justice to the testimony which he gave and to the manner in which he gave it. He swore to Berry: he swore to me: and in all honesty he swore to the car. For this, since Ping and Pong were duplicates, he may be forgiven. He described the morning's incident with a wealth of picturesque detail and an abundance of vivid imagery, while an astute cross-examination only served to adorn the sincerity of his tale.

Finally, in response to his entreaties, police and all, we followed him into the street, where, displaying a histrionic ability which was truly French, he proceeded to reconstruct and rehearse his great adventure with the enthusiasm of a zealot.

Watch in hand, Berry touched the chief of the police upon the shoulder.

"By now," he said, "I think my cousin may have reached Pau. If you would like to telephone. . . ."

He stopped suddenly to peer right and left into the darkness. The gentry had disappeared.

\*       \*       \*       \*       \*

Ten minutes later, with a *gendarme* on either step, we picked up an anxious Adèle. Then we filled up with petrol, had my makeshift connection replaced by a new wire, and started for home.

As we passed the scene of our meeting with Herbert—

"Which goes to prove," said my brother-in-law, "the wisdom of catching at straws. I noticed his likeness to Herbert the moment we entered the room, and, for what it was worth, I kept my eye on him. Then a *gendarme* came in and whispered. I caught the words '*votre frère.*' Laffargue shrugged his shoulders and glanced at the clock. It looked as if his brother was waiting for him to come off duty. I began to wonder whether the two were going to blow my ten francs. During one of the arguments I shot my bolt. I asked him to tell his twin-brother that the Count Blowfly was here and would be glad if he'd wait. He stared rather, but, after a little hesitation, he slipped out of the room. I think my heart stopped beating until he returned. When he looked at me and nodded, I could have screamed with delight. . . ."

For a kilometre or so we sat in silence.

Then—

"It reminds me of poker on board ship," said I. "Our friend of the square jaw cuts in and, with the luck of an outsider, picks up four kings."

"That's it," said Berry. "And we hold three aces."

"Exactly," said I.

"But four kings beat three aces," said Adèle.

"You're forgetting Herbert," said I.

"No, I'm not," said my wife. "Herbert's the Ace of Spades."

"No, sweetheart," said Berry. "He's the joker."

\*　　　\*　　　\*　　　\*　　　\*

It was early upon the following morning that a letter was brought by hand to our door.

Dear Mrs. Pleydell,

I'm afraid you must have thought all sorts of things about me after I'd gone yesterday, but I've just this moment had a telegram, and I'm so excited I can hardly write. I know my name now. You see, I used to be the Marquis Lecco. Then, when Father died, they said he'd never been the Duke at all, and so I had no name. But now it's all settled, and they've lost their case. And I can sign myself always,

Yours very sincerely,

Padua.

## CHAPTER VI

# How Berry Ran Contraband Goods, and the Duke of Padua Plighted Jill his Troth

That Jill was in love with the Duke of Padua was only less manifest than that the Duke of Padua was in love with Jill. Something, however, was wrong. So much our instinct reported. Our reason refused to believe it, and, with one consent, we pretended that all was well. For all that, there lay a shadow athwart the babies' path. Yet the sky was cloudless. . . . The thing was too hard for us.

With a sigh, I opened my case and took out a cigarette. Then I handed the case to Berry. The latter waved it aside and wrinkled his nose.

"I'm through," he said shortly. "Offal's all very well in an incinerator, if the wind's the right way, but, as a substitute for tobacco—well, it soon palls."

I closed the case and slid it into my pocket.

"I must confess," I said, "that I'm nearing the breaking-point."

"Well, I wish you'd be quick and reach it," said Adèle. "How you can go on at all, after finding that fly, I can't imagine."

She shuddered at the memory.

Less than a week ago a suspicious protuberance in the line of a local cigarette had attracted my attention. Investigation had revealed the presence of a perfect, if somewhat withered, specimen of the *musca domestica* imbedded in the vegetation which I had been proposing to smoke. This was too much for the girls, none of whom had since touched a cigarette, and when my brother-in-law suggested that the fly had probably desired cremation, and urged that, however obnoxious, the wishes of the dead should be respected, Daphne had reviled her husband and requested Jonah to open the door, so that she could sit in a draught.

We were in a bad way.

Now that we were in France, the difficulty of obtaining cigars, cigarettes, or tobacco, such as we were used to enjoy, seemed to be insuperable. The prohibitive duty, the uncertainty and by no means infrequent failure of the French mails, brought the cost of procuring supplies from England to a figure we could not stomach : attempts at postal smuggling had ended in humiliating failure : the wares which France herself was offering were not at all to our taste. We were getting desperate. Jonah, who had smoked the same mixture for thirteen years, was miserable. Berry's affection for a certain brand of cigars became daily more importunate. My liver was suffering. . . .

"We'd better try getting a licence to import," I said heavily. "It may do something."

"Ah," said my brother-in-law, drawing a letter from his pocket, "I knew I had some news for you. I heard from George this morning. I admit I don't often take advice, but this little missive sounds an unusually compelling call.

"Above all, do not be inveigled into obtaining or, worse still, acting upon, a so-called 'licence to import'. It is a copper-bottomed have. I got one, when I was in Paris, gleefully ordered five thousand cigarettes from Bond Street, and started to count the days. I soon got tired of that. Three months later I got a dirty form from the Customs, advising me that there was a case of cigarettes, addressed to me, lying on the wharf at Toulon—yes, Toulon. They added that the charges to be paid before collection amounted to nine hundred francs by way of duty, eleven hundred and sixty-five by way of freight, and another three francs forty for every day they remained in the Custom House. In this connection, they begged to point out that they had already lain there for six weeks. Friend, can you beat it? But what, then, did I do? Why, I took appropriate action. I wrote at once, saying that, as I was shortly leaving for New York, I should be obliged if they would forward them via Liverpool to the Piræus : I inquired whether they had any objection to being paid in roubles : and I advised them that I was shortly expecting a pantechnicon, purporting to contain furniture, but, in reality, full of mines. These I begged them to handle with great care and to keep in a temperature never higher than thirty-seven degrees Fahrenheit, as they were notoriously sensitive, and I particularly wished to receive them intact. I added that the pantechnicon would be consigned to me under another name. A fair knowledge of the French temperament suggests to me that the next two or three furniture vans which arrive at Toulon will be very stickily welcomed."

I threw away my cigarette and stared at the mountains.

" 'Though every prospect pleases,' " I murmured, " 'and only fags are vile.' "

"The only thing to do," said Adèle, "is to have a little sent out from England from time to time, and ration yourselves accordingly."

Berry shook his head.

"Easier to stop altogether," he said. "Tobacco's not like food. (I'm not speaking of the stuff you get here. Some of that is extremely like food—of a sort. I should think it would, as they say, 'eat lovely'.) Neither is it like liquor. You don't carry a flask or a bottle of beer in your hip-pocket—more's the pity. But nobody's equipment is complete without a case or a pouch. Why? So that the moment this particular appetite asserts itself, it can be gratified. No. Smoking's a vice; and as soon as you clap a vice in a strait-jacket, it loses its charm. A cigar three times a day after meals doesn't cut any ice with me." He tilted his hat over his eyes and sank his chin upon his chest. "And now don't talk for a bit. I want to concentrate."

Adèle laid a hand upon his arm.

"One moment," she said. "If the car arrives before you've finished, are we to interrupt you?"

"Certainly not, darling. Signal to the driver to stop in the middle distance. Oh, and ask approaching pedestrians to keep on the grass. Should any children draw near, advise their nurse that I have the mumps."

We were sitting upon a seat in the Parc Beaumont, revelling in the temper of the sunshine and the perfection of the air. A furlong away, Daphne, Jill, and Jonah were playing tennis, with Piers, Duke of Padua, to make a fourth. Nobby and a fox-terrier were gambolling upon an adjacent lawn.

Pau has many virtues, all but one of which may, I suppose, be severally encountered elsewhere upon the earth. The one, however, is her peculiar. The place is airy, yet windless. High though she stands, and clear by thirty miles of such shelter as the mountains can give, by some queer trick of Nature's, upon the map of Æolus Pau and her pleasant precincts are shown as forbidden ground. There is no stiff breeze to rake the boulevard : there are no gusts to buffet you at corners : there are no draughts in the streets. The flow of sweet fresh air is rich and steady, but it is never stirred. A mile away you may see dust flying; storm and tempest savage the Pyrenees : upon the gentlest day fidgety puffs fret Biarritz, as puppies plague an old hound. But Pau is sanctuary. Once in a long, long while some errant blast blunders into the town. Then, for a second of time, the place is Bedlam. The uncaught shutters are slammed, the unpegged laundry is sent whirling, and, if the time is evening, the naked flames of lamps are blown out. But before a match can be lighted, the air is still again. And nobody cares. It was an accident, and Pau knows it. Probably the gust had lost its way and was frightened to death. Such a thing will not happen again for two or three months. . . .

"I like Piers," said Adèle suddenly. "But I think he might kiss my hand."

"How dare you?" said I.

"I do really," said Adèle. "He kisses Daphne's and he actually kisses Jill's."

"That's all wrong," said I. "You don't kiss a maiden's hand."

"Of course you do," grunted Berry. "A well-bred son of Italy——"

"But he isn't a son of Italy. He's English on both sides."

"I'm not talking of his sides," said Berry. "It's a matter of bosom. You may have English forbears, but if they've been Italian dukes for two centuries, it's just possible that they've imbibed something besides Chianti. Personally, I think it's a very charming custom. It saves wiping your mouth, and——"

"Well, why doesn't he kiss my hand?" said Adèle.

"Because, sweetheart, you are—were American. And—he's very punctilious—he probably thinks that a quondam citizen might have no use for such circumstance."

"I should," said Adèle. "I should just love it. I like Piers."

I looked across at my brother-in-law.

"D'you hear that?" I inquired. "She likes him."

Berry shrugged his shoulders.

"I told her not to marry you," he said.

"No, you didn't," said Adèle. "You egged me on."

"Oh, you wicked story," said Berry. "Why, I fairly spread myself on the brutality of his mouth."

"You said he was honest, sober, and hard-working."

"Nonsense," said Berry. "I was talking of somebody else. I have seen him sober, of course, but—— Besides, you were so precipitate. You had an answer for everything. When I spoke of his ears, you said you'd get used to them : and when I asked you if you'd noticed——"

"I shan't," said Adèle. "I mean, I didn't. However, it's done now. And, after all, he's very convenient. If we hadn't got married, I shouldn't have wintered at Pau. And if I hadn't wintered at Pau, I shouldn't have met Piers."

"True," said Berry, "true. There's something in that." He nodded in my direction. "D'you find he snores much?"

"Nothing to speak of," said Adèle. "Used he to?"

"Like the devil," said Berry. "The vibration was fearful. We had to have his room underpinned."

"Oh, he's quite all right now," said my wife. "Indeed, as husbands go, he's—he's very charming."

"You don't mean to say you still love him?"

"I—I believe I do."

"Oh, the girl's ill," said Berry. "Put your head between your knees, dear, and think of a bullock trying to pass through a turnstile. And why 'as husbands go'? As a distinguished consort, I must protest against that irreverent expression."

"Listen," said Adèle, laughing. "All women adore ceremonious attention—even Americans. The ceremonious attentions of the man they love are the sweetest of all. It's the tragedy of every happy marriage that, when comradeship comes in at the door, ceremony flies out of the window. Now, my husband's my king. Once he was my courtier. I wouldn't go back for twenty million worlds, but—I've got a smile for the old days."

"I know," said Berry softly. "I know. Years ago Daphne told me the same. And I tried and tried. . . . But it wouldn't work somehow. She was very sweet about it, and very wise. 'Ceremony,' she said, 'gets as far as the finger-tips.' I vowed I'd carry it further, but she only smiled. . . . We retired there and then, ceremoniously enough, to dress for dinner. I'd bathed and changed and got as far as my collar, when the stud fell down my back. I pinched it between my shoulder-blades. At that moment she came to the door to see if I was ready. . . ." He spread out expressive hands. "They talk about the step from the sublime to the ridiculous. We didn't use any stairs: we went down in the lift. After that I gave up trying. A sense of humour, however, has pulled us through, and now we revile one another."

"And so, you see," said Adèle, slipping an arm through mine, "Piers has wares to offer me which you haven't. The shame of it is, he won't offer them. Still, he's very nice. The way in which he solemnly takes us all for granted is most attractive. He's as natural as a baby a year old. He just bows very courteously and then joins in the game. The moment it's over, he makes his bow and retires. We call him Piers : he calls us by our Christian names —and we haven't known him a week. It's not self-confidence; it's just pure innocence."

"I confess it's remarkable," said I. "And I don't wonder you like him. All the same, I'm sorry——"

"There!" cried Adèle suddenly pointing across the lawn. "Boy, he's gone in again."

I reached the edge of the ornamental water in time to observe the Sealyham emerge upon the opposite bank.

"You naughty dog" said I. "You naughty, wicked dog." Nobby shook himself gleefully. "No, don't come across. Go round the other way. Go *back*!"

The dog hesitated, and, by way of turning the scale, I threw my stick for him to retrieve. As this left my hand, the hook caught in my cuff, and the cane fell into mid-stream. . . .

As Nobby climbed out with the stick, the park-keeper arrived— a crabbed gentleman, in a long blue cloak and the deuce of a stew.

The swans, he said, would be frightened. (There was one swan, three hundred yards away.) Always they were being pursued by bold dogs. *Mon Dieu*, but it was shameful. That hounds should march unled in the Parc Beaumont was forbidden —absolutely. Not for them to uproot were the trees and flowers planted. Where, then, was my attachment? And I had encouraged my dog. Actually I had made sport for him. He had seen the deed with his eyes. . . .

One paw raised, ears pricked, his little head on one side, his small frame quivering with excitement, his bright brown eyes alight with expectation, a dripping Nobby regarded us. . . .

I took a note from my pocket.

"He is a wicked dog," I said. "There. He pays his fine. As for me, I shall be punished enough. My home is distant, and I was to have driven. Now he is wet and must grow dry, so I must walk. I will think out his punishment as I go." And, with that, I hooked my cane to the delinquent's collar and turned away.

"*Pardon Monsieur*." The old fellow came shambling after us. "*Pardon*, but do not punish him, I pray you." Nobby screwed round his head and looked at him. "Oh, but how handsome he is! Perhaps he did not understand. And I should be sorry to think . . ." Nobby started towards him and moved his tail. "See how he understands. He has the eyes of a dove." He stooped to caress his *protégé*. "Ah, but you are cold, my beauty. Unleash him, *Monsieur*, I pray you, that he may warm himself. I shall not notice him." As I did his bidding, and Nobby capered away, "*Bon*," he said pleasedly. "*Bon. Au revoir, mon beau*." He straightened his bowed shoulders and touched his hat. "*A votre service, Monsieur*."

I returned thoughtfully to where Adèle and Berry were sitting, watching us closely and pretending that we did not belong to them. So far as personal magnetism was concerned, between Nobby and the Duke of Padua there seemed to be little to choose. To judge by results, the two were equally irresistible. In the race for the Popularity Stakes the rest of the males of our party were simply nowhere.

With a sigh, a blue coupé slid past me and then slowed down. The grey two-seater behind it did the same. When I say that Daphne, who loathes mechanics, was seated in the latter conveyance, submitting zealously to an oral examination by Piers regarding the particular functions of the various controls, it will be seen that my recent conclusions were well founded.

"Letters," said Jill, getting out of the coupé. "One for Berry and two for Adèle." She distributed them accordingly. "Fitch brought them up on his bicycle. And Piers' aunt is coming— the one whose villa he's at. I forgot her name, but he says she's awfully nice."

"Splendid," said I. "And now congratulate me. Having tramped the town all the morning, I've got to walk home."

"Why?"

I pointed to Nobby.

"That he may warm himself," I said.

My cousin gave a horrified cry.

"Oh, Boy! And we only washed him last night."

"I'll take him," cried Piers. "I'd like to. And you can drive Daphne back."

I shook my head, laughing.

"It's his master's privilege," I said. "Besides, he's had his scolding, and if I deserted him he'd be hurt. And he's really a good little chap."

"But——"

"My dear Piers," said Daphne, laying a hand on his arm, "rather than risk hurting that white scrap's feelings, my brother would walk to Lyons."

"You will all," said Berry, "be diverted to learn that I am

faced with the positively filthy prospect of repairing to London forthwith. After spending a quarter of an hour in an overheated office in New Square, Lincoln's Inn, in the course of which I shall make two affidavits which nobody will ever read, I shall be at liberty to return. Give me the Laws of England."

"Never mind, old chap," said Daphne. "We'll soon be back again. I shall go with you, of course. Ought we to start to-night?"

Considering that there was snow in London, that the visit would entail almost continuous travelling for nearly thirty hours each way, and that my sister cannot sleep in a train, it seemed as if Berry, at any rate, was pulling out of the ruck.

"My sweet," replied my brother-in-law, "I won't hear of it. However, we'll argue it out in private. Yes, I must start to-night."

"You must go?" said Jonah softly.

"Can't get out of it."

"Right." My cousin leaned out of the car. "I'll give you my tobacconist's address. The best way will be to have the stuff decanted and sewn in your coat."

There was a pregnant silence.

Then—

"Saved!" I cried exultantly. "Saved!"

"What d'you mean—'Saved'?" said Berry.

"Hush," said I, looking round. "Not an 'h' mute! This summons of yours is a godsend. With a litte ingenuity, you can bring enough contraband in to last us till May."

\*    \*    \*    \*    \*

If our efforts to induce my brother-in-law to see reason were eventually successful, this was no more than we deserved. We made light of the risk of detection, we explained how the stuff could be concealed, we told him the demeanour to assume, we said we wished we were going, we declared it was done every day, we indemnified him against fines, we entreated, we flattered, we cajoled, we appealed to him "as a sportsman", we said it was "only right", we looked unutterable things, and at last, half an hour before it was time for him to start for the station, he promised, with many misgivings and expressions of self-reproach, to see what he could do. Instantly, from being his suppliants, we became his governors; and the next twenty minutes were employed in pouring into his ears the most explicit directions regarding his purchase and disposal of our particular fancies. Finally we made out a list. . . .

He had absolutely refused to allow my sister to accompany him, but we all went down to the station to see him off.

As we were pacing the platform—

"Have you got the list?" said Jonah.

The same question had been asked before—several times.

"Yes," said Berry, "I have. And if anybody asks me again, I shall produce it and tear it into shreds before their eyes."

"Well, for Heaven's sake, don't lose it," said I, "because——"

"To hear you," said Berry, "anybody would think that I was mentally deficient. Anybody would think that I was going to enclose it in a note to the Customs, telling them to expect me on Saturday, disguised in a flat 'at and a bag of gooseberries, and advising them to pull up their socks, as I should resist like a madman. I don't know what's the matter with you."

We endeavoured to smooth him down.

"And if," purred Daphne, "if there should be any—that is— what I mean is, should any question arise——"

Berry laughed hysterically.

"Yes," he said, "go on. 'Any question'. Such as whether they can give me more than five years' hard labour. I understand."

"Get on the telephone to Berwick. He knows the President personally and can do anything."

"Sweetheart," replied her husband, "you may bet your most precious life. . . . If Berwick wasn't in Paris I wouldn't touch the business with the end of a forty-foot pole."

"I wish I was going with you," said Daphne wistfully.

Berry took off his hat.

"You are," he said gently, "you are." He laid his hand upon his heart. "I wish I could put the tobacco in the same poor place. But that's impossible. For one thing, lady, you've all the room there is."

Which was pretty good for a king who hadn't been a courtier for nearly nine years.

\*　　\*　　\*　　\*　　\*

It was upon the following afternoon that Adèle, who was brushing Nobby, sat back on her heels.

"When Jill," she said, "becomes the Duchess of Padua, what bloods we shall be."

"She isn't there yet," said I.

"Where?"

"My sweet," said I, "I apologise. I was using a figure of speech, which is at once slipshod and American."

"That," said my wife, "is the worst of being English. You're like the Indian tailor who was given a coat to copy and reproduced a tear in the sleeve. Imitation can be too faithful. Never mind. I forgive you."

"D'you hear that, Nobby?" The terrier started to his feet. "Did you hear what the woman said? That we, who have founded precedents from time immemorial—that you and I, who taught America to walk——"

"He's Welsh," said Adèle.

"I don't care, It's scandalous. Who defiled the Well of English? And now we're blamed for drinking the water."

Adèle looked out of the window and smiled at a cloud.

"Once," she said slowly, "once I asked you if you would have known I was an American. . . . And when you said 'Yes', I asked you why. . . . Do you remember your answer? . . . Of course," she added swiftly, "that was before we were married."

"You beautiful witch," said I. "You unkind, beautiful witch. You've only to touch the water with the tip of your little red tongue to make it pure. You've only to put your lips to it to make it the sweetest music that ever a poor fool heard. You've only to smile like that to make me proud to kiss your shining foot."

"Nobby!" cried Adèle. "Oh, Nobby! Did you hear that? Did you hear what the man said? A real courtier's speech! But how can he kiss my feet when I'm sitting on them?"

I stepped to her side, picked her up, and swung her on to a table.

Then I kissed her sweet insteps.

From her perch my wife addressed the Sealyham.

"It's all right, Nobby," she said relievedly. "He is a king, after all. Only a king would have done that."

As I sat down by her side—

"I'd love to be a queen," cried a voice. "Love to. Wouldn't you like to be a king?"

It was Jill speaking.

The fresh tones came floating up and in at the open window. She could not have heard our words. It was pure coincidence.

Adèle and I sat very still.

"I don't know," said Piers slowly.

"I'll tell you what I'd do," said Jill. "I'd—Piers, what is the matter?"

"Nothing," said Piers.

"There is," said Jill accusingly. "You know there is. I can see it in your eyes. What are you thinking about?"

"I—I don't know," stammered her swain.

"I think you might tell me," said Jill aggrievedly. "I always tell you everything. Once or twice lately you've got all quiet suddenly—I can't think why. Is it because your aunt's coming?"

Piers laughed bitterly.

"Good Heavens, no," he said.

"Well, why is it, then?"

For a moment there was no answer.

Then all of a sudden the sluice-gate of speech was pulled up.

"Oh, Jill, Jill, Jill . . . I could go on saying your name for the rest of my life! I say it all the way home. I say it as I'm going to sleep. I say it when I wake in the morning. . . . I saw you first at Biarritz. You never knew. I was staying with some Italian people. They've got a place there. And I was alone in the grounds. And then I saw you—with Boy. You looked so wonderful. . . . All in green you were, standing with your feet close together, and your head on one side. Your hair was coming down, and the sun was shining on it. . . . I found out who you were, and came to Pau. I wanted to get to know you. I felt I must. And, whenever you all went out, I followed in the two-seater. And then—I got to know you—at St. Bertrand—that wonderful, wonderful day. . . . I—was—so—awfully—happy. . . . And now"—his voice sank to a wail—"I wish I hadn't. If only I'd stopped to think. . . . But I didn't. I just knew I wanted to be with you, and that was all. Oh," he burst out suddenly, "why did I ever do it? Why did I ever follow you—that wonderful day? If I'd dreamed how miserable it'd make me, how miserably wretched I'd be . . . It's the dreadful hopelessness, Jill, the dreadful hopelessness. . . . But I can't help it. It's something stronger than me. It's not enough to be with you. I want to touch you : I want to put my arms round your neck : I want to play with your hair. . . . Of course I'm terribly lucky to be able to kiss your hand, but—— Ah, don't be frightened. I was—only playing, Jill, only pretending. And now I'm going to be all serious again—not quiet, but serious. Goodbye, Madonna. Have you ever seen *Pagliacci*? Where the fellow bursts into tears? I think I could do that part this afternoon. . . ."

A light padding upon the gravel came to our ears.

Then a car's door slammed.

A moment later Piers' two-seater purred its way down the drive. . . .

Adèle and I continued to sit very still.

Presently I turned to her and raised my eyebrows.

"Hopelessness?" I whispered. "Hopelesseness? What on earth does he mean?"

My wife shrugged her shoudlers helplessly.

Then she laid a finger upon her lips.

I nodded obediently.

\*   \*   \*   \*   \*

"Yes," said Berry, "you see in me a nervous wreck. My heart's misfiring, I'm over at the knees, and with the slightest encouragement I can break out into a cold sweat."

He sank into a chair and covered his eyes. . . .

I had meant to meet him at the station, but the early train had beaten me, so Fitch had gone with the car. Indeed, it was not yet eight o'clock, and Daphne was still abed. That had not prevented us from following Berry into her room, any more than had the fact that no one of us was ready for breakfast. I had no coat or waistcoat : so far as could be seen, Jonah was attired in a Burberry and a pair of trousers : a glance at Adèle suggested that she was wearing a fur coat, silk stockings, and a tortoise-shell comb, while Jill was wrapped in a kimono, with her fresh fair hair tumbled about her shoulders.

Jonah voiced our anxiety.

"You—you've got the goods?"

"They're downstairs," said Berry. "But don't question me. I can't bear it. I'll tell you all in a minute, but you must let me alone. Above all, don't thwart me. I warn you, my condition is critical."

He sighed heavily.

Apparently impressed by his demeanour, Nobby approached, set his paws upon his knee, and licked his face.

"There you are," said Berry, lifting the dog to his lap. "The very fowls of the air pity me. No, it's not a sore, old chap. It's where I cut myself yesterday. But I'm just as grateful. And now lie still, my beauty, and poor old Sit-tight the Smuggler will tell you such a tale as will thicken your blood.

"Upon Friday morning last I purchased a uniform-case. Not a new one—the oldest and most weather-beaten relic I could procure. On Friday evening I packed it. One thousand cigars, five thousand cigarettes, and six pounds of tobacco looked very well in it. My sword, a pair of field boots, breeches, coat—carefully folded to display the staff badges—and my red hat looked even better. I filled up with socks, shirts, puttees, slacks, spurs and all the old emblems of Mars that I could lay my hands on. Finally I leavened the lot with a pound of the best white pepper—to discourage the moths, my fellow, to discourage the moths."

His tone suggesting the discomfiture of the wicked, the Sealyham barked his applause.

"Quite so. Well, I locked the case up and corded it, and precisely at ten o'clock I retired to bed.

"I never remember feeling so full of beans as I did the next morning. I could have bluffed my way across Europe with a barrel of whiskey on a lead. I felt ready for anything. Sharp at a quarter to eleven I was at the station, and one minute later a porter, with the physique of a blacksmith, had the box on his shoulder and my dressing-case in his hand.

"It was as he was preparing to lay his spoils at the feet of the registration-monger that my bearer trod upon a banana-skin. . . . To say that he took a toss, conveys nothing at all. It was the sort of fall you dream of—almost too good to be true. And my uniform-case, of which he never let go, described a very beautiful parabola, and then came down upon the weigh-bridge, as the swiple of an uplifted flail comes down upon grain. . . .

"Both hinges went, of course. It says much for the box that the whole thing didn't melt then and there. If I hadn't corded it, most of the stuff would have been all over the Vauxhall Bridge Road.

"Well, I was so rattled that I could hardly think. I joined mechanically in the laughter, I assured complete strangers that it didn't matter at all, I carried through the registration like a man in a dream, and I tipped everybody I could see. It was as I was thrusting blindly towards the gates that I first realised that half the people in the place were sneezing to glory. I was still digesting this phenomenon when I sneezed myself. . . .

"Still it never occurred to me. There are times when you have to be told right out. I didn't have to wait long.

"As I presented my ticket, a truck full of luggage was pushed through the gate next to mine. The porters about it were sneezing bitterly. 'Snuff?' said one of them contemptuously. 'Snuff be blarsted! *It's pepper!*'

"Whether at that moment my stomach in fact slipped or not I am unable to say, but the impression that my contents had dropped several inches was overwhelming.

"I staggered into the Pullman, more dead than alive. . . . After a large barley and a small water, I felt somewhat revived, but it was not until the train was half-way to Dover that I had myself in hand. I was just beginning under the auspices of a second milk and soda, to consider my hideous plight, when a genial fool upon the opposite side of the table asked me if I had 'witnessed the comedy at Victoria'. Icily I inquired : 'What comedy?' He explained offensively that 'some cuckoo had tried the old wheeze of stuffing pepper in his trunk to put off the Customs', and that the intended deterrent had untimely emerged. My brothers, conceive my exhilaration. 'The old wheeze'. I could have broken the brute's neck. When he ordered me a filthy cigar with a kink in it, and said with a leer that I shouldn't 'get many like that on the other side of the Chops', I could have witnessed his mutilation unmoved. . . .

"Still, it's an ill wind. . . . The swine's swords were like a spur. I became determined to get the stuff through.

"Grimly I watched the case go on to the boat, to the accompaniment of such nasal convulsions as I had never believed to be consistent with life itself. By way of diverting suspicion, I asked one of the crew what was the matter. His blasphemous answer was charged with such malignity that I found it necessary to stay myself with yet another still lemonade.

"Arrived at Calais, I hurried on board the train.

"The journey to Paris was frightful. The nearer we got, the more dishevelled became my wits. The power of concentration deserted me. Finally, as we were running in, I found that I had forgotten the French for 'moths'. I'd looked it out the night before : I'd been murmuring it all day long : and now, at the critical moment, it had deserted me. I clasped my head in my hands and thought like a madman. Nothing doing. I thought all round it, of course. I thought of candles and camphor and dusk. My vocabulary became gigantic, but it did not include the French equivalent for 'moths'. In desperation I approached my *vis-à-vis* and, in broken accents, implored him to tell me 'the French for the little creatures which you find in your clothes'. . . .

"I like the French. If I'd asked an Englishman, he'd have pulled the communication-cord, but this fellow never so much as stared. He just released a little spurt of good-will and then started in, as if his future happiness depended on putting me straight. 'But I was meaning the fleas. Oh, indubitably. Animals most gross. Only last November he himself. . . .' It took quite a lot of persuasion to get him off fleas. Then he offered me lice. I managed to make him understand that the attack was delivered when the clothes were unoccupied. Instantly he suggests rats. With an effort I explained that the things I meant were winged. As the train came to a standstill, he handed me '*chauvesouris*'. Bats! I ask you. . . .

"I stepped on to the platform as if I was descending into my tomb. How I got to the baggage-room, I'm hanged if I know; but I remember standing there, shivering and wiping the sweat off my face. Truck by truck the registered baggage appeared. . . .

"I heard my case coming for about a quarter of a mile.

"The architecture of the baggage-room at the *Gare du Nord* may be crude, but its acoustic properties are superb. The noise which accompanied the arrival of the cortège was simply ear-splitting. I was in the very act of wondering whether, if I decided to retire, my legs would carry me, when, with a crash, my uniform-case was slammed on to the counter three paces away. . . .

"A cloud of pepper arose from it, and in an instant all was confusion. Passengers and porters in the vicinity dropped everything and made a rush for the doors. A Customs official, who was plumbing the depths of a basket-trunk, turned innocently enough to see the case smoking at his elbow, dropped his cigar into some blouses, let out the screech of a maniac and threw himself face downward upon the floor. Somebody cried : 'Women and children first!' And, the supreme moment having arrived, I—I had the brain-wave.

"I stepped to the case and, with most horrible oaths, flung my hat upon the ground, smote upon the counter with my fist and started to rave like a fanatic. I made the most awful scene. I roared out that it was my box, and that it and its contents were irretrievably ruined. Gradually curiosity displaced alarm, and people began to return. I yelled and stamped more than ever. I denounced the French railways, I demanded the station-master, I swore I'd have damages, I tore off the cords, I lifted the lid, I alternately sneezed and raged, and, finally, I took out my tunic and shook it savagely. In vain the excisemen insisted that it was not their business. I cursed them bitterly, jerked an ounce of pepper out of a pair of brogues, and replied that they were responsible. . . .

"It was after I had shaken my second pair of slacks that the officials, with streaming eyes, began to beseech me to unpack the case no further. If only they'd known, I didn't need much inducing. I could see the shape of a cigarette-box under one of my shirts. Of course I argued a bit, for the look of the thing, but eventually I allowed myself to be persuaded and shoved the kit back. Finally they scrawled all over the lid with pieces of chalk, and, vowing the most hideous vengeance of invoking the British Ambassador, I stalked in the wake of my box out of the station.

"I was through.

"I had my dinner in bed. I think I deserved it. Still, I suppose it was indiscreet to have ordered lobster *à la Newburg*. I have slept better. I *was* sleeping better at half-past eight the next morning, when a waiter entered to say the *there was an official to see me from the Gare du Nord.* . . .

"Believing it to be another dream, I turned over and shut my eyes. The waiter approached and, touching me on the arm, repeated his ghastly communication. With a frightful effort I explained that I had the ague and could see nobody for some days. Mercifully he retired, and for a little space I lay in a sort of trance. After a bit I began to wonder what, in the name of Heaven, I was to do. I was afraid to get up, and I was afraid to stay in bed. I was afraid to stop in the hotel, and I was terrified of meeting the official downstairs. I was afraid to leave the case there, and I was still more afraid to take it away. I was getting hungry, and I was afraid to ring for breakfast. It was a positively poisonous position. Finally, after a lot of thought, I got up, bolted the door, unpacked the blasted box and shoved all the tobacco in the drawers of the wardrobe. Luckily there was a key. The kit I disposed naturally enough. Then I had a bath and dressed.

"As I was fastening my collar, the telephone went. It was the *Gare du Nord*. I jammed the receiver back.

"As I passed through the hall, a clerk dashed after me 'The *Gare du Nord*,' he said, 'were insisting upon seeing me about a case of mine.' I replied that I was busy all day, and could see nobody before six o'clock. I didn't mention that my train went at five. It was as well I didn't argue, for, as I left the hotel, a station official entered. I leapt into a taxi and told the driver to go to Notre Dame. Not that I felt like Church, but it was the first place I could think of. Somebody shouted after me, but—well, you know how they drive in Paris. I stopped round the second corner, discharged the taxi, and walked to a restaurant. By rights, I should have been ravenous. As it was, the food stuck in my throat. A bottle of lime-juice, however, pulled me together. After luncheon I went to a cinema—I had to do something. Besides, the darkness attracted me. . . . I fancy I dozed for a bit. Any way, the first thing I remember was a couple of men being arrested in the lounge of a hotel. It was most realistic. What was more, the clerk who had run after me in the morning and the clerk on the screen might have been twins. . . . I imagine that my hair rose upon my head, and for the second time it seemed certain that I had mislaid my paunch.

"I got out of the place somehow, to find that it was snowing. For the next hour I drove up and down the Champs Elysées. I only hope the driver enjoyed it more than I did. At last, when pneumonia seemed very near, I told him to drive to the hotel.

"I fairly whipped through the hall and into the lift. As this ascended, a page arrived at the gate and spoke upward. I didn't hear what he said.

"When I was in a hot bath, the telephone went. I let the swine ring. Finally somebody came and knocked at the door. Of my wisdom I hadn't bolted it, so, after waiting a little, they entered. I lay in the bath like the dead. After a good look round, they went away. . . .

"By twenty-past four I'd dressed, and repacked the case. I rang for a porter, told him to shove it on a taxi, and descended to settle my bill. Mercifully, the clerk who had stopped me in the morning was off duty. I could have squealed with delight. I paid my reckoning, tipped about eight people I'd never seen before, and climbed into the cab. Ten minutes later I was at the quai d'Orsay.

"By the time I was in the *wagon lit* it was ten minutes to five. . . .

"I sank down upon the seat in silent gratitude. The comfortable glow of salvation began to steal over my limbs. I looked benevolently about me. I reflected that, after all, the last thirty hours of my life had been rich with valuable experience. Smilingly I decided not to regret them. When I thought of the scene in the baggage-room, I actually laughed. Then the conductor put his head in at the door and said that there was somebody to see me from the *Gare du Nord*."

Berry suspended his recital and buried his face in his hands.

"I shall never be the same again," he said brokenly. "Never again. Up to then I had a chance—a sporting chance of recovery. At that moment it snapped. In a blinding flash I saw what a fool I'd been. If I'd only stayed on the platform, if I'd only gone into the restaurant car, if I'd only locked myself in a lavatory till the train had started, I should have been all right. As it was, I was caught—bending.

"It was the official I'd seen in the morning all right. After a preliminary flurry of ejaculation, he locked the door behind him and began to talk. . . . Don't ask me what he said, because I didn't hear. When the rope's round your neck, you're apt to miss the subtleties of the hangman's charge. After a time I realised that he was asking me a question. I stared at him dully and shook my head. With a gesture of despair, he glanced at his watch.

" '*Monsieur*,' he said, 'the train departs. I have sought you all day. The superintendent has told me to speak with you at all costs —to beg that you will lodge no complaint. He is desolated that your luggage was injured. It is a misfortune frightful. He cannot think how it has occurred. But to complain—no. I will tell *Monsieur* the truth. Twice in the last half-year an English officer's baggage has gone astray. But one more complaint from your Embassy, and the superintendent will be replaced. And in ten short days, *Monsieur*, he will have won his pension. . . . Ah, *Monsieur*, be merciful.'

"I was merciful.

"I waved the fellow away and swore haltingly that I would say nothing. We mingled a few tears, and he got out as the train was moving. . . .

"And there you are. I'd got my reprieve. Everything in the garden was lovely. But I couldn't enjoy it. My spirits failed to respond." He took the Sealyham's head between his hands and gazed into his eyes.

> "O Nobwell, Nobwell!
> Had I but seen the fool at half-past eight
> As he desired, he would not in the train
> Have put the wind up me so hellishly."

There was a moment's silence.

Then Jonah stepped to my brother-in-law and clapped him on the back.

"Brother," he said, "I take my hat off. I tell you frankly I couldn't have done it. I wouldn't have claimed that case at Paris for a thousand pounds"

Clamorously we endorsed his approval.

By way of acknowledgment the hero groaned.

"What you want," said I, "is a good night's rest. By mid-day to-morrow you'll be touching the ground in spots."

"I shan't be touching it at all," said Berry. "If it's nice and warm, I shall have a Bath chair, which you and Jonah will propel at a convenient pace. Nobby will sit at my feet as a hostage against your careless negotiation of gradients." He drew a key from his pocket and pitched it on to a table. "I fancy," he added, "I heard them put the case on the landing: and as I propose, decorative though it is, to remove my beard, perhaps one of you wasters will fetch me a cigarette."

There was a rush for the door.

True enough, the uniform-case was outside.

Jonah and I had its cords off in twenty seconds.

One hinge was broken and some khaki was protruding.

Adèle thrust the key into the lock. This was too stiff for her fingers, so after a desperate struggle, she let me have at the wards. . . .

After an exhausting two minutes we sent for a cold-chisel. . . . As the lock yielded, Berry appeared upon the scene.

For a moment he stared at us. Then—

"But why not gun-cotton?" he inquired. "That's the stuff to open a broken box with, if you don't like the look of the key. You know, you're thwarting me. And don't try to turn the lid back, because there aren't any hin——"

The sentence was never finished.

As I lifted the lid, my brother-in-law fell upon his knees. With trembling hands he plucked at a Jaeger rug, reposing, carefully folded, upon the top of some underclothes. Then he threw back his head and took himself by the throat.

"Goats and monkeys!" he shrieked. *"It's somebody else's case!"*

\*　　\*　　\*　　\*　　\*

When, twenty-four hours later, a letter arrived from Pier's aunt, inviting us all to tea, we accepted, not because we felt inclined to go junketing, but because we did not wish to seem rude.

We were in a peevish mood. For this the loss of our forbidden fruit was indirectly responsible. The immediate cause of our ill-humour was the exasperating reflection that we were debarred from taking even those simple steps which lead to the restoration of lost luggage. We stood in the shoes of a burglar who has been robbed of his spoils. As like as not, our precious uniform-case was lying at the station, waiting to be claimed. Yet we dared not inquire, because of what our inquiries might bring forth. Of course the authorities might be totally ignorant of its contents. But then, again, they might not. It was a risk we could not take. The chance that, by identifying our property, we might be at once accusing and convicting ourselves of smuggling a very large quantity of tobacco, was too considerable. There were moments when Jonah and I, goaded to desperation, felt ready to risk penal servitude and "have a dart" at the bait. But Berry would not permit us. If things went wrong, he declared, he was bound to be involved—hideously. And he'd had enough of thin ice. The wonder was, his hair wasn't white. . . . By the time we had swung him round, our own courage had evaporated.

As for Piers, no one of us had seen or heard from him for five whole days. Ever since his extraordinary outburst upon the verandah, the boy had made himself scarce. While we were all perplexed, Jill took his absence to heart. She mourned openly. She missed her play-fellow bitterly, and said as much. And when three days had gone by and the last post had brought no word of him, she burst into tears. The next morning there were rings beneath her great grey eyes. She was far too artless to pretend that she did not care. Such a course of action never occurred to her. She had no idea, of course, that she was in love.

All the same, when upon Wednesday afternoon the cars were waiting to take us to tea with Mrs. Waterbrook, my cousin leaned over the banisters with a bright red spot upon either cheek.

"I say," she cried, "I'm not coming."

One and all, we stared up amazedly.

"Not coming?" cried Daphne. "But, darling——"

Jill stamped her small foot.

"N-no," she said shakily. "I'm not. And—and, if he asks after me, say I'm awfully well, but I felt I wanted a walk. I'm going to take Nobby out."

Her skirts whirled, and she was gone.

Adèle flew after her, while the rest of us stood whispering in the hall. Five minutes later the two descended together. But while we others climbed into the cars, Jill twitched a lead from the rack and took her stand upon the steps, with Nobby leaping for joy about her sides. And when she cried "Good-bye", there was a ring in her tone which sounded too glad to be true.

Mrs. Waterbrook was perfectly charming.

As we were ushered into a really beautiful salon, she rose from a little bureau—a tall, graceful figure, with masses of pretty grey hair and warm brown eyes.

"My dear," she said to Daphne, "what a beautiful creature you are!" She turned to Adèle. "As for you, if I were your husband, I'm afraid I should have a swelled head. Which is he? Ah, I see by the light in his eyes. . . . Of course, I ought to have called upon you, but I'm lazy by nature, and my car won't be here till to-morrow. And now I must thank you for being so kind to Piers. He ought to be here, of course. But where he is, I don't know. I've hardly seen him since I arrived. He seems to be crazy about his uncomfortable car. Went to Bordeaux and back yesterday— three hundred miles, if you please. I feel weak when I think of it. And now please tell me about yourselves. Beyond that you're all delightful, I've heard nothing from him."

I would not have believed that one woman could entertain five strangers with such outstanding success. Within five minutes Jonah and Daphne were by her side upon the sofa, Adèle was upon the hearth at their feet, Berry was leaning against the mantelpiece, and I was sitting upon the arm of an adjacent chair, describing our meeting with Piers a fortnight ago.

"I don't know his age," I concluded. "I take it he's about nineteen. But he's got the airs and graces of Peter Pan."

"Piers," said Mrs. Waterbrook, "is twenty-five. His mother was my sister. She married his father when she was seventeen. He was twenty years older than she, but they were awfully happy. The blood's pure English, although the title's Italian. The fief of the duchy goes with it. They were given to Piers' great-grandfather—he was a diplomat—for services rendered. A recent attempt to dispossess the boy mercifully failed." She looked round about her. "By the way, I thought there were six of you. Piers gave me the number, but neither gender nor anything else."

"There's a female to come," said Berry. "But I don't think she will to-day. She's a wayward child. We'll send her round to apologise to-morrow."

Here coffee and chocolate were served.

"I must apologise," said Mrs. Waterbrook, "for giving you no tea. But there you are." She sighed. "What tea you can get in France reminds me of grocer's port. I won't touch it myself, and I haven't the face to offer it to my guests. I usually bring some from England; but I—I didn't this time." She passed a hand across her eyes, as though to brush away a memory. "After all, you needn't come again, need you?"

"But we do the same," said Daphne. "We've given up tea. Up to last week, I clung to a cup before breakfast. But now I've stopped it."

"Yes," said Berry. "It was affecting her brain. Ten minutes after she'd swallowed it, she used to begin to wonder why she married me."

"I believe you," said Mrs. Waterbrook. "You can't drink French tea and be resigned. Now, a cup of well-made chocolate affords relief."

Before Berry could reply, she had pointed to an old china box and said that it contained cigarettes.

If she had said that it was full of black pearls, she could not have created more excitement. Besides, there was a confidence in her tone that set my nerves tingling. It was, I felt sure, no "grocer's port" that she was commending. And I—we, with the exception of Berry, had not smoked a good cigarette for nearly six weeks. . . .

As Jonah handed the box to Daphne, I strove to look unconcerned.

"And if anybody likes cigars," added Mrs. Waterbrook, "there are some in that silver box by Major Pleydell."

Berry started, said, "Oh—er—thanks very much," and opened the box. Then he took out a cigar, idly enough.

I became conscious that Daphne's and Adèle's eyes were upon me as Jonah brought me the cigarettes. I took one without looking, and stared back. Instantly their eyes shifted to the cigarette in my hand. I followed their gaze, to behold one of the brand which I had smoked invariably for seven years.

Dazedly I looked across at Berry, to see him regarding his cigar with bulging eyes. . . .

As in a dream, I heard Jonah's voice.

"You must forgive my cousins. They're not being rude. To tell you the truth, we've recently had a bereavement. A particularly cherished friend, who was to furnish us all with tobacco for several months, disappeared in sickening circumstances only two days ago. The cigar and the cigarette have revived some painful memories."

Our hostess opened and closed her mouth before replying. Then—

"What," she said faintly, "what was your—er—cherished friend like?"

Berry started to his feet.

"Both hinges gone," he shouted, "tied up with rope—reeking of pepper——"

Mrs. Waterbrook interrupted him with a shriek.

"He's outside my bedroom," she wailed. "By the side of the tall-boy. I suppose it's too much to hope that you've got my tea."

"Tea?" we screamed.

"Tea," piped our hostess. "Beautiful China tea. Thirty-five pounds of it. Under the camisoles."

Berry raised his eyes to heaven.

"Modesty forbade us," he said, "to go further than the b-b-b-bust b-b-b-bodices."

\* \* \* \* \*

It was in the midst of our rejoicing that Piers set foot on the verandah. For a moment he stood staring, pardonably bewildered, at the two smugglers, who were saluting one another respectively with a profound curtsey and the most elaborate of bows. Then he pulled open the great window and stepped hesitatingly into the room.

As he did so, the door was flung open, and a man-servant appeared.

"Mees Mansel," he announced.

Nobby entered anyhow, pleasedly lugging Jill into the room.

"Why, Jill!" cried Daphne. "My dear. . . . Mrs. Waterbrook, let me introduce——"

"*But that's not Miss Mansel!*"

It was Piers' voice.

With one accord we turned, staring. . . .

With arm outstretched, the boy was pointing at Jill.

For a moment nobody moved.

Then Piers sprang forward and caught Jill's hands in his.

"Jill!" he panted. "Jill, you're not Miss Mansel?"

"Yes, I am," said Jill steadily.

"But I thought you were married to Boy. I thought—I thought Adèle was Miss Mansel."

"Oh, Piers," said Jill reproachfully. "And she's got a wedding-ring on."

Piers stared at Jill's hand.

"I—I never thought of that," he said slowly. "I am silly." A wonderful smile came tearing to light his face. "But oh, Jill," he faltered, "I—am—so—awfully—glad!"

Never, I fancy, was love so simply declared.

For a moment Jill looked at him. Then her eyes fell, and an exquisite blush came stealing into her cheeks.

For an instant Piers hesitated. Then he let fall her fingers and turned about, flushing furiously. . . .

Before he had found his tongue, my cousin advanced to her hostess and put out her hand.

"I'm afraid I'm awfully late," she said quietly.

Mrs. Waterbrook stooped and kissed her.

"My darling," she said softly, "it was worth waiting for."

CHAPTER VII

## *How Daphne Lost her Bedfellow, and the Line of Least Resistance Proved Irresistible*

Order, so to speak, having been restored, and the path of love made straight beyond all manner of doubt, we decided festively to make an excursion to Spain. The fact that Piers could speak Spanish suggested that all the arrangements should be left in his hands. We embraced the suggestion cordially. Then, at the eleventh hour, a courteously imperative wire from his solicitors had deprived us of our courier. . . .

The Duke of Padua had left Pau that evening, and all six of us had gone to the station to speed him to Paris and Rome. My cousin's farewell to her future husband had been ridiculously affecting. Polonius' advice to his son was above rubies, but Jill's charge came pelting out of an eager heart.

"Oh, and Piers darling, you will take care, won't you? And do wear warm things. I'm sure it's still most awfully cold up there, and—and I don't know what men wear extra, but couldn't you put on a bodybelt?"

"Binder, dear, binder," corrected Berry.

"Well, binder, then. I remember Jonah saying——"

"Never," said her brother.

"Yes, you did. You said the great thing was to keep warm round the—er—round the hips."

Berry looked round.

"All women and children," he said, "will leave the Court."

"Piers, you will, won't you? For my sake. Oh, and don't forget you've got to get some sock-suspenders, because your left one comes down. And be very careful crossing the streets. Wait till there's a gap—always. And don't drink the water, will you? Don't even use it for your teeth. Daphne won't."

"That's right," said Berry. "Do as she does. Combine business with pleasure and clean them in a small Worthington."

"Oh, and lock your door at night. Just in case. And, Piers darling, I love you very much, and—and God bless you, dear, and I shall just wait and wait for you to come back again."

Hat in hand, Piers put her fingers to his lips.

"Good-bye, Madonna."

They kissed one another passionately.

The next moment the train was moving, and the Duke swung himself on to the step of the *wagon lit*.

Jill began to trot by his side. . . .

When she could run no faster, my cousin gave up the attempt and stood waving her tiny handkerchief and then staring after the train.

As we came up, she turned to us bravely.

"I hope," she said shakily, "I hope he'll get on all right. He's such a child," she added, knitting her pretty brow. "I wish to goodness we were married. Then I could have gone with him." She stumbled, and I caught her. She looked up at me with her grey eyes swimming. "I've often seen you off, Boy, but I wasn't silly like this."

"It's a question of interest, darling. Piers is your very own pigeon."

Jill wiped her eyes thoughtfully.

"I suppose that's it," she said slowly. "My very own. . . . Boy, will you take me to a tailor's? I want to get a binder."

Ere we sat down to dinner that night, two stout bodybelts had been dispatched to Paris by registered post.

*       *       *       *       *

"Satisfactorily," said Berry, restoring his napkin to his knees, "to consume oxtail, one should be stripped to the waist."

"That'll do," said Daphne.

"As a rule," said her husband, "it will. Of course, for a really careless feeder, still further divestment may be desirable. Afterwards he can be hosed. And now about Spain. Of course, without Piers to talk for us, we shall be mocked, misled, and generally stung to glory. But there you are. If you're landed with half a kingdom, I guess it's up to you to take possession."

"As at present arranged," said Jonah, "we start the day after to-morrow, spend one night at Pampeluna, two at San Sebastian, and get back on Saturday."

"One clear day," murmured Daphne. "I suppose that'll give us time."

"What's there to do," said Adèle, "besides packing?"

"Not much," said Jonah. "The passports have been visa-ed, and that's the main thing. We must get some money at the bank—Spanish money, I mean—book rooms, run over the cars . . . I can't think of anything else."

"We'd better take some insecticide," said Berry. "Spain's very conservative."

"Nonsense," said Daphne.

"All right," said her husband. "Only, on the command 'Terrot', don't wake me to inspect the bodyguard. Have we any castanets? And what about some sombreros? I mean, I want to do the thing properly."

"Thanks," said his wife. "But if you're going in fancy dress, I'd rather remain at Pau. I haven't forgotten our second Sunday here."

"I shall always maintain," was the reply, "that I was suitably dressed. On the previous Sunday I had carefully studied the fashions upon the Boulevard, and I flatter myself that, had I been permitted to appear in public, my attire would have found immediate favour."

"If," said I, "I remember aright, it consisted of a white bowler, a morning-coat, golf-breeches, blue silk stockings and cloth-topped boots."

"That's right," said Berry. "And an alpenstock. I ought really to have had my cuffs trimmed with skunk," he added wistfully, "but I thought of it too late."

"I tell you what," said Adèle. "We must take some films."

"That's right," said Jill. "I promised Piers we'd send him some snapshots."

Jonah groaned.

"Surely," he said, "our passport photographs are bad enough."

"The camera," said Berry, "can never lie. Besides, I'm very fond of your passport portrait. I admit I hadn't previously noticed that your right ear was so much the larger of the two, but the cast in your left eye is very beautifully insisted upon. Mine, I must confess is less successful. Had I been told that it was a study of the Honorary Treasurer of the Splodgeworth Goose Club on bail, I should have held it an excellent likeness. Daphne's is very good. She's wearing that particularly sweet expression of hers. You can almost hear her saying, 'Mine's a large port'. Apart, they're bad enough, but with both of them on the same document—well, why we weren't turned back at Boulogne I shall never know. Boy's, again, is lifelike."

"Shame," said Adèle. "He looks all bloated."

"I know he does, sweetheart. But that's his own fault. What's put in the mouth comes out in the flesh. The camera can never lie. And now don't choke. It's unmaidenly. And I cannot think of you as a matron. Let's see. Oh, yes. Films. Anything else?"

"Soap," said Daphne.

"Fountain-pen," said Jill.

"Cards," said Adèle.

"Tea," said Daphne.

"Beer-opener," said I.

"Plate and linen," said Berry. "That's nine. Let's go by train."

"Anybody," said Jonah, "would think that we were going into the bush. If you must have a camera—well, take one. But as for soap and tea and beer-openers and fountain-pens—oh, you make me tired."

"And me," said Berry unctuously. "A plain man of few words, all this vulgar mouth-wash about creature comforts——"

It was hardly to be expected that he would get any further. . . .

It was when the storm of indignation was at its height that the electric light failed.

Four of us breathed the same expletive simultaneously. Then—

"Lost," said Berry's voice. "Two cheese-straws and a blob of French mustard. Finder will be——" The crash of glass interrupted him. "Don't move, Falcon, or you'll wreck the room. Besides, it'll soon be dawn. The nights are getting shorter every day."

"Very good, sir," replied the butler.

"They'll bring some candles in a minute," said Daphne.

"What we really want," said my brother-in-law, "is a prismatic compass."

"What for?" said Jill.

"To take a bearing with. Then we should know where the port was, and I could peel you a banana. Or would you rather suck it?"

"Brute!" said Jill, shuddering. "Oh, why is the dark so horrid?"

"The situation," said I, "calls for philosophy."

"True," said Berry. "Now, similarly placed, what would Epicurus have done?"

"I think," said Adèle, "he'd have continued his discourse, as if nothing had happened."

"Good girl," said Jonah. "Any more queries about Pampeluna?"

"Yes," said my sister. "How exactly do we go?"

"We go," said I, "to St. Jean-Pied-de-Port. There we get a permit to take the cars into Spain. Then we go over the mountains by Roncevaux. It's a wonderful drive, they say, but the very deuce of a climb. Pampeluna's about fifty kilometres from the top of the pass. If we get off well, we ought to be there in time for tea."

"Easily," said Jonah. "It's only a hundred and twenty miles."

I shrugged my shoulders and resumed a surreptitious search for the chocolates.

"I expect we shall strike some snow," I said.

"Snow?" cried Jill.

"Rather," said Berry. "And avalanches. The cars will be roped together. Then, if one falls, it'll take the other with it. Will somebody pass me the grape-tongs? I've found a walnut."

"Why on earth," said Daphne, "don't they bring some candles? Falcon!"

"Yes, madam?"

"Try to find the door, and go and see what they're doing."

"Very good, madam."

With infinite care the butler emerged from the room. As the door closed—

"And now," said Adèle, "I can't bear it any longer. Where *are* the chocolates?"

"My dear," said my sister, "I've been feeling for the wretched things ever since the light went out. Hasn't anybody got a match?"

Nobody had a match.

At length——

"They can't have been put on the table," said Jill. "I've——"

"Here they are," said Berry.

"Where?"

"Here. Give me your pretty white hand."

"This isn't them," said Jill. "They're in—— Oh, you brute! You've done it on purpose."

"I'm awfully sorry," said Berry. "I quite thought——"

"You liar!" said Jill heatedly. "You did it on purpose. You know you did. Daphne, he's gone and put my hand in the ginger."

"It'll wear off, dear," said Berry. "It'll wear off. By the time Piers is back, you'll hardly know. . . ."

The apologetic entry of Falcon with two inches of candle upon a plate cut short the prophecy.

As he solemnly set the brand in the centre of the table, the light returned with a flash. . . .

It was when the butler had placed the wine before Berry and was about to withdraw, that Daphne asked for the chocolates.

Falcon peered at the table.

"They were there, madam," he said.

Berry looked round uneasily.

"I think, perhaps," he began stooping to feel under his chair, "I think—I mean, fearing lest in the confusion. . . ."

He broke off, to stare at a small silver bowl which was as bare as his hand.

Daphne took a deep breath.

"And that was full," she said witheringly. "And you sat there and let us feel all over the table, and pretended you were looking, and put Jill's hand in the ginger, and all the time——"

"I never ate one," said Berry. "I never. . . ." He stopped short and looked round the room. "Nobby!"

The Sealyham emerged from beneath the table, wide-eyed, expectant.

Sternly my brother-in-law held out the bowl.

Never was guilt more plainly betrayed.

The pricked ears fell flat: the bright brown eyes sank to the floor: the pert white tail was lowered incontinently. Nobby had hauled down his flag.

"Oh, Nobby!"

The terrier squirmed, laid his head upon the ground, and then rolled over upon his back. . . .

"You can't blame the dog," said I. "Besides, he'll pay for it. Quarter of a pound of chocolates'll fairly——"

"I've just remembered," said Daphne, "that they weren't chocolates at all. They were *marrons glacés*—the last of the bunch. They won't make any more this year."

Berry wiped his forehead.

"Are you saying this," he demanded, "to torment me? Or is it true?"

"It's a C.B. fact."

"But what about tea?" screamed her husband. "Tea without a *marron glacé* will be like—like Hell without the Prince of Darkness."

"I can't help it. France has a close season for them."

Berry hid his face in his hands.

"Under my chair!" he wailed. "The last of the bunch (sic). And I never ate one!"

"Come, come," said I. "Similarly placed, what would Epicurus have done?"

"I know," said Adèle.

"What?" said Berry.

My wife smiled.

"He'd 've made tracks for Spain," she said.

\*     \*     \*     \*     \*

The French sergeant saluted, Daphne nodded, Berry said, "Down with everything", I touched my hat, and we rolled slowly over the little bridge out of one country into another.

Our reception was very serious.

So far as our papers were concerned, the Spanish N.C.O. knew his job and did it with a soldierly, if somewhat trying, precision. Pong was diligently compared with the tale of his *triptyque*. Our faces were respectively compared with the unflattering vignettes pasted upon our passports. The visas were deliberately inspected. Our certificates wer unfolded and scrutinised. Our travelling pass was digested. To our great relief, however, he let the luggage go. We had no contraband, but we were two hours late, and to displace and replace securely a trunk and a dressing-case upon the back of a coupé takes several minutes and necessitates considerable exertion of a very unpleasant kind. Finally, having purchased a local permit for five pesetas, we were suffered to proceed.

We were now at the mouth of a gorge and the pass was before us. Had the gorge been a rift in the range, a road had been cut by the side of the torrent, and our way, if tortuous, had been as flat as your hand. But the gorge was a *cul de sac*—a beautiful blind alley, with mountains' flanks for walls. So the road had been made to scale one side of the alley—to make its winding way as best it could, turning and twisting and doubling upon itself, up to a windy saddle which we could hardly see.

I gave the car its head, and we went at a wicked hill as a bull at a gate.

Almost immediately the scenery became superb.

With every yard the walls of the gorge were drawing further apart, slowly revealing themselves in all their glory. Forests and waterfalls, precipices and greenswards, grey lichened crags and sun-bathed terraces, up, above all, an exquisite vesture of snow, flawless and dazzling—these stood for beauty. All the wonder of height, the towering proportions of the place, the bewildering pitch of the sky—these stood for grandeur. An infinite serenity, an imperturbable peace, a silence which the faint gush of springs served to enrich—these stood for majesty. Nature has throne-rooms about the world, and this was one of them.

I started the engine again—for we had instinctively stopped—and Pong thrust on.

Up, up, up we toiled, through the hanging village of Valcarlos, past a long string of jingling mules, under stupendous porches of the living rock, round hair-pin bends, by woods and coppices, over grey bridges—wet and shining and all stuck with ferns—now looking forward to the snow-bound ridge, now facing back to find the frontier village shrunk to a white huddle of dots, the torrent to a winking thread of silver, and our late road to a slender straggling ribbon, absurdly foreign, ridiculously remote.

On we stormed, higher and higher, past boulders and poor trees wrung with the wind, and presently up and into and over the snow, while slowly, foot by foot, depth dragged height down to nothing.

For the third time it occurred to me that the engine was unwarrantably hot, and, after a moment's consideration, I took out the clutch and brought the car to a standstill.

"What is it?" said Daphne.

"She's hot," said I. "Hotter than she should be. At least, I think so. Of course it's a deuce of a pull." And, with that, I opened the door.

"You're not going to get out in this snow?"

"Only a second, dear."

Upon observing that the fan-belt was broken, it was natural that I should regret very much that I had not looked for the trouble when first I suspected its presence. Had I done so, I should have spared the engine, I should have been able to correct the disorder without burning myself to hell, and I should not have been standing, while I worked, in four inches of snow.

Gloomily I made my report.

"I'm sorry," I concluded, "but I shall have to have Berry. I've got a new strap in the boot, but I can't shift the luggage alone."

Berry closed his eyes and sank his chin upon his breast.

"Go on, old chap," said Daphne. "I'm very sorry for you, but——"

"I—I don't feel well," said Berry. "Besides, I haven't got my gum-boots."

"Will you get out?" said his wife.

At last, between us, we got him as far as the running board.

"Come on," I said impatiently.

"Don't rush me," said Berry, staring at the snow as if it were molten lead. "Don't rush me. How fresh and beautiful it looks, does not it?" He took a deep breath and let himself down upon his toes. "A-A-ah! If you can do sixty kilometres with a pound of snow in each shoe, how many miles is that to the gallon?"

The belt was at the very back of beyond, but I found it at last. As we replaced the luggage—

"And while," I said, "I'm fixing the strap, you might fill up the radiator."

"What with?" said Berry.

"Snow, of course. Just pick it up and shove it in."

" 'Just pick it up and sho——' Oh, give me strength," said Berry brokenly. Then he raised his voice. "Daphne!"

"What's the matter?"

"I've got to pick up some snow now."

"Well, rub your hands with it, dear—well. Then they won't get frost-bitten."

"You—er—you don't mind my picking it up, then? I mean, my left foot is already gangrenous."

"Well, rub that, too," called Daphne.

"Thanks." said Berry grimly. "I think I'd rather wait for the dogs. I expect there are some at Roncevaux. In the pictures they used to have a barrel of whisky round their necks. The great thing was to be found by about five dogs. Then you got five barrels. By the time the monks arrived, you were quite sorry to see them."

"Will you go and fill up the radiator?" said I, unlocking the tool box. . . .

The fitting of the new belt was a blasphemous business. My fingers were cold and clumsy, and everything I touched was red-hot. However, at last it was done.

As I was looking over the engine—

"We'd better pull up a bit," said Berry. "I've used all the snow round here. Just a few feet, you know. That drift over there'll last me a long time."

"What d'you mean?" said I. "Isn't it full yet?"

"Well, I thought it was just now, but it seems to go down. I've put in about a hundredweight to date."

An investigation of the phenomenon revealed the unpleasant truth that the radiator was leaking.

I explained this to Berry.

"I see," he said gravely. "I understand. In other words, for the last twenty minutes I have been at some pains to be introducing water into an inconveniently shaped sieve?"

"That," said I, "is the idea."

"And, for all the good I've been doing, I might have been trying to eat a lamb cutlet through a couple of straws?"

"Oh, no. You've cooled her down. In fact . . ."

It took five minutes and all the cajolery at my command to induce my brother-in-law to continue his Danaidean task, until I had started the engine and we were ready to move.

Then he whipped its cap on to the radiator and clambered into the car.

I was extremely uneasy, and said as much.

It was now a quarter to five. Pampeluna was some thirty miles away, and Heaven only knew what sort of country lay before us. We were nearly at the top of the pass, and, presumably, once we were over we should strike a lot of "down hill". But if the leak became worse, and there was much more collarwork. . . .

Desperately I put Pong along.

The snow was deeper now and was affecting the steering. The wheels, too, were slipping constantly. I had to go very gingerly. Two deep furrows ahead told of Ping's passage. I began to wonder how Adèle, Jill, and Jonah were getting on. . . .

It was when the snow was perhaps a foot deep that we snarled past a ruined cabin and, stumbling over the very top of the world, began to descend.

Ten minutes later we came to Roncevaux. Where Abbey began or village ended, it was impossible to say, and there was no one to be seen. The place looked like a toy some baby giant had carried into the mountains, played with awhile, and then forgotten.

Here was the last of the snow, so I crammed some more into the radiator, tried very hard to think I could see the water, and hoped for the best. While I was doing this, Berry had closed the car—a wise measure, for, though we should lose a lot of scenery, the sun was sinking and Evening was laying her fingers upon the fine fresh air.

Navarre seemed very handsome. It was, indeed, all mountains —bleaker, less intimate than France, but very, very grand. And the road was splendidly laid : its long clean sweeps, its graceful curves, the way in which its line befitted the bold landscape, yet was presenting a style of its own, argued a certain poetry in the hearts of its engineers.

We swept through a village that might have been plucked out of Macedonia, so rude and stricken it looked. There was no glass in the windows : filth littered the naked street : pigs and poultry rushed for the crazy doorways at our approach.

Pampeluna being the nearest town, I realised with a shock what sort of a night we should spend if we failed to get there.

I began to hope very hard that there were no more hills. Presently the road forked and we switched to the right. Maps and guide declared that this was the better way.

"What's *carretera accidentada* mean?" said my sister, looking up from the *Michelin Guide*.

"I think *carretera* means 'road,' " said I. "As for *accidentada* —well, it's got an ugly sound."

"Well, do look out," said Daphne. "We shall be there any minute. This must be Espinal, and that's where it begins."

Berry cleared his throat.

"The art of life," he announced, "is to be prepared. Should the car overturn and it become necessary to ply me with cordial, just part my lips and continue to pour until I say 'When'. Should—— What are you stopping for?"

"Very slightly to our rear," said I, "upon the right-hand side of the road stands a water-trough. You may have noticed it."

"I did," said Berry. "A particularly beautiful specimen of the palæolithic epoch. Shall we go on now?"

"Supposing," said I relentlessly, "you plied the radiator. Just take the cap off and continue to pour till I say 'When'."

"I should be charmed," was the reply. "Unfortunately I have no vessel wherewith to——"

"Here you are," said Daphne, thrusting a hotwater bottle into his hand. "What a mercy I forgot to pack it!"

As I lighted a cigarette—

"It is indeed," said I, "a godsend."

With an awful look, Berry received the godsend and emerged from the car.

After perhaps two minutes he reappeared.

"No good," he said shortly. "The water's too hard or something. The brute won't look at it."

"Nonsense," said Daphne.

"All right," said her husband. "You go and tempt it. I'm through, I am."

"Squeeze the air out of it and hold it under the spout."

"But I tell you——"

I took out my watch.

"In another half-hour," I said, "it'll be dark, and we've still forty kilometres——"

Heavily Berry disappeared.

When I next saw him he was filling the radiator from his hat. . . .

After six journeys he screwed on the cap and made a rush for the car.

"But where's my bottle?" screamed Daphne.

"I rejoice to say," replied Berry, slamming the door, "that full fathom five the beggar lies."

"You've never dropped——"

"If it's any consolation," said Berry, as I let in the clutch, "he perished in fair fight. The swine put about a bucket up each of my sleeves first, and then spat all over my head. Yes, it is funny, isn't it? Never mind. Game to the last, he went down regurgitating like a couple of bath-rooms. And now I really am flea-bitten. I can't feel anything except my trunk."

It was as well that we had taken in water, for very soon, to my dismay, we began to climb steadily. . . .

Once again we watered—Heaven knows how high up—at a hovel, half barn, half cottage, where a sturdy mother came lugging a great cauldron before we had named our need. In all conscience, this was obvious enough. The smell of fiery metal was frightening me to death.

Mercifully, that terrible ascent was the last.

As the day was dying, we dropped down a long, long hill, round two or three death-trap bends, and so, by gentle stages, on to a windy plain. . . .

It was half-past six when we ran into Pampeluna.

After paying an entrance fee, we proceeded to the Grand Hotel. It was intensely cold, and a wind cut like a knife. The streets were crowded, and we moved slowly, with the result that the eight urchins who decided to mount the running-boards did so without difficulty. The four upon my side watched Berry evict their fellows with all the gratification of the immune.

"Little brutes," said Daphne. "Round to the left, Boy. That's right. Straight on. Look at that one. He's holding on by the lamp. Boy, can't you—— Now to the right. . . . Here we are."

"Where?" said I, slowing up.

"Here. On the right. That must be it, with the big doors."

As I climbed out of the car, seven more boys alighted from the dickey, the wings, the luggage, and the spare wheels.

A second later I found myself in a bank.

The edifice appeared to be deserted, but after a moment or two an individual came shuffling out of the shadows. My inability to speak a word of Spanish and his inability to speak a word of any-thing else disfavoured an intelligent conservation, but at last I elicited first that the Grand Hotel was next door, and secondly that it would not be open until July.

I imparted this pleasing information to the others.

"Closed?" said Berry. "Well, that is nice. Yes. He's quite right. Here it is in the Guide. 'Open from July to October.' I suppose a superman might have put it more plainly, but it's a pretty broad hint. And now what shall we do? Three months is rather long to wait, especially as we haven't had any tea. Shall we force an entry? Or go on to Madrid?"

"Fool," said Daphne. "Get in, Boy. I'm getting hungry."

I got in and started the engine.

Then I got out again with a stick.

This the seven boys, who had remounted, were not expecting.

I got in again, feeling better. . . .

The second hotel we visited was admirably concealed.

As we were passing it for the second time, Jonah came stepping across the pavement.

"Lucky for you we got in early," he said. "We've got the last two rooms. They're on the fourth floor, they're miles apart, they're each about the size of a minute, and I don't think the beds are aired. The lift's out of order, there's no steam heat, and there are no fire-places. Both the bath-rooms have been let as bedrooms, and the garage is conveniently situated about a mile and a half away. The porter's cut his hand, so you'll have to carry up your luggage and help me with ours. Nobody speaks anything but Spanish, but that doesn't matter as much as it might, because the waiters have struck. And now look sharp, or we shan't get any dinner."

\*      \*      \*      \*      \*

Bearer will bring you to where we are. Don't talk. Don't do anything. Just get into the car.

JONAH.

I stared at the words stupidly.

Then I looked at the chauffeur standing, hat in hand, and step-ped into the depths of a luxurious limousine.

A moment later we were whipping over the cobbles.

It was nearly half-past seven, and I had just walked back from the garage where I had deposited Pong. Whether my instructions that the radiator was to be mended and the car to be washed had been understood and would be executed, I was almost too tired to care. I was also abominably cold. The prospect of an evening and night attended with every circumstance of discomfort was most depressing. For the fiftieth time I was wishing that we had never come.

And then at the door of the hotel I had been handed the message. . . .

There was a foot-warmer in the limousine and a voluminous fur-rug. I settled myself contentedly. What it all meant, I had not the faintest idea. Enough that I was comfortable and was beginning to grow warm. My faith, moreover, in Jonah was profound.

The car drew up with a rush before a mansion.

As I stepped out, the chauffeur removed his hat, and the front door was opened.

I passed up the steps into the grateful shelter of a tremendous hall.

At once my coat and hat were taken from me and I was reverently invited to ascend the huge staircase. I did so in silence. At the top of the flight a waiting-woman received me and led the way.

Everywhere luxury was in evidence. There were plenty of lights, but they were all heavily shaded. So thick were the carpets that I could hardly hear my own footfalls. The atmosphere was pleasantly warm and full of the sweet scent of burning wood. What furniture I saw was very handsome. Three exquisite stalls, filched from some old cathedral, stood for a settle. A magnificent bronze loomed in a recess. At the head of the stairs was glowing a great Canaletto.

I followed my guide wonderingly. . . .

A moment later she stopped to knock upon a door.

"Who is it?" cried Adèle.

I raised my voice, and she called to me to enter.

I opened the door into the finest bedroom that I have ever seen.

Upon the walls were panels of yellow silk, and all the silks and stuffs were grey or golden. A soft grey carpet, a deep sofa, a giant four-poster, a mighty press, a pier-glass, chairs, mirrors, table-lamps—all were in beautiful taste. An open door in one corner, admitting the flash of tiles, promised a bath-room. On the bed my dress-clothes, which I had packed for San Sebastian, lay orderly. And there, upon a chair, in front of a blazing fire, sat Adèle, lightly clothed, looking extraordinarily girlish, and cheerfully inveigling a stocking on to a small white foot.

I looked round dazedly.

"Isn't it priceless?" said Adèle. "Isn't it all priceless?" She danced across the room and flung her arms round my neck. "And I thought you were never coming. I wanted to wait for you, lad, but they wouldn't let me. But I've run a bath for you and put out all your clothes. By the way, I can't find your links anywhere. Are you sure——"

"No," I said, "I'm not. I'm not sure of anything. I'm not sure I'm awake. I'm not sure I'm alive. I'm not sure I'm not mad. 'Sure'? I don't know the meaning of the word. What are you doing here? What am I doing here? Where are we? What's it all mean?"

"My darling," said Adèle, "I've not the faintest idea."

"But——"

"Listen. You hadn't been gone five minutes before a man came into the hotel and up to Jonah. He seemed very nervous and excited, but he was very polite. He couldn't speak a word of anything but Spanish, but at last we gathered that he was asking us if we were the people who had wired to the Grand Hotel. When we said that we were, he talked faster than ever, and at last we began to understand that he'd got some rooms for us elsewhere. You can imagine our joy. Once we understood, he didn't have to ask us whether we'd come. The next minute two chauffeurs were slinging the baggage on to a couple of cars, and, after we'd managed to explain that you were coming back, Berry paid some sort of a bill and we all pushed off. When we saw this wonderful house, we nearly fainted. As far as I can see, we've got it all to ourselves. Berry and Daphne are in another room like this, about two doors away, and Jill's between us. I don't know where Jonah is. I can only imagine that the man who came is the manager of the Grand Hotel, and that this is where they put people when their own place is closed."

Unsatisfactory as it was, this seemed, roughly, the only possible explanation. Indeed, but for the magnificence of our lodging, it would have been reasonable enough. Still, we knew nothing of Spain. Perhaps this was their idea of hospitality. I began to like Pampeluna very much. . . .

By the time I had had a hot bath I had begun to wonder whether it was worth while going on to San Sebastian.

\* \* \* \* \*

We had dined in state. We had eaten an eight-course dinner, superbly cooked and admirably served. At the conclusion of our meal, folding doors had been opened, and we had passed into the shadowed comfort of a gorgeous library, where only the ceaseless flicker of a great log fire had lighted us to deep-cushioned chairs and a rich sofa, where coffee and liqueurs were set upon a low table and the broad flash of silver showed a massive cigar-box reposing conveniently upon an ebony stool.

With one consent, sitting at the feet of Epicurus, we had thrust uncertainty aside, and, thanking Heaven that we had fallen so magically upon our own, confined our conversation to the events of our journey, and compared enthusiastic notes regarding the wonders, entertainments, and perils of our drive.

From behind a big cigar Berry was slowly enumerating the accessories without which, to make life worth living, no car should ever take the road, when the door opened and a servant, bearing a salver, entered the room.

Stopping for an instant to switch on the light, the man stepped to my brother-in-law.

For a moment Berry glanced at the card. Then—

"English," he said. " 'Mr. Hubert Weston Hallilay, 44 Calle de Serrano, Madrid.' Better have him in, hadn't we?" He turned to the servant and nodded. "Ask him to come in," he said.

The servant bowed and withdrew.

A moment later a fair-haired boy, perhaps twenty-three years old, was ushered into the room.

He greeted us respectfully, but with an open-hearted delight which he made no attempt to conceal.

"How d'you do? I'm most awfully glad to see you. Officially, I'm here by request. The comic mayor got hold of me. He's worried to death because he can't converse with you. I don't suppose you mind, but it's shortening his life. I've had a fearful time with him. There are about a thousand things he wants to know and he's commissioned me to find them out without asking any questions. That, he says, would be most rude. Unofficially, I'm—well, I'm at your service. If I'd known you were coming, I'd have been here before. I'm attached to Madrid, really, but I'm putting in six weeks here—for my sins."

"You're very kind," said Berry. "Incidentally, you're a godsend —the second we've had to-day. The first, I may say, lies in five feet of water on a particularly blasted mountain-side. But don't be disconcerted. We shouldn't think of drowning you. For one thing, you're much too valuable. And now sit down, and have some cold coffee and a glass of kümmel."

As he sank into a seat—

"Mr. Hallilay," said Daphne, twittering, "I can't bear it. *Why are we here?*"

The boy looked at her curiously. Then—

"Well," he said, "there was no other place. Even if the Grand had been open, I gather it's hardly fit. . . . Of course there's been the most awful mix-up. Trust Spain for that. The Post Office knew they couldn't deliver the wire. Instead of telling somebody, or communicating with Pau, they let it lie in the office till this afternoon. Then they took it to the mayor. Of course he nearly died. But, being a man of action, he got a move on. He flew round here and laid the facts before the steward—the owner happens to be away—and arranged to put this house at your disposal. Then he rushed round, borrowed a couple of cars, and spent what time he had left splitting his brain over your wire and hovering between the station and the various approaches to Pampeluna. As an inevitable result, he missed you, and when he finally had the brain-wave of inquiring at the Grand and found you'd already arrived, he nearly shot himself."

"But why—I mean," I stammered, "it's devilish good of the mayor and you and everyone, but why—in the first place, why did the Post Office take the wire to the mayor?"

Hallilay raised his eyebrows.

"Well," he said slowly, "when they saw the telegram, they realised——"

"Who sent the wire?" said Berry.

"I did," said Jonah. "I said,

Retenez lundi soir, deux grandes deux petites chambres avec salle de bain en suite, arrive en auto.    Mansel."

For a moment I thought the boy was going to faint. Then he covered his face and began to shake with laughter. . . .

Presently he plucked a form from his pocket, unfolded it, and handed it to me.

"That may have been what you sent," he said jerkily, "but here's how the wire arrived."

Retenez lundi soir, deux grandes deux petites chambres avec salle de bain, suite arrive en auto.    Manoel.

After I had read it aloud there was a long, long silence.

At length—

"I see," said Berry. "I knew our journey would be eventful, because my wife put her teeth in upside down this morning, but I little dreamed it was to be a royal progress. However. I take it one of the things the mayor would like to know is—er—what has become of—of——"

Hallilay nodded tearfully.

"That, sir," he said, "is the first and foremost question upon an unanswerable list."

\* \* \* \* \*

We left Pampeluna upon the following afternoon, in response to a wire from San Sebastian peremptorily desiring us immediately to repair to that resort.

Hallilay, as good as his word, was of inestimable service. He had, indeed, dealt with the delicate situation with admirable judgment. Finally he covered our retreat in a masterly manner.

From the first he had insisted that the *rôle* we had unconsciously assumed must be deliberately maintained. Our scruples he had brushed to one side.

"Whatever happens, Pampeluna must never know the truth. It'd be most unpleasant for you—obviously. For the mayor—well, Spaniards are very proud, and I think it'd kill him. Very well, then. Your course, plainly, is the line of least resistance. O friends, Romans, countrymen, it's—it's too easy." He broke off and glanced meaningly about him. "I'm not much of a diplomat, but —well, the best is good enough for me."

Talk about Epicurus. . . .

CHAPTER VIII

## *How Adèle Bought a Bottle of Perfume which had No Smell, and I Cut Eulalie Dead*

"I must have a paper," said Berry. "I haven't read the news for fifty-five hours, and—and anything may have happened. Supposing the rouble and the shilling have changed over. The tie I'm wearing 'ld be worth about six hundred pounds."

I set down my cup and picked up the receiver.

"So you're really off to-morrow, are you?" said an attractive voice. "Well, don't miss Fuenterrabia. It's only five miles out of your way, and it's worth seeing. They sell most lovely scent in the Calle del Puerto. Ask for their 'Red Violets'."

With a chunk I was disconnected, and a second later a bureau clerk had promised to procure an English paper and send it up to my room.

Less than an hour ago we had arrived at San Sebastian—according to plan. A very handsome run had ended becomingly enough in the drive of a palatial hotel, and, though it was growing dusk as we had slipped into the town, we had seen quite enough of our surroundings to appreciate that, where Nature had succeeded so admirably, man had by no means failed.

And now we were taking tea in my sister's bedroom and discussing what Berry called "the order of going in".

"We'd better decide right away," said my brother-in-law, "to stay here a week. It's perfectly obvious that two nights are going to be no earthly."

"All you're thinking of," said Daphne, "is the Casino. I knew it would be like this."

"All right," replied her husband, "look at the guide-book. We haven't seen this place yet, and there are twelve excursions—all highly recommended. We can cut out Tolosa, because I see we did that this afternoon. That was where the child lobbed the jam-tin into the car. I fancy I passed the cathedral when I was chasing him. Any way, I shall say so."

"I am told," said I, "that Fuenterrabia's worth seeing."

"It's the show place about here," said Jonah. "Old as the hills. That'll take a morning alone."

I yawned.

"There's a shop there," I said, "in the Calle del Puerto, where they sell some wonderful scent. I believe it's all good, but their 'Red Violets' is simply ravishing."

The girls pricked up their ears.

"Who told you all this?" said Adèle.

"I can't imagine," said I truthfully. "But she had a nice voice. You know—one of those soft mellifluous ones, suggesting that she's bored to distraction with everything except you." I took out a cigarette and looked about me. "Anyone got a match?" I added.

"Blow the matches," said my sister. "When did all this happen?"

"This afternoon," said I. "I'd always heard that San Sebastian——"

"Is she staying here?" said Adèle.

"In the hotel? She didn't say."

"But how did you come to speak to her?" demanded my wife.

"I didn't," I said. "She spoke to me. I tell you I've always heard that San——"

"And you communed with her?" said Berry. "With your lawful wife working herself to death on the first floor unpacking your sponge-bag, you exchanged secrets of the toilet with a honey-toned vamp? Oh, you vicious libertine. . . . Will she be at the Casino to-night?"

"I didn't ask her."

Berry raised his eyes to heaven.

"You don't know her name; you never asked where she's staying, and you've fixed nothing up." He sighed heavily. "Some people don't deserve to get on."

"I hadn't time," I pleaded. "We got on to scent almost at once."

"Why scent?" said Jonah. "Or is that an indiscreet question?"

"Oh, that's easy," said Berry. "The scent was on the handkerchief he picked up. It's been done before."

"I don't understand," said Jill.

"I'm glad you don't, darling. One expert in the family is bad enough." He nodded at me. "I used to think I was useful, till I'd seen that Mormon at work. Talk about getting off. . . . Why, he'd click at a jumble sale."

"Would he really?" said Adèle interestedly. "I'd no idea he was so enterprising."

Berry shrugged his shoulders.

"My dear," he said, "he's a blinkin' marvel. Where you and I 'ld be standing outside a stage-door with a nervous grin and a bag of jujubes, he'd walk straight up to a Marchioness, say, 'I feel I must tell you that you've got a mouth in a million', and —*get away with it*. But there you are. In the present case——"

"—for once in a way," said Adèle, "the lady seems to have made the running." She turned to me with a smile. "Well, Juan me lad, tell us some more about her. Was she fair or dark?"

I nodded at Berry.

"Better ask him," I said. "He knows more about it than I do."

"She was dark," said Berry unhesitatingly. "A tall willowy wench, with Continental eyes and an everlasting pout. Am I right, sir?"

"You may be," said I. "Not having seen the damsel. . . ."

There was an outburst of incredulous objection.

"Sorry," I added, "but the liaison was conducted upon the telephone. Just now. When I ordered the paper. The lady had no idea she was giving me counsel. So, you see, we're both blameless. And now may I have a match"

"Well, I am disappointed," announced Adèle. "I quite thought we were off."

"So did I," said Daphne. "And you never even——Oh, it's spoiled my tea."

Even Jill protested that I had "led them on".

In some dudgeon, I began to wonder if I should ever understand women.

\*     \*     \*     \*     \*

An hour and a half had slipped by.

Ready for dinner with twenty minutes to spare, I had descended to the lounge. There a large writing-table had suggested the propriety of sending a postcard to the sweetest of aunts, who, in the absence of evidence to the contrary, invariably presumed our death after fourteen days.

There being no postcards available, I started a letter. . . .

For a page and a half my pen ran easily enough, and then, for no reason whatever, my epistolary sense faltered, laboured, and ceased to function.

I re-read what I had written, touched up the punctuation, and fingered my chin. I reviewed the past, I contemplated the future, I regarded my finger-nails—all to no effect. There was simply nothing to say. Finally I rose and went in search of a waiter. There was, I felt, a chance that a Martini might stimulate my brain. . . .

I returned to my seat to find that, while I had been gone, a heifer from another herd had come to drink at the pool.

Immediately upon the opposite side of the writing-table sat one of the prettiest women that I have ever seen. Her colouring was superb. Beneath a snow-white skin all the wild beauty of a mountain-rose glowed in her cheeks; each time she moved, a flashing mystery of red and golden lights blazed from the auburn crown piled on her head; stars danced an invitation in the great grey eyes. Her small straight nose, the exquisite line of her face, her fairy mouth alone would have redeemed the meanest countenance. A plain black velvet dress, cut rather high at the throat, but leaving her lovely arms bare from the shoulder, and a complete absence of jewellery, showed that my lady knew how pictures should be framed. . . .

With an effort I bent to my letter. From being difficult, however, the composition of another two pages of coherent prose had
become formidable. Turning to the past, I could remember nothing. Looking into the future, I found myself blind. As for the
present, I felt instinctively that a description of the curve of my
*vis-à-vis'* mouth would be out of place and might be misunder-
stood.

I observed suddenly that my lady had stopped writing.

After a moment she read over what she had written and put in
two commas. Then she put a dash at the end of her last sentence.
Such an addition had not occurred to me. For what it was worth,
I adopted it surreptitiously. When I looked up, the tips of four
pointed fingers were being regarded with some severity. Finally
the girl laid down her pen, and, propping her chin on two ridiculous fists, stared dismally upon the neutral zone between our
respective blotting pads.

"Have you dealt with the weather?" said I.

The stars, which had stopped dancing, leaped again into life.

"Fully," she said.

"And the place?"

She nodded.

"And the people staying in the hotel?"

"I've just said they're all very dull."

I wrote rapidly. Then—

" 'The people here,' " I read, " 'are nearly all very dull.' "

For a moment she looked at me. Then she picked up her pen.

"How," she demanded, with a dazzling smile, "do you spell
'nearly'?"

"Only one 'r'," I replied. "Same as 'adorable.' "

"Nearly" went down—rather shakily.

I pulled up my cuffs.

" 'Spanish furniture,' " I said, following my pen, " 'is like the
Spanish—on the large side. Everything is too big.' "

" '—too big'," said my lady, with her head on one side. "You
see, my confidence in you is supreme."

"One moment," said I. "There's only one 'w' in 'sweet', isn't
there?"

"Yes," she said, bubbling. "Same as 'awful'."

I cleared my throat.

" 'The table, for instance,' " I continued, " 'at which we—I am
writing, is simply huge. If it were only half as wide, it would be
much more—er—convenient.' "

The two white shoulders began to shake with laughter.

I thought very swiftly. Then—

"New paragraph," I said.

"Half a page more," breathed my companion.

I frowned.

" 'They have,' " I announced, " 'quite a good Casino here.' "

Our two pens recorded the statement.

" 'The great thing to do is to go there after dinner.' "

The custom was reported in duplicate.

" 'But I'm not going to-night,' " said the girl, " 'because——' "

"But——"

" '——I've got to do my packing.' "

I groaned. Then—

" 'But I shan't go to-night,' " I declared, " 'because I'm going to help a friend pack.' " I looked up cheerfully. "Yes?"

" 'I shall look forward,' " she said, smiling, " 'to seeing you again—some time.' "

" 'Soon.' "

The pretty head went to one side.

" 'With my love,' " she said quietly.

" 'Your devoted servant,' " said I.

For a second my lady hesitated. Then she signed a name, crammed her letter into an envelope, and rose to her feet.

The stars in the wonderful eyes had become misty, and there was a strange wistful curve to the exquisite lips.

For an instant we looked at one another. Then—

"Just 'Eulalie'," she said.

The next moment she was gone.

I turned to see Daphne, Adèle, and Berry a dozen paces away....

I advanced with what composure I could summon.

"I have been endeavouring," I said, "to atone for this afternoon."

There was a frosty silence. Then—

"So I see," said my sister icily.

Berry passed a hand across his eyes.

"Ugh!" he said shuddering. "I've gone all goosegogs—I mean, gooseflesh. Will she be at the Casino to-night?"

My wife set a hand upon my arm.

"I must admit," she said, smiling, "that she had a mouth in a million."

\*    \*    \*    \*    \*

By half-past ten the next morning we were again upon the road.

The almanack swore it was March, but here was a summer's day. Not a cloud was floating in the great blue sky : down to the tenderest breeze, the winds were sleeping : the sun was in all his glory. For earth herself, the stains of winter were being done away. Out of the country's coat the greys and browns, lately so prominent, were fading notably. As thick as fast, the green was coming in. As we rounded a bend and sailed down a long sweet hill towards the frontier, the road was all dappled with the shadows of youngster leaves.

Our way seemed popular. Car after car swept by, waggons and lorries went rumbling about their business, now and again two of the Guardia Civil—well-horsed, conspicuously armed and point-device in their accoutrements—sat stiff, silent, and vigilant in the mouth of an odd by-road.

Come to the skirts of Irun we switched to the left, and five minutes later we were at Fuenterrabia.

A city with a main street some four yards wide, keeping a king's palace, if hatchments be evidence, remembering more dukes than shopkeepers, its house-walls upholding a haphazard host of balconies and overhung with monstrous eaves—a pocket stronghold, set on the lip of Spain, staring at sea and land, each sunlit rood of which is fat with History—a lovely star upon the breast of Fame, chosen by English poets to enrich their songs, Fuenterrabia is among the crown jewels of Europe.

We thrust up the Calle Mayor and into the Plaza de Armas. There we put the cars in the shade and alighted eagerly to view the town at close quarters.

"Look at that little boy," cried Jill, "eating an apple. Where's the camera? Get him to stand in the sun, Boy, against that old wall."

"That's right," said Berry. "And there's a dog scratching himself. Ask him to devil his tenants beside the Post Office. If we get a good picture, we can call it *Local Affection, or The Old, Old Story* and send it to *The Field*."

To humour my cousin's whim, I approached a dirty-looking child. . . .

Despite my assurances of good-will, however, the urchin retired as I advanced, all the time consuming his apples with a nervous energy, which suggested at once a conviction that I had my eye upon his fruit and a determination to confound my strategy. The apple was dwindling fast, and, redoubling my protests, I quickened my pace. For a second the boy hesitated. Then he took two last devastating bites, flung the core in my face, and took to his heels.

Pursuit being out of the question, I returned furiously to the others, to find them, as was to be expected, quite weak with laughter.

"It w-was good of you, Boy," declared Jill, tearfully. "And I got such a precious picture—just as he threw it."

"I suppose you know," I said stiffly, "that he hit me upon the nose."

"There must," said Berry, "have been some misunderstanding. The Spaniard's courtesy is proverbial. You're sure you weren't rude to him, brother?"

"Certain," said I grimly.

"Dear, dear," said my brother-in-law, opening a guide-book. "It's most mysterious. Just listen to this. *The stranger is at first to be carried away by the obliging tone of society, by the charming spontaneity of manner, and by the somewhat exaggerated politeness of the people he meets.* There now. Were you carried away at all? I mean, if you were——"

" I was not," said I.

Berry returned to the book.

"*He should return these civilities in kind, but he should avoid turning the conversation on serious matters, and should, above all, refrain from expressing an opinion on religious or political questions.* I do hope you didn't. . . ."

I shook my head.

"Then," said Berry, "should we meet the child again, I shall cut him dead. And that's that. And now let's go and find a dairy. You'll be wanting a pick-me-up."

For an hour and a half we went about the city.

We marked her bulwarks, we told her towers, we observed her mansions, we strolled upon her terraces, we enjoyed her prospects.

Last of all, we visited the Calle del Puerto.

Before we had taken a dozen paces along the aged alley, a faint odour of perfume began to assert itself, and a few seconds later we were standing before a tiny shop, scrupulously sweet and clean to look upon, absurdly suggestive of the patronage of marionettes. A curtain of apple-green canvas was swaying in the low doorway, while an awning of the same stuff guarded a peepshow window, which was barely three feet long and less than one foot high. Herein, ranged behind a slab of fine plate-glass, stood three plain, stoppered phials, one rose-coloured, one green, and one a faint yellow. Below, on a grey silk pillow, was set a small vellum-bound book. This was open. In capitals of gold upon the pages displayed were two words only—PARFUMS FRANÇAIS.

The effect was charming.

We gathered about the window, ejaculating surprise.

"*Urbs in rure,*" said Jonah. "And then you're wrong. The rue de la Paix isn't in it."

Which is a description I cannot better.

Daphne lifted the *portière*, and we followed her in.

Passing suddenly out of the brilliant sunshine, we could at first see nothing. Then gradually the interior of the shop took shape.

There was no counter, but an oblong mahogany glass-topped table, standing in the centre of the polished floor, evidently was discharging that office. Upon this stood three other phials, similar to those displayed in the window, but fitted with sprays instead of stoppers. In front of each a grey gold-lettered slip of silk, laid between the glass and the mahogany, declared its contents—ROSE BLEUE . . . LYS NOIR . . . JASMIN GRIS.

The room was very low, and the walls were panelled. Upon these, except for that framing the door and window, were rows of shelves. On these, at decent intervals, stood phials of four different sizes. To judge from the colour of their glass, each wall was devoted to one of the three scents. That facing us was green, that on our left rose-coloured, that upon our right a faint yellow. A black curtain in a corner suggested a doorway leading to another part of the house. The air, naturally enough, was full of perfume.

We stared about us in silence.

After waiting perhaps five minutes, peering unsuccessfully behind the curtain, raising our voices in talk, and finally rapping upon the table without attracting attendance, we decided to return to where we had left the cars and visit the shop again on our way out of the town.

As we came to the Plaza, the clock of the great church announced the hour. A quarter to one.

"Good Heavens!" cried Daphne, checking the time by her wrist-watch. "I'd no idea it was so late. And I left word for Evelyn to ring me up at the hotel at one o'clock." We made a rush for the cars. "Can it be done, Jonah?"

"Only by air," said my cousin. "Outside a track, thirteen miles in fourteen minutes is just a shade too thick. Still, there's nothing the matter with the road after Irun, and Evelyn may be delayed getting through."

He swung himself into Ping and started her up. My sister and Jill scrambled aboard while he was turning her round. As he headed for the Calle Mayor—

"Stop!" shrieked his sister. "The scent, Jonah, the scent. We've got to go back."

Jonah threw out the clutch.

"We'll get that!" cried Adèle. "You go on, and we'll follow."

"Right."

The next moment Ping had dropped out of sight.

It was perhaps five minutes later that, after conjuring Berry to stay where he was and move the car for nobody, I assisted my wife on to the pavement.

When Fuenterrabia was planned, an eleven-feet-six wheel-base was not considered. To wheedle Pong to the mouth of the Calle del Puerto had been a ticklish business, and I had berthed her deliberately with an eye to our departure for the city gate, rather than to the convenience of such other vehicles as might appear. Besides, for my brother-in-law to have essayed manœuvres in such surroundings would have been asking for trouble.

As Adèle and I hastened along the street—

"We must look sharp," I insisted. "She's half across the fairway. If anybody with anything broader than a mule feels they can't wait, there'll be murder done."

We came to the shop, panting. . . .

The place was just as we had left it, and—there was no one there.

I looked round impatiently.

"What on earth," I began, "is the good of a——"

As I spoke, the curtain in the corner was pushed to one side, and a French girl entered the room.

Her manner was most curious.

For a moment she hesitated, as though she would turn and fly. Then, with her eyes upon Adèle, she moved slowly forward. She seemed to be making an effort to come and serve us. That she was most apprehensive was perfectly plain. . . .

Half-way between curtain and table she stopped. Then she put a hand to her throat.

"*Madame* desires something?"

"Some scent please," said Adèle reassuringly.

Her cheerful tone appeared to encourage the girl. And when my wife pointed to the green phial and asked to be sprayed with its contents, I could have sworn her attitude was that of relief.

In a flash she had produced a small square of linen. This she handed to Adèle.

"Smell, *Madame*. See, it is scentless. *Pardon*." She sprayed it with scent. "*Voilà*. That is the 'Black Lily'."

Adèle passed it to me. The scent was exquisite.

"It's delicious," said Adèle.

"Yes, *Madame*, it is good. Will *Madame* sample the others?"

"If you please."

Fresh squares of linen were produced, offered for inspection, and sprayed. . . .

Each perfume seemed more ravishing than its predecessor. To test the worth of this impression, we reverted to the 'Black Lily'. One breath of this satisfied us that it was the best of the lot. To be quite sure, we smelt the 'Blue Rose', and were instantly convinced of its superiority to its fellows. A return to the 'Grey Jasmine' persuaded us that there was only one scent in the shop. It was, indeed, impossible to award the palm. Each perfume had some irresistible virtue which the others lacked.

When, at last, Adèle implored me to help her to a decision, I spoke to the point.

"There's only one thing to do. We can't wait now, so have a big bottle of each. Then you and Jill and Daphne can fight it out at home."

Adèle asked the price of the scents.

"They are all the same price, *Madame*. The large bottle, one hundred *pesetas*—the others, seventy, fifty, and thirty, according to size."

"Very well. I'll take a large bottle of each."

"Thank you, *Madame*."

A prolonged and vicious croak from the end of the street argued that Berry's patience was wearing thin, but to have asked the girl to make haste would have been supererogatory.

In a trice three phials had been taken down from their shelves, and three stout silk-lined cases, of the pattern of safety-match boxes, had been produced. The phial went into its tray, the tray into its sheath, the case complete into a sheet of rough grey paper, and the whole was girt with cord in next to no time.

As the last knot was being tied Adèle touched me upon the arm.

"I almost forgot," she said. Then she turned to the girl. "I have been told to ask for your 'Red Violets'."

The scissors the girl was using fell to the floor. As she recovered them—

"Certainly, *Madame*," she whispered, laying a trembling hand upon the curtain behind.

She disappeared, to reappear almost immediately with a package precisely similar to those she had just made up. She placed it with the others.

"Oh," said Adèle, "but you haven't——"

A perfect hurricane of croaks, mingled with cries of anger, interrupted her.

"Never mind," I cried, gathering up the parcels. "How much is it now? Four hundred, I suppose."

As I was counting the notes, a yell of anguish in Berry's unmistakable accents fell upon my ears.

I threw the money upon the table and bolted out of the shop with Adèle at my heels. . . .

As we came to the corner, I ran full tilt into—Eulalie. For an instant our eyes met, but she looked away pointedly, slipped to one side, and passed on. . . .

Then—

"*Obstàculos* to you, sir!" roared Berry. "Look at my wing. . . . Yes, I see the cabriolet. But what of that? It's perfectly happy. . . . No, it *didn't* want to get by. And if it had—— Oh, go and push yourself off somewhere." Here he caught sight of me. "See what this greasy pantaloon's done? I told him he hadn't room, but he wouldn't wait. And now he's shoving it on to that cabriolet. . . . Oh, why can't I speak Spanish? I'd give him earache."

I thrust our packages into the fold of the hood and ran to examine the wing. Happily the damage was slight. I announced this relievedly.

"I daresay it is," raged Berry, as we resumed our seats. "What I object to is the poisonous hostility of the brute. He blinkin' well meant to do it."

"Dear, dear," said Adèle, bubbling. "There must have been some misunderstanding. The Spaniard's courtesy is proverbial."

"Exactly," said I. "The stranger is at first apt to be carried away by the exaggerated politeness of the——"

"You may be," said Berry, "as blasphemous as you like, but, for the love of the home for little children, let's get out of this town."

I let in the clutch. . . .

We were passing out of the beautiful armoried gateway, when an approaching peasant signalled to us to stop, and pointed excitedly back the way we had come. The fellow's manner suggested that we had dropped something.

I pulled up the car, opened my door, and jumped out.

As I did so, a breathless Eulalie appeared upon the other side of the car.

"I never thought I should catch you," she said uncertainly. "My car got mixed up with that waggon, so I chanced it and ran. And, now I'm here, I hardly know how to tell you. . . ." She addressed herself to Adèle. "But I fancy you've got my scent—'Red Violets'. It's rather—rather special. They only make it by request. And a friend of mine had ordered a bottle for me. It was put ready for me to call for, and, as far as I can make out, they've given it to you by mistake. I'm—I'm afraid I'm asking an awful lot, but might I have it? I'm leaving Spain altogether in half an hour, so I shan't have another chance."

I never remember feeling so utterly disillusioned. Recalling the telephone conversation of the day before, I was frankly disgusted. Such sharp practice as this smacked of a bargain sale.

The scent was ours. We had bought it fairly. Besides, it had *not* been reserved. If either Adèle or Eulalie had to go empty away, Law and Equity alike were pronouncing in favour of my wife.

Adèle was speaking.

"Oh, certainly. Boy, will you . . .?" I stepped into the car and thrust a hand into the fold of the hood. "I shall know which it is. The paper it's wrapped in is different. There's a line running through it, and the others were plain." I plucked out a case and gave it to her to examine. "That's right." Gravely she handed it to Eulalie. "I'm sorry you had to run so," she added gently.

The other shrugged her shoulders.

"I caught you," she said simply, "and that's the great thing." She glanced over her shoulder. "And here comes my car. I'm really most awfully grateful. . . ."

With a swish the cabriolet swept alongside, skidded with locked wheels upon the pavement, and fetched up anyhow with its bonnet across our bows. It was a piece of driving for which the chauffeur ought to have been flogged.

". . . most awfully grateful," repeated Eulalie, swinging the case by its cord. "You—you might have made it much harder. . . ."

The next moment she was in the cabriolet. . . .

Dazedly I watched the latter float out of sight.

"B-but she hasn't paid," I stammered. "She's never given us the money. Four pounds that bottle cost. . . ."

We stared at one another in dismay.

At length—

"Stung," said Berry. "But what a beautiful bit of work! Four pounds' worth of scent for the asking. No unpleasantness, no sleight of hand, no nothing. Just a glad eye last night and a two-minute run this morning. I don't wonder she was grateful."

\*     \*     \*     \*     \*

We had spent the afternoon traversing San Sebastian, and had found the place good—so good, in fact, that it was past six before we returned to the hotel.

I followed Adèle upstairs rather wearily.

"I shall never get over this morning," I said. "Never." Arrived at our door, I fitted the key to the lock. "To think that I stood there and let you hand—— Oh, blast! We've left the scent in the car."

"So we have," said Adèle. "What an awful nuisance! I knew we should. It's fatal to put anything in that hood. You don't see it."

I pushed open the door.

"As soon as I've changed," I said, switching on the light. "I'll go and——"

The sentence was never finished.

Had I been told that a cyclone had struck our bedroom, I should not have been surprised.

Adèle and I stood staring at such a state of disorder as I had never dreamed of.

The bed had been dragged from the wall, and its clothes distributed about the room; the wardrobe and cupboards stood open : every drawer in the room was on the floor : our clothing had been flung, like soiled linen, into corners : my wife's dressing-case had been forced, and now lay open, face downward, upon the carpet, while its contents sprawled upon a mattress : a chair had fallen backwards into the empty cabin-trunk, and the edge of a sheet had caught on one of its upturned legs. . . .

"Adèle! Boy!" The swish of a skirt, and there was my sister behind us. "Our room's been—— Good Heavens, yours is the same! Whatever's the meaning of it?"

Within three minutes two managers and three clerks were on the scene. To do them justice, they were genuinely perturbed. Fresh rooms—a magnificent suite—were put at our disposal : under our own eyes our belongings were gathered into sheets and carried to our new quarters : maids were summoned and placed at the girls' service : valets were sent for : the dressing-case was sent to be repaired : we were begged at our convenience to report whether there were any valuables we could not find, and over and over again we were assured that the management would not rest until the thieves were taken : jointly and severally we were offered profound apologies for so abominable an outrage.

Berry and Jonah, who had been taking the cars to the garage, arrived in the midst of the removal.

Upon the circumstances being laid before my brother-in-law, he seemed for some time to be deprived of the power of speech, and it was only upon being shown the contents of a sheet which had just been conveyed by two valets into his wife's bedroom that he at last gave tongue.

Drawing a pair of dress trousers from beneath a bath towel, a pair of brogues, and a box of chocolates, he sobbed aloud.

"You all," he said brokenly, "do know these trousers : I remember the first time ever I put them on; 'twas on a summer's evening, in the Park. . . ."

With one accord and some asperity my sister and I requested him to desist.

"All right," he said. "But why worry? I know there's nothing valuable gone, because in that case I should have been told long ago. We've been shocked and inconvenienced, of course; but, to balance it, we've got a topping suite, a private sitting-room thrown in, and a whole fleet of bottle-washers in attendance, all stamping to wash and iron and brush our clothes as they've never been brushed before. Jonah's and Jill's rooms all right?"

"Yes."

"Well, let them move along, any way. Then we shall all be together. And now, if we've got any sense, we shall let this sympathetic crowd straighten up everything—they're simply bursting for the word 'Go !'—and gather round the fire, which I see they've lighted, and talk about something else."

This was sound advice.

A close acquaintance with crime—the feeling that a robber has handled her personal effects, mauled her apparel, trodden her own sanctuary—is bound to jangle a sensitive woman's nerves. The less the girls thought upon the matter, the better for them. . . .

Orders were given, a sofa was drawn towards the hearth, Jonah went to seek some champagne, and I slipped on a coat and left the hotel for the garage.

When I returned some twenty minutes later, Adèle had discovered a piano and was playing "Whispering", while the others were dancing with as much freedom from care as they might have displayed at a night-club.

When I laid the scent on the table, the dance died, and Daphne, Adèle, and Jill crowded about me.

"One for each of you," I said. "With my love. But wait one moment." I turned to Adèle. "How did you tell the 'Red Violets' from the others?"

"It's paper had a line——"

I pointed to the three parcels.

"So have they all," I said. "It depends on the way the light strikes it. One moment you see it, and the next you can't.

My wife examined the packages in turn.

"You're perfectly right," she said. Then, "Good Heavens!" she cried. "Perhaps I gave that woman the wrong one, after all."

I shrugged my shoulders.

"I don't suppose she cared. What's in a name? They're each of them worth four pounds."

"That's true," said Adèle musingly. "Still. . . ."

We opened them one by one.

The first was the Black Lily.

Then came the Grey Jasmine.

I ripped the paper off the third case and laid it upon the table. With my fingers about the cardboard, I paused.

"And what," said I, "is the betting?"

"Blue Rose," cried Jill.

"Red Violets," said Adèle.

I opened the case.

They were both wrong.

The tray contained no perfume at all.

Crammed into the form of a scent-bottle was a dirty huddle of wash-leather.

I lifted it out between my finger and thumb.

The diamond and emerald necklace which lay beneath must have been worth a quarter of a million.

\*     \*     \*     \*     \*

"Yes," said the British Vice-Consul, some two hours later, "this little seaside town is a sort of Thieves' Parlour. Four-fifths of the stuff that's stolen in Spain goes out of the country this way. As in the present case, the actual thief daren't try to cross the frontier, but he's always got an accomplice waiting at San Sebastian. We know the thieves all right—at least, the police do, but the accomplices are the devil. Often enough, they go no further than Biarritz,

and there are so many of the Smart Set constantly floating between the two towns that they're frightfully hard to spot. In fact,
about the only chance is to trace their connection with the thief.
What I mean is this. A's got the jewels and he's got to pass them to
B. That necessitates some kind of common denominator. Either
they've got to meet or they've got to visit—at different times, of
course—the same bureau. . . .

"Well, there you are.

"By the merest accident you stumbled upon the actual communication of the password by A to B. The voice you heard upon
the telephone was that of the original thief, or of his representative.
This morning you visited the actual bureau. I know the place well.
My wife's bought scent there. It's always been a bit of a mystery,
but I never suspected this. I've not the slightest doubt it's been
used as a bureau for years. Well, in all innocence you gave the
password, and in all innocence received the gems. B arrives too
late, finds that you have them, and starts in pursuit. I've no doubt
she really ran on to see which way you'd gone. She couldn't have
hoped to catch you on foot. Of course, she couldn't understand
how you'd come by the password, but the few words you'd had
with her the night before made her *suspect your innocence*. Still,
she wasn't sure, and that's why her chauffeur fetched up across
your bows."

"You don't mean——"

"I do indeed. If you hadn't handed them over, they'd have been
taken by force. . . .

"Well, finding that either by accident or design she's been sold
a pup, B communicates with the gang, and, while you're out, your
rooms are ransacked."

"And I walked," I said, "after dark from the Calle de Miracruz
to this hotel with the baubles under my arm."

The Vice-Consul laughed.

"The armour of ignorance," he said, "will sometimes turn the
keenest wits. The confidence it gives its wearer is proverbial."

"But why," said Adèle, "was the shop-girl so terribly nervous?
I mean, if she's used to this sort of traffic. . . ."

The Vice-Consul fingered his chin.

Then he picked up the jewels.

"Perhaps," he said slowly, "perhaps she knew where they came
from."

"Where was that?" said Daphne.

The Vice-Consul frowned.

"When I last saw them," he said, "they were in the Royal Treasury."

*   *   *   *   *

At half-past ten the next morning I was walking upon the golf links of St. Jean-de-Luz.

I was not there of choice.

Two very eminent detectives—one French and one Spanish—were upon either side of me.

We were close to the seventh green, when the Frenchman touched me upon the arm.

"Look, sir," he said, pointing. "There is a golf party coming. They are making, no doubt, for this spot. When they arrive, pray approach and look at them. If you should recognise anyone, I beg that you will take off your hat."

He bowed, and a moment later I was alone.

I sat down on the turf and took out a cigarette. . . .

With a plop, a golf ball alighted upon the green, trickled a few feet, and stopped a yard from the hole. Presently, another followed it, rolled across the turf, and struggled into the rough.

I got upon my feet and strolled towards the green. . . .

It was a mixed foursome.

In a cherry-coloured jumper and a white skirt, Eulalie looked prettier than ever.

She saw me at once, of course, but she took no notice.

Her companions glanced at me curiously.

Putter in hand, Eulalie walked to her ball—the far one—and turned her back to me. After a little consideration, she holed out.

It was a match shot, and her companions applauded vigorously.

Eulalie just smiled.

"I'm always better," she said, "when I've something at stake."

"And what," said her partner, a large blue-eyed Englishman with a grey moustache, "have you got at stake this time?"

Eulalie laughed mischievously.

"If I told you," she said, "you wouldn't believe me."

Light-heartedly enough, they passed to the eighth tee.

I watched them go thoughtfully.

When the detectives came up—

"I didn't take off my hat," I explained, "because I wasn't sure. But I'm almost certain that somewhere before I've seen that great big fellow with the grey moustache."

My companions were not interested.

## CHAPTER IX

# How Jonah Took Off his Coat, and Berry Flirted with Fortune for all He was Worth

"My dear," said Berry, "be reasonable."

"With pleasure," said Daphne. "But I'm not going to let you off."

Her husband frowned upon a roll.

"When I say," he said, "that I have a feeling to-day that my luck is in, I'm not being funny. Only once before have I had that conviction. I was at Cannes at the time—on the point of leaving for Paris. I went to Monte Carlo instead. . . . That night I picked up over six hundred pounds."

"I know," said his wife. "You've often told me. But I can't help it. I made you give me your word before we came here, and I'm not going to let you off."

"I gave it without thinking," declared her husband. "Besides, I never dreamed I should have this feeling."

"I did," said Daphne shortly. "That's why I made you promise. Have some more coffee?"

Pointedly ignoring the invitation, Berry returned to his roll and, after eyeing it with disgust which the bread in no way deserved, proceeded to disrupt and eviscerate it with every circumstance of barbarity. Covertly, Jonah and I exchanged smiles. . . .

Forty-eight hours had elapsed since I had cut Eulalie, and this was the morning of our last day at San Sebastian.

During our short stay the weather had been superb, and we had been out and about the whole day long. Of an evening—save for one memorable exception—we had been to the Casino. . . .

For as long as I could remember, Berry had had a weakness for Roulette. For Baccarat, *Petits Chevaux*, and the rest he cared nothing: fifty pounds a year would have covered his racing bets: if he played Bridge, it was by request. My brother-in-law was no gambler. There was something, however, about the shining wheel, sunk in its board of green cloth, which he found irresistible.

Remembering this fascination, my sister had broached the matter so soon as we had decided to visit San Sebastian, with the happy result that, ere we left Pau, her husband had promised her three things. The first was to leave his cheque-books at home; the second, to take with him no more than two hundred pounds; the third, to send for no more money.

And now the inevitable had happened.

The two hundred pounds were gone—every penny; we were not due to leave until the morrow; and—Berry was perfectly satisfied that his luck had changed. As for the promises his wife had extracted, he was repenting his rashness as heartily as she was commending her prevision.

"Nothing," said Berry, turning again to the charge, "was said about borrowing, was it?"

"No."

"Very well, then. Boy and Jonah'll have to lend me something. I'm not going to let a chance like this go."

"Sorry, old chap," said Jonah, "but we've got to pay the hotel bill. Thanks to your activities, we're landed with——"

"How much have you got?" demanded Berry.

I cut in and threw the cards on the table.

"Brother," I said, "we love you. For that reason alone we won't lend you a paper franc. But then you knew that before you asked us."

My brother-in-law groaned.

"I tell you," he affirmed, "you're throwing away money. With another two hundred and fifty I could do anything. I can feel it in my bones."

"You'd lose the lot," said Jonah. "Besides, you've eaten your cake. If you'd limited yourself last night and played rationally, instead of buttering the board. . . ."

"I'm sure," said Jill, "you ought to have played on a system. If you'd put a pound on 'RED' and kept on doubling each time you lost——"

"Yes," said Berry. "That's an exhilarating stunt, that is. Before you know where you are, you've got to put two hundred and fifty-six pounds on an even chance to get one back. With a limit of four hundred and eighty staring you in the face, that takes a shade more nerve than I can produce. I did try it once—at Madeira. Luck was with me. After three hours I'd made four shillings and lost half a stone. . . . Incidentally, when a man starts playing Roulette on a system, it's time to pray for his soul. I admit there are hundreds who do it—hundreds of intelligent, educated, thoughtful men and women. Well, you can pray for the lot. They're trying to read something which isn't written. They're studying a blank page. They're splitting their brains over

158

a matter on which an idiot's advice would be as valuable. I knew a brilliant commercial lawyer who used to sit down at the table and solemnly write down every number that turned up for one hour. For the next sixty minutes he planked still more solemnly on the ones that had turned up least often. Conceive such a frame of mind. That wonderful brain had failed to grasp the one simple glaring point of which his case consisted—that Roulette is lawless. He failed to appreciate that he was up against Fortune herself. He couldn't realise that because '7' had turned up seven times running at a quarter past nine, that was no earthly reason why '7' shouldn't turn up eight times running at a quarter past ten. Heaven knows what fun he got out of it. For me, the whole joy of the thing is that you're flirting with Fate." He closed his eyes suddenly and flung back his head. "Oh," he breathed, "I tell you she's going to smile to-night. I can see the light in her eyes. I have a feeling that she's going to be very kind . . . very kind . . . somehow. . . ."

We let him linger over the fond reflection, eyeing one another uneasily. It was, we felt, but the prelude to a more formidable attack.

We were right.

"I demand," barked Berry, "that I be allowed the wherewithal to prosecute my suit."

"Not a farthing," said Daphne. "To think that that two hundred pounds is gone makes me feel ill."

"That's exactly why I want to win it back—and more also." He looked round desperately. "Anybody want a birthright? For two hundred and fifty quid—I'd change my name."

"It sounds idiotic, I know," said I, "but supposing—supposing you lost."

"I shan't to-night," said Berry.

"Sure?"

"Positive. I tell you, I feel——"

"And you," said Jonah scornfully, "you have the temerity to talk about praying for others' souls. You sit there and——"

"I tell you," insisted Berry, "that I have a premonition. Look here. If I don't have a dart to-night, I shall never be the same man again. . . . Boy, I implore you——"

I shook my head.

"Nothing doing," I said. "You'll thank us one day."

"You don't understand," wailed Berry. "You've never known the feeling that you were bound to win."

"Yes, I have—often. And it's invariably proved a most expensive sensation."

There was a moment's silence. Then—

"Right," said my brother-in-law. "You're one and all determined to see me go down. You've watched me drop two hundred, and not one of you's going to give me a hand to help me pick it up. It may be high-minded, but it's hardly cordial. Some people might call it churlish. . . . Upon my soul, you are a cold-blooded crowd. Have you ever known a deal I wouldn't come in on? And now, because you are virtuous, I'm to lose my fun. . . . Ugh! Hymn Number Four Hundred and Seventy-Seven, 'The Cakes and Ale are Over'."

Struggling with laughter, Adèle left her seat and, coming quickly behind him, set her white hands upon his shoulders.

"Dear old chap," she said, laying her cheek against his, "look at it this way. You're begging and praying us to let you down. Yes, you are. And if we helped you to break your word, neither you nor we would ever, at the bottom of our hearts, think quite so much of us again. And that's not good enough. Even if you won five thousand pounds it wouldn't compensate. Respect and self-respect aren't things you can buy."

"But, sweetheart," objected Berry, "nothing was said about borrowing. Daphne admits it. If I can raise some money without reference to my bankers, I'm at liberty to do so."

"Certainly," said Adèle. "But *we* mustn't help. If that was allowed, it 'ld knock the bottom out of your promise. You and Daphne and we are all in the same stable: and that—to mix metaphors—puts us out of Court. If you ran into a fellow you knew, and he would lend you some money, or you found a hundred in the street, or a letter for you arrived——"

"—or one of the lift-boys died, leaving me sole legatee . . . I see. Then I should be within my rights. In fact, if anything which can't happen came to pass, no one would raise any objection to my taking advantage of it. You know, you're getting too generous."

"That's better," said Adèle. "A moment ago we were cold-blooded."

Berry winced.

"I take it back," he said humbly. "Your central heating arrangements, at any rate, are in perfect order. Unless your heart was glowing, your soft little cheek wouldn't be half so warm."

"I don't know about that," said Adèle, straightening her back. "But we try to be sporting. And that's your fault," she added.

"You've taught us."

The applause which greeted this remark was interrupted by the entry of a waiter bearing some letters which had been forwarded from Pau.

A registered package, for which Berry was requested to sign, set us all thinking.

"Whatever is it?" said Daphne.

"I can't imagine," replied her husband, scrutinising the post-mark. " 'Paris'? I've ordered nothing from Paris that I can remember."

"Open it quick," said Jonah. "Perhaps it's some wherewithal."

Berry hacked at the string. . . .

The next instant he leaped to his feet.

"Fate!" he shrieked. "Fate! I told you my luck was in!" He turned to his wife breathlessly. " 'Member those Premium Bonds you wanted me to go in for? Over a month ago I applied for twenty-five. I'd forgotten about the trash—and *here they are*!"

\*　　\*　　\*　　\*　　\*

Two hours and a half had gone by, and we were rounding a tremendous horse-shoe bend on the way to Zarauz, when my wife touched Berry upon the arm.

"Aren't you excited?" she said.

"Just a trifle," he answered. "But I'm trying to tread it under. It's essential that I should keep cool. When you're arm in arm with Fortune, you're apt to lose your head. And then you're done. The jade'll give me my cues—I'm sure of it. But she won't shout them. I've got to keep my eyes skinned and my ears pricked, if I'm going to pick them up."

"If I," said Adèle, "were in your shoes, I should be just gibbering."

It was, indeed, a queer business.

The dramatic appearance of the funds had startled us all. Had they arrived earlier, had they come in the shape of something less easily negotiable than Bearer Bonds, had they been representing more or less than precisely the very sum which Berry had named in his appeal, we might have labelled the matter "Coincidence", and thought no more of it. Such a label, however, refused to stick. The affair ranked with thunder out of a cloudless sky.

As for my sister, with the wind taken out of her sails, she had hauled down her flag. The thing was too hard for her.

It was Jonah who had sprung a mine in the midst of our

amazement.

"Stop," he had cried. "Where's yesterday's paper? Those things are Premium Bonds, and, unless I'm utterly mistaken, there was a drawing two days ago. One of those little fellows may be worth a thousand pounds."

The paper had confirmed his report. . . .

The thought that, but for his wit, we might have released such substance to clutch at such a shadow, had set us all twittering more than ever.

At once a council had been held.

Finally it had been decided to visit a bank and, before we disposed of the Bonds, to ask for and search the official bulletin in which are published the results of all Government Lottery Draws.

Inquiry, however, had revealed that the day was some sort of a holiday, and that no banks would be open. . . .

At last a financier was unearthed—a changer of money. In execrable French he had put himself at our service.

"Yes, he had the bulletin. It had arrived this morning. . . ."

Feverishly we searched its pages.

Once we had found the column, a glance was enough. Our Bonds bore consecutive numbers, of which the first figure was "o". The series appeared to be unfortunate. The winning list contained not a single representative.

More reassured than disappointed, we raised the question of a loan.

Our gentleman picked at the Bonds and wrinkled his nose. After a little he offered one hundred pounds.

This was absurd, and we said so.

The Bonds were worth two hundred and fifty pounds, and were as good as hard cash. The fellow had no office, and, when we wanted him again, as like as not he would have disappeared. His personal appearance was against him.

When we protested, his answer came pat.

"He was no money-lender. In the last ten years he had not advanced ten pesetas. He was a changer of money, a broker, and nothing else."

Finally he offered one hundred and fifty pounds—at sixty per cent. a year *or part of a year*.

For one so ignorant of usury, this was not bad. We thanked him acidly, offered the Bonds for sale, and, after a little calculation, accepted two hundred and forty-three pounds in Spanish notes.

Half an hour later we had climbed into the cars, anxious to

make the most of our last day in Spain. . . .

If the way to Zarauz was handsome, that from Zarauz to Zumaya was fit for a king. Take us a range of mountains—bold, rugged, precipitous, and bring the sea to their foot—no ordinary sea, sirs, but Ocean himself, the terrible Atlantic to wit, in all his glory. And there, upon the boundary itself, where his proud waves are stayed, build us a road, a curling shelf of a road, to follow the line of that most notable indenture, witnessing the covenant 'twixt land and sea, settled when Time was born.

Above us, the ramparts of Spain—below, an echelon of rollers, ceaselessly surging to their doom—before us, a ragged wonder of coast-line, rising and falling and thrusting into the distance, till the snarling leagues shrank into murmuring inches and tumult dwindled into rest—on our right, the might, majesty, dominion and power of Ocean, a limitless laughing mystery of running white and blue, shining and swaying and swelling till the eye faltered before so much magnificence and Sky let fall her curtain to spare the failing sight—for over six miles we hung over the edge of Europe. . . .

Little wonder that we sailed into Zumaya—all red roofs, white walls and royal-blue timbers—with full hearts, flushed and exulting. The twenty precious minutes which had just gone by were charged with the spirit of the Odyssey.

Arrived at the village, we stopped, to wait for the others. So soon as they came, we passed on slowly along the road to Deva. Perhaps a mile from Zumaya we ate our lunch. . . .

The comfortable hush which should succeed a hearty meal made in the open air upon a summer's day was well established. Daphne and Adèle were murmuring conversation : in a low voice Jill was addressing Berry and thinking of Piers : pipe in mouth, Jonah was blinking into a pair of field-glasses : and I was lying flat upon my back, neither smoking nor sleeping, but gradually losing consciousness with a cigarette in my hand.

I had come to the point of postponing through sheer lethargy the onerous duty of lifting the cigarette to my lips, when, with an oath that ripped the air, Jonah started to his feet.

Sleep went flying.

I sat up amazedly, propping myself on my hands. . . .

With dropped jaw, my cousin was staring through the glasses as a man who is looking upon sudden death. While I watched, he lowered them, peered into the distance, clapped them again to his eyes, let them fall, glanced swiftly to right and left, shut his mouth with a snap, and made a dash for the cars. . . .

With his hand upon Ping's door, he turned and pointed a trembling forefinger along the valley.

"There's Zed," he cried. "My horse. Haven't seen him since Cambrai. Leading a team, and they're flogging him."

I fancy he knew I should join him, for he never closed Ping's door. As he changed into second, I swung myself inboard. A moment later we were flying along the dusty road. . . .

Zed had been Jonah's charger for over three years. Together, for month after month, the two had endured the rough and revelled in the smooth. They had shared misery, and they had shared ease. Together, many times, they had passed through the Valley of the Shadow of Death. And, while the animal must have loved Jonah, my cousin was devoted to the horse. At last came Cambrai. . . .

Jonah was shot through the knee and sent to England. And Zed —poor Zed disappeared.

My cousin's efforts to trace him were superhuman. Unhappily his groom had been killed, when Jonah was wounded, and, though all manner of authorities, from the Director of Remounts downwards, had lent their official aid, though a most particular description had been circulated and special instructions issued to all the depots through which the horse might pass, to his lasting grief Jonah had never heard of Zed again.

And now. . . . I found myself praying that he had not been mistaken.

Jonah was driving like a man possessed.

We tore up a rise, whipped round a bend and, coming suddenly upon a road on our right, passed it with locked wheels.

The noise my cousin made, as he changed into reverse, showed that his love for Zed was overwhelming.

We shot backward, stopped, stormed to the right and streaked up a shocking road at forty-five. . . . We flashed into a hamlet, turned at right angles, missed a waggon by an inch and flung up a frightful track towards a farm. . . .

Then, before I knew what had happened, we had stopped dead, and Jonah's door was open and he was limping across the road.

In the jaws of a rude gateway stood a waggon of stones. Harnessed to this were three sorry-looking mules and, leading them, the piteous wreck of what had been a blue roan. The latter was down—and out.

For this the immediate reason was plain.

The teamster, better qualified for the treadmill, had so steered his waggon that the hub of its off fore wheel had met the gatepost. This he had not observed, but, a firm believer in the omnipotency of the lash, had determined to reduce the check, whatever might be its cause, by methods of blood and iron. Either because he was the most convenient or by virtue of his status, the leader had received the brunt of the attack. That is, of course, one way of driving. . . .

The blue roan was down, and his master had just kicked him in the belly when Jonah arrived.

The Spaniard was a big fellow, but my cousin has wrists of steel. . . . He took the whip from its owner as one takes a toy from a baby. Then with the butt he hit him across the mouth. The Spaniard reeled, caught his foot on a stone and fell heavily. Jonah threw down the whip and took off his coat.

"I don't want to kill him," he said quietly.

When the other rose, he looked extremely ugly. This was largely due to the fact that most of his front teeth were missing and that it was difficult, because of the blood, to see exactly where his face ended and his mouth began. The look in his eyes, however, was suggesting the intent to kill.

He had no idea, of course, that he was facing perhaps the one man living who could have thrashed a champion. . . .

It is not often that you will see half a dozen of the most illustrious members of the National Sporting Club attending an Assault-at-Arms held at a public school. Three years running I had that honour. The gentlemen came to see Jonah. And though no applause was allowed during the boxing, they always broke the rule. . . . In due season my cousin went to Oxford. . . . In his second year, in the Inter-University contest, he knocked his opponent out in seven seconds. The latter remained unconscious for more than six hours, each crawling one of which took a year off Jonah's life. From that day my cousin never put on the gloves again. . . .

All, however, that the Spaniard saw was a tall lazy-looking man with a game leg, who by his gross interference had taken him by surprise.

He lowered his head and actually ran upon his fate. . . .

I have never seen "punishment" at once so frightful and so punctiliously administered. Jonah worked with the swift precision of the surgeon about the operating table. He confessed afterwards that his chief concern was to keep his opponent too blind with rage to see the wisdom of capitulation. He need not have worried. . . .

When it had become obvious that the blessed gifts of sight, smell, and hearing had been almost wholly withdrawn from the gentleman, when, in fact, he had practically ceased attempting to defend himself, and merely bellowed with mortification at every stinging blow, Jonah knocked him sprawling on to the midden, and drew off his wash-leather gloves.

The next moment he was down on his knees beside the roan, plucking at the rough harness with trembling fingers.

Once the horse sought to rise, but at Jonah's word he stopped and laid down his head.

Between us we got him clear. Then we stood back, and Jonah called him.

With a piteous effort the roan got upon his legs. That there was back trouble and at least one hock was sprung I saw at a glance. The horse had been broken down. He was still blowing badly, and I ran for the flask in the car. When I came back, Jonah was caressing his charger with tears running down his cheeks. . . .

There is a listlessness, born of harsh treatment, suckled on dying hopes, reared on the bitter memory of happier days, which is more eloquent than tears. There is an air of frozen misery, of a despair so deep that a kind word has come to lose its meaning, which none but horses wear.

Looking upon Zed, I felt ashamed to be a man.

Gaunt, filthy, and tottering, the flies mercilessly busy about three shocking sores, the roan was presenting a terrible indictment to be filed against the Day of Judgment. ". . . And not one of them is forgotten before God. . . ." But there was worse than pain of body here. The dull, see-nothing eyes, the heavy-laden head, the awful-stricken mien, told of a tragedy to make the angels weep— an English thoroughbred, not dead, but with a broken heart.

We had administered the brandy, Jonah was bathing a sore, and I had made a wisp and was rubbing Zed down, when—

"Good day," said a voice.

With his arms folded upon the sill, a little grey-headed man was watching us from a window.

I looked up and nodded.

"Good day," I said.

"Ah like boxing," said the man. "Ah've bin twelve years in the States, an' Ah'd rather see boxing than a bull-fight. You like baseball?"

I shook my head.

"I've never seen it," I said.

"Haven't missed much," was the reply. "But Ah like boxing. You visiting Spain?"

"For a few days."

" 'S a fine country. Bin to Sevilla?"

Entirely ignoring the violence which he had just witnessed, to say nothing of our trespass upon his property and our continued attention to his horse, the farmer proceeded to discuss the merits and shortcomings of Spain with as much detached composure as if we had met him in a tavern.

At length Jonah got up.

"Will you sell me this horse?"

"Yes," said the man. "Ah will."

"What d'you want for him?"

"Five hundred pesetas."

"Right," said Jonah. "Have you got a halter?"

The man disappeared. Presently he emerged from a door halter in hand.

The twenty pounds passed, and Zed was ours.

Tenderly my cousin fitted the halter about the drooping head.

"One more effort, old chap," he said gently, turning towards the gate. . . .

Out of compassion for the mules, I drew the farmer's attention to the hub which was nursing the gatepost.

He just nodded.

"Pedro could never drive," he said.

"I should get a new carter," I said.

He shrugged his shoulders. Then he jerked his head in the direction of the carcase upon the midden.

"He is my step-father. We do not speak," he said simply.

We found the others in the hamlet through which we had passed. There I handed over Ping to Adèle, and thence Jonah and Zed and I walked to Zumaya.

To find a box at the station was more than we had dared hope for, but there it was—empty and waiting to be returned to San Sebastian. Beneath the influence of twenty-five pesetas, the station-master saw no good reason why it should not be returned by the evening train.

We left Jonah to accompany his horse and hurried home by car to seek a stable.

When we sat down to dinner that night at eight o'clock, Jonah called for the wine-list and ordered a magnum of champagne.

When the wine was poured, he raised his glass and looked at me.

"Thank you for helping me," he said. He glanced round with his eyes glowing. "And all of you for being so glad." He drank and touched Adèle upon the shoulder. "In a loose-box, up to his knees in straw, with an armful of hay to pick over, and no congestion. . . . Have you ever felt you wanted to get up and dance?" He turned to Berry. "Brother, your best. May you spot the winner to-night, as I did this afternoon."

"Thank you," said Berry, "thank you. I must confess I'd been hoping for some sort of intuition as to what to do. But I've not had a hint so far. Perhaps, when I get to the table. . . . It's silly, of course. One mustn't expect too much, but I had the feeling that I was going to be given a tip. You know. Like striking a dud egg, and then putting your shirt on a horse called 'Attar of Roses'. . . . Never mind. Let's talk about something else. Why did you call him 'Zed'?"

"Short for 'Zero'," said Jonah. "I think my groom started it, and I——"

"Zero," said Berry quietly. "I'm much obliged."

\*       \*       \*       \*       \*

It was a quarter to eleven, and Berry had lost one hundred and seventy pounds.

Across her husband's back Daphne threw me a despairing glance. Upon the opposite side of the table, Adèle and Jill, one upon either side of Jonah, stared miserably before them. I lighted my tenth cigarette and wondered what Berry had done. . . .

The table was crowded.

From their points of vantage the eight croupiers alternately did their business and regarded the assembly with a bored air.

A beautifully dressed American, who had been losing, observed the luck of her neighbour, a burly Dutchman, with envious eyes. With a remonstrance in every fingertip, a debonnair Frenchman was laughingly upbraiding his fellow for giving him bad advice. From above his horn-rimmed spectacles an old gentleman in a blue suit watched the remorseless rake jerk his five pesetas into "the Bank" in evident annoyance. Cheek by jowl with a dainty Englishwoman, who reminded me irresistibly of a Dresden shepherdess, a Spanish Jew, who had won, was explosively disputing with a croupier the amount of his stake. Two South Americans were leaning across the table nonchalantly "plastering the board". A little old lady, with an enormous bag, was thanking an elegant

Spaniard for disposing her stake as she desired. Finger to lip, a tall Spanish girl in a large black hat was sizing her remaining counters with a faint frown. A very young couple, patently upon their honeymoon, were conferring excitedly. . . .

"*Hagan juego, Señores.*"

The conference between the lovers became more intense.

"*Esta hecho?*"

"Oh, be quick!" cried the girl. "Between '7' and '8', Bill. Between . . ."

As the money went on—

"*No va mas,*" cried the croupier in charge.

Two pairs of eyes peered at the revolving wheel. They did not notice that the Dutchman, plunging at the last moment upon "MANQUE", had touched their counter with his cuff and moved it to '9'.

The ball lost its momentum, poppled across the ridges, and leaped to rest.

"*Neuve.*"

Two faces fell. I wondered if a new frock had vanished into air. . . .

With the edge of his rake a croupier was tapping their counter and looking round for the claimant.

For a second the Jew peered about him. Then he pointed to himself and stretched out his hand.

I called to the croupier in French.

"No. It belongs to Monsieur and Madame. I saw what happened. That gentleman moved it with his cuff."

"*Merci, Monsieur.*"

With a sickly leer the pretender rallied the croupier, confidentially assured the dainty Englishwoman that he did not care, and, laughing a little too heartily, waved the thirty-five pounds towards their bewildered owners.

"B-but it isn't mine," stammered the boy.

"Yes," I said, smiling. "Your counter was moved. I saw the whole thing." I hesitated. Then, "If you'll take an old hand's advice, you'll stop now. A thing like that's invariably the end of one's luck."

I was not "an old hand", and I had no authority for my dictum. My interference was unpardonable. When the two stopped to thank me, as they passed from the room, I felt like a criminal. Still, they looked very charming; and, after all, a frock on the back is worth a score at the dressmaker's.

"I am going," said Berry, "to suspend my courtship and smoke a cigarette. Possibly I'm going too strong. If I give the lady a rest, she may think more of me."

"I suppose," said Daphne, "you're bent on losing it all."

Her husband frowned.

"Fortune favours the bold," he said shortly. "You see, she's just proving me. If I were to falter, she'd turn me down."

It was impossible not to admire such confidence.

I bade my sister take heart.

"Much," I concluded, "may be done with forty pounds."

"Fifty," corrected Berry. "And now let's change the subject. How d'you pronounce Lwow? Or would you rather tell me a fairy tale?"

I shook my head.

"My power," I said, "of concentration is limited."

"Then I must," said Berry. "It's fatal to brood over your fortune." He sat back in his chair and let the smoke make its own way out of his mouth. "There was once a large king. It wasn't his fault. The girth went with the crown. All the Koppabottemburgs were enormous. Besides, it went very well with his subjects. Looking upon him, they felt they were getting their money's worth. A man of simple tastes, his favourite hobby was fowls.

"One day, just as he'd finished cleaning out the fowl-house, he found that he'd run out of maize. So he slipped on his invisible cloak and ran round to the grocer's. He always wore his invisible cloak when shopping. He found it cheaper.

"Well, the grocer was just recovering from the spectacle of two pounds of the best maize shoving themselves into a brown-paper bag and pushing off down the High Street, when a witch came in. The grocer's heart sank into his boots. He hated witches. If you weren't civil, before you knew where you were, you were a three-legged toad or a dew-pond or something. So you had to be civil. As for their custom—well, it wasn't worth having. They wouldn't look at bacon, unless you'd guarantee that the pig had been killed on a moonless Friday with the wind in the North, and as for pulled figs, if you couldn't swear that the box had been crossed by a one-eyed man whose father had committed arson in a pair of brown boots, you could go and bury them under the lilacs.

"This time, however, the grocer was pleasantly surprised.

" 'I didn't know,' said the witch, 'that you were under the patronage of Royalty.'

" 'Oh, didn't you?' said the grocer. 'Why, the Master of the

Horse has got his hoof-oil here for nearly two days now.'

" 'Master of the Horse be snookered,' said the witch. 'I'm talking about the king.'

" 'The K-King?' stammered the grocer.

" 'Oh, cut it out,' said the witch, to whom an invisible cloak meant nothing. 'No doubt you've been told to keep quiet, but I don't count. And I'll bet you did the old fool over his maize.'

"The grocer's brain worked very rapidly. The memory of a tin of mixed biscuits and half a Dutch cheese, which had floated out of his shop only the day before, and numerous other recollections of mysteriously animated provisions came swarming into his mind. At length—

" ' We never charge Royalty,' he said loftily.

" 'Oh, don't you?' snapped the witch. 'Well, supposing you change this broomstick. You swore blue it was cut on a rainless Tuesday from an ash that had supported a murderer with a false nose. The very first time I used it, it broke at six thousand feet. I was over the sea at the time, and had to glide nearly four miles to make a landing. Can you b-beat it?'

"When the grocer put up his shutters two hectic hours later, he was a weary man. In the interval he had been respectively a toad, a picture post-card, and a tin of baked beans. And somebody had knocked him off the counter during his third metamorphosis, so he felt like death. All the same, before going to bed, he sat down and wrote to the Lord Chamberlain, asking for permission to display the Royal Arms. Just to make it quite clear that he wasn't relying on hoof-oil, he added that he was shortly expecting a fine consignment of maize and other commodities.

"The postscript settled it.

"The permission was granted, the king 'dealt' elsewhere in future, and the witch was given three hours to leave the kingdom. So the grocer lost his two worst customers and got the advertisement of his life. Which goes to show, my children, that if only—— Hullo! Here's a new shift."

It was true.

The eight croupiers were going off duty. As they vacated their seats, eight other gentlemen in black immediately replaced them.

Berry extinguished his cigarette and handed me his last bunch of notes. In exchange for these, with the peculiar delicacy of his kind, the croupier upon my right selected, arrayed and offered me counters of the value of forty English pounds.

He might have been spared his pains.

As I was piling the money by Berry's side—

"*Zero,*" announced a nasal voice.

"We're off," said my brother-in-law. "Will you see that they pay me right?"

One hundred and seventy-five pounds.

Ere I had completed my calculation—

"*Zero,*" repeated the nasal voice.

"I said so," said Berry, raising his eyebrows. "I had the maximum that time. Will you be so good? Thank you."

Trembling with excitement, I started to count the equivalent of four hundred and ninety pounds.

Berry was addressing the croupier.

"No. Don't touch the stake. She's not finished yet."

"*Esta hecho?*"

"Don't leave it all," begged Daphne. "Take——"

"*No va mas.*"

Desperately I started to check the money again. . . .

"*Zero.*"

There was a long gasp of wonderment, immediately followed by a buzz of exclamation. The croupiers were smiling. Jill was jumping up and down in her seat. Adèle was shaking Jonah by the arm. My sister was clinging to Berry, imploring him to "stop now". The two Frenchmen were laughing and nodding their congratulations. The little old lady was bowing and beaming goodwill. Excepting, perhaps, the croupiers, Berry seemed less concerned than anyone present.

"No. I'm not going to stop," he said gently, "because that would be foolish. But I'll give it a miss this time, because it's not coming up. It's no longer a question of guessing, dear. I tell you, I *know.*"

The ball went flying.

After a moment's interval—

"*Ocho* (eight)," anounced the croupier.

"You see," said Berry. "I should have lost my money. Now this time my old friend Zero will come along."

On to the white-edged rectangle went fourteen pounds.

A few seconds later I was receiving four hundred and ninety. . . .

I began to feel dazed. As for counting the money, it was out of the question. Idiotically I began to arrange the counters in little piles. . . .

"35" turned up.

"That's right," said Berry quietly. "And now . . . It's really very monotonous, but . . ."

With a shrug of his shoulders, he set the limit on "Zero".

I held my breath. . . .

The ball ceased to rattle—began to fall—ricocheted from stud to stud—tumbled into the wheel—nosed "32"—and . . . fell with a click into "o".

Berry spread out his hands.

"I tell you," he said, "it's too easy. . . . And now, again."

"Don't!" cried Daphne. "Don't! I beg you——"

"My darling," said Berry, "after to-night—No. Leave the stake, please—I'll never play again. This evening—well, the money's there, and we may as well have it, mayn't we? I mean, it isn't as if I hadn't been given the tip. From the moment I woke this morning—— Listen, dear. Don't bother about the wheel—the lady's been hammering away. You must admit, she's done the job thoroughly. First the intuition : then the wherewithal : then, what to back. I should be a bottle-nosed mug if I didn't——"

"*Zero.*"

Upon the explosion of excitement which greeted the astounding event, patrons of the Baccarat Table and of the other Roulette Wheel left their seats and came crowding open-mouthed to see what was toward. Complete strangers were chattering like old friends. Gibbering with emotion, the Spanish Jew was dramatically recounting what had occurred. The Dutchman was sitting back, laughing boisterously. The Frenchmen were waving and crying, "*Vive l'Angleterre*". Jonah was shouting as though he had been in the hunting field. Adèle and Jill were beating upon the table.

Berry bowed his acknowledgements.

As in a dream, I watched them send for more money.

When it arrived, they gave me four hundred and ninety pounds.

"*Hagan juego, Señores.*"

Berry shook his head.

"Not this time," he said quietly.

He was right. After a look at "o" the ball ran with a click into "15".

A long sigh of relief followed its settlement.

"You see?" said Berry, picking up fourteen pounds . . .

"Don't," I said weakly. "Don't. I can't bear it. The board's bewitched. If it turns up again, I shall collapse."

"You mean that?" said Berry, putting the money on.

"*No va mas.*"

"I do. My heart——"

"Then say your prayers," said my brother-in-law. "For, as I live, that ball's going to pick out——"

"*Zero.*"

I never remember such a scene.

Everybody in the room seemed to be shouting. I know I was. Respectable Spaniards stamped upon the floor like bulls. The Frenchmen, who with Berry and several others had backed the winner, were clasping one another and singing the Marseillaise. The beautifully dressed American was wringing Adèle's hand. The old gentleman in the blue suit was on his feet and appeared to be making a speech. The Spanish girl was standing upon her chair waving a handkerchief. . . .

In vain the smiling croupiers appealed for order. . . .

As the tumult subsided—

"Seven times in ten spins," said Berry. "Well, I think that'll do. We'll just run up the board on the even chances. . . ."

There was no holding him.

Before I knew where I was, he had set twelve thousand pesetas apiece on "RED", "ODD", and "UNDER 19".

Some fourteen hundred pounds on a single spin.

I covered my eyes. . . .

As the ball began to lose way, the hush was awful. . . .

"*Siete* (seven)," announced the spokesman.

With my brain whirling, I sought to garner the harvest. . . .

My brother-in-law rose to his feet.

"One last throw," he said. " '*PASSE*' for 'The Poor'."

He leaned forward and put the maximum on "OVER 18".

A moment later, counter by counter, four hundred and seventy pounds went into the poor-box.

As I pushed back my chair, I glanced at my watch.

In exactly sixteen minutes Berry had stung "the Bank" to the tune of—as near as I could make it—four thousand nine hundred and ninety-five pounds.

*       *       *       *       *

Some ten hours later we slipped out of San Sebastian and on to the famous road which leads to Biarritz. Berry, Daphne, and Jill were in one car, and Adèle and I were in the other. Jonah and Zed were to travel together by train. It was improbable that they would leave for Pau before the morrow.

As we climbed out of Béhobie, we took our last look at Spain, that realm of majestic distances and superb backgrounds. . . .

You may peer into the face of France and find it lovely; the more you magnify an English landscape, the richer it will become; but to find the whole beauty of Spain, a man must stand back and lift up his eyes.

Now that we had left it behind, the pride and grandeur of the scenery beggared description. It was as though for days we had been looking upon a mighty canvas, and while we had caught something of its splendour, now for the first time had we focussed it aright. The memory we took away was that of a masterpiece.

Anxious to be home in time for luncheon, I laid hold of the wheel. . . .

We whipped through St. Jean de Luz, sang through Bidart, and hobbled over a fearful stretch of metalling into Bayonne. . . .

As we were nearing Bidache—

"How much," said Adèle suddenly, "is Berry actually up?"

"Allowing for everything," said I, "that is, his losses, what he gave to the poor, and the various rates of exchange, about two hundred and forty thousand francs."

"Not so dusty," said Adèle thoughtfully. "All the same——"

A report like that of a gun blew the sentence to blazes.

Heavily I took the car in to the side of the road. . . .

A second tyre went upon the outskirts of Pau.

Happily we had two spare wheels. . . .

As I was wearily resuming my seat, Berry, Daphne, and Jill went by with a cheer.

Slowly we followed them into the town. . . .

It was not until we were stealing up our own villa's drive that at length I remembered the question which for over an hour I had been meaning to put to my wife.

As I brought the car to a standstill—

"What was it," I demanded, "that you had begun to say when we had the first burst near Bidache? We were talking about how much Berry was up, and you said——"

The most blood-curdling yell that I have ever heard fell upon our ears.

For a moment we stared at one another.

Then we fell out of the car by opposite doors and flew up the steps. . . .

Extended upon a chair in the hall, Berry was bellowing, clawing at his temples and drumming with his heels upon the floor.

Huddled together, Daphne and Jill were poring over a letter with starting eyes.

DEAR SIR,

In case the fact has not already come to your notice, we hasten to inform you that as a result of the drawing, which took place on Monday last, one of the Premium Bonds, which we yesterday dispatched to you per registered post, has won the first prize of fr. 500,000 (five hundred thousand francs).

By way of confirmation, we beg to enclose a cutting from the official Bulletin.

We should, perhaps, point out that, in all announcements of the results of drawings, the "o" or "zero", which for some reason invariably precedes the number of a Premium Bond, is disregarded.

Awaiting the pleasure of your instructions,

We beg to remain, dear sir,

Your obedient servants,

———————

\* \* \* \* \*

It was perhaps five hours later that my memory again responded, and I turned to Adèle.

"The dam burst," said I, "at the very moment when you were going to tell me what you had been about to say when the first tyre went outside Bidache. Sounds like 'The House that Jack built', doesn't it?"

"Oh, I know," said Adèle, laughing. "But it's no good now. I was going to say——"

The door opened and Falcon came in with a wire.

I picked up the form and weighed it thoughtfully.

"Wonderfully quick," I said. "It was half-past two when I was at the Bank, and I couldn't have been at the Post Office before a quarter to three. I looked at my watch. Just under four hours."

"The Bank?" said Adèle, staring. "But you said you were going to the Club."

I nodded.

"I know. I was anxious to raise no false hopes. All the same, I couldn't help feeling that half a million francs were worth a tenpenny wire. Therefore I telegraphed to Jonah. His answer will show whether that tenpenny wire was worth half a million francs."

My wife snatched the form from my hand and tore it open.

It was very short.

*Bonds repurchased Jonah.*

\* \* \* \* \*

But my memory never recovered from the two-fold slight.

To this day I cannot remember to ask Adèle what it was that she had been about to say when the first tyre burst outside Bidache.

CHAPTER X

# How Berry Sought Comfort in Vain, and Nobby Slept upon a Queen's Bed

Time was getting on.

The season at Pau was approaching the end of its course. Already villas and flats and servants were being engaged for the winter to come. We had been asked definitely whether we proposed to return and, if so, whether we wished again to occupy the excellent villa we had. Not knowing what answer to make to the first question, we had passed to the second—somewhat illogically. The second had proved more heatedly disputable than the first. Finally Jill had looked up from a letter to Piers and put in her oar with a splash.

"The villa's all right," she announced. "Everyone says it's the best, and so should we, if we didn't live in it. It's what's inside that's so awful. Even one decent sofa would make all the difference."

In silence we pondered her words.

At length—

"I confess," said Berry, "that the idea of having a few chairs about in which you can sit continuously for ten minutes, not so much in comfort as without fear of contracting a bed-sore or necrosis of the coccyx, appeals to me. Compared with most of the 'sitzplatz' in this here villa, an ordinary church pew is almost voluptuous. The beastly things seem designed to promote myalgia."

"Yet they do know," said I. "The French, I mean. Look at their beds."

"Exactly," replied my brother-in-law. "That's the maddening part of it. Every French bed is an idyll—a poem of repose. The upholsterer puts his soul into its creation. A born genius, he expresses himself in beds. The rest of the junk he turns out . . ." He broke off and glanced about the room. His eye lighted upon a couch, lozenge-shaped, hog-backed, featuring the Greek-Key pattern in brown upon a brick-red ground and surrounded on three

177

sides by a white balustrade some three inches high. "Just consider that throne. Does it or does it not suggest collusion between a private-school workshop, a bricklayer's labourer, and the Berlin branch of the Y.W.C.A.?"

"If," said Daphne, "it was only the chairs, I wouldn't mind. But it's everything. The sideboard, for instance——"

"Ah," said her husband, "my favourite piece. The idea of a double cabin-washstand is very beautifully carried out. I'm always expecting Falcon to press something and a couple of basins to appear. Then we can wash directly after the asparagus."

"The truth is," said Adèle, "these villas are furnished to be let. And when you've said that, you've said everything."

"I agree," said I. "And if we liked Pau enough to come back next autumn, the best thing to do is to have a villa of our own. I'm quite ready to face another three winters here, and, if everyone else is, it 'ld be worth while. As for furniture, we can easily pick out enough from Cholmondeley Street and White Ladies."

There was a moment's silence.

Then—

"I'm on," said Jonah, who had caught three splendid salmon in the last two days. "This place suits me."

"And me," said Adèle warmly.

My sister turned to her husband.

"What d'you think, old chap?"

Berry smiled beatifically. A far-away look came into his eyes.

"I shall personally superintend," he announced, "the removal and destruction of the geyser."

Amid some excitement the matter was then and there decided.

The more we thought upon it, the sounder seemed the idea. The place suited us all. To have our things about us would be wholly delightful. Provided we meant for the future to winter abroad, we should save money.

Pleasedly we proceeded to lunch.

Throughout the meal we discussed what manner of house ours must be, situation, dimensions, aspect. We argued amiably about its garden and curtilage. We determined to insist upon two bath-rooms. By the time the cheese was served, we had selected most of the furniture and were bickering good-temperedly about the style of the wall-papers.

Then we rang up a house-agent, to learn that he had no un-furnished villa "to let" upon his books. He added gratuitously that, except for a ruined château upon the other side of Tarbes, he had nothing "for sale" either.

So soon as we had recovered, we returned to the charge. . . .

The third agent we addressed was not quite certain. There was, he said, a house in the town—*très solide, très serieuse, dans un quartier chic.* It would, he thought, be to our liking. It had, for instance, *une salle de fête superbe.* He was not sure, however, that it was still available. A French gentleman was much attracted, and had visited it three times.

We were greatly disgusted and said so. We did not want a house in the town. We wanted . . .

Finally we succumbed to his entreaties and promised to view the villa, if it was still in the market. He was to ring us up in ten minutes' time. . . .

So it happened that half an hour later we were standing curiously before the great iron gates of a broad shuttered mansion in the rue Mazagran, Pau, while the agent was alternately pealing the bell for the caretaker and making encouraging gestures in our direction.

Viewed from without, the villa was not unpleasing. It looked extremely well-built, it stood back from the pavement, it had plenty of elbow room. The street itself was as silent as the tomb. Perhaps, if we could find nothing else. . . . We began to wonder whether you could see the mountains from the second floor.

At last a caretaker appeared, I whistled to Nobby, and we passed up a short well-kept drive.

A moment later we had left the sunlight behind and had entered a huge dim hall.

"Damp," said Berry instantly, sniffing the air. "Damp for a monkey. I can smell the good red earth."

Daphne sniffed thoughtfully.

"I don't think so," she said. "When a house has been shut up like this, it's bound to——"

"It's wonderful," said her husband, "what you can't smell when you don't want to. Never mind. If you want to live over water, I don't care. But don't say I didn't warn you. Besides, it'll save us money. We can grow moss on the floors instead of carpets."

"It does smell damp," said Adèle, "but there's central heating. See?" She pointed to a huge radiator. "If that works as it should, it'll make your carpets fade."

Berry shrugged his shoulders.

"I see what it is," he said. "You two girls have scented cupboards. I never yet knew a woman who could resist cupboards. In a woman's eyes a superfluity of cupboards can transform the most poisonous habitation into a desirable residence. If you asked a woman what was the use of a staircase, she'd say, 'To put cupboards under'."

By now the shutters had been opened, and we were able to see about us. As we were glancing round, the caretaker shuffled to a door beneath the stairs.

"Here is a magnificent cupboard," she announced. "There are many others."

As we passed through the house, we proved the truth of her words. I have never seen so many cupboards to the square mile in all my life.

My wife and my sister strove to dissemble their delight. At length Cousin Jill, however, spoke frankly enough.

"They really are beautiful. Think of the room they give. You'll be able to put everything away."

Berry turned to me.

"Isn't it enough to induce a blood-clot? 'Beautiful'. Evil-smelling recesses walled up with painted wood. Birthplaces of mice. Impregnable hot-beds of vermin. And who wants to 'put everything away'?"

"Hush," said I. "They can't help it. Besides—Hullo! Here's another bathroom."

"Without a bath," observed my brother-in-law. "How very convenient! Of course, you're up much quicker, aren't you? I suppose the idea is not to keep people waiting. Come along." We passed into a bedroom. "Oh, what a dream of a paper! 'Who Won the Boat-race, or The Battle of the Blues'. Fancy waking up here after a heavy night. I suppose the designer was found 'guilty, but insane'. Another two cupboards? Thanks. That's fifty-nine. And yet another? Oh, no. The backstairs, of course. As before, approached by a door which slides to and fro with a gentle rumbling noise, instead of swinging. The same warranted to jam if opened hastily. Can't you hear Falcon on the wrong side with a butler's tray full of glass, wondering why he was born? Oh, and the bijou spiral leads to the box-room, does it? I see. Adèle's American trunks, especially the five-foot cube, will go up there beautifully. Falcon will like this house, won't he?"

"I wish to goodness you'd be quiet," said Daphne. "I want to think."

"It's not me," said her husband. "It's that Inter-University wall-paper. And now where's the tower? I suppose that's approached by a wire rope with knots in it?"

"What tower?" said Adèle.

"*The* tower. The feature of the house. Or was it a ballroom?"

"Ah," I cried, "the ballroom! I'd quite forgotten." I turned to the agent. "Didn't you say there was a ballroom?"

"But yes, *Monsieur*. On the ground-floor. I will show it to you at once."

We followed him downstairs in single file, and so across the hall to where two tall oak doors were suggesting a picture-gallery. For a moment the fellow fumbled at their lock. Then he pushed the two open.

I did not know that, outside a palace, there was such a chamber in all France. Of superb proportions, the room was panelled from floor to ceiling with oak—richly carved oak—and every handsome panel was outlined with gold. The ceiling was all of oak, fretted with gold. The floor was of polished oak, inlaid with ebony. At the end of the room three lovely pillars upheld a minstrels' gallery, while opposite a stately oriel yawned a tremendous fireplace, with two stone seraphim for jambs.

In answer to our bewildered inquiries, the agent explained excitedly that the villa had been built upon the remains of a much older house, and that, while the other portions of the original mansion had disappeared, this great chamber and the basement were still surviving. But that was all. Beyond that it was once a residence of note, he could tell us nothing.

Rather naturally, we devoted more time to the ballroom than to all the rest of the house. Against our saner judgment, the possession of the apartment attracted us greatly. It was too vast to be used with comfort as a sitting-room. The occasions upon which we should enjoy it as *une salle de fête*, would be comparatively few. Four ordinary salons would require less service and fuel. Yet, in spite of everything, we wanted it very much.

The rest of the house was convenient. The parlours were fine and airy; there were two bathrooms; the bedrooms were good; the offices were admirable. As for the basement, we lost our way there. It was profound. It was also indubitably damp. There the dank smell upon which Berry had remarked was most compelling. In the garden stood a garage which would take both the cars.

After a final inspection of the ballroom, we tipped the caretaker, promised to let the agent know our decision, and, to the great inconvenience of other pedestrians, strolled talkatively through the streets towards the Boulevard.

"I suppose," said Adèle, "those were the other people."

"Who were the other people?" I demanded.

"The two men standing in the hall as we came downstairs."

"I never saw them," said I. "But if you mean that one of them was the fellow who's after the house, I fancy you're wrong, because the agent told me he'd gone to Bordeaux."

"Well, I don't know who they were, then," replied my wife. "They were talking to the caretaker. I saw them through the banisters. By the time we'd got down, they'd disappeared. Any way, it doesn't matter. Only, if it was them, it looks as if they were thinking pretty seriously about it. You don't go to see a house four times out of curiosity."

"You mean," said Berry, "that if we're fools enough to take it, we'd better get a move on."

"Exactly. Let's go and have tea at Bouzom's, and thrash it out there."

No one of us, I imagine, will ever forget that tea.

Crowded about a table intended to accommodate four, we alternately disputed and insulted one another for the better part of two hours. Not once, but twice of her agitation my sister replenished the teapot with Jill's chocolate, and twice fresh tea had to be brought. Berry burned his mouth and dropped an apricot tartlet on to his shoe. Until my digust was excited by a nauseous taste, I continued to drink from a cup in which Jonah had extinguished a cigarette.

Finally Berry pushed back his chair and looked at his watch.

"Ladies and gentlemen," he said, "we came here this memorable afternoon to discuss the advisability of taking a certain messuage—to wit, the Villa Buichi—for the space of three years. As a result of that discussion I have formed certain conclusions. In the first place, I am satisfied that to dwell with you or any of you in the Villa Buichi or any other habitation for the space of three years presents a prospect so horrifying as to belittle Death itself. Secondly, while my main object in visiting the said messuage was to insure, if possible, against the future contraction of some complaint or disease of the hams, I have, I fear, already defeated that object by sitting for upwards of ninety minutes upon a chair which is rather harder than the living rock, and whose surface I have reason to believe is studded with barbs. Thirdly, whilst we are all agreed that a rent of fourteen thousand francs is grotesque, I'd rather pay twice that sum out of my own pocket than continue an argument which threatens to affect my mind. Fourthly, the house is not what we want, or where we want it. The prospect of wassailing in your own comic banqueting-hall is alluring, but the French cook believes in oil, and, to us, living in the town, every passing breeze will offer indisputable evidence, not only of the lengths to which this belief will go, but of the Pentateuchal effects which can be obtained by a fearless application of heat to rancid blubber. Fifthly, since we can get nothing else, and the thought of another winter in England is almost as soul-shaking as that of living again amid French furniture, I suppose we'd better take it, always provided they fill up the basement, put on a Mansard roof, add a few cupboards, and reduce the rent. Sixthly, I wish to heaven I'd never seen the blasted place. Lastly, I now propose to repair to the *Cercle Anglais*, or English Club, there in the privacy of the *lavabo* to remove the traces of the preserved apricot recently adhering to my right shoe, and afterwards to ascertain whether a dry Martini, cupped in the mouth, will do something to relieve the agony I am suffering as the direct result of concentrating on this rotten scheme to the exclusion of my bodily needs. But there you are. When the happiness of others is at stake, I forget that I exist."

With that, he picked up his hat and, before we could stop him, walked out of the shop.

With such an avowal ringing in our ears, it was too much to expect that he would remember that he had ordered the tea, and had personally consumed seven cakes, not counting the apricot tart.

However . . .

I followed him to the Club, rang up the agent, and offered to take the house for three years at a rent of twelve thousand francs. He promised to telephone to our villa within the hour.

He was as good as his word.

He telephoned to say that the French gentleman, who had unexpectedly returned from Bordeaux, had just submitted an offer of fourteen thousand francs. He added that, unless we were prepared to offer a higher rent, it would be his duty to accept that proposal.

After a moment's thought, I told him to do his duty and bade him adieu.

＊　　　＊　　　＊　　　＊　　　＊

That night was so beautiful that we had the cars open.

As we approached the Casino—

"Let's just go up the Boulevard," said Daphne. "This is too

lovely to leave."

I slowed up, waited for Jonah to come alongside, and then communicated our intention to continue to take the air.

The Boulevard being deserted, Ping and Pong proceeded slowly abreast. . . .

A sunset which had hung the sky with rose, painted the mountain-tops and turned the West into a blazing smeltery of dreams, had slowly yielded to a night starlit, velvety, breathless, big with the gentle witchcraft of an amber moon. Nature went masked. The depths upon our left seemed bottomless; a grey flash spoke of the Gave de Pau : beyond, the random rise and fall of a high ridge argued the summit of a gigantic screen—the foothills to wit, odd twinkling points of yellow light, seemingly pendent in the air, marking the farms and villas planted about their flanks. And that is all. A row of poplars, certainly, very correct, very slight, very elegant, by the way that we take for Lourdes—the row of poplars should be recorded; the luminous stars also, and a sweet white glow in the heaven, just where the ridge of the foothills cuts it across—a trick of the moonlight, no doubt. . . . Sirs, it is no such trick. That misty radiance is the driven snow resting upon the peaks of the Pyrenees. The moon is shining full on them, and, forty miles distant though they are, you see them rendering her light, as will a looking-glass, and by that humble office clothing themselves with unimaginable splendour.

As we stole into the place Royale—

"Every minute," announced Adèle, "I'm more and more thankful that we're quit of the Villa Buichi. We should have been simply mad to have taken a house in the town."

"There you are," said Berry. "My very words. Over and over again I insisted——"

"If you mean," said Jonah, "that throughout the argument you confined yourself to destructive criticism, deliberate confusion of the issues, and the recommendation of solutions which you knew to be impracticable, I entirely agree."

"The trouble with you," said Berry, "is that you don't appreciate the value of controversy. I don't blame you. Considering the backlash in your spinal cord, I think you talk very well. It's only when——"

"What exactly," said Adèle, bubbling, "is the value of controversy?"

"Its unique ability," said Berry, "to produce the truth. The hotter the furnace of argument, the harder the facts which eventually emerge. That's why I never spare myself. I don't pretend it's easy, but then I'm like that. Somebody offers you a drink. The easiest way is to refuse. But I don't. I always ask myself whether my health demands it."

There was an outraged silence.

Then—

"I have noticed," I observed, "that upon such occasions your brain works very fast. Also that you invariably choose the—er— harder path."

"Nothing is easier," said Berry, "than to deride infirmity." Having compassed the palace Royale, we returned to the Boulevard. "And now, if you've quite finished maundering over the beauties of a landscape which you can't see, supposing we focussed on the object with which we set out. I've thought out a new step, I want to show you. It's called 'The Slip Stitch'. Every third beat you stagger and cross your legs above the knee. That shows you've been twice to the Crusades. Then you purl two and cast four off. If you're still together, you get up and repeat to the end of the row knitways, decreasing once at every turn. Then you cast off very loosely."

Happily the speaker was in the other car, so we broke away and fled up the rue du Lycée. . . .

The dancing-room was crowded. Every English visitor seemed to be there, but they were not all dancing, and the floor was just pleasantly full.

As we came in, I touched Adèle on the arm.

"Will you dance with me, lass?"

I was not one moment too soon.

As I spoke, two gallants arrived to lodge their claims.

"I've accepted my husband," said Adèle, smiling.

She had to promise the next and the one after.

Whilst we were dancing, she promised the fourth and the fifth.

"I can see," said I, "that I'm in for my usual evening. Of course, we're too highly civilised. I feed you, I lodge you, I clothe you"— I held her off and looked at her—"yes, with outstanding success. You've a glorious colour, your eyes are like stars, and your frock is a marvel. In fact, you're almost too good to be true. From your wonderful, sweet-smelling hair to the soles of your little pink feet, you're an exquisite production. Whoever did see such a mouth? I suppose you know I married you for your mouth? And your throat? And—but I digress. As I was saying, all this is due to me. If I fed you exclusively on farinaceous food, you'd look pale. If I locked you out of nights, you'd look tired. If I didn't clothe you, you'd look—well, you wouldn't be here, would you? I mean, I know we move pretty fast nowadays, but certain conventions are still observed. Very well, then. I am responsible for your glory. I bring you here, and everybody in the room dances with you, except myself. To complete the comedy, I have only to remind you that I love dancing, and that you are the best dancer in the room. I ask you."

"That's just what you don't do," said Adèle, with a maddening smile. "If you did. . . ."

"But——"

"Certain conventions," said Adèle, "are still observed. Have I ever refused you?"

"You couldn't. That's why I don't ask you."

"O-o-oh, I don't believe you," said Adèle. "If it was Leap Year——"

"Pretend it is."

"—and I wanted to dance with you——"

"Pretend you do."

The music stopped with a crash, and a moment later a Frenchman was bowing over my wife's hand.

"May I come for a dance later?" he asked.

"Not this evening. I've promised the next four——"

"There will, I trust, be a fifth?"

"—and, after that, I've given my husband the lot. You do understand, don't you? You see, I must keep in with him. He feeds me and lodges me and clothes me and——"

The Frenchman bowed.

"If he has clothed you to-night, Madame, I can forgive him anything."

We passed to a table at which Berry was superintending the icing of some champagne.

"Ah, there you are!" he exclaimed. "Had your evening dance? Good. I ordered this little hopeful *pour passer le temps.* They've two more baubles in the offing, and sharp at one-thirty we start on fried eggs and beer. Judging from the contracts into which my wife has entered during the last six minutes, we shall be here till three." Here he produced and prepared to inflate an air-cushion. "The great wheeze about these shock-absorbers is not to——"

There was a horrified cry from Daphne and a shriek of laughter from Adèle and Jill.

"I implore you," said my sister, "to put that thing away."

"What thing?" said her husband, applying the nozzle to his lips.
"That cushion thing. How could you——"

"What! Scrap my blow-me-tight?" said Berry. "Darling, you
rave. You're going to spend the next four hours afloat upon your
beautiful toes, with a large spade-shaped hand supporting the
small of your back. I'm not. I'm going to maintain a sitting posture,
with one of the 'nests for rest' provided by a malignant Casino
directly intervening between the base of my trunk and the floor.
Now, I know that intervention. It's of the harsh, unyielding type.
Hence this air-pocket."

With that, he stepped on to the floor, raised the air-cushion as
if it were an instrument of music, and adopting the attitude and
manners of a cornet soloist, exhaled into the nozzle with his might.

There was a roar of laughter.

Then, mercifully, the band started, and the embarrassing attention of about sixty pairs of eyes was diverted accordingly.

A moment later my brother-in-law and I had the table to ourselves.

"And now," said Berry, "forward with that bauble. The Rump
Parliament is off."

Perhaps, because it was a warm evening, the Casino's furnaces
were in full blast. After a while the heat became oppressive. Presently I left Berry to the champagne and went for a stroll in the
Palmarium.

As I was completing my second lap—

"Captain Pleydell," said a dignified voice.

I turned to see Mrs. Waterbrook, leaning upon a stick, accompanied by a remarkably pretty young lady with her hair down her
back.

I came to them swiftly.

"Have you met with an accident?" I inquired.

"I have. I've ricked my ankle. Susan, this is Captain Pleydell,
whose cousin is going to marry Piers. Captain Pleydell, this is
Susan—my only niece. Now I'm going to sit down." I escorted her
to a chair. "That's better. Captain Pleydell, have you seen the
Château?"

"Often," said I. "A large grey building with a red keep, close to
the scent-shop."

"One to you," said Mrs. Waterbrook. "Now I'll begin again.
Captain Pleydell, have you seen the inside of the Château?"

"I have not."

"Then you ought," said Mrs. Waterbrook, "to be ashamed of

yourself. You've been six months in Pau, and you've never taken the trouble to go and look at one of the finest collections of tapestries in the world. What are you doing to-morrow morning?"

"Going to see the inside of the Château," I said.

"Good. So's Susan. She'll meet you at the gate on the Boulevard at half-past ten. She only arrived yesterday, and now her mother wants her, and she's got to go back. She's wild to see the Château before she goes, and I can't take her because of this silly foot."

"I'm awfully sorry," said I. "But it's an ill wind, etc."

"Susan," said Mrs. Waterbrook, "that's a compliment. Is it your first?"

"No," said Susan. "But it's the slickest."

"The what?" cried her aunt.

"I mean, I didn't see it coming."

I began to like Susan.

" 'Slickest'," snorted Mrs. Waterbrook. "Nasty vulgar slang. If you were going to be here longer, Captain Pleydell's wife should give you lessons in English. She isn't a teacher, you know. She's an American—with a silver tongue. And there's that wretched bell." She rose to her feet. "If I'd remembered that *Manon* had more than three acts, I wouldn't have come." She turned to me. "Is Jill here to-night?"

"She is."

"Will you tell her to come and find us in the next interval?"

"I will."

"Good. Half-past ten to-morrow. Good night."

On the way to the doors of the theatre she stopped to speak with someone, and Susan came running back.

"Captain Pleydell, is your wife here?"

I nodded.

"Well, then, when Jill's with Aunt Eleanor, d'you think I could —I mean, if you wouldn't mind, I'd—I'd love a lesson in English."

I began to like Susan more than ever.

"I'll see if she's got a spare hour to-morrow," I said. "At half-past ten."

Susan knitted her brows.

"No, don't upset that," she said quickly. "It doesn't matter. I want to be able to tell them I had you alone. But if I could say I'd met your wife, too, it'd be simply golden."

As soon as I could speak—

"You wicked, forward child," I said. "You——"

"Toodle-oo," said Susan. "Don't be late."

Somewhat dazedly I turned in the direction of the *salle de danse* so dazedly, in fact, that I collided with a young Frenchman who was watching the progress of *le jeu de boule*. This was hardly exhilarating. Of the seven beings gathered about the table, six were croupiers and the seventh was reading *Le Temps*.

I collided roughly enough to knock a cigarette out of my victim's hand.

"Toodle-oo—I mean *pardon, Monsieur. Je vous demande pardon.*"

"It's quite all right," he said, smiling. "I shouldn't have been standing so far out."

I drew a case from my pocket.

"At least," I said, "you'll allow me to replace the cigarette"— he took one with a laugh—"and to congratulate you upon your beautiful English."

"Thank you very much. For all that, you knew I was French."

"In another minute," said I, "I shall be uncertain. And I'm sure you'd deceive a Frenchman every time."

"I do frequently. It amuses me to death. Only the other day I had to produce my passport to a merchant at Lyons before he'd believe I was a foreigner."

"A foreigner?" I cried, with bulging eyes. "Then you *are* English."

"I'm a pure-bred Spaniard," was the reply. "I tell you, it's most diverting. Talk about ringing the changes. I had a great time during the War. I was a perfect mine of information. It wasn't strictly accurate, but Germany didn't know that. As a double-dyed traitor, they found me extremely useful. As a desirable neutral, I cut a great deal of ice. And now I'm loafing. I used to take an interest in the prevention of crime, but I've grown lazy."

For a moment or two we stood talking. Then I asked him to come to our table in the dancing-room. He declined gracefully.

"I'm Spanish enough to dislike Jazz music," he said.

We agreed to meet at the Club on the following day, and I rejoined Berry to tell him what he had missed.

I found the fifth dance in full swing and my brother-in-law in high dudgeon.

As I sat down, he exploded.

"This blasted breath-bag is a fraud. If you blow it up tight, it's like trying to sit on a barrel. If you fill it half full, you mustn't move a muscle, or the imprisoned air keeps shifting all over the place till one feels sick of one's stomach. In either case it's as hard as petrified bog-oak. If you only leave an imperial pint in the vessel, it all goes and gathers in one corner, thus conveying to one the impression that one is sitting one's self upon a naked chair with a tennis-ball in one's hip-pocket. If one puts the swine behind one, it shoves one off the seat altogether. It was during the second phase that one dropped or let fall one's cigar into one's champagne. One hadn't thought that anything could have spoiled either, but one was wrong."

I did what I could to soothe him, but without avail.

"I warn you," he continued, "there's worse to come. Misfortunes hunt in threes. First we fool and are fooled over that rotten villa. Now this balloon lets me down. You wait."

I decided that to argue that the failure of the air-cushion could hardly be reckoned a calamity would be almost as provocative as to suggest that the immersion of the cigar should rank as the third disaster, so I moistened the lips and illustrated an indictment of our present system of education by a report of my encounter with Susan.

Berry heard me in silence, and then desired me to try the chairs at the Château, and, if they were favouring repose, to inquire whether the place would be let furnished. Stifling an inclination to assault him, I laughed pleasantly and related my meeting with the engaging Spaniard. When I had finished—

"How much did you lend him?" inquired my brother-in-law. "Or is a pal of his taking care of your watch?"

The fox-trot came to an end, and I rose to my feet.

"The average weight," I said, "of the spleen is, I believe, six ounces. But spleens have been taken weighing twenty pounds."

"Net or rod?" said Berry.

"Now you see," I continued, "why you're so heavy on the chairs."

With that, I sought my wife and led her away to watch the Baccarat. . . .

Before we had been in the gaming room for twenty seconds, Adèle caught me by the arm.

"D'you see that man over there, Boy? With a bangle on his wrist?"

"And a shirt behind his diamond? I do."

"That's one of the men I saw in the Villa Buichi."

"The devil it is," said I. "Then I take it he's the new lessee. Well, well. He'll go well with the ballroom, won't he?"

It was a gross-looking fellow, well-groomed and oily. His fat hands were manicured and he was overdressed. He gave the impression that money was no longer an object. As if to corroborate this, he had been winning heavily. I decided that he was a bookmaker.

While I was staring, Adèle moved to speak with a friend.

"And who," said a quiet voice, "is attracting such faithful attention?"

It was the Spaniard.

"You see that fat cove?" I whispered. "He did us out of a house to-day. Overbid us, you know."

My companion smiled.

"No worse than that?" he murmured. "You must count yourselves lucky."

I raised my eyebrows.

"You know him?"

The other nodded.

"Not personally, of course," he said. Then : "I think he's retired now."

"What was he?" said I.

"The biggest receiver in France."

\*     \*     \*     \*     \*

Ere we retired to rest, my brother-in-law's prophecy that there was "worse to come" was distressingly fulfilled.

As the "evening" advanced, it improved out of all knowledge. The later the hour, the hotter became the fun. Berry's ill humour fell away. Adèle and I danced furiously together. Vain things were imagined and found diverting. Hospitality was dispensed. The two spare "baubles" were reinforced. . . .

Not until half-past two was the tambourine of gaiety suffered to tumble in its tracks.

We climbed into the cars flushed and hilarious. . . .

Late though we were, whenever we had been dancing there was one member of the household who always looked for our return and met us upon our threshold.

Nobby.

However silently the cars stole up the drive, by the time the door was opened, always the Sealyham was on parade, his small feet together, his tail up, his rough little head upon one side, waiting to greet us with an explosion of delight. In his bright eyes the rite was never stale, never laborious. It was the way of his heart.

Naturally enough, we came to look for his welcome. Had we

looked in vain some night, we should have been concerned. . . .

We were concerned this night.

We opened the door to find the hall empty.

Nobby was not upon parade.

Tired as we were, we searched the whole house. Presently I found a note upon my pyjamas.

> Sir,
>
> Must tell you we cannot find Nobby, the chauffeur and me looking everywhere and Fitch as been out in Pau all evening in quest. Hoping his whereabouts is perhaps known to you,
>
> Yours respectfully,
>
> J. Falcon.

\*       \*       \*       \*       \*

I was at the Villa Buichi the following morning by a quarter to ten.

It seemed just possible that the terrier was there a captive. That he was with us before we visited the house we well remembered. Whether he had entered with us and, if so, left when we did, we could not be sure. We had had much to think about. . . .

The caretaker took an unconscionable time to answer the bell, and when I had stated my business, stoutly refused to let me search the villa without an order. My offer of money was offensively refused. I had to content myself with standing within the hall and whistling as loud as I could. No bark replied, but I was not satisfied, and determined to seek the agent and obtain a permit, the moment that Susan and I had "done" the Château.

It was in some irritation that I made my way to the Boulevard. I had no desire to see the inside of the Château then or at any time; I particularly wished to prosecute my search for the Sealyham without delay. I had had less than four hours' sleep, and was feeling rotten.

In a smart white coat and skirt and a white felt hat over one eye, Susan looked most attractive. Her fresh, pretty face was glowing, her wonderful golden hair was full of lights, and the line of her slim figure, as—hands thrust deep into her coat-pockets—she leaned her small back against the balustrade, was more than dainty. Her little feet and ankles were those of a thoroughbred.

As I descended from the car—

"I say," said Susan, "I've got a stone in my shoe. Where can I get it out?"

I eyed her severely.

"You will have a lot to tell them," I said, "won't you? Go on. Get into the car."

She climbed in, sat down and leaned back luxuriously. Then she thrust out a foot with the air of a queen. . . .

When I had replaced her shoe, she thanked me with a shy smile. Then—

"I say," she said suddenly, "don't let's go to the Château. I don't want to see the rotten place. Let's go for a drive instead—somewhere where you can let her out. And on the way back you can take me to get some gloves."

"Susan," said I, "there's nothing doing. I know a drive in a high-powered car sounds a good deal more *chic* than being shown round a Château, but you can't have everything. Orders is orders. Besides, I've lost my dog, and I want to get a move on. But for that, you should have done the Château and had your drive into the bargain. As it is. . . ."

Susan is a good girl.

The moment she heard of my trouble, she was out of the car and haling me up to the Château as if there was a mob at our heels. . . .

I was not in the mood for sightseeing, but my annoyance went down before the tapestries as wheat before the storm.

Standing before those aged exquisites—those glorious embodiments of patience infinite, imagination high, and matchless craftsmanship, I forgot everything. The style of them was superb. They had quality. About them was nothing mean. They were so rich, so mellow, so delicate. There was a softness to the lovely tones no brush could ever compass. Miracles of detail, marvels of stately effect, the panels were breathing the spirit of their age. Looking upon them, I stepped into another world. I heard the shouts of the huntsmen and the laughter of the handmaidens, I smelled the sweat of the chargers and the sweet scent of the grapes, I felt the cool touch of the shade upon my cheeks. Always the shouts were distant, the scent faint, the laughter low. I wandered up faery glades, loitered in lazy markets, listened to the music of fountains, sat before ample boards, bowed over lily-white hands. . . .

Here, then, was magic. Things other than silk went to the weaving of so potent a spell. The laborious needle put in the dainty threads: the hearts of those that plied it put in most precious memories—treasures of love and laughter . . . the swift brush of lips . . . the echo of a call in the forest . . . a patch of sunlight upon the slope of a hill . . . such stuff, indeed, as dreams are made on. . . .

And there is the bare truth, gentlemen, just as I have stumbled upon it. The tapestries of Pau are dreams—which you may go and share any day except Sundays.

We had almost finished our tour of the apartments, and were standing in the Bedroom of Jeanne d'Albret, staring at a beautiful Gobelin, when I heard the "flop" of something alighting upon the floor.

With one consent, the keeper, Susan, and I swung on our heels.

Advancing stiffly towards us and wagging his scrap of a tail was a small grey-brown dog. His coat was plastered with filth, upon one of his ears was a blotch of dried blood, his muzzle and paws might have been steeped in liquid soot. He stank abominably.

I put up a hand to my head.

"Nobby?" I cried, peering. And then again, "*Nobby?*"

The urchin crept to my feet, put his small dirty head on one side, lowered it to the ground, and then rolled over upon his back. With his legs in the air, he regarded me fixedly, tentatively wagging his tail.

Dazedly I stooped and patted the mud upon his stomach. . . .

The bright eyes flashed. Then, with a squirm, the Sealyham was on his feet and leaping to lick my face.

"B-b-but," shrieked Susan, shaking me by the arm, "is this the —the dog you'd lost?"

"Yes," I shouted, "it is!"

Not until then did the custodian of the apartments find his tongue.

"It is your dog, then!" he raved. "He has marched with us all the time, and I have not seen him. Without an attachment in all these noble rooms! *Mon Dieu!* Dogs may not enter even the grounds, but he must junket in the Château, all vile as he is and smelling like twenty goats."

"Listen," said I. "It's my dog all right, but I never brought him. I've been looking all over Pau. What on earth——"

"But you must have brought him. It is evident. Myself I have shut all the doors. No one has the keys except me. It is impossible."

I pointed to the carved bedstead.

"See for yourself," said I. "He's just jumped down."

The keeper ran to the bed and peered behind the gorgeous parapet. Then he let out a scream of agony.

"Ah, it is true. Ten thousand devils! That so beastly a dog

should have soiled Jeanne d'Albret's bed! Observe the nest he has made in her counterpane. *Mon Dieu!* It is scandalous. *Monsieur,* you will answer for this."

"I shall do nothing of the sort," said I. "But, unless you keep your mouth shut, you will. You shouldn't have let him get in."

I thought the fellow would have choked.

"But it was not I that—— A-a-ah!" he screamed. "See how he approaches the Queen's screen, to destroy it as he has destroyed her bed."

"Nonsense," I said shortly. "He's very struck with the furniture. That's all. Anybody would be. But how the deuce. . . ."

With tears in his eyes the keeper besought me to remove my dog forthwith.

In the circumstances, it seemed best to comply, so, wishing very much that Nobby could speak for himself, I tied my handkerchief to his collar and, with Susan chattering excitedly and clinging to my arm, followed our gibbering guide to the foot of the great staircase.

"He *must* have followed him in," cried Susan. "He simply must. I looked at the chimney, but it's stopped up, and the man says there's no other door. And you know he unlocked each one as we came to it this morning."

"But why's he so filthy?" I said. "And how did he fetch up here? Let's see. He must have come with us as far as Bouzom's. That's only five minutes from here. Then we forgot all about him and left him outside. We were there for ages. I suppose he got fed up with waiting or found a pal or something, and drifted down here. All the same. . . ." I turned to the custodian and took out a fifty-franc note. "He doesn't usually pay so much for a room, but, as this isn't a hotel and he had Jeanne d'Albret's bed. . . ."

The money passed in silence.

I fancy the keeper dared not trust himself to speak.

After all, I was very thankful that Nobby was found.

As we passed out of the gate, a sudden thought came to me, and I turned back.

"I say," I cried, "when last did you visit that room?"

"The Queen's room, Monsieur?"

I nodded.

"Yesterday morning, Monsieur. At nine o'clock."

You could have knocked me down.

I walked towards the car like a man in a dream.

The business smacked of a conjuring trick.

Having lost the terrier in the town, I had been sent to view the Château against my will, there to discover my missing chattel in a locked chamber upon the second floor.

To add to the confusion of my wits, Susan was talking furiously.

". . . I've read of such things. You know. In case of a revolution, for the king to escape. They say there's one at Buckingham Palace."

"One what?" said I abstractedly.

"Underground passage," said Susan. "Leading out into the open. The one from Buckingham Palace goes into a house, I suppose it was country once, and then the ground was built over, or, of course, it might always have led into the house, and they just had loyal people living there or someone from the Court, so that——"

"Heaven and earth!" I roared. "The Villa Buichi."

Susan recoiled with a cry.

I caught her white arm.

"Susan," I yelled, "you've got it in one! The last time we saw him was there. It's a house we saw yesterday. We thought of taking it, but, as soon as he saw us coming, another chap got in quick."

"What a shame!" said Susan. "If only you'd had it, you'd 've been able to go and look at the tapestries whenever you—— Oh, whatever's the matter?"

I suppose my eyes were blazing. I know my brain was.

The murder was out.

"I must see my friend, the Spaniard," I said. "He's made a mistake. *The biggest receiver in France has not retired.*"

Susan stared at me with big eyes.

With a smile, I flung open its door and waved her into the car. . . .

I followed her in.

Then I put my arm round her waist and kissed her pink cheek.

"Now," said I, "you *will* have something to tell them."

Susan gurgled delightedly.

*　　*　　*　　*　　*

The French are nothing if not artistic. They are also good showmen.

It was largely due to the interest of Señor Don Fedriani that, five days later, I had the privilege of sitting for fifty minutes upon an extremely uncomfortable chair in the Oratory of Jeanne d'Albret, and listening at intervals, by means of a delicate instrument, to the biggest receiver in France and his confederates stumbling still more uncomfortably along a dank and noisome passage towards penal servitude for life.

Had he known that the Villa Buichi was surrounded, that the caretaker was already in custody, that a file of soldiers was following a quarter of a mile in his rear, and that the van which was to take him to prison was waiting in the Château's courtyard, my gentleman, who had "lived soft", could not have been more outspoken about the condition of his path.

Not until he had quite finished and had inquired in a blasphemous whisper if all were present, was the strip of magnesium ignited and the photograph made. . . .

I have a copy before me.

The knaves are not looking their best, but the grouping is superb.

*The Toilet of Venus* makes a most exquisite background.


CHAPTER XI

# How Berry Put Off his Manhood, and Adèle Showed a Fair Pair of Heels

But for Susan, I should not have seen the Château, and, but for the merest accident, we should not have revisited Gavarnie. And that would have been a great shame.

It was the day before we were spared this lasting reproach that my brother-in-law stood stiffly before a pier-glass in his wife's bed-chamber. Deliberately Berry surveyed himself.

We stood about him with twitching lips, not daring to trust our tones.

At length—

"But what a dream!" said my brother-in-law. "What an exquisite, pluperfect dream!" Jill shut her eyes and began to shake with laughter. "I suppose it was made to be worn, or d'you think someone did it for a bet? 'A Gentleman of the Court of Louis XIV'. Well, I suppose a French firm ought to know. Only, if they're right, I don't wonder there was a revolution. No self-respecting nation could hold up its head with a lot of wasters shuffling about Versailles with the seats of their breeches beginning under their hocks. That one sleeve is three inches shorter than the other and that the coat would comfortably fit a Boy Scout, I pass over. Those features might be attributed to the dictates of fashion. But I find it hard to believe that even in that fantastic age a waistcoat like a loose cover ever really obtained."

Adèle sank into a chair and covered her eyes.

With an effort I mastered my voice.

"I think, perhaps," I ventured, "if you wore them for an hour or two, they might—might shake down. You see," I continued hurriedly, "you're not accustomed——"

"Brother," said Berry gravely, "you've got it in one. I'm not accustomed to wearing garments such as these. I confess I feel strange in them. Most people who are not deformed would. If I hadn't got any thighs, if my stomach measurement was four times that of my chest, and I'd only one arm, they'd be just about right. As it is, short of mutilation——"

"Can't you brace up the breeches a little higher?" said Daphne.

"No, I can't," snapped her husband. "As it is, my feet are nearly off the ground."

Seated upon the bed, Jonah rolled over upon his side and gave himself up to a convulsion of silent mirth.

"The sleeves and the waistcoat," continued my sister, "are nothing. Adèle and I can easily alter them. What worries me is the breeches."

"They'd worry you a damned sight more if you had 'em on," said Berry. "And if you think I'm going to wear this little song-without-words, even as amended by you and Adèle, you're simply unplaced. To say I wouldn't be seen dead in it conveys nothing at all."

"My dear boy," purred Daphne, "be reasonable. It's far too late to get hold of anything else : it's the ball of the season, and fancy dress is *de rigueur*. I'm sure if you would only brace up——"

With an unearthly shriek, Berry collapsed in my arms.

"Take her away !" he roared. "Take her away before I offer her violence. Explain my anatomy. Tell her I've got a trunk. Conceal nothing. Only . . ."

Amid the explosion of pent-up laughter, the rest of the sentence was lost.

As soon as we could speak coherently, we endeavoured to smooth him down.

At length—

"It's transparently plain," said Jonah, "that that dress is out of the question." Here he took out his watch. "Let's see. It's now three o'clock. That gives us just seven hours to conceive and execute some other confection. It shouldn't be difficult."

"Now you're talking," said Berry. "I know. I'll go as a mahout. Now, that's easy. Six feet of butter muslin, four pennyworth of woad, and a harpoon. And we can lock the elephant's switch and park him in the rhododendrons."

"Why," said Jonah, "shouldn't you go as Mr. Sycamore Tight? You're not unlike him, and the excitement would be intense."

After a little discussion we turned the suggestion down.

For all that, it was not without merit.

Mr. Sycamore Tight was wanted—wanted badly. There was a price upon his head. Two days after he had landed in France, a large American bank had discovered good reason to believe that Mr. Tight had personally depleted its funds to the tune of over a million.

Daily, for the last four days, the gentleman's photograph had appeared in every French paper, illustrating a succinct and compelling advertisement, which included a short summary of his characteristics and announced the offer of a reward of fifty thousand francs for such information as should lead to his arrest.

The French know the value of money.

If the interest excited at Pau was any criterion, every French soul in France went about his business with bulging eyes. Indeed, if Mr. Sycamore Tight were yet in the country, there was little doubt in most minds that his days were numbered.

"No," said Berry. "It's very nice to think that I look so much like the brute, but I doubt if a check suit quite so startling as that he seems to have affected could be procured in time. Shall I go as Marat—on his way to the bath-room? With a night-shirt, a flannel, and a leer, I should be practically there. Oh, and a box of matches to light the geyser with."

"I suppose," said Daphne, "you wouldn't go as a clown? Adèle and I could do that easily. The dress is nothing."

"Is it, indeed?" said her husband. "Well, that would be simplicity itself, wouldn't it? A trifle classical, perhaps, but most arresting. What a scene there'd be when I took off my overcoat. 'Melancholy' would be almost as artless. I could wear a worried look, and there you are."

"Could he go as a friar?" said Jill. "You know. Like a monk, only not so gloomy. We ought to be able to get a robe easily. And, if we couldn't get sandals, he could go barefoot."

"That's right," said Berry. "Don't mind me. You just fix everything up, and tell me in time to change. Oh, and you might write down a few crisp blessings. I shall get tired of saying '*Pax vobis-cum*' when anyone kicks my feet."

"I tell you what," said Adèle. "Would you go as 'a flapper'?"

"A what?" said my brother-in-law.

" 'A twentieth-century miss'," said Adèle. " ' The Golf Girl', if you like. Daphne and I can fit you out, and you can wear your own shoes. As for a wig—any *coiffeur*'ll do. A nice fluffy bobbed one would be best—the same shade as your moustache."

Instinctively none of us spoke.

The idea was so admirable—the result would be so triumphant, that we hardly dared to breathe lest Berry should stamp upon our hopes.

For one full slow-treading minute he fingered his chin. . . .

Then he wrinkled his nose.

"Not 'The Golf Girl'," he said. "That's much too pert. I couldn't deliver the goods. No. I must go as something more luscious. What about 'The Queen of the May'?"

*   *   *   *   *

At twenty-five minutes to ten that evening I was writing a note, and wondering, while I did so, whether the original "Incroyables" ever sat down.

I had just decided that, rather than continually risk dislocation of the knee, they probably either reclined or leaned against pillars when fatigued, when something impelled me to glance over my shoulder.

Framed in the doorway was standing Berry.

A frock of pale pink georgette, with long bell-shaped sleeves and a black velvet girdle knotted at one side, fitted him seemingly like a glove. A large Leghorn hat, its black velvet streamers fastened beneath his chin, heavily weighted with a full-blown rose over one eye, threatened to hide his rebellious mop of hair. White silk stockings and a pair of ordinary pumps completed his attire. A miniature apron, bearing the stencilled legend "AN ENGLISH ROSE" upon its muslin, left no doubt about his identity.

Beneath my gaze he looked down and simpered, swinging his bead bag ridiculously.

I leaned back in my chair and began to laugh like a madman. Then I remembered my knee-caps, and got up and leaned against the wall, whence I could see him better.

As if his appearance alone were not enough, he spoke in an absurd falsetto.

"No, I'm not supposed to be out till after Easter. But don't let that stop you. I mean—you know I do say such dreadful things, and all the time. . . . Father always calls me a tom-cat—I mean, tom-boy, but I don't care. Haven't you any sisters? What not even a 'step'? Oh, but what luck—I mean, I think we'll sit this one out, shall I? I know a lovely place—in the inspection pit. I often go and sit there when I want to have a good fruity drink—I mean, think. I always think it's so wonderful to look up and see the gear-box, and the differential, and the dear old engine-shield and feel you're alone with them all—absolutely alone. . . ."

The tempestuous arrival of Adèle, looking sweet as "Pierrette", and Jonah in the traditional garb of "Harlequin", cut short the soliloquy. . . .

It was ere the two had recovered from their first paroxysm of laughter that Berry minced to the fire-place and, with the coyest of pecks, rang the electric bell.

A moment later Falcon entered the room.

My brother-in-law laughed and looked down, fingering his dress.

"Oh, Falcon," he said archly, "about to-morrow. I don't know whether Mrs. Pleydell's told you, but there'll be four extra to lunch."

I have seen Falcon's eyes twinkle, and I have seen his mouth work—times without number. I have seen him thrust a decanter upon the sideboard and disappear shaking from the apartment. But never before have I seen his self-control crumple as a ripped balloon.

For a second he stared at the speaker.

Then he flung us one desperate, appealing glance, emitted a short wail, and, looking exactly as if he was about to burst into tears, clapped both hands to his mouth and made a rush for the door.

As he reached it, a little Dutch Jill danced into the room, looking adorable.

Use holds.

Falcon straightened his back, stepped to one side, and bowed his apologies. The temporary check, however, was his undoing. As Jill flashed by, he turned his face to the wall and sobbed like a child. . . .

When Daphne made her appearance, amazingly beautiful as "Jehane Saint-Pol", we climbed into the cars and slipped down the sober drive into the fragrant dalliance of an April night.

\*    \*    \*    \*    \*

The ball was over.

It would have been a success any way, but from the moment that Berry had, upon arrival, been directed to the ladies' cloak-room, its enduring fame had been assured.

When, with my wife and sister, reluctant and protesting, upon either arm, he erupted into the ballroom, giggling excitedly and crying "Votes for Women!" in a shrill treble, even the band broke down, so that the music died an untimely and tuneless death. When he danced a Tango with me, wearing throughout an exalted expression of ineffable bliss and introducing a bewildering variety of unexpected halts, crouchings and saggings of the knees—when, in the midst of an interval, he came flying to Daphne, calling her "Mother", insisting that he had been insulted, demanding to be taken home forthwith, and finally burying his face in her shoulder and bursting into tears—when, during supper, with a becoming diffidence, he took his stand upon a chair and said a few words about his nursing experiences in Mesopotamia and spoke with emotion of the happy hours he had spent as a Sergeant-Minor of the Women Police—then it became manifest that my brother-in-law's construction of the laws of hospitality had set up such a new record of generosity as few, if any, of those present would ever see broken.

". . . Oh, and the flies, you know. The way they flew. Oh, it was dreadful. And, of course, no lipstick would stick. My dears, I was simply terrified to look in the biscuit box. And then we had to wash in bits—so embarrassing. Talk about divisional reserve. . . . And they were so strict with it all. Only ten little minutes late on parade, and you got it where auntie wore the gew-gaws. I lost my temper once. To be sworn at like a golf-sphere, just because one day I couldn't find my *Poudre d'Amour*. . . . And, when he'd quite finished, the Colonel asked me what powder was for. I just looked round and gave him some of his own back. 'To dam your pores with,' I said. . . ."

It was past three o'clock before our departure was sped.

Comfortably weary, we reached our own villa's door to make the grisly discovery that no one had remembered the key. . . .

There was no knocker : a feeble electric bell signalled out distress to a deserted basement : the servants were asleep upon the second floor.

After we had all reviled Berry and, in return, been denounced as "a gang of mut-jawed smoke-stacks", accused of "blasphemy" and compared to "jackals and vultures about a weary bull", we began to shout and throw stones at the second-floor windows. Perhaps because their shutters were closed, our labour was lost.

To complete our disgust, for some mysterious reason Nobby refused to bark and so sound the alarm. In the ordinary way the Sealyham was used to give tongue—whatever the hour and no matter what indignation he might excite—upon the slightest provocation. This morning we perambulated the curtilage of the villa, alternately yelling like demoniacs and mewing like cats, without the slightest result.

Eventually it was decided that one of us must effect an entrance by climbing on to the balcony of my sister's room. . . .

Jonah had a game leg: the inflexibility of my pantaloons put any acrobatics out of the question : Berry's action, at any rate, was more than usually unrestricted. Moreover, it was Berry whom we had expected to produce the key.

It became necessary to elaborate these simple facts, and to indicate most definitely the moral which they were pointing, before my brother-in-law was able to grasp the one or to appreciate the other. And when it had been, as they say, borne in upon him that he was for the high jump, another ten minutes were wasted while he made one final, frantic, solitary endeavour to attract the servants' attention. His feminine personality discarded, he raved about the house, barking, screeching and braying to beat the band ; he thundered upon the door with his fists ; he flung much of the drive in the direction of the second floor. Finally, when we were weak with laughter, he sat down upon the steps, expressed his great satisfaction at the reception of his efforts to amuse, and assured us that his death-agony, which we should shortly witness, would be still more diverting.

By now it was a quarter to four, and, so soon as Jonah and I could control our emotion, we took our deliverer by the arms and showed him "the best way up".

He listened attentively.

At length—

"Thanks very much," he said weakly. "Let's just go over it again, shall I? Just to be sure I've got it cold. First, I swarm up that pillar. Good. I may say I never have swarmed. I never knew anybody did swarm, except bees or people coming out of a football match. Never mind. Then I get hold of the gutter and draw myself up with my hands, while continuing to swarm with my legs.

If—if the gutter will stand my weight. . . . Of course, that's easily ascertained. I just try it. If it will, it does. If it won't, I should like a penny-in-the-slot machine erected in my memory outside the English Club. Yes, I've got that. Well, if it will, I work—I think you said 'work'—round until I can reach the down-pipe. The drain—down-pipe will enable me to get my feet into the gutter. Sounds all right, doesn't it? 'The drain-pipe will enable'. A cryptic phrase. Quite the Brigade-Office touch. Where were we? Oh, yes. The drain-pipe having enabled me, etc., I just fall forward on to the tiles, when my hands will encounter and grasp the balustrade. Then I climb over and pat Nobby. Yes, except for the cesspool—I mean the drain-pipe—interlude, it's too easy."

We helped him off with his coat. . . .

We watched his reduction of the pillar with trembling lips; we heard his commentary upon gutters and those who make them with shaking shoulders; but it was when, with one foot in the air and the other wedged behind the down-pipe, the English Rose spoke of the uncertainty of life and inquired if we believed in Hell —when, after an exhausting and finally successful effort to get his left knee into the gutter, he first knelt upon a spare tile to his wounding and then found that his right foot was inextricably wedged between the down-pipe and the wall—when, as a result of his struggles, a section of the down-pipe came away in his hand, so that he was left clinging to the gutter with one foot in the air and twelve feet of piping swaying in his arms—then our control gave way and we let ourselves run before a tempest of Homeric laughter. We clasped one another; we leaned against walls; we stamped upon the ground; we fought for breath; tears streamed from our eyes. All the time, in a loud militant voice, Berry spoke of building and architects and mountain goats, of France and of the French, of incitement to suicide, of inquests and the law, of skunks and leprosy, and finally of his descent. . . .

When we told him tearfully to drop, he let out the laugh of a maniac.

"Yes," he said uncertainly. "To tell you hell-hounds the truth, that solution had already occurred to me. It's been occurring to me vividly ever since I began. But I'm against it. It isn't that I'm afraid, but I want something more difficult. Oh, and don't say, 'Work round the gutter', first, because it's bad English, and, secondly, because no man born of woman could 'work round' this razor-edged conduit with a hundredweight of drain-pipe round his neck. What I want is a definite instruction which is neither murderous nor futile. Burn it, you handed me enough slush when I was rising. Why the hell can't you slobber out something to help me down?"

By the time his descent was accomplished, it was past four o'clock—summer time—and there was a pale cast about the sweet moonlight that told of the coming of another dawn.

"I say," said Jill suddenly, "don't let's go to bed."

"No, don't let's," said Berry, with a hysterical laugh. "Let's—let's absolutely refuse."

Jill went on breathlessly—

"Let's go for a run towards Lourdes and see the sun rise over the mountains."

Our first impulse was to denounce the idea. Upon examination, however, its hidden value emerged.

We were sick and tired of trying to wake the servants; to effect an entrance was seemingly out of the question; to spend another two hours wandering about the garden or wooing slumber in the cars was not at all to our liking.

Finally, we decided that, since we should be back before the world proper was astir, our appearance, if it was noticed at all, would but afford a few peasants an experience which they could relate with relish for many years, and that, since the sky was cloudless, so convenient an occasion of observing a very famous effect should not be rejected.

Five minutes later Ping and Pong slid silently under the Pont Oscar II, and so down a winding hill, out of the sleeping town and on to the Bizanos road.

Our headlights were powerful, the road was not too bad, and the world was empty. . . .

I let Jonah, who was leading, get well away, and then gave the car her head.

Well as we knew it, our way seemed unfamiliar.

We saw the countryside as through a glass darkly. A shadowy file of poplars, a grey promise of meadowland, a sable thicket, far in the distance a great blurred mass rearing a sombre head, a chain of silent villages seemingly twined about our road, and once in a long while the broad, brave flash of laughing water—these and their ghostly like made up our changing neighbourhood. Then came a link in the chain that even Wizard Night could not transfigure—sweet, storied Coarraze, fencing our way with its peculiar pride of church and state; three miles ahead, hoary Bétharram, defender of the faith, lent us its famous bridge—at the toll of a break-neck turn, of which no manner of moonshine can cheat the memory.

We were nearing Lourdes now, but there was no sign of Jonah. I began to wonder whether my cousin was faring farther afield. . . .

It was so.

Lourdes is a gate-house of the Pyrenees; it was clear that my sister and cousins had threaded its echoing porch. Their way was good enough for us. We swung to the right, dived into and out of the sleeping town, and flung up the pale, thin road that heads for Spain. . . .

It was when we had slipped through Argelès, and Jonah was still before us, that we knew that if we would catch him we must climb to Gavarnie.

The daylight was waxing now, and when we came to Pierre-fitte I switched off the lights.

There is a gorge in the mountains some seven miles long. It is, I think, Nature's boudoir. Its tall, steep walls are hung with foliage—a trembling, precious arras, which spring will so emblazon with her spruce heraldry that every blowing rod breathes a refreshing madrigal. Its floor is a busy torrent—fretting its everlasting way by wet, grey rocks, the vivid green of ferns, and now and again a little patch of greensward—a tender lawn for baby elves to play on. Here is a green shelf, ladies, stuck all with cowslips; and there, another—radiant with peering daffodils. In this recess sweet violets grow. Look at that royal gallery; it is fraught with crocuses—laden with purple and gold. Gentians and buttercups, too, have their own nurseries. But one thing more—this gorge is full of fountains. They are its especial glory. All the beauty in the world of falling water is here exhibited. Tremendous falls go thundering: long, slender tresses of water plunge from a dizzy height, lose by the way their symmetry, presently vanish into sparkling smoke; cascades, with a delicate flourish, leap from ledge to ledge; stout heads of crystal well bubbling out of Earth; elegant springs flash musically into their brimming basins of the living rock. The mistress of this shining court is very beautiful. A bank is overhanging a little bow-shaped dell, as the eaves of an old house lean out to shelter half a pavement. As eaves, too, are thatched, so the brown bank is clad with emerald moss. From the edge of the moss dangles a silver fringe. Each gleaming, twisted cord of it hangs separate and distinct, save when a breath of wind plaits two or three into a transient tassel. The fringe is the waterfall.

Enchanted with such a fairyland, we lingered so long over our passage that we only reached Gavarnie with a handful of moments to spare.

As we had expected, here were the others, a little apart from the car, their eyes lifted to the ethereal terraces of the majestic Cirque.

The East was afire with splendour. All the blue dome of sky was blushing. Only the Earth was dull.

Suddenly the topmost turret of the frozen battlements burst into rosy flame. . . .

One by tremendous one we saw the high places of the world suffer their King's salute. Little wonder that, witnessing so sublime a ceremony, we forgot all Time. . . .

The sudden clack of shutters flung back against a wall brought us to earth with a jar.

We turned in the direction of the noise.

From the window of a cottage some seventy paces away a woman was regarding us steadily. . . .

We re-entered the cars with more precipitation than dignity.

A glance at the clock in the dashboard made my heart sink.

A quarter past six—summer time.

It was clear that Gavarnie was lazy. Argelès, Lourdes, and the rest must be already bustling. Long ere we could reach Pau, the business of town and country would be in full swing. . . .

The same reflection, I imagine, had bitten Jonah, for, as I let in the clutch, Ping swept past us and whipped into the village with a low snarl.

Fast as we went, we never saw him again that memorable morning. Jonah must have gone like the wind.

As for us, we wasted no time.

We leapt through the village, dropped down the curling pass, snarled through Saint-Sauveur, left Luz staring, and sailed into Argelès as it was striking seven.

From Argelès to Lourdes is over eight miles. It was when we had covered exactly four of these in six minutes that the engine stuttered, sighed, and then just fainted away.

We had run out of petrol.

This was annoying, but not a serious matter, for there was a can on the step. The two gallons it was containing would easily bring us to Pau.

What was much more annoying and of considerable moment was that the can, when examined, proved to be dry as a bone.

After a moment's consideration of the unsavoury prospect, so

suddenly unveiled, I straightened my back, pushed my ridiculous
hat to the nape of my neck, and took out a cigarette-case.

Adèle and Berry stared.

"That's right," said the latter bitterly. "Take your blinking time.
Why don't you sit down on the bank and put your feet up?"

I felt for a match.

Finger to lip, Adèle leaned forward.

"For Heaven's sake," she cried, "don't say there's none in the
can!"

"My darling," said I, "you've spoken the naked truth."

There was a long silence. The gush of a neighbouring spring
was suggesting a simple peace we could not share.

Suddenly—

"Help!" shrieked the English Rose. "Help! I'm being com-
promised."

So soon as we could induce him to hold his tongue, a council was
held.

Presently it was decided that I must return to Argelès, if possible, procure a car, and bring some petrol back as fast as I could.
Already the day was growing extremely hot, and, unless I encountered a driver who would give me a lift, it seemed unlikely
that I should be back within an hour and a half.

We had, of course, no hope of salvation. Help that arrived now
would be too late. Lourdes would be teeming. The trivial round
of Pau would be in full blast. The possible passage of another car
would spare us—me particularly—some ignominy, but that was
all.

It was arranged that, should a car appear after I had passed
out of sight, the driver should be accosted, haply deprived of petrol,
and certainly dispatched in my pursuit.

Finally we closed Pong, and, feeling extremely self-conscious
and unpleasantly hot, I buttoned my overcoat about me and set
out for Argelès.

The memory of that walk will stay with me till I die.

If, a few hours before, I had been satisfied that "Incroyables"
seldom sat down, I was soon in possession of most convincing evidence that, come what might, they never did more than stroll.
The pantaloons, indeed, curtailed every pace I took. It also became painfully obvious that their "foot-joy" was intended for use
only upon tiled pavements or parquet, and since the surface of
the road to Argelès was bearing a closer resemblance to the bed
of a torrent, I suffered accordingly. What service their headgear

in any conceivable circumstances could have rendered, I cannot pretend to say. As a protection from the rays of the sun, it was singularly futile. . . .

Had I been wearing flannels, I should have been sweltering in a quarter of an hour. Dressed as I was, I was streaming with honest sweat in less than five minutes. . . . Before I had covered half a mile I tore off my overcoat and flung it behind a wall.

My reception at the first hamlet I reached was hardly promising.

The honour of appreciating my presence before anyone else fell to a pair of bullocks attached to a wain piled high with wood and proceeding slowly in the direction of Lourdes.

Had they perceived an apparition shaking a bloody goad, they could not have acted with more concerted or devastating rapidity.

In the twinkling of an eye they had made a complete *volte-face*, the waggon was lying on its side across the fairway, and its burden of logs had been distributed with a dull crash upon about a square perch of cobbles.

Had I announced my coming by tuck of drum, I could not have attracted more instant and faithful attention.

Before the explosion of agony with which the driver—till then walking, as usual, some thirty paces in rear—had greeted the catastrophe, had turned into a roaring torrent of abuse, every man, woman, and child within earshot came clattering upon the scene.

For a moment, standing to one side beneath the shelter of a flight of steps, I escaped notice. It was at least appropriate that the luckless waggoner should have been the first to perceive me. . . .

At the actual moment of observation he was at once indicating the disposition of his wood with a gesture charged with the savage despair of a barbaric age and letting out a screech which threatened to curdle the blood.

The gesture collapsed. The screech died on his lips.

With dropped jaw and bulging eyes, the fellow backed to the wall. . . . When I stepped forward, he put the waggon between us.

I never remember so poignant a silence.

Beneath the merciless scrutiny of those forty pairs of eyes I seemed to touch the very bottom of abashment.

Then I lifted my ridiculous hat and cleared my throat.

"Good day," I said cheerfully, speaking in French. "I'm on my way back from a ball—a fancy-dress ball—and my car has run out of petrol. I want to hire a cart to go to Argelès."

If I had said I wanted to hire a steam-yacht, my simple

statement could not have been more apathetically received. . . .

Happily, for some unobvious reason, no one seemed to associate me with the bullocks' waywardness, but it took me ten minutes' cajolery to elicit the address of a peasant who might hire me a cart.

At last I was told his lodging and pointed the way.

Such direction proved supererogatory, first, because we all moved off together, and, secondly, because it subsequently transpired that the gentleman whom I was seeking was already present. But that is France.

Upon arrival at his house my friend stepped out of the ruck and, with the utmost composure, asked if it was true that I was desiring to be driven to Argelès. Controlling my indignation, I replied with equal gravity that such was my urgent ambition. Taking a wristwatch from my pocket, I added that upon reaching a garage at Argelès, I would deduct the time we had taken from half an hour and cheerfully give him a franc for every minute that was left.

I can only suppose that so novel a method of payment aroused his suspicion.

Be that as it may, with an apologetic bow, the fellow requested to see the colour of my money.

Then and then only did I remember that I had not a brass farthing upon my person.

What was worse, I felt sure that Adèle and Berry were equally penniless . . .

My exit from that village I try to forget.

I found that the waters of humiliation were deeper than I could have believed. They seemed, in fact, bottomless.

It is, perhaps, unnecessary to say that I returned by the way I had come. I had had enough of the road to Argelès. My one idea was to rejoin Adèle and Berry and to sit down in the car. Mentally and physically I was weary to death. I craved to set my back against the buttress of company in this misfortune, and I was mad to sit down. Compared with standing any longer upon my feet, the contingency of dislocation became positively attractive. . . .

The first thing that met my eyes, as I limped round the last of the bends, was the bonnet of a dilapidated touring car.

I could have thrown up my rotten hat.

A few feet further from Lourdes than Pong himself was an aged grey French car. Standing in the white road between the two was a strapping figure in pale pink georgette and a large Leghorn hat, apparently arguing with three blue-covered mechanics. From

Pong's offside window the conical hat and extravagant ruff of "Pierrette" were protruding excitedly.

My companions' relief to see me again was unfeigned.

As I came up, Adèle gave a whimper of delight, and a moment later she was pouring her tale into my ears.

"You hadn't been gone long when these people came by. We stopped them, of course, and——"

"One moment," said I. "Have they got any petrol?"

"Listen," said Berry. "Four *bidons* of what they had are in our tank. It was when they were in, that we found we hadn't a bean. That didn't matter. The gents were perfectly happy to take my address. A pencil was produced—we had nothing, of course—and I started to write it all down on the edge of yesterday's *Le Temps*. They all looked over my shoulder. As I was writing, I *felt* their manner change. I stopped and looked round. *The fools were staring at me as if I were risen from the dead.* That mayn't surprise you, but it did me, because we'd got through that phase. For a moment we looked at one another. Then one picked up the paper and took off his hat. 'It is unnecessary,' he said, 'for *Monsieur* to give us his name. We know it perfectly.' The others nodded agreement. I tell you, I thought they'd gone mad. . . ."

He pushed his hat back from his eyes and sat down on the step.

"But—but what's the trouble?" I gasped.

Berry threw out his hands.

"Haven't you got it?" he said. "*They think I'm Sycamore Tight.*"

\*          \*          \*          \*          \*

I soon perceived the vanity of argument.

With my brother-in-law in the hand and fifty thousand francs in the bush, the three mechanics were inexorable.

They accepted my statements; they saw my point of view; they uncovered; they bowed; they laughed when I laughed; they admitted the possibility, nay, likelihood of a mistake; they deplored the inconvenience we were suffering. But, politely and firmly, they insisted that Berry should enter their car and accompany them to Lourdes.

That this their demand should be met was not to be thought of.

Adèle and I could not desert Berry; from the police at Lourdes nothing was to be expected but suspicion, hostility, and maddeningly officious delays; Berry's eventual release would only be obtained at a cost of such publicity as made my head swim.

Any idea of force was out of the question. But for the presence of my wife, we would have done what we could. With Adèle in our care, however, we could not afford to fail, and—they were three to two.

I racked my brain desperately. . . .

Presently one of the trio lugged out a watch. When he showed his fellows the hour, they flung up their arms. A moment later they were clearing for action.

*Le Temps* was carefully folded and stuffed out of sight. Berry was informed, with a bow, that, so soon as their car was turned round, they would be ready to leave. The slightest of the three stepped to the starting-handle. . . .

The next moment, with a deafening roar, their engine was under way.

I was standing with my hand upon our off hind wing, and as the driver ran to his throttle, I felt a steady tremor.

*Under cover of the other car's roar, Adèle had started Pong's engine.*

What was a great deal more, *she had given me my cue.*

I thought like lightning.

There was not a moment to lose. Already the driver was in his seat and fumbling with his gear-lever. . . .

As slowly as I dared, I strolled to the off-side door.

Adèle's and my eyes met.

"When you hear me say, 'Look'," I said.

With the faintest smile, "Pierrette" stared through the wind-screen. . . .

I returned to the rear of the car.

The way we were using was narrow, but fifty paces away in the direction of Argelès was a track which left our road to lead to a farm. For this spot the driver was making. There he would be able to turn with the acme of ease.

His two companions were standing close to Berry.

As luck would have it, the latter was standing with his back to our car, perhaps a foot from the tail-lamp.

Not one of the three, I fancy, had any idea that our engine was running.

I addressed the mechanics in French.

"I have been talking with *Madame*, and, tired as she is, she agrees that it will be best if we follow you to Lourdes. Please don't go too fast when you get to the town, or we shall lose our way."

As they assured me of their service, I turned to Berry, as though to translate what I had said.

"There are two steps to the dickey. The lower one is two paces to your right and one to your rear. It is not meant for a seat, but it will do. Throw your arm round the spare wheels and sit tight."

Berry shrugged his shoulders.

A glance up the road showed me the other car being turned into the track.

I crossed to the near side of Pong and stopped as though to examine the exhaust. The two mechanics were watching me. . . .

With the tail of my eye I saw Berry glance behind him, sink down upon the step, drop his head miserably into the crook of his arm, and set that arm upon the spare wheels.

Suddenly I straightened my back, glanced past the two warders, and flung out a pointing arm.

"*Look!*" I shouted, and stepped on to the running-board.

As I spoke, Adèle let in the clutch. . . .

It was really too easy.

By the time our two friends had decided to turn and inquire what had excited my remark, we were ten paces away and gathering speed . . .

Of course they ran after us, yelling like men possessed.

That was but human.

Then they recovered their wits and raced for their car.

I cried to Berry to sit tight, and opened the door. . . .

"Is he on?" said Adèle, as I took my seat by her side.

I nodded.

"As soon as we're far enough on, we must take him inside. He ought to be safe enough, but I'll bet he's blessing his petticoats. As for you, sweetheart, I don't know which is the finer—your nerve or your wit."

A cool hand stole into mine.

Then—

"But we're not there yet," said Adèle.

This was unhappily true.

Pong was the faster car, and Adèle was already going the deuce of a pace. But there was traffic to come, and two level crossings lay between us and Lourdes.

I turned and looked out of the glass in the back of the hood. The English Rose had thrust herself inelegantly on to the petrol tank. Her right foot was jammed against a wing, so that her shapely leg acted as a brace : her arms clasped the two spare wheels convulsively : her head was thrown back, and her lips were moving. . . .

Of our pursuers there was no sign. That moment we had rounded a bend, but when a moment later we rounded another they were still out of sight.

I began to wonder whether it was safe to stop and take Berry inboard. . . .

Then the Klaxon belched, and a cry from Adèle made me turn.

Two hundred yards ahead was a flock of sheep—all over the road.

We had to slow down to a pace which jabbed at my nerves.

I did not know what to do.

I did not know whether to seize the chance and take Berry inside, or whether to put the obstacle between Pong and the terror behind, and I felt I must look at the sheep.

The speedometer dropped to twenty . . . to fifteen . . . to ten. . . .

Then the tyres tore at the road, and we practically stopped.

Adèle changed into second speed.

I opened the door instantly, only to see that to collect Berry now was out of the question. The sheep were all round us—like a flood—lapping our sides.

Adèle changed into first.

I was physically afraid to look behind.

The next moment we were through.

We stormed round a curve to see a level crossing a quarter of a mile ahead.

*The gates were shut.*

Adèle gave a cry of despair.

"Oh, Boy, we're done!"

"Not yet," said I, opening the door again. "Go right up to them, lass. At least, it'll give us a chance to get Berry inside."

We stopped with a jerk three feet from the rails.

As I ran for the gate, I glanced over my shoulder.

"Now's your chance!" I shouted. "Get . . ."

I never completed the sentence.

*The English Rose was gone.*

I stopped still in my tracks.

Then I rushed back to the car.

"He's gone!" I cried. "We've dropped him! Quick! Reverse up the way we've come, for all you're worth."

Adèle backed the car with the speed and skill of a professional. I stood on the running-board, straining my eyes. . . .

The next moment a dilapidated touring car tore round the bend we were approaching and leapt towards us.

It passed us with locked wheels, rocking to glory.

At a nod from me, Adèle threw out the clutch. . . .

As the mechanics came up—

"I'm sorry, *Messieurs*," I said, "but I fear you've passed him. No, he's not here. Pray look in the car. . . . Quite satisfied? Good. Yes, we dropped him a long way back. We thought it wiser."

With that I wished them "Good day", and climbed into our car.

"But what shall we do?" said Adèle.

"Get home," said I, "as quick as ever we can. So long as we stay hereabouts, those fellows'll stick to us like glue. We must go and get help and come back. Berry'll hide somewhere where he can watch the road."

As we passed over the level crossing, I looked behind.

The dilapidated grey car was being turned round feverishly.

*   *   *   *   *

Forty-five minutes later we sped up the shadowy drive and stopped by our own front door.

"Pierrette" switched off the engine and sat looking miserably before her.

"I wish," she said slowly, "I wish you'd let me go with you. I did hate leaving him so, and I'd feel——"

With a hand on the door, I touched her pale cheek.

"My darling," said I, "you've done more than your bit—far more, and you're going straight to bed. As for leaving him—well, you know how much I liked it, but I know when I'm done."

" 'Tis the last rose of summer,<br>Left blooming alone. . . ."

Delivered with obvious emotion in a muffled baritone voice, Moore's famous words seemed to come from beneath us.

Adèle and I stared at one another with starting eyes. . . .

Then I fell out of the car and clawed at the flap of the dickey. . . .

My hands were trembling, but I had it open at last.

Her head pillowed upon a spare tube, the ruin of "An English Rose" regarded me coyly.

"I think you might have knocked," she said, simpering. "Supposing I'd been *en déshabille*!"

## CHAPTER XII

## *How a Telegram Came for Jill, Piers Demanded his Sweetheart, and I Drove After my Wife*

My Darling Jill,

It's all finished now, and I can start for Paris to-morrow.
I must stay there one night, to sign some papers, and then I
can leave for Pau. And on next Sunday morning as ever is,
we'll have breakfast together. Perhaps—— No, I won't say
it. Any way, Sunday morning at latest. Everyone's been awfully kind, and—you'll never guess what's coming—Cousin
Leslie's turned out a white man. He's the one, you know, who
brought the suit. The day I got back from Irikli I got a note
from him, saying that, while he couldn't pretend he wasn't
sorry he'd lost his case, he knew how to take a beating, and,
now that it was all over, couldn't we be friends, and asking
me to come and dine with him and his wife at the Grand
Hotel. Old Vissochi didn't want me to go, and kept quoting
something out of Virgil about "fearing the Greeks", but, of
course, I insisted. And I am so glad I did. Leslie and his wife
were simply splendid. Nobody could have been nicer, and
considering that, if he'd won, he'd 've had the title, estates,
money and everything, I think it speaks jolly well for them
both. They've got two ripping little boys, and they were
frightfully interested to hear about you. They'd no idea, of
course, but I just had to tell them. They were so astonished
at first they could hardly speak. And then Mrs. Trunk
picked up her glass and cried out, "Hurray, Hurray", and
they both drank to us both, and everybody was staring, and
Leslie got quite red with embarrassment at their having made
such a scene. Then they made me tell them what you looked
like, and I did my best, and they laughed and said I was
caking it on, so I showed them your photograph. And then
Mrs. Trunk made me show her a letter of yours, and told
your character from your handwriting, and we had a great
time. Oh, Jill, I'm longing for you to see Irikli. Of course I
love Rome, but I think we'll have to be at Como a lot. Father
always liked it the best, and I think you will. It's so lovely, it

makes you want to shout. It only wants a princess with golden hair to make it fairyland, and now it's going to have one. Oh, my darling, I'm just living to see your beautiful face again and your great grave grey eyes. Jill, have you any idea what wonderful eyes you've got? I say, we are going to be happy, aren't we? So happy, we shan't have time for anything else. But I can't wear a body-belt, dear. Not after this. I promised I would till I came back, but I'm almost melted. I don't think Jonah can be right. Any way, I'll bet he doesn't wear one.

Your very loving

PIERS.

My cousin showed us the letter with the artless confidence of a child.

Excepting herself, I don't think any one of us shared the writer's enthusiasm about Mr. Leslie Trunk. We quite agreed with Signor Vissochi. It was hard to believe that the man who had instituted such an iniquitous suit could so swiftly forgive the costly drubbing he had received, or, as heir-presumptive to the dukedom, honestly welcome the news of Piers' engagement. Sweetheart Jill, however, knew little of leopards and their spots. Out of respect for such unconsciousness, we held our peace. There was no hurry, and Piers could be tackled at our convenience. . . .

The conversation turned to our impending departure from France.

"I take it," said Jonah, "that we go as we came. If we're going to Paris for the Grand Prix, there's not much object in stopping there now. In any event, it 'ld mean our going by train and sending the cars by sea. I'm not going to drive in Paris for anyone. I'm too old."

After a little discussion, we decided that he was right.

"Same route?" said Adèle.

"I think so," said Jonah. "Except that we miss Bordeaux and go by Bergerac instead."

"Is that shorter or longer?" said Berry. "Not that I really care, because I wouldn't visit Bordeaux a second time for any earthly consideration. I've seen a good many poisonous places in my time, but for inducing the concentrated essence of depression, that moth-eaten spectre of bustling commerce has them, as the immortal B-B-B-Wordsworth says, beat to a b-b-b-string-bag."

"I don't seem to remember," said Daphne, "that it was so awful."

"It wasn't," said I. "But the circumstances in which he visited it were somewhat drab. Still, it's not an attractive town, and, as the other way's shorter and the road's about twice as good——"

"I'm glad it's shorter," said Berry. "I want to get to Angoulême in good time."

"Why?" said Jill.

Berry eyed her reproachfully.

"Child," he said, "is your gratitude so short-lived? Have you in six slight months forgotten that at Angoulême we were given the very finest dinner that ever we ate? A meal without frills—nine tender courses long? For which we paid the equivalent of rather less than five shillings a head?"

"Oh, I remember," said Jill. "That was where they made us use the same knife all through dinner."

"And what," demanded Berry, "of that? A conceit—a charming conceit. Thus was the glorious tradition of one course handed down to those that followed after. I tell you, that for me the idea of another 'crowded hour' in Angoulême goes far to ameliorate the unpleasant prospect of erupting into the middle of an English spring."

"It's clear," said I, "that you should do a gastronomic tour. Every department of France has its particular dainty. With a reliable list, an almanac, and a motor ambulance, you could do wonders."

My brother-in-law groaned.

"It wouldn't work," he said miserably. "It wouldn't work. They'd clash. When you were in Picardy, considering some *pâtés de Canards*, you'd get a wire from Savoy saying that the salmon trout were in the pink, and on the way there you'd get another from Gascony to say that in twenty-four hours they wouldn't answer for the flavour of the ortolans."

"Talking of gluttony," said Jonah, "if they don't bring lunch pretty soon, we shall be late. It's past one now, and the meeting's the other side of Morlaas. First race, two-fifteen."

I rose and strolled to the Club-house, to see the steward. . . .

This day was the sixteenth of April, and Summer was coming in. Under our very eyes, plain, woods and foothills were putting on amain her lovely livery. We had played a full round of golf over a blowing valley we hardly knew. Billowy emerald banks masked the familiar sparkle of the hurrying Gave; the fine brown lace of rising woods had disappeared, and, in its stead, a broad hanging terrace of delicate green stood up against the sky; from being a

jolly counterpane, the plain of Billère itself had become a cheerful quilt; as for the foot-hills, they were so monstrously tricked out
with fine fresh ruffles and unexpected equipage of greenery, with
a strange epaulet upon that shoulder and a brand-new periwig
upon that brow, that if high hills but hopped outside the Psalter
you would have sworn the snowy Pyrenees had found new
equerries.

Luncheon was served indoors.

Throughout the winter the lawn before the Club-house had
made a dining-room. To-day, however, we were glad of the shade.

"Does Piers know," said Adèle, "that he's coming home with
us?"

Jill shook her head.

"Not yet. I meant to tell him in my last letter, but I forgot." She
turned to Daphne. "You don't think we could be married at once?
I'm sure Piers wouldn't mind, and I'd be so much easier. He does
want looking after, you know. Fancy his wanting to leave off that
belt thing."

"Yes, just fancy," said Berry. "Apart from the fact that it was a
present from you, it'd be indecent."

"It isn't that," said Jill. "But he might get an awful chill."

"I know," said Berry. "I know. That's my second point. Keep
the abdominal wall quarter of an inch deep in lamb's wool, and
in the hottest weather you'll never feel cold. Never mind. If he
mentions it again, we'll make its retention a term of the marriage
settlement."

Jill eyed him severely before proceeding.

"It could be quite quiet," she continued; "the wedding, I mean.
At a registry place——"

"Mrs. Hunt's, for instance," said Berry.

"——and then we could all go down to White Ladies together,
and when he has to go back to fix things up in Italy, I could go,
too."

"My darling," said Daphne, "don't you want to be married
from home? In our own old church at Bilberry? For only one
thing, if you weren't, I don't think the village would ever get over
it."

Jill sighed.

"When you talk like that," she said, "I don't want to be married at all. . . . Yes, I do. I want Piers. I wouldn't be happy without him. But . . . If only he hadn't got four estates of his own, we
might——"

"Five," said Berry. Jill opened her big grey eyes. "Four now, and a share in another upon his wedding day."

Jill knitted her brow.

"I never knew this," she said. "What's the one he's going to have?"

Berry raised his eyebrows.

"It's a place in Hampshire," he said. "Not very far from Brooch. They call it White Ladies."

The look which Jill gave us, as we acclaimed his words, came straight out of Paradise.

"I do wish he could have heard you," she said uncertainly. "I'll tell him, of course. But it won't be the same. And my memory isn't short-lived really. I'd forgotten the Angoulême dinner, but I shan't forget this lunch in a hundred years."

"In another minute," said Berry, "I shall imbrue this omelet with tears. Then it'll be too salt." He seized his tumbler and raised it above his head. "I give you Monsieur Roland. May he touch the ground in spots this afternoon. Five times he's lent me an 'unter-'oss out of sheer good nature; his taste in cocktails is venerable; and whenever I see him he asks when we're going to use his car."

We drank the toast gladly.

Roland was a good sportsman, and throughout the season at Pau he had been more than friendly. He was to ride two races at the meeting this afternoon.

"And now," said I, "get a move on. St. Jammes is ten miles off, and the road is vile. If we'd got Roland's flier, it'ld be one thing, but Ping and Pong'll take their own time."

My brother-in-law frowned.

"Business first," he said shortly. "Business first. I spoke to the steward about the cutlets, and I won't have them rushed. And if that's our Brie on the sideboard—well, I, too, am in a melting mood, and it's just asking for trouble."

*       *       *       *       *

There was a fresh breeze quickening the air upon the uplands beyond old Morlaas, to whip the flags into a steady flutter and now and again flick a dark tress of hair across Adèle's dear cheeks.

As we scrambled across country—

"Why, oh, why," she wailed, "did ever I let it grow? I'll have it cut again to-morrow. I swear I will."

"And what about me?" said I. "You're a joint tenant with me.

You can't commit waste like that without my consent."

"I'm sure I can abate—is that right?—a nuisance."

"It's not a nuisance. It's a glory. When I wake up in the morning and see it rippling all over the pillow, I plume myself upon my real and personal interest in such a beautiful estate. Then I start working out how many lockets it 'ld fill, and that sends me to sleep again."

"Does it really ripple?" said Adèle. "Or is that a poet's licence?"

"Rather," said I. "Sometimes, if I'm half asleep, I feel quite seasick."

Adèle smiled thoughtfully.

"In that case," she announced, "I'll reconsider my decision. But I wish to Heaven it 'ld ripple when I'm awake."

"They're off!" cried Jonah.

A sudden rush for the bank on which we were standing confirmed his report. We had much ado to escape being thrust into the deep lane the bank was walling.

The lane was about a mile long, and so was the bank. The latter made a fair "grand stand". As such it was packed. Not only all the visitors to Pau, but every single peasant for twenty miles about seemed to have rallied at St. Jammes to see the sport. The regular business of the race-course was conspicuously missing. Pleasure was strolling, cock of an empty walk. For sheer *bonhomie*, the little meeting bade fair to throw its elder brethren of the Hippodrome itself into the shadowy distance.

Roland rode a fine race and won by a neck.

We left the bank and walked up the lane to offer our congratulations.

"Thank you. Thank you. But nex' year you will bring horses, eh? An' we will ride against one another. Yes? You shall keep them with me. I 'ave plenty of boxes, you know. An' on the day I will give your horse his breakfast, and he shall give me the race. That's right. An' when are you going to try my tank? I go away for a week, an' when I come back yesterday, I ask my people, 'How has Captain Pleydell enjoyed the car?' 'But he 'as not used it.' 'No? Then that is because the Major has broken her up?' 'No. He has not been near.' I see now it is not good enough. I tell you I am hurt. I shall not ask you again."

"Lunch with us to-morrow instead," laughed Daphne.

"I am sure that I will," said Roland.

After a little we sauntered back to our bank. . . .

It was nearly a quarter to five by the time we were home. That was early enough, but the girls had grown tired of standing, and we had seen Roland win twice. Jonah we had left to come in another car. This was because he had found a brother-fisherman. When last we saw him, he had a pipe in one hand, a lighted match in the other, and was discussing casts. . . .

Falcon met us at the door with a telegram addressed to "Miss Mansel".

The wording was short and to the point.

*Have met with accident can you come Piers Paris.*

The next train to Paris left Pau in twelve minutes' time.

Adèle and a white-faced Jill caught it by the skin of their teeth.

They had their tickets, the clothes they stood up in, a brace of vanity bags, and one hundred and forty-five francs. But that was all. It was arranged feverishly upon the platform that Jonah and I should follow, with such of their effects as Daphne gave us, by the ten-thirty train.

Then a horn brayed, I kissed Adèle's fingers, poor Jill threw me a ghost of a smile, and their coach rolled slowly out of the station. . . .

I returned to the car dazedly.

Thinking it over, I decided that we had done the best we could. On arrival at Bordeaux, my wife and cousin could join the Spanish express, which was due to leave that city at ten-fifteen; this, if it ran to time, would bring them to the French capital by seven o'clock the next morning. Jonah and I would arrive some five hours later. . . .

The Bank was closed, of course, so I drove to the Club forthwith to get some money. Jonah was not there, but, as he was certain to call, I left a note with the porter, telling him what had occurred. Then I purchased our tickets—a lengthy business. It was so lengthy, in fact, that when it was over I called again at the Club on the chance of picking up Jonah and bringing him home. He had not arrived. . . .

I made my way back to the villa dismally enough.

My sister and Berry were in the drawing-room.

As I opened the door—

"Wherever have you been?" said Daphne. "Did they catch it?"

I nodded.

"You haven't seen Jonah, I suppose?"

I shook my head.

"But where have you been, Boy?"

I spread out my hands.

"Getting money and tickets. You know their idea of haste. But there's plenty of time—worse luck," I added bitterly. Then: "I say, what a dreadful business!" I sank into a chair. "What on earth can have happened?"

Berry rose and walked to a window.

"Jill's face," he said slowly. "Jill's face." He swung round and flung out an arm. "She looked old!" he cried. "Jill—that baby looked old. She thought it was a wire to say he was on his way, and it hit her between the eyes like the kick of a horse."

Shrunk into a corner of her chair, my sister stared dully before her.

"He must be bad," said I. "Unless he was bad, he 'ld never have wired like that. If Piers could have done it, I'm sure he 'ld have tempered the wind."

" 'Can you come?' " quoted Berry, and threw up his arms.

Daphne began to cry quietly. . . .

A glance at the tea-things showed me that these were untouched. I rang the bell, and pleasantly fresh tea was brought. I made my sister drink, and poured some for Berry and me. The stimulant did us all good. By common consent, we thrust speculation aside and made what arrangements we could. That our plans for returning to England would now miscarry seemed highly probable.

At last my sister sighed and lay back in her chair.

"Why?" she said quietly. "Why? What has Jill done to earn this? Oh, I know it's no good questioning Fate, but it's—it's rather hard."

I stepped to her side and took her hand in mine.

"My darling," I said, "don't let's make the worst of a bad business. The going's heavy, I know, but it's idle to curse the jumps before we've seen them. Piers didn't send that wire himself. That goes without saying. He probably never worded it. I know that's as broad as it's long, but, when you come to think, there's really no reason on earth why it should be anything more than a broken leg."

There was a dubious silence.

At length—

"Boy's perfectly right," said Berry. "Jill's scared stiff—naturally. As for us, we're rattled—without good reason at all. For all we know. . . ."

He broke off to listen. . . . The front door closed with a crash.

"Jonah," said I. "He's had my note, and——"

It was not Jonah.

It was Piers, Duke of Padua, who burst into the room, looking extraordinarily healthy and very much out of breath.

We stared at him, speechless.

For a moment he stood smiling. Then he swept Daphne a bow.

"Paris to Pau by air," he said, "in four and a quarter hours. Think of it. Clean across France in a bit of an afternoon. You'll all *have* to do it: it's simply glorious." He crossed to my sister's side and kissed her hand. "Don't look so surprised," he said, laughing. "It really is me. I didn't dare to wire, in case we broke down on the way. And now where's Jill?"

We continued to stare at him in silence.

\* \* \* \* \*

It was Berry— some ten minutes later—who hit the right nail on the head.

"By George!" he shouted. "By George! I've got it in one. *The fellow who sent that wire was Leslie Trunk.*"

"*Leslie?*" cried Piers. "But why——"

"Who knows? But your cousin's a desperate man, and Jill's in his way. So are you—more still, but, short of murder itself, to touch you won't help his case. With Jill in his hands. . . . Well, for one thing only, I take it you'd pay pretty high for her—her health."

Piers went very white.

For myself, I strove to keep my brain steady, but the thought of Adèle—my wife, in the power of the dog, would thrust itself, grinning horribly, into the foreground of my imagination.

I heard somebody say that the hour was a quarter past seven. I had my watch in my hand, so I knew they were right. Vainly they repeated their statement, unconsciously voicing my thoughts. . . .

Only when Daphne fell on her knees by my side did I realise that I was the speaker.

Berry and Piers were at the telephone.

I heard them.

"Ask for the Bordeaux Exchange. Burn it, why can't I talk French? Do as I say, lad. Don't argue. Ask for the Bordeaux Exchange. Insist that it's urgent—a matter of life and death."

Piers began to speak—shakily.

"Yes. The Bordeaux Exchange. . . . It's most urgent, *Mademoiselle*. . . . A matter of life and death. . . . Yes, yes. The Exchange itself. . . . What? My God! But, *Mademoiselle*——"

A sudden rude thresh of the bell announced that his call was over.

Berry fell upon the instrument with an oath.

"It's no good!" cried Piers. "It's no good. She says the line to Bordeaux is out of order."

My sister lifted her head and looked into my face.

"Can you do it by car?" she said.

I pulled myself together and thought very fast.

"We can try," I said, rising, "but—— Oh, it's a hopeless chance. Only three hours—*less than* three hours for a hundred and fifty miles. It can't be done. We'd have to do over seventy most of the way, and you can't beat a pace like that out of Ping and Pong. On the track, perhaps. . . . But on the open road——"

The soft slush of tyres upon the drive cut short my sentence.

"Jonah, at last," breathed Daphne.

We ran to the window.

It was not Jonah.

It was Roland.

So soon as he saw us, he stopped and threw out his clutch.

"I say, you know, I am mos' distress' about your lunch to-morrow. When you ask me——"

"Roland," I cried, "Roland, will you lend me your car?"

"But 'ave I not said——"

"Now—at once—here—to drive to Bordeaux?"

Roland looked up at my face.

The next moment he was out of his seat.

"Yes, but I am not going with you," he said. Then: "What is the matter? Never mind. You will tell me after. The lights are good, and she is full up with gasolene. I tell you, you will be there in three hours."

"Make it two and three-quarters," said I.

\*　　　\*　　　\*　　　\*　　　\*

The day's traffic had dwindled to a handful of home-going gigs, and as we swung out of the rue Montpensier and on to the Bordeaux road, a distant solitary tram was the only vehicle within sight.

I settled down in my seat. . . .

A moment later we had passed the Octroi, and Pau was behind us.

Piers crouched beside me as though he were carved of stone. Once in a while his eyes would fall from the road to the instrument-board. Except for that regular movement, he gave no sign of life. As for Berry, sunk, papoose-like, in the chauffeur's cockpit in rear, I hoped that his airman's cap would stand him in stead. . . .

The light was good, and would serve us for half an hour. The car was pulling like the mares of Diomedes. As we flung by the last of the villas, I gave her her head. . . .

Instantly the long straight road presented a bend, and I eased her up with a frown. We took the corner at fifty, the car holding the road as though this were banked for speed. As we flashed by the desolate race-course and the ground on which Piers had alighted two hours before, I lifted a grateful head. It was clear that what corners we met could be counted out. With such a grip of the road and such acceleration, the time which anything short of a hairpin bend would cost us was almost negligible.

As if annoyed at my finding, the road for the next five miles ran straight as a die. For over three of those miles the lady whose lap we sat in was moving at eighty-four.

A hill appeared—a long, long hill, steep, straight, yellow—tearing towards us. . . . We climbed with the rush of a lift—too fast for our stomachs.

The road was improving now, but, as if to cancel this, a steep, winding hill fell into a sudden valley. As we were dropping, I saw its grey-brown fellow upon the opposite side, dragging his tedious way to the height we had left.

We lost time badly here, for down on the flat of the dale a giant lorry was turning, while a waggon was creeping by. For a quarter of a precious minute the road was entirely blocked. Because of the coming ascent the check hit us hard. In a word, it made a mountain out of a molehill. What the car might have swallowed whole she had to masticate. She ate her way up the rise, snorting with indignation. . . .

A mile (or a minute, Sirs, whichever you please) was all the grace she had to find her temper. Then the deuce of a hill swerved down to the foot of another—long, blind, sinuous. The road was writhing like a serpent. We used it as serpents should be used. Maybe it bruised our heels : we bruised its head savagely. . . .

We were on the level now, and the way was straight again. A dot ahead was a waggon. I wondered which way it was going. I saw, and we passed it by in the same single moment of time. That I may not be thought inobservant, forty-five yards a second is a pace which embarrasses sight.

A car came flying towards us. At the last I remarked with a smile it was going our way. A flash of paint, a smack like the flap of a sail, and we were by.

A farm was coming. I saw the white of its walls swelling to ells from inches. I saw a hen, who had seen us, starting to cross our path. Simultaneously I lamented her death—needlessly. She missed destruction by yards. I found myself wondering whether, after all, she had held on her way. Presently I decided that she had and, anxious to retrace her steps, had probably awaited our passage in some annoyance. . . .

We swam up another hill, flicked between two waggons, slashed a village in half and tore up the open road.

The daylight was waning now, and Piers switched on the hooded light that illumined the instrument-board. With a frown I collected my lady for one last tremendous effort before the darkness fell.

She responded like the thoroughbred she was.

I dared not glance at the speedometer, but I could feel each mile as it added itself to our pace. I felt this climb from ninety to ninety-one. Thickening the spark by a fraction, I brought it to ninety-two . . . ninety-three. . . .

In a quiet, steady voice, Piers began to give me the benefit of his sight.

"Something ahead on the right . . . a waggon . . . all clear . . . cart, I think, on the right . . . no—yes. It's not moving. . . . A bicycle on the left . . . and another . . . a car coming . . . all clear . . . no—a man walking on the right . . . all clear. . . ."

So, our narrowed eyes nailed to the straight grey ribbon streaming into the distance, the sea and the waves roaring in our ears, folded in the wings of the wind, we cheated Dusk of seven breathless miles and sent Nature packing with a fork in her breech.

Sore at this treatment, the Dame, as ever, returned, with Night himself to urge her argument.

I threw in my hand with a sigh, and Piers switched on the lights as we ran into Aire-sur-l'Adour.

I heard a clock striking as we swung to the left in the town. . . .

Eight o'clock.

Two more hours and a quarter, and a hundred and nineteen miles to go.

I tried not to lose heart. . . .

We had passed Villeneuve-de-Marsan, and were nearing, I knew, cross-roads, when Piers forestalled my inquiry and spoke in my ear.

"Which shall you do? Go straight? Or take the forest road?"

"I don't know the Roquefort way, except that there's pavement there. What's it like?"

"It's pretty bad," said Piers. "But you'll save about fifteen miles."

"How much pavement is there? Five or six miles?"

"Thirty about," said Piers.

"Thanks very much," said I. "We'll go by the forest."

I think I was right.

I knew the forest road and I knew its surface was superb. Thirty miles of pavement, which I did not know, which was admittedly rough, presented a ghastly prospect. The "luxury" tax of fifteen precious miles, tacked on to the way of the forest, was really frightening, but since such a little matter as a broken lamp would kill our chances, I dared not risk the rough and tumble of the pavement upon the Roquefort road.

At last the cross-roads came, and we swung to the right. We had covered a third of the ground.

I glanced at the gleaming clock sunk in the dash.

Twenty-five minutes past eight.

An hour and fifty minutes—and a hundred miles to go.

With a frightful shock I realised that, *even with the daylight to help me, I had used a third of my time.*

I began to wish frantically that I had gone by Roquefort. I felt a wild inclination to stop and retrace my steps. Pavement? Pavement be burned. I must have been mad to throw away fifteen miles—fifteen golden miles. . . .

Adèle's face, pale, frightened, accusing, stared at me through the wind-screen. Over her shoulder, Jill, white and shrinking, pointed a shaking finger.

With a groan, I jammed my foot on the accelerator. . . .

With a roar, the car sprang forward like a spurred horse.

Heaven knows the speed at which St. Justin was passed. I was beyond caring. We missed a figure by inches and a cart by a foot. Then the cottages faded, and the long snarl of the engine sank to the stormy mutter she kept for the open road.

We were in the forest now, and I let her go.

Out of the memories of that April evening our progress through the forest stands like a chapter of a dream.

Below us, the tapering road, paler than ever—on either side an endless army of fir trees, towering shoulder to shoulder, so dark, so vast, and standing still as Death—above us, a lane of violet, all pricked with burning stars, we supped the rare old ale brewed by Hans Andersen himself.

# I Drive after my Wife

Within this magic zone the throb of the engine, the hiss of the carburettor, the swift brush of the tyres upon the road—three rousing tones, yielding a thunderous chord, were curiously staccato. The velvet veil of silence we rent in twain; but as we tore it, the folds fell back to hang like mighty curtains about our path, stifling all echo, striking reverberation dumb. The strong, sweet smell of the woods enhanced the mystery. The cool, clean air thrashed us with perfume. . . .

The lights of the car were powerful and focussed perfectly. The steady, bright splash upon the road, one hundred yards ahead, robbed the night of its sting.

Rabbits rocketed across our bows; a bat spilled its brains upon our wind-screen; a hare led us for an instant, only to flash to safety under our very wheels. As for the moths, the screen was strewn with the dead. Three times Piers had to rise and wipe it clear.

Of men and beasts, mercifully, we saw no sign.

If Houeilles knew of our passage, her ears told her. Seemingly the hamlet slept. I doubt if we took four seconds to thread its one straight street. Next day, I suppose, men swore the devil was loose. They may be forgiven. Looking back from a hazy distance, I think he was at my arm.

As we ran into Casteljaloux, a clock was striking. . . .

Nine o'clock.

We had covered the thirty-five miles in thirty-five minutes dead.

"To the left, you know," said Piers.

"*Left?*" I cried, setting a foot on the brake. "Straight on, surely. We turn to the left at Marmande."

"No, no, *no*. We don't touch Marmande. We turn to the left here." I swung round obediently. "This is the Langon road. It's quite all right, and it saves us about ten miles."

Ten miles.

I could have screamed for joy.

Only fifty-five miles to go—and an hour and a quarter left.

The hope which had never died lifted up its head. . . .

It was when we were nearing Auros that we sighted the van.

This was a hooded horror—a great, two-ton affair, a creature, I imagine, of Bordeaux, blinding home like a mad thing, instead of blundering.

Ah, I see a hundred fingers pointing to the beam in my eye. Bear with me, gentlemen. I am not so sightless as all that.

I could steer my car with two fingers upon the roughest road. I could bring her up, all standing, in twice her length. My lights, as

229

you know, made darkness a thing of nought. . . . I cannot answer for its headlights, nor for its brake-control, but the backlash in the steering of that two-ton van was terrible to behold.

Hurling itself along at thirty odd miles an hour, the vehicle rocked and swung all over the narrow surface—now lurching to the right, now plunging to the left, but in the main, holding a wobbling course upon the crown of the road—to my distraction.

Here was trouble enough, but—what was worse—upon my sounding the horn, the driver refused to give way. He knew of my presence, of course. He heard me, he saw my headlights, and—he sought to increase his pace. . . .

I sounded the horn till it failed : I yelled till my throat was sore : Piers raged and howled : behind, I heard Berry bellowing like a fiend. . . . I cursed and chafed till the sweat of baffled fury ran into my eyes. . . .

For over five hideous miles I followed that bucketing van.

I tried to pass it once, but the brute who was driving swerved to the left—I believe on purpose—and only our four-wheel brakes averted a headline smash.

At that moment we might not have been on earth.

My lady stopped as a bird stops in its flight. With the sudden heave of a ship, she seemed to hang in the air. Wild as I was, I could not but marvel at her grace. . . .

Out of the check came wisdom.

It was safe, then, to keep very close.

I crept to the blackguard's heels, till our headlights made two rings upon his vile body.

With one foot on the step, Piers hung out of the car, watching the road beyond.

Suddenly the van tilted to the right. . . .

I knew a swerve must follow, if the driver would keep his balance.

As it came, I pulled out and crammed by, with my heart in my mouth. . . .

A glance at the clock made me feel sick to death.

Fifteen priceles minutes that van had stolen out of my hard-earned hoard. I had risked our lives a score of times to win each one of them. And now an ill-natured churl had flung them into the draught. . . .

I set my teeth and put the car at a hill at eighty-five. . . .

We flashed through Langon at twenty minutes to ten.

Thirty-five minutes left—and thirty miles to go.

We were on the main road now, and the surface was wide, if rough. What little traffic there was, left plenty of room.

I took the ashes of my caution and flung them to the winds.

Piers told me afterwards that for the first twenty miles never once did the speedometer's needle fall below seventy-two. He may be right. I knew that the streets were coming, and the station had to be found. It was a question, in fact, of stealing time. That which we had already was not enough. Unless we could pick some out of the pocket of Providence, the game was up.

I had to slow down at last for a parcel of stones. The road was being re-made, and thirty yards of rubble had to be delicately trod. As we forged through the ruck at twenty, Piers stared at the side of the road.

"BORDEAUX 16," he quoted.

Ten more miles—and nineteen minutes to go.

The traffic was growing now with every furlong. Belated lorries rumbled about their business : cars panted and raved into the night : carts jolted out of turnings into the great main road.

When I think of the chances I took, the palms of my hands grow hot. To wait for others to grant my request for room was out of the question. I said I was coming. . . . I came—and that was that. Times out of number I overtook vehicles upon the wrong side. As for the frequent turnings, I hoped for the best. . . .

Once, where four ways met, I thought we were done.

A car was coming across—I could see its headlights' beam. I opened the throttle wide, and we raced for the closing gap. As we came to the cross of the roads, I heard an engine's roar. . . . For an instant a searchlight raked us. . . . There was a cry from Berry . . . an answering shout . . . the noise of tyres tearing at the road . . . and that was all.

A moment later I was picking my way between two labouring waggons and a trio of straggling carts.

"BORDEAUX 8," quoted Piers.

Five more miles—and eleven minutes to go.

Piers had the plan of the city upon his knees. He conned it as best he could by the glow of the hooded light. After a moment or two he thrust the book away.

"The station's this end of the town. We can't miss it. I'll tell you when to turn."

Three minutes more, and our road had become a street. Two parallel, glittering lines warned me of trams to come.

As if to confirm their news, a red orb in the distance was eyeing us angrily. . . .

"We turn to the right," said Piers. "I'll tell you when."

I glanced at the clock.

The hour was nine minutes past ten.

My teeth began to chatter of sheer excitement. . . .

There was a turning ahead, and I glanced at Piers.

"Not yet," he said.

With a frantic eye on the clock, I thrust up that awful road. The traffic seemed to combine to cramp my style. I swerved, I cut in, I stole an odd yard, I shouldered other drivers aside, and once, confronted with a block, I whipped on to the broad pavement and, amid scandalised shouts, left the obstruction to stay less urgent business.

All the time I could see the relentless minute-hand beating me on the post. . . .

At last Piers gave the word, and I switched to the right.

The boulevard was empty. We just swept up it like a black squall.

Left and right, then, and we entered the straight—with thirty seconds to go.

"Some way up," breathed Piers.

I set my teeth hard and let my lady out. . . .

By the time I had sighted the station, the speedometer's needle had swung to seventy-three. . . .

I ran alongside the pavement, clapped on the brakes, threw out the clutch.

Piers switched off, and we flung ourselves out of the car.

Stiff as a sleepy hare, I stumbled into the hall.

"*Le train pour Paris!*" I shouted. "*Où est le train pour Paris?*"

"This way !" cried Piers, passing me like a stag.

I continued to shout ridiculously, running behind him.

I saw him come to a barrier . . . ask and be answered. . . . try to push through. . . .

The officials sought to detain him.

A whistle screamed. . . .

With a roar I flung aside the protesting arms and carrying Piers with me, floundered on to the platform.

A train was moving.

Feeling curiously weak-kneed, I got carefully upon the step of a passing coach. Piers stepped on behind me and thrust me up to the door.

Then a conductor came and hauled us inside.

\*     \*     \*     \*     \*

I opened my eyes to see Adèle's face six inches away.

"Better, old chap," she said gently.

I tried to sit up, but she set a hand upon my chest.

"Don't say I fainted?" I said.

She smiled and nodded.

"But I understand," she said, "that you have a wonderful excuse."

"Not for ser-wooning," said I. "Of course we did hurry, but. . . ."

Piers burst in excitedly.

"There isn't another driver in all——"

"Rot," said I. "Jonah would have done it with a quarter of an hour to spare."

So he would.

My cousin would have walked to the train and had a drink into the bargain.

\*     \*     \*     \*     \*

While the train thundered northward through a drowsy world, a council of five sat up in a *salon lit* and laid its plans. By far its most valuable member was Señor Don Fedriani, travelling by chance from Biarritz to the French capital. . . .

It was, indeed, in response to his telegram from Poitiers that, a few minutes before seven o'clock the next morning, two detectives boarded our train at the Gare Austerlitz.

Five minutes later we steamed into the Quai d'Orsay.

Jill, carefully primed, was the first to alight.

Except for Piers, Duke of Padua, the rest of us followed as ordinary passengers would. It was, of course, plain that we had no connection with Jill. . . .

That Mr. Leslie Trunk should meet her himself was quite in order. That, having thus put his neck into the noose, he should proceed to adjust the rope about his dew-lap, argued an unexpected generosity.

"Yes, he had sent the wire. He had taken that responsibility. How was Piers? Well, there was plenty of hope." He patted her delicate hand. "She must be brave, of course. . . . Yes, he had just left him. He was in a nursing-home—crazy to see her. They would go there at once."

We all went "there" at once—including Piers, Duke of Padua.

Mr. Leslie Trunk, Señor Don Fedriani, and the two police-officers shared the same taxi.

"There" we were joined by Mrs. Trunk.

The meeting was not cordial, neither was the house a nursing-home. I do not know what it was. A glance at the proportions of the blackamoor who opened the door suggested that it was a bastile.

\*  \*  \*  \*  \*

It was thirty hours later that Berry pushed back his chair.

It was a glorious day, and, viewed from the verandah of the Club-house, that smiling pleasaunce, the rolling plain of Billère was beckoning more genially than ever.

So soon as our luncheon had settled, we were to prove its promise for the last time.

"Yes," said Berry, "puerile as it may seem, I assumed you were coming back. My assumption was so definite that I didn't even get out. For one thing, Death seemed very near, and the close similarity which the slot I was occupying bore to a coffin, had all along been too suggestive to be ignored. Secondly, from my coign of vantage I had a most lovely view of the pavement outside the station. I never remember refuse looking so superb. . . .

"Well, I don't know how long I waited, but when it seemed certain that you were—er—detained, I emerged from my shell. I didn't like leaving the car unattended, but as there wasn't a lock, I didn't know what to do. Then I remembered that just as the beaver, when pursued, jettisons some one of its organs—I forget which—and thus evades capture, so the careful mechanic removes some vital portion of his engine to thwart the unauthorised. I had a vague idea that the part in question was of, with, or from the magneto. I had not even a vague idea that the latter was protected by a network of live wires, and that one had only to stretch out one's finger to induce a spark about a foot long and a shock from which one will never wholly recover. . . . I reeled into the station, hoping against hope that somebody *would* be fool enough to steal the swine. . . .

"Yes, the buffet was closed. Of such is the city of Bordeaux. . . . When I recovered consciousness I sought for you two. I asked several officials if they had seen two gentlemen. Some walked away as if nettled : others adopted the soothing attitude one keeps for the inebriated. Upon reflection, I don't blame them. I had a weak case. . . .

"At last I returned to the car. Alas, it was still there. I then had recourse to what is known as 'the process of exhaustion'. In fact, I found it extremely useful. By means of that process I was eventually successful in starting the engine, and, in the same elementary way, I got into top gear. I drew out of that yard with a running backfire nearly blowing me out of my seat.

"Well, the general idea was to find a garage. The special one was to hear what people said when I stopped to ask them the way. The fourth one I asked was a chauffeur. Under his direction, one first of all reduced the blinding stammer of the exhaust to an impressive but respectable roar, and then proceeded in his company to a dairy, a garage, another dairy and a hotel—in that order. I gave that chap a skinful and fifty francs. . . .

"Yesterday I drove home. I can prove it. All through the trams, like a two-year-old. I admit I took over six hours, but I lunched on the way. I trust that two of the poultry I met are now in Paradise. Indeed, I see no reason to suspect the contrary. So far as I could observe, they looked good, upright fowls. And I look forward confidently to an opportunity of apologising to them for their untimely translation. They were running it rather fine, and out of pure courtesy I set my foot positively on the brake. Unfortunately, it wasn't the brake, but the accelerator. . . . My recollection of the next forty seconds is more than hazy. There is, so to speak, a hiatus in my memory—some two miles long. This was partly due to the force with which the back of the front seat hit me in the small of the back. Talk about a blue streak. . . . Oh, it's a marvellous machine—very quick in the uptake. Give her an inch, and she'll take a hell of a lot of stopping. However. . . ."

"Have you seen Roland?" I said.

"Yes. He dined last night. I told him you'd broken down his beauty and that I had administered the *coup de grâce*. He quite believed it."

"What did he say?" said Adèle.

"Since you ask me," said Berry, "I'll give you his very words. I think you'll value them. 'I tell you,' he said, 'I am very proud. You say she is done. Well, then, there are other cars in the *usine*. But she has saved something which no one can buy in the world— the light in a lady's eyes.' "

There are things in France, besides sunshine, which are not for sale.

**THE END**